SONG
of
SACRIFICE

Homeric Chronicles

JANELL
RHIANNON

Legacies spring from love and blood...
For my father, Thomas,
My son, Joshua,
& his son,
Kolton Howard-Thomas

Men are the dreams of shadows.

PINDAR

PART ONE
Sacrifice and Sorrow

Sing, Muse, of dreams and sorrows
Sing, Muse, of great sacrifices made
for love and war
for justice and revenge

Sing of Troy's Forgotten Prince
his mother's empty arms
his father's empty stare
and the silver she-bear

Sing of Phthia's Golden Warrior
son of a king and a nymph
burdened by a dual fate
he must choose his length of years
or glory hefted with a spear

Sing of Sparta's Princess
cursed twice over by Aphrodite
her beauty a poison
her beauty a prison
his love the antidote and the key

Sing of sad Mycenae
its king bent on gold and war
its daughter bent across an altar
its queen bent with heavy grief
forging vengeance beneath her shroud

Sing, Muse, sing their songs
from beginning to bittersweet end

SONG
of
SACRIFICE

ONE

smoke and dreams

TROY—1290 BCE

"There now, you're safe," Hecuba whispered, standing in a pool of silver moonlight. A cool breeze fluttered the privacy draping surrounding the royal balcony. Heavy with child, she craved the cool night air on her face and against her damp skin. "If I should lose you, my heart …" The baby kicked at her protective hands.

Reaching for the polished stone railing, she leaned into the night. Hecuba scanned the entire skyline of the Trojan citadel, reaching far into the blackness of the night. Throughout the city, the orange glow of oil lamps broke through the black night, dotting windows of merchant shops and citizens, reassuring her that Troy was at peace. The child stretched as the pull of the Moon Goddess stirred her unborn child. She closed her eyes to the city. *By all the gods, I beg you, let this child live.*

When Hektor came to the light, she rejoiced in his black curls and hazy blue eyes. She'd kissed each finger and each toe. It was the only time she'd ever seen her husband weep. Hektor was the Golden Prince of Troy. The beloved son. She quickly conceived again, but the joyous birth ended in mourning. And then again with the third. Hecuba, grief stricken and desperate, routinely made sacrifices to Apollo and Artemis. She'd even set up a private shrine to Eleithyia, Goddess of Childbirth, in her private quarters. But not until now had her womb quickened for a fourth time with the king's seed.

Hecuba rubbed her naked belly again, and ran her hands up to cup each aching breast. Beneath the inky blue sky dusted with stars, she prayed. *Please. What must I do?*

Only recently had she even dared to believe that this child would come to the light as another proud young prince or princess for Troy. But as soon as she embraced the thin hope of happiness, the gods sent her a troubling vision. The jumbled images held no clear meaning, but try as she might, she couldn't dismiss them. The figure of the foreign warrior, armored all in gold, haunted her even in the light of Apollo. "*There can be no promises between lions and men.*"

A light caught in the corner of her eye and she turned to see the dark outline of her husband's body as he slid from their bed, holding a small oil lamp in his hand.

"What is it, Hecuba?" King Priam's voice, rough with sleep soothed her from across the room. The king came up behind her, pressing his warm, naked skin against her nude backside. He set the lamp on the balcony railing.

Hecuba shrugged. "It's nothing, my love. The child is restless."

Reaching for her himation draped over a sitting bench, he wrapped the finely spun cloth around her shoulders. "You and our son will catch a chill." Priam's hands slid down the familiar curves of his wife's widening waist, then up to the sides of her heavy breasts. His lips brushed against the nape of her neck, his warm breath raising the fine hairs along her arms. "You're too tempting without a covering."

She took his hands in hers, placing them on the widest part of her belly. "Surely, one of your concubines would please you more than I. What if it is a daughter?"

King Priam chuckled. "I love all our children." He gently nipped Hecuba's neck with his teeth. "You know there is no one I desire more than you."

She swatted at his exploring hands. "Leave me be."

He gently pinched her nipples, until they wrinkled into tight buds. "We're no strangers to these discomforts are we, my love?"

Hecuba reluctantly accepted the tradition that as Queen of Troy, she'd never be the only woman in her husband's life. After the loss of two heirs, the king's councilors urged Priam to take other wives and concubines. Custom, after all, decreed that the King of Troy should have as many children as possible, securing the royal line and breeding strong, valiant Trojan commanders and warriors. When Priam had agreed, Hecuba realized for the first time what it meant to truly be queen. The king would be her whole world, but he'd enjoy a life separate from the one he shared with her.

In these moments of weakness and self-doubt, she reminded herself that he'd chosen her for love, not simply duty or lust. He proved his loyalty to her by sharing the royal bed only with her, his queen, every night without fail. No concubines or other wives desecrated their private chambers. Priam had never remained long in the arms of another woman after mating, always returning to her freshly bathed. She'd never caught the lingering scent of another woman on her husband's skin or dress. But, from time to time, she'd catch sight of a beautiful woman with a rounded belly. And soon, little children with dark curls and dimpled chins ran about the halls and courtyard. Hecuba knew in her heart they belonged to Priam, but she could never voice her agony or speak of betrayal. The king would do what he must for the city.

"Why are you standing here, naked for all of Troy to see?"

"I couldn't sleep."

Priam sighed. "Is it the vision?"

Hecuba nodded. "I can't forget it." She pulled his arms tighter around her. "It frightened me," she admitted. "I hear that warrior's voice roaring in my head. *No promises between lions and men.* What does it mean? We're at peace, finally. Aren't we?"

"War is inevitable, Hecuba. I know why you're fearful."

"What if—"

"It means nothing, sweet wife."

She shivered in his arms. "But the warrior—"

He leaned his cheek against hers. "Consult Iphicrates in the morning, if it will ease your mind. Now, come to bed, wife. I grow cold."

Hecuba turned in his arms, catching the mischievous gleam in his eye. "You will keep me with child until I am old and grey."

Priam stung her buttocks with a firm slap. "That would not be such a bad thing." He swooped up his pregnant wife, protesting and laughing, and carried her to their bed. The himation slipped to the floor. Despite her growing belly, she wrapped her legs around his still narrow waist. He growled into her neck, biting and kissing her.

Hecuba nipped the square of his chin, and then grabbed his curly black hair at the nape of his neck, pulling his head closer so her teeth could find his earlobe. She kissed softly down his neck.

Untangling her legs from his waist, he positioned her against the pillows. "You're a playful woman," he laughed. "And you'll pay for teasing your king with such kisses."

Hecuba cocked an eyebrow. "How shall I pay you? I have no gold or silver, my lord."

The king knelt between her legs; his eyes burned with passion. "You have buried your treasure and …" Priam bent down, kissing the insides of her thighs, nibbling her soft flesh, moving his tongue to her center, "I will find it." His tongue slid slowly up the soft inner flesh of her body, finding the swollen bud of her pleasure. Skillfully, he teased it, until she begged him to stop, squeezing her knees around his head.

"Are you so easily satisfied?" Sliding his body up between her legs, he plunged deep inside of her. Moving with a deliberately slow pace, he stroked until his wife's desire was reawakened. When Hecuba's fingers dug into his shoulders and her breath caught, he quickened his thrusts.

Hecuba wrapped her legs around his thighs, digging her heels into his upper thighs. "Priam, by Apollo … *now*."

When her pleasured moans echoed across the chamber, Priam roared his release over hers. They collapsed together, their legs tangled in the bed linen. With a contented sigh, Priam collapsed on his side and fell back into an easy sleep.

Hecuba stared into the dark for a long while, until sheer exhaustion pulled her into the restless world of nightmares.

Apollo's light, flashing off the golden helm and shield of the foreigner, blinded Hecuba as she gazed down from the dizzy heights of Troy's southern wall. The stranger caught her stare, his eyes flashing blue fire, chilling her to the bone. She pulled her dark veil tighter around her face. The warrior hefted a bronze-tipped spear, leveling it at the man armored as a Trojan warrior. *His helm hides his face. But I know him … how do I know him? It's not Priam. But who?*

From below, the foreigner's voice thundered through the air, shaking the stone foundation beneath her feet. "There can be no promises between lions and men!"

Hecuba watched in horror as the golden armored man charged with shield tilted and spear leveled for a fatal strike. *We are not at war? How can this be?* The men crashed into one another, splintering their shields, tossing the remnants to the ground. With a roar, the tall, golden warrior circled and attacked like a lion. Death sang clearly in the clash of their silver swords. The queen's heart pounded frantically, knowing one of them would surely die.

The queen opened her mouth to scream the burning questions: *Who are you? Why do you fight?* But, the words dusted on her tongue. She clasped her hands beneath her heavy belly. *Not now. Not now.* Dust swirled about the combatant's feet, as they danced to their death. The shining warrior lunged with grace, his spear finding the soft flesh beneath the Trojan warrior's shoulder. The foreigner laughed as the spray of blood splattered across his armor. The man whose face remained in shadow dropped hard to his knees, his chin bobbing close to his chest. *Is he dead? Who are you? Why are you here?* In that moment; Hecuba realized she stood alone on the rampart. *Where is Priam?* She turned to see smoke rising from the citadel. *What is happening? Priam! Priam! Where have you gone?*

Why have you left me alone?

Warm liquid trickled down her inner thighs. Hecuba glanced down to see a pool of blood at her feet. Her fingertips bled as she gripped the edge of the stone wall, bracing for the birth. *I cannot have the child on the wall.* A searing pain tore through her, dropping her to all fours. *Not yet. Not yet.* She placed a trembling hand to her sacred opening, feeling for the baby. Her fingers touched a rounded object emerging. Screaming, she pushed for relief. In triumph, she pulled it forth, only to find she held not her long-awaited son, but a burning log. She dropped it, screaming and running from the wall.

"Mama? mama, wake up now." Little Hektor peered over the edge of his mother's bed, placing his chubby hand on her arm. "Mama?"

Hecuba opened her eyes to see her eldest child. Hektor was a glorious boy. His eyes shone like two polished stones of lapis lazuli, a gift from the gods. The rest of him exuded Priam's stock—the black curls framing a handsome face, the slight dip in the middle of his tiny chin, and the bump of Priam's strong nose. Hecuba loved her son's contagious lopsided smile the most. Whenever Hektor asked his father why they both shared the same chin, Priam regaled him with the story of how Zeus touched the chin of all those of royal Trojan blood. "It is a mark of honor," he would say. "A mark of the princes and kings of Troy."

The queen gently placed her hand over her son's. "I am awake now, Hektor. Tell me, what have you been doing all morning?"

Hektor's eyes rounded with excitement. "I was in the stables with Xenos," he took a big breath, "helping with the horses."

"As a Trojan prince should. What else did you do?"

Hektor's face beamed. "I rode Ares for the first time." The young prince loved his horse. Priam had purchased the stallion as a colt from the southern Troad where the finest war horses were bred. The colt's sleek obsidian coat and the luminous white crescent stamped on its forehead set him apart from all the others in the royal stable. Hektor and Ares had become inseparable. Life existed this way for the princes of Troy. The Trojan tradition of breaking horses was a gift admired far and wide, reaching even across the storming seas. Some worlds revered their fast ships and others their monuments stretching toward the heavens, but the Trojans venerated their magnificent horses. A warrior's worth extended to the mount he rode into battle, honor and nobility bonding the rider and the steed. And for a chosen few, the god Apollo gifted the ability of communicating directly with the majestic beasts by whispering secret words into their ears. The gift had not come to Hektor, but Hecuba hoped it might be granted to the son she now carried.

"And how is Mighty Ares?"

"He grows strong, Mama. He ate all of the oats I carried to him."

Queen Hecuba sat up, pulling the boy to her side. "Did you ride long, then, this morning?"

"Yes." Hektor's gaze fell to his hands. "But I fell off."

Hecuba tilted her son's chin up. "Xenos tells me all warriors fall off. Even princes and sometimes, even kings." She tapped his nose. "With my own eyes I have seen your father tossed more times than I have fingers." She held up both hands showing all ten fingers, wiggling each one for emphasis.

Hektor squinted in disbelief at his mother. "My father fell off that many times?"

"Yes," the queen laughed. "Breaking horses is difficult when you do not grow up together as you and Mighty Ares have. Some horses never feel the weight of a man until they are already grown. They are wild, free spirited beasts."

Hektor shrugged his little shoulders. "Someday, I will break the horses."

"Yes, I am certain you will."

Hektor's eyes sparkled with the anticipation only an innocent could have. "And learn to fight." He spoke of war as a game he'd play, running safety back to his mother's arms.

Icy fingers squeezed the queen's heart. Her dream of the foreign warrior, lunging gracefully with a spear poised for a lethal strike loomed behind her eyes. His voice thundering, *"There can be no promises between lions and men."* Hecuba willed the image to a shadow with a shake of her head. She recalled what Priam had said about war being inevitable. *Was it a god-sign? A warning? A mother's fear?* Looking at her little boy, her heart ached. She wanted her husband to be wrong, to believe that war was an invention of greed that diplomacy and honor could wipe from their world.

The moment passed as quickly as it had overwhelmed her. *It's a woman's burden knowing men will one day go to war.* Since girlhood, she'd been raised knowing this was the way of life, but now, as a mother, she agonized over it. Men wished to be proud warriors, heeding the call to battle, holding their shields and spears aloft, and roaring their blood lust for battle to Ares as they charged headlong into the face of possible death. Fathers raised sons, and those sons raised more sons … all glorifying the field of battle and the dark God of War, Ares, for honor and song.

All women, even queens, faced the agonies of war's aftermath.

Bodies broken beyond recognition, bloody wounds requiring a steady hand to stitch them closed, and ruined minds to mend. All that paling in comparison to washing and dressing the dead for the funeral pyres, and when the smell of burning flesh filled the air, men swore under their breath it would be the last. Until the next season brought new challenges, and it all began again.

Hecuba pulled Hektor's little head toward hers and kissed him on top of his curls. He smelled of hay. "You will be a great warrior someday, my little Hektor, breaker of horses, my golden prince."

Hektor wrinkled his nose at his mother and crossed his slender arms across his chest. "I'm not little."

Hecuba pinched his cheek. "Only to me, sweet boy." Hektor leapt into his mother's bed. She tickled him under his arms. Rounds of cheerful giggles bounced across the chamber, echoing out the open windows. Hecuba forced all of the frightening prospects of the future from her mind. She poured her affection and joy into the moment with her son laughing next to her.

He put his hand on his mother's rounded belly. "Is he truly inside of you?"

"Yes, he is," Hecuba said. "But, don't be disappointed if it's a girl. Kings need daughters, too."

Hektor laughed. "I can't break horses with a sister. I see a brother for me. We will ride together. Fight together."

Hecuba's eyes filled with tears. "Then, a boy it must be."

Hecuba's vision disturbed Priam more than he allowed her to believe, stealing his peace with each passing day. When the priests summoned him, he traveled alone cloaked through the city he loved, the stone streets winding toward the citadel's center where Apollo's temple stood. The city's inhabitants regaled their patron god's part in building their fortress home in songs, holding many festivals in his honor.

Apollo's temple dazzled with marble pillars towering to dizzying heights set against the expanse of the heavens. Paintings of gods and goddesses and their heroic deeds spiraled every marble column from cap to base around the outer perimeter of the temple. On each corner, a magnificent sculpture of Apollo held up the temple's roof with the structure resting on each statue's shoulders. A carved relief depicting Apollo and Poseidon building Troy's great ramparts adorned the immense pediment above the temple's entrance and black marble paved the entry.

As Priam passed beneath the great triangle, entering Apollo's sacred space, he thought of his legacy, his immortality. For him, it lay in the hope that his sons and grandsons depicted his life in some glorious measure on a wall or column or in a song of his great deeds. Trojan kings may rule the city, but in the end it was the city itself that was the true inheritance of all Trojan kings. He must protect it.

The king walked to the cella, the sacred chamber, readying his offering on the plinth stone. Setting down the small basket of pearls and the shimmering gold crown of laurel leaves, he wondered if it was enough. *In the morning, I will bring a fatted bull as well.*

An errant pearl slipped through the basket, bouncing behind the wall of blue curtains where Apollo's secrets floated as whispers into the ears of eager priests and priestesses. Sheer blue fabric shielded the sacred adyton from the direct gaze of supplicants, preserving the sanctity and the mystery of the god. Priam heard the pearl roll to silence. *I have not brought nearly enough. I cannot carry the entire treasury on my back. Why was I summoned? Was it Hecuba's vision?*

A priestess with hair as pale as summer honey emerged holding the lost pearl in her palm. Her dark grey eyes looked on him with pity, as she placed the gem in his outstretched hand.

Priam placed it back with the others. "Gratitude."

When her steady gaze probed his face, the black ice of her pupils pierced through all of his fears. "You are troubled, King Priam."

"It is not every day one is summoned to the god."

The priestess nodded. "That is true."

"Why am I here?"

"Apollo demands a great sacrifice. Troy must be saved."

King Priam shook his head in confusion. "But we are not at war?"

"The city will fall before a descendant of Aeacus, unless the boy dies."

"Troy has no quarrel with the western tribes. Pirating along the southern Troad coast has died down to nothing. We bear the west no ill will," Priam argued. Then … "What boy?"

"Your unborn son."

Priam's knees buckled and he caught himself on the altar's edge. "It is a boy?"

"He is."

The king's mind reeled. "I cannot kill my own child. My son." *How could I do such a thing? How would I tell Hecuba?*

"Then, Troy will perish."

"Why does Apollo punish me with this task? Have I not made all of the offerings? Does Troy not venerate the Shining One above all others?"

The priestess folded her hands. "Do you remember your sister, Priam?"

Guilt surged through Priam's heart. "I lost my entire family the day Hesione was taken from Troy. How could I forget?" The image of Hesione's pale blue gown fluttering in the wind, her head bowed low, as Herakles dragged her off to his ship still haunted him all these years later. "Priestess, Apollo must know what happened to Hesione was not my fault. My father—"

"Your father's legacy is yours as well. A royal daughter of Troy now lives among the Greeks. What was it, Priam? Cowardice or greed?"

Priam clenched his jaw, his face flushed with frustration. "I had been away. I am not responsible for my father's dishonor. What else could I do in that moment?"

"What could you have done? That is what Apollo wishes to know. Gods test mortals in many ways. And you doubted Apollo."

Priam's face shook, the vein on his forehead bulged. "Where was Apollo when Herakles and his Greeks came to Troy? What happened was not because of me."

The priestess remained unmoved. "Unless you obey him, Troy will be burnt to ashes, wiped clean from mortal memory. The wall will crumble to ruin and dust. The sand will drink the blood of Trojan warriors. And its women and children condemned to slavery. Is refusing this sacrifice worth the lives of thousands upon thousands?"

Priam's hope of saving his unborn son slipped from his fingers. "Is there no other way, Priestess? I beg Apollo to take my life in his place. Just let my son live."

"If he lives, Troy will burn. It's that simple. There can be no oaths between lions and men." She disappeared behind the blue veil.

Suddenly, it struck him. He'd heard that warning before in Hecuba's vision. "Wait! What does that mean? About lions and men?" But the priestess was gone and he dared not follow her.

Priam's heart sank, knowing Apollo refused a compromise. As the king, there would be only one choice, and as a father it was no choice at all. Priam understood, now, his complicity in the episode looming before his family and city. *I was a coward.* And deeper yet, he knew he craved the power of kings. *I have brought this on myself. Hecuba … she'll never forgive me.* Perhaps he would yet find a way around this. *Maybe Apollo tests me again? Maybe he will stay my hand in the final moment?* There was time to win Apollo's favor.

"What news from Apollo's priests?" Hecuba could stand the silence between them no longer. "We keep no secrets between us."

Priam stared into the hearth fire.

Hecuba could see the flames reflecting in his stony dark eyes. "Priam?"

"They say the babe must die, or Troy will fall."

The words pierced Hecuba's heart, stealing her breath away. Tears burned at the edges of her eyes. "Surely, you don't intend to listen."

Priam turned his wounded eyes to his wife. "I don't know what I intend. If Apollo does not relent, I must choose between one life and thousands."

"But it's our child."

Priam's nostrils flared and his chin shook. "Do you think I am unaware of that? That I haven't grieved in my heart for our lost children? Do you think I want this?"

Placing her hands on her rounded middle, Hecuba choked down her tears. "I beg you, make more sacrifices. Whatever Apollo wants, give it to him."

Priam took a long drink of his wine. "He asks only for our son, nothing less."

"Is there … no hope?" Tears fell from her eyes like summer rain.

"Hope." He drained his cup. "That's all we have left to us."

TWO

farewell my son

TROY—1290 BCE

I t begins. *Why Apollo? Why must you demand my son?* Recognizing the familiar dull ache squeezing down her lower back and wrapping around her hips, she rolled onto her side. The pain eased and passed. The full moon tugged the child to her light. Her eyes leveled with the feet of the Eleithyia's shrine barely visible in the half-light. *Goddess, please,* she begged. Precious little time remained before she'd be forced to call Tessa to fetch the midwife. *How can Priam take our son?* Iecuba gripped a handful of the linen cover, until her knuckles whitened.

Hecuba wept into her pillow, as the babe struggled to the light. His innocence would be her life's burden. *I will never feel him suckle life from my breasts. I will never know the sweet smell of his skin. Never feel his weight in my arms as he sleeps. Never see him smile. I won't know him at all.* He would be stolen from her and lost forever. With each new pain, she clenched her teeth, breathing as quietly as possible.

As the pressure and pain mounted, she shifted to the opposite side, trying desperately not to cry out.

The moonlight slipped past the high window. A pain pierced Hecuba's pelvis, forcing a shrill scream into the stillness shattering the silver calm. The warm wetness of the birthing waters washed between her thighs, soaking the linen. *Eleithyia you waste no time bringing the child along. Why, Goddess? Let him stay with me a while longer, I beg you.* Her plea hung unheeded in that space between earth and sky.

Priam bolted upright at her shriek. As he reached for her, his hand touched the wet linens. "How long have you labored in the dark without the women?"

Hecuba grabbed his arm, digging her fingernails into his flesh, leaving red-crescent welts on his skin. She screamed and cried again. "Now, Priam! He's coming now!"

The king leapt from the bed, tossing a simple chiton over his head just as Tessa flew into the chamber followed by the women. "The child, Tessa. Make haste. The queen nears delivery," Priam barked at the women, as he walked passed them to the door where he grabbed the guard's shoulder. "Fetch Agelaus to me."

The guard's surprise was evident in his wide eyes. "My lord, the royal herder?"

"Just bring him to me." Priam shut the door so quickly the guard barely had time to move his foot before the heavy timbers smashed it. He ran with all haste to do as his king commanded.

Priam returned to his wife's side. "Is it too early, Tessa? Another moon perhaps?" If, by chance, the child should die on its own, then he would be spared the task of killing it himself.

"Children come when they are ready. When the gods are ready. The moon is full; it should not surprise you, my lord. But, yes, it is early."

The midwife—a short, rounded woman—rushed to Hecuba's side as another pain tore across the queen's back. Fear filled her eyes. "I don't want to push! HAARRHH—AAAH!" Hecuba fought the urge with her entire being, weeping and moaning.

"My queen, you must. You can't stop the child coming to the light."

Hecuba wept, miserable and in agony. "I must. He will die."

The midwife gently shoved the king aside. "My lord, I remind you this is a woman's work."

Priam shook his head. "I will stay regardless."

The midwife shrugged, turning her attention to Hecuba. "My queen, this will hurt but for a moment. I must feel for the baby's position." Gently, she slid her hand inside of the queen. The child's crown was just a few finger joints from the light of life. "When the next pain comes, bear down as hard as you can."

"Priam, no, no … I beg you, do not take our son." Hecuba's body betrayed her. The urge to birth the boy mounted stronger than before. She held her breath, trying as she might to stop the birth, her legs shaking with the effort.

The midwife shook her head. "Tessa, she cannot fight it. She may harm the babe."

Tessa encouraged her queen. "My lady, you must move to the edge of the bed. Sit up, help the child out." The two women eased Hecuba to the edge, propping her into a semi-sitting position with her back side resting on the mattress. The urge to push overtook Hecuba's body and she strained mightily. A gush of blood and water splashed her bare feet.

"Priam," Hecuba cried out. "Priam, save our son!"

The midwife put her hand between the queen's spread thighs.

"You are crowning him with your glory. Eleithyia blesses you. The child is coming, my queen."

"Priam! He's our—HAARRHH!" Hecuba's final effort brought forth a squalling baby boy covered in the scum of new life. Tessa supported the queen when her legs collapsed, easing her gently back into the bed, as the midwife cradled the child still connected by its life cord.

The midwife smiled, holding the newborn up so Hecuba could see him. "He is perfect!" Pulling a sharp blade from her pocket, she deftly cut the life cord, handing the infant to Tessa. "Clean the prince and take him to his mother. Put haste in your step, woman." The midwife tended to the queen with steady, experienced hands. The last stage of birth remained. The midwife massaged Hecuba's stomach to help her body expel the sacred afterbirth without tearing the womb. It was dangerous work—if not done with care, a mother could hemorrhage to death. The midwife knew the seers would want the bloody membrane for divination and she wanted a healthy queen.

Tessa gently washed the infant's body. His wrinkly face purpled with his distress, flinging his arms and legs out in fright, startling him into more screaming. Once Tessa tightly swaddled the newborn, his crying subsided to a soft whimper. "Such a beautiful boy. Surely, the goddess has endowed you with many gifts, little one."

Tessa crossed the chamber, handing the child to the queen. "Here is your prince, my lady."

Hecuba opened her arms, embracing her son. Sensing her love and warmth, the new prince settled into a wide-eyed silence. The baby's hazy blue eyes locked onto Hecuba's face, shattering her already broken heart. "He knows who I am." After kissing him tenderly on the forehead, she kissed his little fingers clinging to one of her own.

The queen dared a glance at her husband. Priam's silence terrified her. He offered no word of encouragement, nor commented about the child. *Please, Apollo, send a sign. Let me keep my son.*

Tessa ordered the bed dressed with fresh linen, and the servants hurried to haul the soiled clothing and the defiled bloody linens. Satisfied that all boded well for the queen, Tessa asked the king, "Shall I call for the heralds, my lord?"

"No." Priam had scarce moved since he'd ordered the guard hours before. He sat unmoving like a stone, watching Hecuba labor and deliver the second prince of Troy with eyes glazed over and distant.

Confused, Tessa said, "But, my lord, is it not—"

"Leave us. All of you," Priam ordered sternly. The women took their leave and the room fell, except for Hecuba's quiet sobbing.

As the child quieted, secured in her embrace, Hecuba's soul ached. "How can I let him go?" she whispered. "He's so beautiful." Wispy black curls framed his cherubic face. She brushed her index finger gently across the tiny indent of the infant's chin. "Look, Priam. He has your chin. Just like Hektor. Why does Apollo want our son? Why not one of your whore's children?" Her desperation forced the question.

Priam's frown deepened. Hecuba searched for some trace of grief or sadness behind the hardness in his eyes. "They are all *my* children, Hecuba. How can you wish death to any of my blood? I have asked for a sign from Apollo for *our* son. But the god is silent in my ears even now. It is clear. I must save Troy."

The queen's tears sprang anew. "How can you do this to our son? After we've lost … the others."

Priam said angrily, "Do you believe I *wish* this? To kill my own son? A prince of Troy? This is Apollo's doing, not mine." The half-lie slipped easily from his tongue.

"What can we do to save him?"

Very quietly Priam said, "I want to hold the boy." Hecuba lifted the tiny babe to him with a hopeful heart that once he felt the weight of the prince in his arms it would be enough to persuade the king to change his mind. The infant looked even smaller wedged in the crook of Priam's giant arm. The king touched the child's little indented chin with his calloused finger. "If only Apollo would allow you to grow into a strong, Trojan warrior."

Hecuba knew then that Priam would enforce the god's commands. He'd reminded her that they weren't the first parents forced to sacrifice a child on command of a god. She'd hoped that their station would save their son, but alas the gods remained unmoved and indiscriminant in their decision. To the gods, there were no princes or peasants, only mortals.

A commotion clanged outside of the royal antechamber. From just beyond the door, Tessa's voice screeched with unmistakable contempt and fear. "You can't go into the chamber!" The loud crash of pottery shattering against the floor startled the infant in Priam's arms. It bawled.

"Get out of my way, woman!" a man's voice bellowed above the unmistakable sound of soldiers' heavy footsteps. "Get out of my way I said! Do you wish Apollo to strike you down where you stand?"

Tessa screamed once more and then fell silent.

Priam handed the baby back to Hecuba, as Iphicrates, the royal seer, stormed into the chamber followed by a confused contingent of palace guards. Royal decree gave Iphicrates direct access to the king day or night. The guards, sensing danger, and confused by the queen's personal servant's protests, tried barring Iphicrates at the door. But, threatening the wrath of Apollo convinced them all to stand aside. Death for disobeying Priam's household orders was worrisome, but Apollo's retribution was far more terrifying.

Iphicrates' face contorted in fear and anger. His eyes, bloodshot and red-rimmed, bulged with concern. "Where is the child?"

Priam reached for his sword, signaling the guards to stand down. "How dare you enter our inner sanctum unannounced and uninvited." Standing between his family and the seer, he leveled his blade at the Iphicrates. "You're not welcomed here."

The seer stared Priam in the eyes. "I must be here to see it done."

The king sneered. "I do not require your oversight."

"Apollo believes otherwise."

The child squalled loudly in his mother's arms. Hecuba pressed her nipple into the newborn's mouth, but the baby's agitation only increased. He refused to latch the soft flesh of his mother's comfort.

"He must be taken now," the seer demanded.

Hecuba tried unsuccessfully to quiet her newborn. "There is no need to rush the deed. Do you see a threat to Troy from the window? Are there enemies at the gates? Troy is in no imminent danger."

The seer challenged the queen, "Did you dream of birthing a burning log?"

Hecuba shivered. "How can you know of that?" She looked to Priam. "I told no one, not even you."

Iphicrates, his robes sweeping the marble floor, stepped closer to the queen. "Apollo sent me a vision. He was clear. The Trojan prince must die this day or Troy will burn."

Hecuba clutched her son closer. "This very day? This very moment?"

Priam lowered his sword. "Surely, this can wait until full dawn. Apollo may yet grant a reprieve. I will make more sacrifices in his honor. I will bring more gold to his temple. I will—"

Iphicrates recognized the hard line of Priam's mouth, and prayed the king wouldn't kill him where he stood. "There will be no concession. My lord, you *know* why."

Hecuba caught Priam's sneer and the flash of fear in his eyes. "Priam, what is he talking about? What have you kept from me that now condemns our son?" The baby struggled and cried in Hecuba's arms, and he still refused to suckle. "Tell me, for love of the gods, I have a right to know. You cannot allow him to be ripped from my arms without revealing everything."

The king sighed deeply in tortured defeat. As his fury faded, his shoulders slumped. "We will obey the god, Iphicrates. Now, leave us," Priam commanded, signaling the guards again. "Or I will have you dragged out and beaten to death." The guards circled Iphicrates, as he spun on his heels, exiting in a rush.

Priam pulled a guard to him. "Bring Agelaus directly to me. He should be waiting by now."

The man hurried to do as commanded, and within moments a solid knock echoed through the chamber.

"Troy must not fall, Hecuba. You know as king I must protect the people."

The knock came again, louder.

"Give me the baby," Priam demanded quietly. The king's mask fell into place like a door slamming shut.

The queen looked down at her son, who'd now managed to take her nipple in his mouth. *How could Apollo demand something so cruel from such an innocent?* "I can't." Her body trembled with fear, as the child finally suckled.

"You must."

Hecuba's pale hands clutched the infant tighter. "I can't. I can't do it." She wept in desperate defeat. Sitting with the newborn in her arms, she begged, "Let him stay with me the night." A fat tear splashed the baby's forehead.

The third knock at the door signaled that the guard stood ready for orders.

"Hecuba, you must understand. This is the command. Though it rips out our hearts, we must obey." He exhaled a tender but firm sigh. "Now, give me the child." Priam reached over the bed, prying the baby from Hecuba's unwilling arms. His little mouth clung to the warm nipple, and when it slipped from his mouth, he squalled anew.

Hecuba begged through her sobs, "Let me feed him."

"No more. We must do what must be done." With the baby in his arms, Priam strode across the room with heavy steps, and finally opened the door. The king handed the child to a surprised Agelaus. Hecuba's wretched sobs echoed behind Priam, breaking his heart because he knew this wound would shatter everything he held precious. He wanted to relent, but he could not. "Take the baby to the foothills of the sacred mountain. Leave him there. Exposed. Turn away from him. Don't look back."

"But, my lord, I'm just a bull herder. I'm not …" Agelaus' eyes widened in horror. "It's misty cold and soon baking heat."

"You know the terrain better than anyone else. You'll know where to leave him so he won't be found by accident." King Priam leaned close to the herder's ear and whispered, "Cut out his tongue and send it to me as proof of your obedience."

Agelaus stood frozen with the warm bundle squirming and whimpering in his arms. "But, I—"

"Are your ears full of wax? For the love of Apollo! Go!" Priam bellowed. At the curse, the king watched Agelaus run from the chamber as if the royal hunting hounds nipped at his heels.

Hecuba wailed hysterically, refusing any comfort from anyone. Her pain echoed throughout the palace and the whispers traveled like a chilly wind that the newborn prince had been taken, sentenced to die by Apollo. Servants and slaves said extra prayers to the gods, and made personal sacrifices to the Shining One, not only for the prince's impending suffering and death, but for their own safety. Not knowing why Apollo exacted such a heavy price from the king and queen frightened them, and they wished any further misfortune to wing passed them.

Priam sat on the edge of their bed, placing a tender hand on his wife's shoulder. "My love, you must eat something."

"I am not hungry."

The king picked up a cup of water. "Drink at least."

Hecuba turned, lifting her head to take a small sip, then lay back down facing away from him.

"It is not our fault," Priam said.

"No, it is not. It is yours."

"There was nothing I could do. Apollo commanded and I obeyed. You do not understand. I cannot let Troy be destroyed."

Hecuba wept again, but her eyes shed no tears. "You would rather our son die, than fight some future war. I understand perfectly."

Priam touched a lock of her dark hair, which was strewn messily across her pillow. "We can have others—"

The queen turned to face him, then, her face swollen with raw grief, her eyes red-rimmed from weeping dry tears, and her voice hoarse from wailing. "You sit and speak to me of other children, when my arms can still feel the weight of him? When my breasts ache with milk he will never suckle? When I yet bleed between my thighs from bringing him to the light? You cannot know my sorrow to speak of such things to me. Get out, Priam. Leave me be."

Priam paced a long while in their chamber, his own heart weighed down by grief and guilt. *It is my fault Apollo took him. My cowardice forced this.* He studied the pale figure curled on their bed. *She will not forgive me for this.* Finally, as darkness filled the room, Priam left Hecuba alone in her bed of sorrow. He needed his own comfort, and that he could find elsewhere, in the arms of one of his concubines. It would be the first time in all of the years of their marriage that he sought solace for his personal anguish in the arms of a woman other than Hecuba.

Agelaus wondered why King Priam wanted such a gruesome end for this new life. What secret did he wish to hide by exposing his son to wind and rain and wild beasts at the foot of Mount Ida? No rumors of adultery on her part warranted such harshness for the tiny prince. Agelaus examined the child's body for defects. Finding none, his confusion deepened. "Why? Why must I do this harsh work for the king?"

Agelaus contemplated the injustice that ordinary men must do what kings chose not to do. Brushing a finger against the child's cheek, he said, "They command and we obey. The gods command and we obey. My entire life is nothing but bowing and scraping to keep mischief from my house." Immediately regretting giving breath to the thought, he scanned the skies. "Apollo, forgive me if now, I bring it to myself." He waited for retribution to strike from Olympus, but none came.

Agelaus had fathered two sons of his own, fine sons both. Harmon, stubborn and headstrong, had seen five winters, while Tymon was a quieter child barely two summers old. He worried his youngest would be more his mother's son, than a bull herder. *Why would the king wish this child, prince, dead?* The child whimpered. It was a sound he knew well enough, and he knew what he must do. His farm wasn't too far from the path he traveled now. Swaddling the baby, he made for home. The child must be fed before the long trek to the mountain, or its wailing would wake the entire wood. *And perhaps wake the wrath of the gods against me.* His youngest, two years older than the prince, still took the breast. *That should be enough.*

Cradling the infant tightly to his chest, he pushed aside his mission. "The king need not know all. What harm can come from one day?" *The gods help me if he should discover what I'm doing. I've no desire to hang jerking at the end of a rope, pissing and shitting until Hades welcomes me.* He shuddered at the thought. Besides, he didn't feel like making the long trek to the sacred mountain before a proper morning meal.

When Agelaus opened the gate to the courtyard, he peered around the corner expecting, but hoping, not to find his family roused and going about morning chores. The royal guards' clamoring had stirred the entire household from sleep, when they came in the dark to snatch him from a rare night of comforting sleep. Pausing at the gate, he strained to hear anything out of the ordinary. A single cricket chirped, then fell silent. A rooster crowed the coming dawn.

The crushed stone crunched beneath his feet like broken pottery shards. Agelaus silently cursed each noisy footstep, until he made it safely to the side door of the house.

Agelaus walked through the kitchen where the cooking flames had burned to smoldering blackened charcoal. Soon, Lexias would be up to stoke the charred wood to flame. He passed around a corner, moving quietly toward his bedchamber. A faint glow outlined the door. With a pounding heart, he took the last few steps. Closing his eyes, Agelaus gently pushed the door open, holding his breath.

When he opened his eyes, Lexias lay sound asleep in their bed. He exhaled slowly. *If I can just position the babe without waking her.* As he approached the bed, he leaned close to Lexias, slowly pulling a swollen breast from her shift. She moaned in her sleep. Agelaus froze, waiting for his wife to open her eyes and find him standing there holding a stranger's child. But, she didn't awaken. Slowly and with great care he laid the baby in the crook of her arm, placing its face near his wife's soft bosom. Maternal instinct took over. A sleepy Lexias pulled the child in to suckle. The prince hungrily latched on to her nipple, filling his belly with warm milk, falling quickly to slumber.

When Apollo's light brightened the heavens over the distant mountains, Agelaus knew he could delay the king's bidding no longer. Fear and dread filled him, as he stood in the doorway staring at the beauty of the sky, wondering if the gods would take the child quickly or if they would force it to linger and suffer. He wished for some reason to justify the deed. The child was deformed. It was a bastard. It was cursed. But, the king provided only the cruel command.

Lost in thought, Agelaus jumped at the shrill voice behind him.

Lexias stood with the sleeping baby in one arm. "Whose child is this? And why did I wake to find it on my breast?"

Continuing to scan the heavens, Agelaus said, "It's best you don't know."

Narrowing her eyes at her husband's back, she dug her free fist into her hip. "I'll not take care of any bastards in my home. By the balls of Zeus, I swear I—"

Agelaus turned, shaking his head. "Calm yourself. He's no bastard of mine, Lexias."

Suspicious, she checked beneath the loin wrapping. "A boy, then. I should've guessed. Whose son is he?"

"He's not sprung from my seed, if that's what worrying you. He wasn't given a name."

Lexias pursed her lips. "So, the gods have a sense of humor after all. I pray only for a girl. And they drop another boy-child in my lap." She smoothed the blanket the child lay nestled in, noting the elegant purple edging. "Where did you get this covering? These threads, only a noble house …" Her voice hushed. "Only a *royal* house would have the luxury of finely spun cloth and purple."

Agelaus grit his teeth, grabbing her arm. "Keep quiet, wife. The child doesn't stay with us."

Lexias pulled her arm free, softening a little. "Well, take this *nobody* so I can feed our own. *If* he left any milk." She squeezed a sagging breast. "He woke me nearly sucking my tit off."

Taking the child from his wife, Agelaus said, "I told you, he's not for us. He's for the gods."

"Rather ominous of you, Agelaus." Her eyes scrutinized his reddening face. "Explain yourself." Her foot tapped the floor.

Sighing, Agelaus brushed the baby's exposed cheek, its murky blue eyes staring up at him. "I've been charged with leaving the child on he slopes of the sacred mountain."

"Exposure?" Lexias blinked back surprise. "Well, I say you cannot do it. That's a heinous deed to do to a child. I'll not let my husband bear the weight of that."

"I must."

"Who can force a man against his will to do such a thing? No one holds that power over you. Who? Who has asked this crime of you?" Every once in a while a rumor passed through the village like a cold mist whispering about some abandoned child here or there. No one ever knew who or why, just that it was. Occasionally, a shepherd would come across a small stack of bleached bones, adding grisly details for good measure. So, the stories of infants left to die survived, spreading mystery and fear. But this, this was different. This was no rumor or random speculation circulating among the town. This was Agelaus, a man who feared all of the gods, a man who loved his children, a man who was now willing to abandon a babe to certain suffering and death.

"It's for your own safety, for our boys, I must keep silent. It was a mistake to come home. I should've traveled straight up the mountain." He stepped nearer to Lexias, leaning his face close to her ear, just in case the gods were listening. "Forget this infant ever crossed your path. That's what's best."

Lexias reached a strong hand to her husband's arm, squeezing it firmly. "Agelaus, don't do this. Look at him. He's helpless. You remember our sons, when they were of an age. I know you, husband, you'll not forgive yourself if you go through with it."

"You're probably right. But, I've no choice. How do I choose between our own little ones, and this … this stranger."

"You know whose child it is, don't you?"

Agelaus nearly choked on his words. "I do, but you must trust me. I have no choice."

"In the end, it's always the consequences that make us do one thing or another. Is the consequence so bad?"

The shepherd nodded. "Death. It would mean my death."

"Well, what's wrong with him, then?"

"Would you please, for the love of Apollo, stop asking questions," Agelaus snapped. "Help me secure a backpack to put him in so I can carry him over my back. It's a long walk where I'm going."

Lexias reluctantly pulled a thin, long blanket from a cupboard and fashioned a sling, securing the little nobody around Agelaus' shoulders and back. She tugged on her handiwork, making certain the little one was safe and comfortable. With a belly full of milk and tight swaddling, the child would likely sleep for several hours. Lexias kissed her husband on the cheek and watched him walk down the path away from their house. Her heart agonized over her husband's decision, hoping it was the right one.

Once Agelaus vanished from her line of sight, she turned her attention to the stable. She gently massaged her sore nipples. "Time to milk the goats before Tymon wakes for his feeding."

———

"My lady, you must try to eat a little something." Tessa set a tray of soft cheese and fresh bread on a table next to the queen's bed. "Some honeyed wine?"

Hecuba lay on her side, facing away from her trusted maid. "I am not hungry, Tessa."

"Just some bread, my lady, please." *This isn't like her at all, languishing abed.* It troubled Tessa that the king had stayed away all morning. He never stayed away all night, but when she'd asked the kings' guards where Priam was, they refused to tell her. And the rumors floating among the household made her skin crawl. *Why does he stay away from her? Why does she weep after such a joyous day?*

The household should be bustling with preparations for festivals and feasts, not quiet and mournful. As Tessa tidied up the linens, she noticed the prince's cradle was not in the chamber. *Strange.* The queen, a fiercely protective and doting mother, had nursed Hektor. She'd not allow her newborn prince out of her sight for a wet nurse. The rumors filled her head. *It can't be true. By the gods, I beg you, don't let it be true.*

Trembling, Tessa walked slowly around the bed. "My queen?"

The afternoon breeze quietly fluttered the edges of the curtains, and light bird song floated in the chamber. The air should be sweet, but only sourness filled Tessa's nose. When she saw the queen's face, she stifled a gasp. Hecuba looked like death with her pale skin and unblinking eyes staring at nothing.

"My lady? Where's the child?"

"Please, leave me be. I want no food. I want nothing except my son," Hecuba whispered.

Tessa grasped the front of her chiton. "Where is he, my lady?"

The queen remained silent.

Tessa dared a step closer, leaning down near her queen. "Has something happened?"

"He is gone, Tessa. Forever."

The faithful maid reached a hand to the queen's forehead. "You aren't fevered."

"Would that it was so simple," the queen said, miserably.

"What has happened, my lady?"

"Priam has taken my son from me."

Tessa froze. "The king?"

The queen sobbed softly. "Stripped him from my arms."

Thin tears spilled down Tessa's wrinkled cheeks. "Why, my lady? Why?"

"Apollo commanded it so."

Tessa strained to control her voice. "Was there some malady?"

Hecuba wailed anew. "My son. My son."

Tessa wrung her hands together. *By the gods, it's true.* "What happened, my lady? I beg you tell me."

Hecuba calmed enough to speak. "Apollo commanded it. For the sake of Troy."

"My lady …" Tessa's hands fell to her side. The queen had lost two children after Hektor, but she couldn't believe that the gods would be so cruel as to take this one as well. He was healthy. Heavy. Handsome. "It's unfair, my lady."

"Who knows why the gods truly do anything?" groaned the queen. "Do not ever speak of him again. His existence is best forgotten."

Tessa backed away from her queen, hiding her horror and disbelief behind a trembling hand. "The gods give and take what they wish and we mortals suffer."

"Yes," murmured Hecuba, as a fresh wave of grief washed over her. "Please, leave me."

"I will come again, my lady. I won't be far if you need me." What balm existed for the broken heart of a mother? What words or nourishment could fill the emptiness of the circle of a mother's arms where a child should be? *There is nothing I can do for her now. Gods be merciful to the child, this prince who would be forgotten by decree.* Tessa left the queen weeping in bed, her own heart breaking with each step she took from her queen. She understood, now, why the king had stayed away. And likely he would for some time, because she couldn't imagine Hecuba ever forgiving Priam for this.

In order to reach the rolling hills that formed the wide base of Mount Ida, Agelaus followed the Scamander River across the boggy plain, where the famous wild horses of Troy roamed. The jostling and swaying of walking kept the infant from crying. In fact, he hadn't heard even the slightest whimper from the prince the entire journey. Except for the occasional gusts of wind and Agelaus' humming, the long trek to the sacred slopes proved a quiet venture. This was the first time, and he prayed the last, he'd be ordered to expose an infant. He knew he must obey or face a nasty death, but soon doubts crept into his troubled mind. *Can I do this?* He thought of little Harmon's face smiling up at him. *The prince is only a babe-in-arms.* He walked until the sun passed its zenith and hovered midway in the western sky. Agelaus traveled along a small dirt trail worn through the weeds and grasses following the river. Soon, the sacred mountain rose up before him and the path became rockier and uneven.

By late afternoon, he'd reached a place where the trees grew more sparsely. Agelaus stopped and untied the swaddling backpack. The child who'd slept the entire morning hike was now awakened by being untied and removed from his comfort. The baby's whimper turned to a loud wail. The newborn's cry echoed up into the trees and into the clear sky. Startled birds flew from the brush, a hare scampered away leaving a thin dust trail behind it. Agelaus set the prince down on the ground beneath the base of an ancient tree. He stared at the little nobody, his eyes filling with pitiful tears. *What can I do? What can I do?* Agelaus knew if he didn't do as commanded, his own family would suffer in blood. His loyalty and obedience pitted him against his own nature. *I am lost no matter which way I turn.*

"I'm sorry, little prince. I've got my own family to worry about." He looked up to the sky, hoping to see Apollo or Zeus racing from above to stop him, but saw only the beauty of blue heavens. "May the gods forgive me. May I forgive myself someday."

He turned quickly, walking away as fast as he could with the child's crying echoing in his ears. After a few moments, the sound of the little prince faded into the surrounding hillsides and groves. Guilt filled Agelaus' heart all the way home. His only solace rested in the knowledge that he had done as commanded. *Artemis, have some mercy on this child. Save him if you can from wild beasts.*

THREE

the silver bear

TROY—1290 BCE

Zeus summoned Artemis to the crystal hall of Olympus. The cries of the infant who would doom the city of Troy tormented his waking ears. As he watched the shepherd abandon the infant, he knew he must intervene. The infant must survive and fulfill his destiny.

Artemis, with her bow slung across her shoulder, entered the hall. "What game holds your rapt attention, Father? I see you are mesmerized by the view below."

"I gave Apollo permission to exact a heavy price from the King of Troy. But the scheme has gone awry."

The goddess smirked. "You and your games. Mortals are unpredictable at best, and Apollo an apt player."

Zeus narrowed his eyes at his daughter. "It is our way. Apollo played his hand, now I must correct the course."

"What has that to do with me?"

"I am sending you to intervene. Apollo must not know." He stroked his silvered beard. "At least not yet. Let him believe he has won his victory for now."

Artemis crossed her arms, unable to deny the Lord of Gods. "Tell me what I must do."

With a swift sweep of his arm, Zeus cleared the clouds for his daughter to see what he saw. He opened her ears to the wailing infant. "There, below, see the mortal child on the mountain?"

The goddess winced. "Exposure. Such a barbaric death. Easier to slit its throat and be done with it."

"Fly down to the infant. Suckle it until the shepherd, Agelaus, returns for it."

"Whose child is it?"

"None of your concern."

Artemis arched a brow. "Mysterious move, Father. Intriguing. I can hardly wait to see how this will end."

"Speak of it no more."

Artemis bowed her head. "As you wish, Father." She flew from Olympus to the newborn that bore no proper name. Passing through clouded skies, she transformed her goddess silhouette into her totem form. Forcing her back to a rounded hump, she pulled her arms and legs squat and strong. Her regal neck thickened and her chest expanded, making the final twist into a silver-coated bear.

With wide paws, she hit the earth and sauntered up to the abandoned child sprawled on the dirt. He'd cried and flailed his way from the safety of the bunting. Dust caught in his thin tears smudging his tiny cheeks. His little belly ached for milk with no relief. His hazy blue eyes, incapable of focusing on the dark form blocking the blinding light of day, filled with tears and crusted with dirt. The pathetic infant stretched out his tiny palm toward the shadow. Silver paws gently scooped up the wretched child. The goddess-bear placed him on her breast and he suckled her rich milk until his limbs went slack with warmth and peaceful slumber. She curled around the sleeping child, her vigil beginning until Zeus sent his servant.

For days, sleep refused to come. Dark shadows crept into the corners of Agelaus' dozing eyes, startling him awake. Haunting cries of the newborn filled his ears, drowning out the sounds of the ordinary day. On the tenth day, Agelaus woke drenched in sweat again.

"What's wrong?" Lexias asked groggily.

"The cattle keep dying in my dreams," he whispered into the dark, fearful the gods plotted to strike him dead or worse. "I see myself walking around their carcasses. What do you think it means?"

Lexias rolled over. "That I shall never sleep again."

"Are children not innocents? He showed no deformity," Agelaus agonized.

"I know. I know. We will never know. Be satisfied, husband. You made your decision. We must look forward, not back. Go back to sleep."

"Lexias?"

"What now, Agelaus?"

"I can't keep it to myself any longer."

Lexias sat up, intrigued and annoyed. "What do you mean?"

"It's about the baby."

"If you're going to tell me the child was your bastard and you left him rotting in the sun—"

Agelaus hissed, "Lower your voice, woman. The child isn't mine." His eyes widened with the horror he was about to speak. "He was the son of Priam."

Lexias, a practical woman, dug her fingers into her husband's arm, pulling him close to her face. "As in a son of *King* Priam?"

"Yes."

Lexias shook him. "By all the gods! By the balls of Zeus! Why didn't you tell me from the start?"

"I was forbidden. I was afraid of—"

"Afraid of what? The gods? The king? You killed a royal prince of Troy. You believe there will be no consequence to pay?"

"I did as the king commanded, Lexias."

She released her hold on his arm. "Men. You have no clue about the hearts of women. The heart of a mother."

Agelaus protested, "Apollo commanded the king do this. He had no choice."

"The gods! The gods! What do they do but rain misery on us? What good are the gods? The poor queen. Her misery." She placed a hand on her milk swollen breast. "I suckled her prince and didn't know it."

"Now that you know it's a prince, you have more pity?"

"I told you not to do it in the first place."

Agelaus, fearful the gods would eavesdrop between a man and wife, put his finger to her lips. "Keep your voice down, woman. *They* may hear you."

"You need to get that baby, or what's left if it."

The bull herder groaned. "What mutilated mess will I find?"

"If there's anything left at all."

"Are you certain I should go back, Lexias? Once done, it can't be undone."

"The child is most likely dead, but if we give it a proper burial, lessen your part in this brutality … if the queen should change her mind, or the king should regret his decision … perhaps you will be spared."

Agelaus grabbed his wife's arm. It had not occurred to him that the king might change his mind, and if he did, he'd need someone to blame. "By the gods! I'm going to die."

"You were so concerned about the gods, you forgot about the world we live in, the world of men."

Agelaus sat bolt upright, the truth quickly dawning on him. "By the balls of Zeus, you speak honestly. I must do what I can. Perhaps, perhaps, it may all come to nothing, but if it should turn the other way …" Agelaus closed his eyes against such imagined punishments. "Are you certain, Lexias?"

"Yes, I am."

A rosy dawn veil swept across the sky, as Lexias packed her husband a hearty lunch of flat bread, sweet purple grapes, and a hunk of wrapped goat cheese. She filled his worn leather flask with a mixture of tart wine and water. Then, she kissed her husband on the cheek, sending him on his way. "Travel with care, my dear."

Agelaus waved and walked away, his burden already heavy on his heart.

Lexias set about her chores, feeding the penned calves, milking the goats, and grinding grain for bread. If she had spare time in the afternoon, she would card wool and weave in the shade. Her brooding husband had proved of little use these past several days around the farm. His worrying had made him ill and her impatient.

She reasoned the tragedy was not her husband's fault. Only the gods knew the truth of Priam's heart and what secrets he held there, so any fault of the king's lay between him and the gods. If a king disobeyed a god, an entire kingdom might crumble to dust and ash. Lexias sighed and looked up at the climbing sun, a few stray tendrils of her hair stuck to her sweating neck and face. She wiped her forehead on her sleeve. *Let Agelaus do what he must and be unstained.*

"Quit these morbid thoughts, woman. Get to your goats," she said to herself. She gave one last glance upwards and went about her day, her thoughts at war in her mind as she worked.

The path along the Scamander passed by faster than before beneath Agelaus' feet, his anxiety and worry pushing him at a frantic pace. He didn't stop to eat the entire way there. His stomach twisted and complained, but he pressed forward, believing any moment spent lingering might make the situation worse. The herdsman's head pounded as the heat of Helios rose higher and higher. Sweat trickled into the corners of Agelaus' mouth and stung his eyes. He trudged forward, undeterred, his mind set stubbornly to purpose that he would at least find the infant to bury it, easing his guilt for his part in its death with a proper burial. King Priam would never know.

Agelaus recognized the terrain as he neared the area he'd abandoned the child. He blinked the heat from his eyes, catching a flash of silver in the sunlight. He froze. A silver-furred bear emerged from a small patch of brush ahead of him. *I've no weapon! What an imbecile I am.* He hid in the brush, hoping the animal wouldn't catch his scent.

Peering through the scraggly branches, Agelaus watched in dismay as the bear headed straight for the very spot he'd left the baby. Horrifying images of the bear sucking the little bones dry filled his head. He scratched at the prickling sweat on his neck. His heart thundered in his ears. He willed himself to stop breathing so hard, fearful the bear would sense him and eat him, too.

In the midst of his panic, a woman's gentle singing carried on the breeze, hypnotizing Agelaus with its sweet melody. He didn't understand her words, but fell to peace inside. It dawned on him. *This is the language of the gods!* In the city temples, he'd heard the divine tongue spoken by the priests and priestesses under the influence of the gods. *What is a woman doing this far up the sacred mountain? How does she know the words?* He pressed closer to the brush. A twig snapped under his foot. He froze. The song hushed.

Agelaus, wide eyed and certain he was about to die, watched as the silver bear reemerged from the brush. Its shaggy coat shimmered in the bright sun. The bear's glittering black eyes scanned the foliage, finding Agelaus' face. The beautiful beast tossed its neck from side to side and then lumbered away. *Could it be?*

He heard a child's cry and rushed to the spot where he'd left the prince. There, lying as peaceful and serene as ever, lay the carefully swaddled prince. He was unharmed by the bear. In Artemis' temple, a large mosaic of her walking next to a bear adorned a part of the floor. Since boyhood, he'd stepped across it many times to make offerings to the goddess. "It must have been," he whispered, picking up the child. "Lexias will never believe this. I'm sorry, little one, to have left you here. You are heavier than before."

He undid the swaddling, checking the baby for injuries. "Why, you're fat!" He pulled the loin wrapping away. "You're not even soiled!" Agelaus had expected to find a carcass or bones or some other gruesome remains of the newborn, maybe even nothing at all if a wild animal had dragged it away. The one thing he never expected was to actually find the baby alive, let alone thriving. The herdsman knew in his heart it was a god-sign. He eyed the sky. "Artemis, you've set the child in my care. I am certain of it. Allow him your protection in my house."

He swaddled the infant and wrapped him tightly in the backpack sling. "Well, my little backpack prince, I'm not certain what happens now, but I'll see that you've not a gruesome end," Agelaus said. "Paris, yes, that's what I'll call you … the little backpack. It's time to go home. One more mouth to feed won't break my back." He looked around; making certain no one spied him, because everything from that point on was treason and certain death. He knew at least one of the gods was watching, and hoped they'd take pity on the child as he did. And take pity on him as well.

FOUR

a small return

TROY—1290 BCE

T he return hike covered miles of quiet farmland and empty spaces. Occasionally, a stray cow or goat crossed his path. Birds flew above looking for freshly sown fields to plunder with eager beaks. When the sun hit its searing zenith, Agelaus worried about stumbling across strangers, or worse, people he actually knew and trying to explain about Paris. In his rush to retrieve the baby, he'd given little thought to the future or the suspicious talk certain to surface. Everyone in the village knew that Lexias was not with child. How would he explain the sudden appearance of an infant? He concocted a story as he walked.

"I am returning with my cousin's child. She died and … gratitude, you're very kind. Well, Lexias insisted that we care for the orphan. You know Lexias." He practiced the lie over and over, adding a convincing *what-can-I-do-about-it* shrug. After a mile of rehearsal, Agelaus convinced himself he could answer anyone's questions.

It wasn't long before fate tested his resolve. A farmer, pulling a cart laden with baskets, approached from the opposite direction. Despite his earlier resolve he jumped off the road and hid behind a tree. "By the balls of Zeus, I'm such a coward," he whispered into the tree's trunk.

A woman's silver voice rang clearly and icily in his ear. "*You are brave to take this child. Fate is served.*"

He shook off the chill, but the words lingered, ripening like a fig in the hot sun. *Brave? Foolhardy, maybe.* The words *Fate is served* weighed ominously on his heart. He still didn't know why the child stood condemned before the world. Perhaps, it didn't matter. King Priam would likely never speak to him, a common man, about the child's death sentence. Agelaus sighed. "You're my son, now, little Paris."

When the farmer passed into the distance, Agelaus pulled the baby off his back to rest. "Just a few more miles, little one. Just a few more miles."

He gently bounced his new *son* in his arms. He'd plenty of practice raising little ones with Lexias. As a father, Agelaus leaned toward tenderness, a rebellion against his own father's harsher methods. "Time to get you home to your new *mother*, little Paris. You'll need a feeding soon enough. Can't have you bawling in my ear."

Agelaus wrapped the infant securely onto his back again and began the last leg of their journey home, not knowing how Lexias would take this surprise. They'd both believed the child would be dead and made no plan for this. Raising a king's son in secret. *The deed is done and can't be undone now.*

Lexias squatted next to a goat for its evening milking. "Come, girl. Let's get it done with." Sliding the clay jar beneath the goat, Lexias pushed the backs of her hands firmly into the engorged udder. Fresh warm milk whizzed into the jar. "There's a good girl." She repeated the process on the opposite side. "Your milk makes the best cheese." She scratched the goat behind the ears before lightly slapping its hind quarters. The goat skittered off into the herd of nannies. *One down, four to go.*

She stood up, wiping the sweat from her face, scanning the narrow path for the fifth time that morning. Low and behold, in the far distance, she caught sight of her husband. *By the gods, I hope he didn't find a mangled mess.* She'd planned a small funeral rite and a quick burial. Hopefully, that would put an end to her husband's suffering and sleeplessness.

She waved with one hand, the other knuckled at her hip. "Hello, husband!" Agelaus waved back, his pace quickening at the sight of her. Her temples throbbed with anticipation. *Hurry up, old man. The wait keeps me from my chores and my stomach in knots. My head!* As he got closer, she couldn't tell whether he carried a small bundle or was slumped over with exhaustion. "Hurry, old man!" she hollered.

"Wife! I bring you a miracle!"

Lexias mumbled to the goats, "What a greeting! How are bleached and pillaged bones miraculous?" She watched him hike the last stretch of dirt path.

As Agelaus neared, his smile broadened. "Look! Lexias! Look, what I have brought home."

Lexias frowned. "What are you doing? Why so—" A muffled cry sounded from the backpack sling.

The bull herder faced his wife and grabbed her by the shoulders.

"He's alive, Lexias."

"But how can that be? Are you certain it is the same child?"

"Of course! The same cloth binding I was given by … well, it is the same." He pulled the dirty purple linen threaded with gold from his pack. The sun glinted off the metallic threads shining the truth of her husband's words.

She ripped the cloth from his grasp and stuffed it into her waistband. "By the balls of Zeus, put that away! Let's see the child. Hurry up. Surely, he's in need of attention." She helped unknot the backpack sling, and the rounded bundle of child lay securely in her arms as the sling fell away. Clouded blue eyes squinted in the brightness and he cried.

"Come to the house, my dear," Agelaus encouraged.

Lexias stood unmoved, checking his little body for injury. She looked up at Agelaus with rounded eyes. "Not a mark on him. Not a scratch. And he's fat!"

Smiling back, Agelaus shrugged his shoulders. "The gods, Lexias. They intervened."

"We must never tell anyone, Agelaus. No one!"

"I'll not speak a word. You believe I wish myself dead?"

Lexias carefully swaddled the baby. "I believe I wish all of us a long life. What will we call him?"

Agelaus took him from the cradle of his wife's arms. "I've named him Paris."

"Your sense of humor astounds." Lexias shook her head. "I'm to raise a son named after the sling he arrived in?"

"There now, Paris, don't mind your mother's sharp tongue."

Lexias scowled at her husband. "Sharp tongue indeed."

"I jest, wife. Come, let's get inside."

She grabbed his arm. "What do we tell everyone?"

"That my long lost cousin died, leaving us caretakers of the infant."

"You have thought this out. Well done, old man."

Agelaus grinned. "Old woman."

Lexias playfully slapped his arm. They walked into the house never once looking back, the future the only path from that day forward. Paris' parentage was safely sheltered in the secrecy only a husband and wife share, for their futures entwined until death.

"Sire, a basket has arrived for you with instructions that your eyes alone should view the contents," Damianos said.

"Who is it from?" asked Priam.

"Agelaus, the herdsman. He claims you alone will know the meaning."

"Give it to me." Dread pounded through his veins upon hearing the ominous message. *Has Agelaus done the deed?* Even as his heart cried out for his son, he knew Troy must be saved. The mask of king didn't protect him from himself.

Damianos returned and presented him with the small basket.

Taking the bundle, Priam asked, "Where is the queen?"

"I don't know, my lord."

"Leave me," Priam commanded, and the slave disappeared on silent feet.

The basket hefted little more than air. He lifted the lid to see a small lump wrapped neatly in a piece of rough spun cloth. Small traces of darkened crimson stained the linen. *Blood. Stains of blood.* As he undid the tiny bundle, a slender piece of meat fell onto the floor. He picked it up between two fingers. It was stiff and bumpy. Priam's throat soured, realizing it was not just a piece of bloody meat, but a small tongue. The king closed his eyes. A child's tongue. His son's tongue. The evidence he commanded Agelaus to send.

Priam carried the basket with him from the hall out to his private gardens. He walked until he found a quiet spot in a wild stand of pomegranate bushes the size of trees. Gathering twigs and small broken limbs, he built a fire. Once the flames burned hot, he removed the tongue from the basket. He tossed it and the stained cloth into the fire. As the smoke curled into the air, Priam wept. *My son. My son. What have I done?*

When the fire burned out, Priam gathered the ashes and scattered them to the winds of Aeolus. *Take my son.*

When priam entered Hecuba's chambers later that evening, he hoped his wife would be in a more forgiving mood than the previous evening. He found her standing on the balcony overlooking the upper citadel and the city and harbor below. Her hands entwined behind her accentuated her long, narrow back. Her dark hair, pinned up in simple coils, exposed the gentle curve of her neck. Priam thought of all the kisses he'd planted there.

"Wife," he said tenderly.

Without turning to face him, Hecuba replied, "What do you want?"

He stepped closer. "Join me for dinner, my love."

"I am not hungry, Priam."

Longing for the closeness they shared to return, Priam stepped behind her, slipping his arms around her still swollen waist. "You must eat. Little Hektor is asking for you."

She stiffened at his touch. With a controlled voice, she said, "You think I wish to sit across from you? Look into your eyes ..." she turned slowly to face him, "and see the very eyes my son had? The son you stole from me?" Anger and grief mingled together in fresh tears. "You have broken me, Priam."

Queen Hecuba looked out, again, at the sprawling city. Clay tiled rooftops stretched as far as the eye could see, the stone-lined streets curved beyond sight, and the hazy blue horizon marked the line where Troy ended. "All of the Trojans are safe tonight because you believed our son a threat to them all."

Priam dropped his arms to the side. "It was Apollo's will, not mine, Hecuba."

"I do not care." Her face twisted with renewed heart break. "He was my son, Priam! Mine!" She wrapped her arms around her middle, hugging the swell of where her son used to be. Her shoulders shook slightly at first and then with violence. "Mine," she wept over and over. Gripping the stone railing with one hand, the queen slid to her knees, sobbing for her son.

Priam stooped to hold her in his arms, wishing to comfort her, but she pushed his hands away. "My son. And you took him from me ..." Her words morphed to an anguished howl.

The king straightened. *I am cursed because of Laomedon. For my own weakness.* From the balcony, he could see Mount Ida rising into a hazy sky. With his wife weeping at his feet, he was overcome with guilt. It was his fault. All of it.

FIVE
Paris and the bulls
TROY—1287 BCE

The morning opened dark and grey. Rain threatened. It mattered not what weather fell from the gods, the bulls needed tending and so did the farm. Agelaus' family relied on the financial surplus his knowledge and skill provided in raising the sacred beasts for sacrifice and the bull arena. The extra coin he earned from King Priam's patronage and his expertise supplemented his family's world, providing more than a meager herder's existence. He tended to the fields, small orchard, and the bulls, longing for the day when his sons attained experience enough to watch the fields and cattle without his company.

Lexias looked after the chickens and goats and their sons … and little Paris Alexander. The boy grew at a rapacious rate, faster than the other two at an equal number of passing seasons. Lexias lamented daily that Paris would be the death of her and the cupboards. At the age of three, Paris now stood as tall as her hip. He never refused a meal and often snuck whatever morsels he scavenged from the wooden cooking table.

"Paris? Paris! Where are you?" Lexias had taken her eyes off him long enough to gather the eggs. She still needed to milk the goats. "Where is that boy?" As she searched the stables, looking behind the bales and storage pots, her ears pricked at a loud snort. She bolted toward the bull pen, skidding to a complete stop, sending dirt flying and breaking her sandal strap. Reaching down, she undid the sandal flopping like a shackle and tossed it, never once taking her eyes from the boy walking without care among the bulls corralled for the next week's sacrifices.

"Gratitude, Apollo, at least you didn't send him to the hen house to get pecked to death. Yes, better he is stomped to bone and guts by bulls!" she said aloud, not caring if the gods heard her. Lexias didn't hold the gods in as high esteem as her husband. Agelaus lived and breathed by signs and omens, made worship and sacrifice, and lived truly to serve and honor his patrons. Pressing needs in the real world were more important than the unseen world of the divine.

"Paris! Come out of there!" she demanded. Fearing she'd startle the massive animals, Lexias moved closer, one step at a time.

Paris, catching the sound of his mother's voice, looked over his shoulder as he reached up and tugged a bull's tail.

Lexias stumbled and clutched the front of her chiton. *Where is Agelaus?* "Paris, stop that."

When the boy released his grip, the bull flicked its tail, meandering away as if nothing more than a fly pestered it. Lexias rolled her eyes, as sweat trickled down her cheeks. "By the gods! How do I get him out in one piece?" She watched with unblinking eyes as Paris moved deeper into the herd of dark hides and hooves of death. Dropping to her knees, she scanned between the bull's legs for the boy's feet.

"Lexias?"

"*Ahhh!*" She jumped up, brushing stands of stray hair from her face, tears immediately springing to her eyes at the sight of her husband.

Agelaus put a steady hand on his wife's shoulder. "I know the look. Where is he this time? What has he done?"

Lexias pointed toward the corral, sinking to her knees, and sobbed, "He's in with the bulls."

The hairs on Agelaus' arms stood on end. Turning toward the enclosure, he heard his young son's babbling. "Paris? Paris? Come here." Agelaus steadied his voice, knowing the dangers of startling the bulls while his son was underfoot. Slowly, he approached the pen. *Strange they are not bothered by his presence.* "Paris Alexander, come here."

A rounded face peeked from under a bulging muscled neck. "There you are. Come." Agelaus held his arms out. "Come here, son." Paris moved toward the edge of the pen. Agelaus moved closer. *Thank the gods.* Then, in a flash, Paris bolted back into the corralled herd. The beasts stomped around, scattering wildly. One bull bucked at another. Lexias screamed.

Agelaus sprang for the corral. He leapt over the fencing, landing hard on his feet. His left ankle immediately throbbed. Ignoring the burn shooting up his leg, Agelaus hobbled his way into the herd, keeping a keen eye trained on the boy and on the giants he not so gently shoved aside. The bulls bellowed and snorted. Then, by the grace of Apollo, the boy's head popped up in front of a bull next to Agelaus. He snatched Paris up by the arm so hard, the boy began crying, which agitated the bulls more than the frantic pushing and shoving.

Lexias sprinted to the corral, pulling Paris from her husband's grasp and over the fencing. She suffocated the boy with a maternal hug, sobbing hysterically into his black curls.

Agelaus climbed the barrier between danger and safety, bruised and rattled, with an ankle swollen to the size of an apple.

"I took my eyes from him for just a moment. Every day it's something new. He's too daring. If the bulls—"

Agelaus hobbled to his wife's side. "But they didn't."

"If you hadn't come, I-I don't know what I would've done."

The herder ruffled the boy's hair. "You must mind your mother, Paris. Do as she says."

Lexias pressed her palms together, wringing her fingers. "I could never forgive myself if something happened to him, but I am tired, Agelaus. Tired of chasing this child down, trying to keep him safe."

"I understand, wife. You're *old* and he is too fast."

Lexias squinted hard at her husband, snapping his legs with her apron. "Old am I?"

Agelaus backed up. "Now, now, Lexias … it was a jest. I will take the boy from now on."

"To the meadows?" she screeched.

"Unless, you've a better plan stuffed there inside of your chiton."

"I have to milk the goats before their udders burst," she quipped. Over her shoulder she added, "May the gods go with both of you."

Agelaus picked Paris up and held him in his arms. His legs dangled to Agelaus' mid-thighs. "What am I to do with you, son? What to do?"

SIX

the gods' gift

TROY—1285 BCE

Paris looked deeply into the dark, watery eyes of the laboring cow as she lay on her side in the field. She snorted when he ran a calming hand between her ears. His young brow knitted with concern for her extended labor.

"Why does the calf not come to the light, father?" Paris asked. "She's frightened."

Agelaus knelt beside his son and shook his head. "Her first water spilled at dawn." Agelaus looked up into the sky. "Apollo's light is high above us now. You're right, son. She should be frightened. Too much time has passed."

Paris always spoke as if he knew what the cattle were thinking. It puzzled Agelaus, yet he never corrected the boy, because he was always right. He watched as Paris continued stroking the cow's forehead. His normally loud and rambunctious son offered gentle hands and words to the cow.

"I must help her bring the calf to light, Paris. It will be distressing for her and the calf. But, if I don't do this, we may lose them both. Can you help her remain calm?"

Paris broke his spell with the cow and looked his father dead in the eye. "I will, Father. Please, help her." Paris bent his head near the animal's ears again, speaking in a low, comforting whisper to her. "Be patient, cow. Father knows how to help you. Be calm." His small hands stroked her head and neck.

Agelaus moved to the hind quarters of the tired mother. He noted her heavy breathing had steadied. He wasn't certain if it was Paris' calming effect or her labor stealing her strength, but he knew he had to reach inside and pull the calf out. Placing a firm hand on the cow's hip, he gently inserted the other hand inside of the birth canal. The beast snorted and groaned and weakly kicked her leg at Agelaus. "Calm her, Paris!"

Paris kissed the cow on the forehead. "Be still. Father is helping you. Soon you'll see your baby."

Agelaus pressed his arm deeper into the birth canal, touching the problem. "Paris, one of the calf's legs is turned back. I'll need to push it back, so she can push the calf without exhausting herself to death. Tell her it will soon be finished."

Paris stroked the cow's head, leaning so close to her ears that Agelaus couldn't hear what his son murmured.

Sweat soaked Agelaus' tunic so it clung like a second skin to his back. Feeling for the calf's head, he gently pushed it back and reached for the bent leg. "Ah! There it is, girl." The cow's body pushed against his arm, impeding his progress in pulling the calf straight. "Tell her to stop pushing her baby to the light. I can't get the calf positioned if she works against me."

Paris murmured into the mother's ears again and her body stopped heaving against Agelaus' arm.

The calf's bent leg slipped from his grasp. "By Zeus you're hard to get hold of." He reached again, moving slowly and carefully, not wanting to risk injuring the cow for the sake of the calf. The cow groaned with her effort to birth her baby, lifting her head to look back at Agelaus. "Paris, keep her down!"

The boy placed both hands on the cow's head. "Be still. Be still." The animal's head dropped back to the grass and she closed her eyes. "Father, she is spent and wishes to give up."

Agelaus reached up to wipe the sweat from his brow with his free hand. "Not long now, Paris. Tell her to be ready to welcome her calf."

"Did you hear my father? You won't have to wait much longer. Be still. Your calf is coming."

Over the years, Agelaus had assisted many cows through difficult deliveries, but he had never had such an able hand to aide him. And such a young one at that. Paris merely five springs on the earth had managed to keep a distressed mother from struggling against his intrusive arm. "Ah! The head and both legs are facing the light!" Agelaus announced triumphantly. He removed his arm gently, wiping the birthing muck on his tunic. "Your mother will not be pleased by the filth and stench."

"Why will she be upset? You helped bring a calf to our farm and saved its mother. You are always saying we are proud herdsmen."

Agelaus gave Paris' shoulder a gentle squeeze. "We are indeed breeders of fine cattle."

"And prize bulls most of all!" Paris exclaimed. "And this new bull will be mine to raise."

"Yes, we've been blessed by the gods with the finest bulls in

Troy. We don't know yet if this one is a bull."

"She does," Paris said.

Agelaus raised his eyebrow. "The cow?"

"Yes, she told me he will be a fine bull. The biggest we've ever bred."

"How can she know this?" Agelaus asked incredulously.

Paris narrowed his eyes at his father. "Wasn't that why you bred her to Theodoros? The god-gift?"

"True, I'd hoped the pairing would breed a fine bull. The finest. She is the best cow we own. And he the biggest bull."

"She said Theodoros is fierce, but her calf will be far bigger."

Agelaus threw his head back and laughed. "Well then, tell her to bring him to the light without delay. Let's see this magnificent beast."

"Did you hear father, cow? Bring your baby to the light!"

Agelaus watched in awe as the cow seemingly understood Paris. Her belly contracted several times, until the calf's front hooves appeared and then its nose pushed into the air, followed by its entire head. "Paris, quickly! Come here!" Agelaus squatted behind the cow. "The calf must take its first breath now."

Paris stood behind his father, observing over his shoulder. "He's not breathing."

"No, he's not. We must clear the nose, so he can take his first breath." Agelaus wiped the slime from the calf's nostrils, encouraging it to breathe.

The cow heaved, struggling to sit up momentarily. The upper body of the calf, covered in a thin, slimy skin, slid out with its black tongue hanging limp from its mouth and eyes closed.

Paris' eyes welled with tears. "Is he dead?"

"No, he's not dead. Soon, Paris we will see if she is right." The cow's wide belly constricted one last time, pushing the rest of the calf from her body, spilling amber-colored water with it. The calf lay still, its black hide glistening wetly in the sun.

"Father! Why does it not breathe?"

Agelaus knelt to clear the debris from the calf's nostrils again and pinched its nose and slapped it firmly on its side.

"What are you doing? You'll hurt him!" Paris hollered.

"I'm helping the calf take its first air. Here." Agelaus grabbed Paris by the wrist, pulling him next to the newborn. "Rub his nose. Pat him until he breathes. Quickly now. The sooner he takes his first breath, the stronger he'll be."

Paris did as his father commanded, wiping the slimy skin from the calf. It snorted. It gagged. It inhaled its first air and picked its head up, coming eye to eye with Paris. "He's well, Father!" Paris' faced beamed.

"She was right, Paris. It's a bull, by Zeus, with balls to rival the god-king himself!" Agelaus smiled proudly at his youngest boy.

As the calf stood on his unsteady legs, his entire body shivered in the warm breeze.

Paris crossed his arms over his chest. "He's cold."

"He'll be warm soon enough. How's his mother?"

Paris whispered the question into the cow's ear. She nudged Paris' shoulder and then licked his hair. "She said she's glad to be done."

"After she delivers the birth sac, she'll be done. I'll take it to Apollo's temple for divination. Let's see how fortunate we'll be with this new addition to our farm."

The cow groaned loudly as she stood, turning her full attention to her baby wobbling next to her. Paris laughed when the mother licked her baby, nearly knocking it over.

Agelaus wondered about the nature of Paris' royal bloodline.

He was convinced, after this afternoon, the boy's connection to the cattle went far beyond simple observation. The king's line was renowned for their god-gift of speaking with horses. And now Agelaus wondered if this god-gift coursed through Paris' blood, making it possible for his son to speak to bulls. *He's already got the dimpled chin of Priam's sons.* A chill ran down his spine. It hadn't occurred to him that the boy's own familial inheritance would out them for their lie. *No one knows but Lexias. I must keep it that way.* When he'd decided to keep the discarded child years ago, he hadn't expected to love him. But there it was. He loved the boy as his own. Thinking that one day he might lose his son to the boy's rightful father pained him, even though he knew he couldn't stop whatever the gods had planned.

"Mother!" Paris hollered approaching the farm with his father. "Mother!" Knowing she'd be milking the goats, Paris ran straight for the stable. Smiling broadly, he said, "Guess what I've done today?"

Lexias looked up from her work to see the boy's brilliant flash of teeth. It wasn't his usual smile of mischief, but pride. She breathed a small sigh of relief. "So, what is this thing you've done?"

"Remember the cow heavy with calf? In the far field?"

Lexias hesitated. "Yes?"

Beaming with accomplishment, he put his fists into his hips. "I helped Father bring her calf to the light."

"Well, then. You've had a busy morning. Cow and calf are doing well?" she asked.

Paris grimaced. "Yes. Father said the leg was turned back, so he had to help her. It was messy."

Agelaus now stood in the stable doorway. "We almost lost them both."

"But we didn't. Mother, it will be the finest bull we've ever had," Paris said.

Lexias slapped the nanny goat on its hind quarters, sending it skittering off. "What say you, Agelaus? Is our young son speaking true?"

"He is. The bull-calf is strong despite his difficult entry into the world."

Lexias nodded her approval. "And you, Paris, helped deliver this bull-calf?"

"Yes, Mother."

"And you didn't shy away from the birth?"

"No, Mother. The cow needed me. I spoke to her to keep her calm."

Lexias looked to her husband for confirmation. He nodded his head. "Then you have done well. I'm proud you didn't turn away. Only the bravest men can appreciate the agonies of birth for animal or woman." She stood from her stool. "You must be famished. The both of you. Go wash up. I'll prepare the evening meal early."

Paris ran to his mother, wrapping his little arms around her waist. Lexias leaned down, smoothing his curly black hair from his face before placing a gentle kiss on his forehead. "You are a son any mother would be proud to call her own." As she said the words, she missed the tear her husband wiped from his eye. "It's his calling to be with you, Agelaus. He grows fine and strong with your care. You'll find our other sons about their chores. Now, off. Off with you both." She hurried them from the stable. Once alone, she took her stool again to finish milking the last goat, smiling as she completed her work. *He is a fine son.*

SEVEN

a prince and his mother

TRO AN PALACE—1285 BCE

Five years, Hecuba thought. Five years and the ache for the son she'd never known still throbbed painfully in her chest. She'd grown accustomed to the hurt. Watching her children romping in the courtyard, the queen sighed. Little Deiphobus entertained his younger twin siblings with his wooden sword and shield. The youngest, Polydorus, nursed at her breast. She'd refused a wet nurse for all of her children after the loss of her second son. Rarely did she allow her children from her sight. The ache for her second son pulled at her again, never giving her peace. In truth, some days she conjured the pain to remind her of his little face, and some days she cursed the sadness and prayed to Apollo and Artemis to wipe her memories of him.

When Hektor appeared at the courtyard gate, she smiled widely despite her melancholy. He waved, making straight for her. Only he had the power to dull the hurt that had become as much a part of her as her hand or foot. The other children, although a source of joy, reminded her of the one she'd lost. Hektor's presence was the only one not marred by grief. He was her Golden Prince.

Hektor approached and kissed his mother's cheek. "Mother," he said, pinching Polydorus' bare foot. The baby kicked at his eldest brother's attempted affection. "Such a strong leg for someone so little," he laughed. "You're sad again, Mother. I can see it in your eyes."

Patting his arm with her free hand, she said, "Nothing can be hidden from my Hektor. Someday you'll be a wise king." Hecuba sighed, and her eyes found her son's. "I'll always be sad. I fear that if I'm not, I'll forget him forever. And that would be worse. His memory is all your father left me of him." She switched the baby to her other breast, adjusting his heavy weight in the crook of her arm.

A commotion across the yard drew Hecuba's attention. "Deiphobus! Be mindful of Helenus! Cassandra, move away from the fountain! Where is Tessa when I need her? Tessa!"

From the balcony above them, Tessa called down to her queen, "Yes, my lady?"

"Come! Take the twins and the baby. They must rest." Deiphobus laughed at his younger siblings. Hecuba added, "And take Deiphobus, as well." The boy threw his wooden armaments down, kicking the ground, and mumbled to himself. "Truth be told, I'm the one in need of rest." She rubbed the side of her swollen belly. "It seems I am forever with child. How was your training?"

Hektor placed his hand on the pommel of his short sword. "I'm much better with the sword than a spear."

Tessa came to take the children. The queen handed her servant a very sleepy baby. "My lady, he is a fat one." The nurse cradled him carefully in her arms and steered the gaggle inside, leaving Hektor and his mother alone.

"Where is my father?" Hektor asked.

Hecuba stiffened. "Where he always is this time of day."

Hektor wrapped his hand around his mother's, dwarfing hers. "I'll have only one wife, Mother."

"We'll find you a fine wife, Hektor. A beauty in heart, as well as face."

"If she's as beautiful as you, I'll be satisfied. But that is a long way off!" Hektor grinned, warming Hecuba's heart. Taking his mother's hand, he pulled her up. "Come. I want to show you my horse."

Hecuba stood reluctantly, putting a hand to the small of her back. "The stables are a long walk from here."

"It's not so far. Besides, you smile more when away from the palace."

The stables dominated the entire southwest of the citadel's lower levels. Spreading out as far as the eye could see, the horse fields were covered in tall, swaying grasses and low brush. From their vantage point, they could see horses running and kicking up clouds of dust. Pausing to admire the horses, Hecuba said, "Can you imagine Troy existing without horses?"

"I wouldn't recognize our city without them," Hektor mindlessly answered. "Mother?"

"Yes?"

"I remember him, too," he said quietly.

Hektor was tall for a boy his age, standing nearly eye to eye with her with his curly black hair shining in the sun. *He is the kindest soul.* She wrapped her arm around his shoulders, pulling him close to her. "You're truly Troy's greatest treasure."

Hektor looked at his mother, beaming. "You only say that because you're my mother. What else would you say?"

"I say it because it's the truth."

Priam pulled the woman in his arms closer, passing his hand across her belly. "You're beautiful rounded with my son."

"My king," Melita blushed. "I hope he's strong."

The king kissed her mouth, letting his lips linger to kiss her again. "All of my sons are strong." *All of my sons …*

Even his lover's arms couldn't keep the old pain from surfacing. Sometimes, when walking the palatial halls, he swore the cries of the Forgotten Prince echoed against the stones. *Will he haunt me forever?* He pushed the dark thought back into the abyss of his mind.

Melita swept the back of her hand softly against Priam's cheek. "As you say, my lord. All fine, strong boys. I'm only sorry he will be a bastard."

"He's my child, bastard or not. And I will love him, as I love all of the others. And you." He leaned down to kiss her again, his hand caressing the mound of her belly and slipping lower as his kiss deepened. His fingers slide into the soft folds of her sacred cross, slipping easily inside of her. When Melita moaned into his neck, he turned her over and mounted her from behind. The king pressed his need for comfort inside of her. A few deep thrusts and his lover's body quivered with her release. Priam grabbed her roughly by the hips and finished quickly after her.

Priam broke their union and rolled to his lover's side, sweating and satisfied. The mask of king descended slowly. "Briseus of Pedasus arrives this evening with his wife. I'll not return, here, until he leaves for home."

Melita frowned against his shoulder. "I understand, my king."

He kissed her cheek. "Don't be sad. It's just a short while."

"Will you be staying with the queen?"

Priam knew the jealousies of his women all too well. Since Hecuba's heart had chilled against him, he'd taken several concubines and minor wives to ease his loneliness. Balancing them all with his own happiness grew a tiresome chore, and yet, he still yearned for Hecuba's love to return to him. He told himself that if her heart ever warmed from winter to spring in his regard, he would forget all of the others.

"Hecuba is my wife and queen. She must give me legitimate sons. It's my duty, as well as hers, that we live as man and wife, king and queen."

"Forgive me, my king," Melita whispered. "My words carry no bitterness."

Priam swung his legs from the bed. "There is nothing to forgive." He washed himself at the water basin, and then pulled his tunic over his head. "The hour grows late. There's much to do before guests arrive."

Melita rose from the bed, pulling a soft ivory robe over her naked body. She didn't bother to close the front, so that Priam could catch glimpses of her naked flesh as she carefully arranged his sash around his waist. Her hands smoothed each pleat to perfection. "This is a beautiful dye, my king. Deepest blue. It complements your eyes."

Looking down at her, the king sighed. "You're most beautiful today." He'd learned that a honeyed word or two would bring him more peace with his hasty departure.

Melita blushed again. "My king."

"Remember, I'll return when I'm able."

"I'll remember."

Priam kissed her again on the mouth, not a deep lover's kiss but a hard certain kiss, his mind turning to his royal duties and away from physical pleasures.

After the king left, Melita wept bitter tears. *I will always be second to the queen.* As a concubine, she had no rights, no say, and nowhere to run. Her life depended solely on the king's favor. Her heart ached knowing Priam would bed his wife tonight. And she knew full well the queen was also with child, so she reasoned that the queen was cold, but not too cold. *Perhaps we are both lonely women in Priam's household. Why do you worry about what you can't change? He's right. You're just a whore carrying his bastard.*

When she was first brought before Priam, she recalled trembling with fear. But his gentleness and sexual appetite won first her body, and then her heart. *I should never have allowed myself to love what I couldn't possess.* A physical ache pierced her chest knowing that she must share the man she loved. She caressed her belly. "He promised to always keep us safe and to love you. That's all that matters."

Hektor tugged at his robe. "Mother, do I have to sit the entire dinner?"

Hecuba nodded, smoothing his wild hair and adjusting his simple golden diadem. "Yes, my son. You're expected to behave as the Prince of Troy tonight. Not Hektor the Breaker of Horses."

The prince frowned. "I'd rather be riding or sword fighting than sitting around listening to old men."

"One day, Hektor, if you're fortunate enough, you'll be an old man gossiping about your glorious days of youth. I promise you, these days will pass with swiftness." Hecuba shivered. In a blink, she saw dust and gold flashing. *Again, I see the dual. Who are they to me?* She rubbed her hands briskly, shaking off the chill. "We must go. Your father will be waiting."

All eyes turned toward Hecuba and Hektor as they entered the main hall.

Priam stood. "My queen! My son, the Prince of Troy!"

Hecuba and Hektor bowed their heads, acknowledging the king. Hektor then escorted his mother to the head of the great table, seating her at his father's right. Servants resumed scurrying about the main hall, carrying silver platters of roasted wild boar and beef, loaves of hot bread, and trays of soft cheeses. Wine stewards funneled sweet wine mixed with honey, mint, and cinnamon into finely crafted silver pitchers, before pouring the fragrant libations into hammered gold and silver kylikes for the guests.

Priam touched his wife's hand, his finger gliding gently over the gold bangle on her wrist. "You are radiant."

Hecuba's face betrayed nothing. "My lord."

Leaning close to her, Priam's breath warmed her cheek. "Come, my queen, surely you find some joy in our company?"

A servant slid between them, refilling the queen's kylix with spiced wine. Hecuba sipped the dark liquid. "This is very good," she said, as it burned sweetly down her throat.

Priam squeezed a fig on his plate. "I'm pleased even if you're not. You've been long absent."

Hecuba glanced to an adjoining hallway, catching a glimpse of a very pregnant servant woman. She noted the woman's comely face and dark, shiny hair. "With good cause," Hecuba replied sharply. "You've not missed my presence over much, if my eyes judge correctly. She has a name, this one?"

Priam followed his wife's line of sight, until his eyes rested on Melita. His lips grazed her ear, as he whispered, "She's small comfort when you refuse me."

Hecuba clenched her jaw, stopping the harsh words at the tip of her tongue. *It's the way of Trojan kings to take more than one wife. You knew this when you married.* In the early years, she'd welcomed his loving embrace, but now she barely endured the weight of him over her as he spilled his seed inside of her. Every coupling resulted in a child, as if the gods wished to mock her grief. The emptiness of the Forgotten Prince in her arms and the grief usurped any tender feelings she'd ever had for her husband. The dark shroud around her heart protected her. *Only in my grief can I find any peace at all.*

A familiar voice interrupted her thoughts. "My Lady Hecuba, are you well?"

The queen looked up into a pair of honey-brown eyes and the kindly face of Shahvash, the wife of Briseus. "Yes, I'm well. Apologies, my thoughts flew elsewhere."

Shahvash smiled warmly. "I see you're again with child. How wonderful for you and the king."

Hecuba placed a hand on her belly, feeling the hard, rounded curve of a new child pressing against her ribs. Soon, eating would become difficult and relieving her waters much more frequent. "Yes. It's a much anticipated joy."

"Briseus and I are expecting our first by summer's end."

"Praise Artemis."

Shahvash raised her kylix of wine to share with the queen. "We're blessed, my lady. But I give my thanks to Apollo."

Forcing a tight smile for her guest's sake, Hecuba asked, "Why Apollo?"

"My husband's brother, Chryse, is a loyal servant and priest of the god. Apollo granted him a vision of this child." She lovingly stroked the sides of her belly. "He said her husband would be the greatest warrior who ever lived and her name would fall from the lips of storytellers for generations to come."

"Then, surely she will be most beautiful," Hecuba said. *Why couldn't Apollo give me such a blessing, even if a girl? Why did he have to take my son from me? Order such a cruel death?* She wanted to curse Apollo, but dared not breathe the words to life. "Have you come to bargain for our horses?"

Shahvash plucked a handful of plump dates from a tray. "You've the mind of a man. Always a head for trading and exchange of coins or horses, my Lady Hecuba."

"Apologies. I can't help but praise our stock. Finer horses can't be found in all the Troad."

Shahvash's laughter rang silver and sweet. "You're correct. I can't deny my husband has come for that purpose."

Hektor clanged his silver cup on the table. "My horse is the finest in all the land." He glanced expectantly between the women.

The queen smiled behind her hand. "My lady Shahvash. My eldest son, Hektor."

Hektor nodded to Shahvash across the table. "I apologize if I've been rude to speak. I've been listening between the men and my mother regarding horses. I'm surrounded by talk of horses."

Shahvash flashed a brilliant smile. Hecuba noted her perfect teeth. "There is nothing to pardon. What else would the Prince of Troy love, but horses?"

"Would you care to see the finest one in all of the land?" Hektor asked. "Mother?"

Queen Hecuba nodded approval. "If our guest should wish it. Fair warning. It's a walk, my lady."

Hektor sweetened the proposition. "He's as black as a starless night. The most hot-blooded of all of the horses owned by my father. Sure-footed. He'll be the finest mount that ever lived."

"How can I refuse such a request?" Shahvash asked.

The eldest son of Priam grinned with pride. "It appears you can't, my Lady Shahvash."

"What do you call this magnificent steed?"

"Ares."

"God of War? A suitable name for a warhorse!" Shahvash exclaimed.

"If only there was a war! I would ride Ares swiftly onto the plains and fight." Hektor's face beamed as he wished for war.

Hecuba shook off another shiver of *gold and dust*, as she placed her hand gently on Priam's arm. "Hektor has a mind to show our guest his horse."

Priam nodded his consent. "He's truly my son. Take an escort."

"We shall." Hecuba left the great hall with Shahvash and Hektor following. "We're for the stables it seems."

Priam watched from the corner of his eye as the queen took her leave of the feast, Hektor talking all the way with the wife of Briseus.

"She's an easy woman … your wife," Priam remarked to his royal dinner companion.

Briseus raised a perfectly arched eyebrow at Priam's assessment. "Don't let her soft voice and manner deceive. The blood of my wife's family breeds fierceness and hot tempers. She's not so easily bent to a husband's will as you may think."

Priam's drunken laughter shook the table, splashing his wine. The dry planks drank the red liquid. He clapped Briseus firmly on the back. "It appears, my friend, that our taste in horses and women is the same! The untamable ones tempt the most."

"True enough, King Priam. I fear the daughter she carries will be the undoing of me."

"How do you know it is a daughter and not a sturdy son?"

"Apollo has spoken the sacred word that it is so."

Priam bristled at the mention of Apollo. "The god's word was … favorable, regarding the child?"

Briseus nodded. "The girl-child will marry the greatest warrior that ever lived."

Priam clasped his guest's arm. "Then, by all means, she should be married to Hektor."

"Nothing would please me more," Briseus said, as they raised their wine in salute and drank.

The king handed his drinking cup to a slave, signaling across the chamber to another slave. "No more talk of horse flesh and women. Bring the dancers!" He settled back into his chair, as the veiled women swirled into the room. Their swaying bodies undulated to the bells and drums, while Priam's foggy mind drifted to Hecuba. It may have been years since she'd enthusiastically wrapped her long legs around him in ecstasy, but his cock still throbbed at the memory.

EIGHT

cattle thieves and the nymph

TROY—1277 BCE

Paris sat with his father under an olive tree eating their evening meal. The branches, heavy with unripe fruit, swayed in the cool breeze above their heads. The campfire burned brightly against the night.

Paris jabbed a stick into the fire, shifting a few larger pieces of wood, encouraging the flames higher. "I'm ready, Father."

"For what?"

"To be a man," Paris said, setting the charred stick aside. He pulled a hunk of goat cheese from the meal basket.

Agelaus scanned the stars scattered and blinking across the imperial dark. "Yes, my son, tonight you'll begin your journey." He met the boy's eyes in the firelight. "It will be different you know, being out here alone."

"I'll make you proud, Father. I want you to be proud of me. Even … even if I'm not really yours."

Agelaus looked down at his son. "You are mine, Paris. From the moment I brought you home. Squalling and fat from the foothills. Do you know what makes a boy a good son?"

Paris shook his head, as all of the times his mother scolded him for not thinking before he acted rushed forward. "No."

"It's not the blood tie, Paris. Even the Olympians, in a moment of madness, turned against Zeus. No, it's not the blood ties." He put his arm around Paris' shoulders. "It's the measure of heart he offers. And you give your mother and me your full heart. We give you ours in return."

"And that makes me a good son?"

"Yes."

"As good as Tymon and Harmon?"

Agelaus chuckled. "Don't tell them, but you give more heart than they do."

"So you give me more heart in return?"

"Shah! That is our secret."

Paris beamed with pride. "I'll keep our secret, Father."

Wrapping up the remaining food, Agelaus packed it in a basket. "Now, about tending these bulls. You must be vigilant for thieves and wolves," Agelaus said.

"I know, Father."

"Do you have your bow?" Agelaus took great pride in his son's lethal ability with the weapon. The art of bow hunting had come easily to Paris at a very young age, felling his first stag at age six. His aim neared perfection. His strength far more advanced than other boys his age.

"I can take care of the herd, Father. Don't worry," Paris said, munching a mouth full of bread. "If I see anything, I'll pierce it with my arrows."

"That's my boy." Agelaus put his hand on his son's curly black hair. "You do that. I can't afford to lose another bull." He stood. "Well, it's a long walk back to the farm. Better get started back home."

Paris stuck his dimpled chin in the air with confidence. "No bulls lost on my watch. I promise. You can sleep well tonight, Father." As he waved his father off, he thought, *I won't even blink if I can help it.*

As the young herder watched the night, he imagined the goddess Asteria, Goddess of Stars, casting each star from a basket like jewels strewn across a meadow. In his mind, she wore a flowing silver gown and had silver hair illuminated by starlight and silver flames for eyes. To keep from falling asleep, he counted each sparkle as it appeared and kept counting until the glimmering specks numbered beyond tracking.

Being out in the fields at night might frighten most boys his age, but he'd been accompanying his father since he could walk. The night sounds of crickets chirping and the eerie calls of owls comforted Paris, letting him know all was well. Once, when he was younger, a black wolf had wandered into their camp. The fire had died low and from the blackness beyond the orange glow a dark shape stepped tentatively into view. Agelaus had jumped up, yelling and waving his arms like a man possessed. The startled wolf spun into the fire by accident, eventually running for its life. When his father had recovered his wits, they'd looked at each other and laughed. So, on this first night of his first unaccompanied watch, he wasn't even afraid of the black wolves.

The night air grew colder as the sky grew darker. Paris stoked the campfire and pulled his wool himation close around his shoulders. In its warmth he could smell the smoke of a dozen campfires and his mother's arms. All he had to do now was remain alert to strange noises or any distressing sounds from the cattle. Being unaccustomed to the touch of man, they would sound the loudest alarm if disturbed.

Paris settled against the olive tree he and Agelaus always camped under. He'd been there so often that his backside had dented the earth. The tree's twisted roots gripped the ground like gnarled fingers. He poked the small campfire again. Delicate cinders floated into the deepening night.

Before long, he blinked the heaviness from his eyes as the night stretched into early morning. As the night insects ceased their musical song, he pulled the bread and cheese from the basket. *Eat, Paris, stay awake*. A wolf howled far in the distance. An owl screeched and he looked up from under the olive canopy to see the white feathered underbelly pass low overhead. *Athena*. The delicate branches shook with the weight of the night hunter, as it perched without knowing he was watching. *I've tricked the goddess*. But, soon the owl's beady, orange eyes caught him in their gaze. The bird leapt from the branch and flew off into the coming dawn.

Like the changing of the tides, the sky began to lighten from black to pale wine. Paris had managed to stay awake all night, despite the chill and the silence, never leaving his post. He stood and stretched his bones, cracked his back with a twist, and shook his legs to wake the muscles.

The sparrows began their morning greetings before they could be seen. He heard them jumping from branch to branch above him. He knew his father would be returning to break the nighttime fast with him. In the quiet of the early morning, a heard a bull bellow. *That's strange*. Another bellow echoed from the far meadow. The hairs on Paris' neck stood on end. Walking out from the camouflage of the olive tree, he strained to hear more. The faint baritone of men's voices carried on the wind. With his heart thumping in his chest, Paris reached for his bow. He'd secretly hoped this might happen. Giddy with the notion of finally having a man's adventure, he prayed to Apollo to guide his arrows if he was fortunate enough to loose them.

The meadow glistened with the breath of morning. His toes slipped against the leather soles of his sandals and soon they were soaked and slapping loosely around his feet. He stumbled as one foot caught the sloppy sandal of the other, hurtling him to the ground with a soggy thud.

Scrambling to his knees, cursing his clumsiness, he unlaced the flimsy leather and cast the sandals aside. Barefooted, he crept along the edge of the meadow toward the narrow gorge. He was careful to pass unseen around the bulls just waking or grazing. Paris knew these bulls hated the sight of men. Once, he and his father had come across a corpse of a would-be cattle thief who'd been gored and stomped into a bloody pile of guts and bones. Without a horse, he'd never get away alive if one should catch sight of him. Paris' breath hung in small clouds as he exhaled his excitement. The wet meadow squished between his toes. He'd never felt so alive in all of his life.

A man shouted, "Watch out, you idiot! He'll gore you that close!"

Paris froze. A bull roared. Someone screamed.

"Lykourgos!" the same man yelled again.

Paris crept even closer to the meadow's edge, peering through the low growing bramble and snags just in time to witness a bull stomping the head of a man into the marshy earth. Vomit burned the back of his throat at the sight of the thief's blood and brains being smashed into the ground. He swallowed the rising bile without making a sound.

He counted three men, now that one was smashed to Hades. *They're fools to try this without horses.* Slowly and with great stealth, Paris pulled an arrow from his hip quiver, resting it against his bow. Setting his arrow into position, he pulled the shaft back with a steady hand. He eyed the biggest man and aimed directly at the man's neck. His fingers curled tightly around the tendon string, steadying the shot. The arrow whistled through the air, slamming into its mark with fatal accuracy. The target threw his arms up with his back awkwardly arched, while blood gurgled over his chin. The man fell to his knees. Blood oozed from both sides of his neck where the arrow had pierced cleanly through it. As the man fell flat on his face, his companions looked around in surprised horror.

"Hades!" the shortest one screamed.

Frantically eyeing the area where Paris hid, the other one yelled, "Where did that come from?" A great rumbled vibrated the air, as the bull whipped his heavy head back and forth.

"Let's get out of here, Licinius. Do you hear me? It's not worth it."

Licinius scoffed. "You puny pigeon shit, Philip! You sound like a frightened woman."

Philip backed into the brush. "I'm not going to die by bull or arrow. Not today or any other day. I—" The thief fell hard, his life's blood gurgling like a brook.

Licinius screamed, dropped his rope, and ran as fast as he could for the opposite side of the gorge. The enraged bull caught sight of him, pursuing him into the distance.

Before long, Paris heard a sickening shriek and knew the last thief had met his end. "The gods have punished you!" His voice echoed in the air, down the hillside, and across the meadow, startling birds and beast alike. Paris plucked the last arrow from his quiver, shooting it jubilantly into the sky, and on its way down landed in a tree. A flash of green gossamer caught in the corner of his eye, as the arrow floated to the ground. Melodic laughter swirled around him like frenzied butterflies.

"Hello! Is someone there?" Beyond the trees, a bull snorted, reminding Paris he must be cautious, if he wanted to eat supper at the day's end. If he got himself killed there would be no one to tell the tale of how he saved the herd. He shrugged the laughter off as his imagination.

"Who are you?"

Paris turned to see a peculiar woman. He reached a hand to touch her. "Who are you?" Paris pulled his bow from his shoulder. "Why do you smile at me like that?"

"No need to bother with your bow. I saw you kill the cattle thieves, but your bow is no match for me."

Paris relaxed his stance, but kept his eyes on her. "You make no noise when you walk."

"I should hope not. Nymphs require absolute stealth to keep watch on their lands."

"These are my father's lands." Paris narrowed his eyes. "You're a nymph? A wood nymph or a water nymph."

"Water."

"Where did you come from?" he asked.

"Where the River Cebron washes over the foothills of the sacred mountain. I sprang to life where the cascading falls make love to the rocks."

"You're immortal, then?"

"Such questions. Do you not have cattle to tend?"

Paris eyed her, undeterred. "Are you or aren't you?"

"Yes, I'm immortal."

"Do you have a name?"

"Yes."

Paris wrinkled his nose. "Well, what is it?"

"Oenone."

"My name is—"

"Paris."

"How do you know my name?"

Oenone smiled, revealing pearly white teeth. "We nymphs know many things. But, why are you named Paris? After a backpack?"

"Because I was carried from these mountains by my father in a backpack. That's why, nymph."

"Oenone," she politely corrected. "And it's as good a name as any other, Paris. I didn't mean to offend you."

"Well, you don't say it like my elder brothers. They intend offense."

The nymph shed a single tear on his behalf to show her sincerity. "That's unfortunate." Catching it on the tip of her delicate finger, it crystallized into a sparkling gem. "Take this, young Paris, to remember me."

The boy suspiciously eyed the token.

"Are you going to take it or not, Paris?" Oenone asked.

He took the offering and put it in his satchel. "Yes. It'll prove I met a nymph. No one believes me when I tell them my stories."

Oenone kissed the top of his head. "Off with you then. Cattle to mind and stories to tell, I suppose."

Paris shrugged, releasing a half grin like one of Eros' deadly arrows. "Will I see you again?"

"I've no doubt, young Paris. Hero of the fields. Defender of man and beast."

Lexias stared at the boy. Their eyes locked in a battle of wills, so he resorted to his smile, as he usually did to win his mother over. Lexias shook her head at his expected maneuver, a grin that could melt the ice fringe from a pond mid-winter. "Clean your hands and put on fresh linen before you sit at my table."

"Why?" He looked down at his clothing. "I am clean enough."

Lexias shook her head. "I can smell you from across the kitchen. All cow dung and wet grass."

Paris exhaled loudly in continued protest, sniffing his armpits and his tunic. "I smell nothing."

"Please, take me at my word, son. Fresh clothing. Then, dinner." Paris acquiesced. "What will I do with this child?" she groaned, turning the flat bread over on the cooking stone. "He grows more headstrong with each passing day. Surely, he'll drag me to an early grave." She tucked a greying lock of hair behind her ear. "Or turn me completely grey."

"What are you mumbling about now, woman? Let me guess, Paris again?" Agelaus chuckled at his wife's exasperation.

Lexias didn't bother turning around. "You may expect a cold wind to blow through your bed this night, Agelaus."

As soon as Paris sat to eat, he regaled his family with the tales of his cattle watch. He told them how he single-handedly drove off a handful of thieves and met a water nymph named Oenone.

Harmon shook his head in disbelief, laughing at his younger brother. "You and your fantastic tales, little sister."

Paris squeezed his eyes to mere slits at his older brother. "I. Am. Not. A. Girl!"

"Prove it then. Prove you've seen this water nymph," Harmon goaded.

Paris produced the silver crystal, holding it out for everyone to see.

His eldest brother, Harmon, snatched the bauble from Paris' hand, examining it closely. "That's nothing but a shiny little rock."

Paris put his bread down. "It's her tear. I saw her make it."

"Just one tear, not two or three?" Tymon, the middle brother, said, fanning the flames between his brothers.

"Nymphs only cry one tear at a time."

"How'd you come by such nonsense? You don't know anything about nymphs or spirits," Tymon insisted.

Agelaus banged his hand on the table. "Boys, that's quite enough. Leave Paris alone. Perhaps, he did meet a nymph." He sipped his wine. "Not all mysteries in this world are revealed to every person."

"Here begins the *Paris is special* story." Harmon shoved his plate away. "That's no nymph tear. It's just a rock."

Lexias reached a calming hand to her husband's arm. "Agelaus, please. Don't antagonize the boys against each other."

Refusing to argue with his wife in front of the boys, Agelaus said, "Paris, I believe you. Now, eat your dinner."

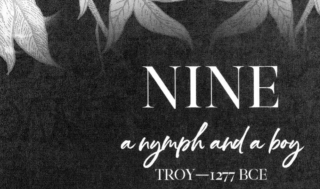

NINE

a nymph and a boy

TROY—1277 BCE

"What lesson do you wish this day?" Oenone asked.

"Whatever you wish," Paris answered.

Rising from her seat on a large rock, the nymph said, "Come, we shall walk then."

Paris also stood, dusting off his tunic. "There's always much to learn with you."

They hiked for a long while without a trail to guide them. The nymph needed no markers for she knew everything about the woods and meadows and hills and streams. Paris kicked loose stones as they went.

Without warning, Oenone grabbed Paris by the shoulders. She bent her head close to his and whispered, "Look." She pointed at a dark speck high above them.

Paris followed the direction of her finger, squinting hard into the bright sun. "I see nothing."

She squeezed his shoulders gently. "Wait, you will."

Paris stared into the sky, and then he saw it. A dark smudge grew until …"It's too big to be a bird. But, surely it has wings." His mouth fell open. "It can't be."

Oenone smiled broadly, releasing her hold on him. "And why can't it? Don't I exist?"

"That's different. You're real, but that's … that's a legend." Paris stood in awe. "I can't believe it's Pegasus."

"He's rare indeed. My father grants him protection here among the hills. He roams wherever he wishes, protected from mortals."

"Why should someone wish to harm Pegasus?" Paris asked.

"Why do mortals do what they do? You're strange creatures. Fickle. Changeable as the wind."

"What is fickle?" Paris asked.

"Fickle is to change your mind without regard for promises made to others."

Paris laughed out loud. "I'll not be fickle. I promise."

"We'll see if your time with me yields a steady head and heart."

Oenone came to a tall plant bearing deep blue, bell-shaped flowers. "Here it is." The plant stalk stood as high as Paris and sprang from between the rocks. "Akoniton."

"I've never heard of this plant," Paris said. "It's pretty." He reached out to touch it, but Oenone slapped his hand away.

"Don't let its beauty fool you. It's deadly. You must learn to handle it with care."

"Where does it come from? Why is it poisonous?" Paris questioned.

The nymph eyed the boy. "I'll tell you, then, and teach you its proper application."

Paris leaned against the rock the plant sprang from, careful not to touch it. "I'm ready."

Oenone folded her arms. "Do you know about Herakles? And his labors?"

"Everyone knows about Herakles, Oenone. What does he have to do with it?"

"One of Herakles' labors was to fetch Kerberos from his post as guard at the entrance of Hades."

"What is a Kerberos? Why did he have to guard the Gate of Hades?"

"So many questions! But that's good. Kerberos was a fierce and wild beast. He had three vicious heads, a thick mane of venomous snakes about his neck, and the tail of a serpent. His purpose was to keep the dead from escaping the Underworld and to keep the living out."

Paris' eyes rounded in horror. "Kerberos is a beast of nightmares."

"Truly, he was, Paris. But, Herakles captured the beast, carrying him to the light of our world at the bidding of King Eurystheus of Argos. Kerberos was so cruel, so evil, that when the foam from his mouth fell, touching the earth, the akoniton sprang up. That's why it has a lethal sap flowing through the beautiful flower."

"The spit of Kerberos," Paris mused.

"It's most often used for hunting wolves. One's arrow must be carefully tipped with the milky poison, the hunter taking great care not to touch the arrow head, or he will die. And the quiver must be destroyed afterward in case any remnant of the poison remains."

"That's a good story, Oenone. I'll remember it."

"Good. Now, go fetch enough wood so I can keep my fire burning bright the entire night."

"I will," Paris said.

As he walked away, Oenone knew that someday he'd need

the knowledge of the plant to aid him, this much she'd seen in her dreams. Who it was intended for wasn't revealed to her. The gods were infuriating that way, telling pieces of a story, while never unfolding all the parts at once. They gave just enough to cause concern and confusion. *A war is coming. I pray it doesn't take his life.*

When paris reached the edge of the wheat field, he slowed. His brothers walked ahead of him and he wished to avoid another argument, or worse a fight. Whenever he returned from the foothills after spending time with the nymph, they harassed him unmercifully. Paris dreaded any conversation at all with his brothers, especially his eldest, Tymon. He hoped they'd continue without noticing him, but Tymon turned in his direction and waited.

Tymon's voice carried on the wind. "Have you been out with your nymph again, little brother?"

Paris wished to be anywhere but dumbly skirting the wheat field. He put his head down and continued forward, dreading the inevitable encounter. As he walked, he noted the golden light of late afternoon skimming the swaying field. He reached out, snapping a head of wheat off in his hand. "You needn't wait for me, brothers!" Paris shouted.

"I wouldn't miss another of your tales!" Tymon laughed. Harmon, standing beside him, laughed less enthusiastically.

When Paris finally closed the gap between them, he looked his eldest brother hard in the eye. Tymon glared back at him so harshly, he knew what was to come. Even though he was several years younger, he stood almost as tall as his eldest brother. "I've no wish to argue, Tymon. Let's just get home before mother punishes us all for being late."

His eldest brother stood, feet shoulder width apart, as immovable as a stone. "Why do you assume I wish to exchange harsh words with you, little brother?"

Paris stood mutely staring at the ground.

"Tell me, boy, why you believe you're better than us?"

"I don't."

Tymon ground the toe of his sandal into the dirt. "You carry on with your made-up stories about a nymph, expecting us to believe the gods somehow favor you by such a gift."

Paris sighed. Tymon's badgering would end when one of them was bloodied, usually him. He longed for the day his size and strength equally matched his eldest sibling. He prayed that just once he could knock Tymon to the ground and pummel his face with a hard fist. "I hiked the trail scouting for places to set traps for game."

Harmon piped in, steering the conversation from a physical encounter, "Good. Did you set any?"

Paris shook his head. "No, just scouted."

Harmon shrugged. "Tomorrow, then. Set your traps. And surprise Mother with a hare or two."

Tymon refused to let his little brother dodge his questioning. "No nymph today? No entertaining us with your stories?"

Looking into Tymon's face, Paris said, "I've no stories to tell." He watched his brother's jaw twitch and his shoulder drop slightly. Paris steadied himself for the heavy blow. Like lightning, Tymon's hand flew with fierceness, cracking Paris on the cheek, knocking him backward into the wheat.

Tymon stood over Paris, hatred dripping with each word.

"You're a *nobody*." He spat at Paris. "A nobody our father was willing to take in. And how do you repay his kindness? By disgracing us with your lies."

Paris' face ached when he screamed back at Tymon, "They aren't lies!"

Harmon stepped between his brothers. "Enough for now. Paris said there's nothing to tell. Leave it at that." He grabbed Tymon's shoulder. "My hunger is going to devour me like a lion if I don't get something to eat." The tension broke, as he reached a hand down to Paris and pulled him to his feet.

"I suppose it's enough … for now." Tymon took a step toward Paris, putting his face just inches from his youngest brother. "There's always tomorrow. Isn't there?"

Paris rubbed his cheek and seethed inside. He wanted nothing more than to punch Tymon in the throat and bash his nose until it spewed red like a fountain.

Harmon nudged Tymon's shoulder again. "Come, let's go home."

"Yes, we shouldn't keep *our* mother waiting."

Paris didn't say a word. He knew Tymon enjoyed watching him trying to defend his place in the family, just so he could lord it over him that he wasn't truly tied by blood to any of them. He was *nobody* and he knew it in his heart, no matter how much Agelaus had tried to reassure him. Thoughts of his real family consumed him. Would he ever know who he was? Would he ever know why they abandoned him for dead? Paris knew Agelaus kept the truth from him. He guessed his mother knew as well. His parents loved him, assuring him he was by all rights one of them. But in his heart, it wasn't enough.

TEN

five years later
TROY—1272 BCE

"I know you're there." Paris didn't even look up as he gathered wood.

"Greetings, Paris." Oenone appeared from behind a slender tree.

By his eighteenth summer, Paris looked increasingly forward to his nights in the fields. He'd never minded the dark or cold, even as a boy. The stars he'd imagined as sparkling tears of gods and goddesses. The night breeze their divine breath. The lyrical buzz of insects' soothing music created for him alone. Paris loved the life he lived on his own, away from his two elder brothers. And recently, he'd come to look forward to Oenone's closeness.

As the sky purpled, signally the twilight of the day, he knew it was time to head back to the camp. According to his calculations, the moon would be rounded to perfection, a pearl set by the gods, casting its silvery beams on him and the contented bulls bedding down for the night. A moth flickered near his face and he batted it into the deepening darkness. The soft bellows of his herd carried on the air, reassuring Paris that everything was as it should be.

Oenone flicked a small pebble in Paris' direction with her bare toe. "How did you know?"

Paris stood, facing her, and smiled. "You can't know all of my secrets." *That I believe you the most enchanting creature ever created.* He stole a glance at her rounded breasts and gentle curves, before turning away. Crimson heat flamed up his neck.

Oenone frowned. "What troubles you, Paris?"

"Nothing. Nothing at all." *Except that I want to feel your lips on mine. Your breasts in my mouth.*

The nymph reached a tender hand in his direction. "If there's truly nothing, then why do you avoid me?"

Paris wiped the sweat from his forehead with his forearm. His leather pallet teemed with logs, as he secured it with leather straps, making unnecessary adjustments here and there. "This will get us through the night, I think."

They walked side by side in silence to Paris' usual campsite. Oenone produced two fish from the twig basket slung around her shoulders.

"Gratitude," Paris mumbled, as he worked on starting a cooking fire.

The nymph handed Paris a bundle of wild sage and rosemary. "And these."

Paris dared another glance at Oenone's breasts, barely concealed in the thin gown of spun flax and flowers. A whoosh of birds flew overhead. Crickets quieted around the perimeter of the camp. *Something's wrong.* Paris pressed a finger to his lips, signaling the nymph.

Beyond the camp a twig snapped under a heavy weight. A stray cricket chirped an isolated warning. Paris stoked the fire as quickly as he could, because wild beasts preferred to avoid the bright heat of flames. Paris remembered how the black wolf sprang into the night encampment Agelaus made all those years ago. Another twig snapped in the dark. He cocked his head in the direction of the noise, as a chill crept up his spine. The hairs on the back of his neck and arm prickled.

Moving slowly next to Oenone, Paris whispered urgently into her ear, "Shah. We're not alone. Slip into the shadows. Stay hidden." In the blink of an eye, the nymph vanished into the darkness.

Paris sat on his haunches, stoking the flames as if nothing were amiss. The unnatural silence swelled with tension. Agelaus' words rang clearly in his head. *"Night creatures stop their chatter only for man."* He chastised himself. *I should've paid attention to the dark, not the nymph's breasts. By the balls of Zeus! How could I be so careless?*

Scanning the black line of brush surrounding the camp, he continued the pretense of stoking the fire. The night creatures remained silent, as Paris waited for who would emerge. A snap of a twig sounded to his left, another to his right. *So, there are two circling …*

Cattle thieves moved among the fields in the night, and it was uncommon for them to be so near the herdsman's camp. *Why are they here? I carry nothing of value.* Everyone who knew him knew that. That thought, however, gave rise to a more sinister scenario. *What do they want with me?* A dark-cloaked figure jumped from the brush behind him, another from in front of him, hunting him like a pair of wolves. He turned just in time to see a wooden club swinging in his direction, before his vision faded into woozy blackness.

"Did he see you?" asked Harmon.

"No." Tymon stood over an unconscious Paris. "Tie up his hands and feet."

"Are you certain that's necessary? What if—"

"Stop fretting like a frightened woman," Tymon snarled. "What do I care for his comfort?" Their father's favoritism of the adopted bastard over his own blood had soured any gentle feelings Tymon had for Paris years ago. "Did you see where that woman slipped off to?"

"No," Harmon answered, as he bound his younger brother's feet. "She's not a woman. Paris' nymph is *real*."

"And what of it? Likely, she's long gone by now, or hiding up some damned tree spying on us," Tymon spat.

Harmon stood, shaking his head in disbelief. "He's been telling the truth all these years."

"No matter, brother. I'm going to teach him humility."

Harmon eyed the black outline of branches against a sky full of blinking stars. "Are you certain we should—"

"Get his legs," Tymon ordered. "Let's move him before he wakes up."

The brothers carried Paris down a small embankment, across a narrow stream, and around an outcropping of boulders. A burning torch, wedged into the crack between two large rocks, lit the entrance of a small cave. Tymon plucked the torch as they walked into the cave.

A narrow path wound its way into the earth, the ceiling decreasing in height as they walked.

"Don't you think it's far enough?" Harmon asked. "This doesn't feel like the jest you said it would be. This is … cruel."

"Yes, it's far enough," Tymon said. "What are you worried about? He'll be fine. It's his arrogance that earned him a sound beating. Always rattling on about his skill with bulls or the damned nymph. All with father's encouragement." He took Harmon by the shoulders. "Who are we? Who are we, but his flesh and blood?"

Harmon chewed the edge of his lip. "He *is* good with the bulls. Better than you or I."

Tymon dropped an unconscious Paris roughly to the ground, his head striking the earth with a solid thud. "Shut your fucking mouth, Harmon, before I close it with my fist."

Harmon gently lay Paris' feet to the ground. He knew better than to challenge Tymon when his temper ran hot. So, he simply nodded. They left Paris there, alone and injured in the dark.

Paris painfully blinked his eyes open, his vision slowly focusing on Oenone leaning over him. His head rested in her lap, as voices filtered through his hazy memory. "What happened?" he asked, struggling to sit up.

"You were ambushed, Paris, and beaten," Oenone said, her eyes shining with unshed tears.

Paris stopped rubbing his chin. "The voices ... it was my brothers." Anger raced through his veins with the realization.

Oenone pulled him closer, one hand resting on his pounding heart. With the other, she inspected his scalp, feeling the congealed blood clot at his temple where he'd been struck. "Shah. All will be set straight."

"I'll make certain of it," Paris said, his jaw clenched and revenge glinting in his eyes.

The nymph's lips brushed against his forehead. "Turn away from anger. You'll find no pleasure in returning harm."

Oenone's closeness distracted him from his aching body. The round softness of her breasts pressed against his arm. He'd never touched a woman's breasts before. He'd seen women in the village nursing their babies. He'd been smashed into his mother's bosom by the occasional embrace, but with Oenone it was different. The smell of wild grass and flowers filled his head with sensual ideas fueled by the images of naked women he'd seen etched in the clay vessels his mother stored the oil in. His cock twitched to life. Out in the fields, he released his seed on the grass without shame. But here, pressed close against the nymph, his cheeks flushed with heat as the familiar urge grew.

"Why do you tremble?"

"You are beautiful, Oenone."

The nymph smiled.

Paris licked his dry lips. His head pounded. "I wish to touch you."

"You may."

With a trembling hand, he caressed her cheek as she looked down into his face.

Oenone placed her hand over his, sliding it over her breast. "You have been thinking of this, too."

"You're … soft," he whispered hoarsely.

The nymph slipped the fabric of her gown from her shoulder, exposing her bare flesh. "You may touch me again."

As Paris caressed the slight swell of her breast, her nipple hardened against his palm. His eyes caught hers in the dim light. Slowly, he raised his head to taste her. He wrapped his tongue around the tight bud, sucking then licking. A small moan escaped the nymph's throat, encouraging him to explore her body in the semi-dark. His loins shuddered, spilling his seed onto his thigh.

Paris' hands stopped exploring.

"Don't worry, Paris. The pleasures you can find with a woman are foreign to you. In time, you'll know all that a mortal can know of that." She kissed him gently on the eyes and on his mouth. "Soon, we'll be united. Rest for now. When you wake, we'll return to the camp."

"I am in love with you," Paris blurted out, not knowing why.

Oenone whispered, "There will be time for that later."

"It's true," Paris promised. "No other woman could be more beautiful than you."

Oenone reached into her shoulder satchel, pulling out a finger-like root. "Bite into this. The pain in your head will dull, so you can sleep." Paris took the root and chewed its bitter flesh. "Now, sleep, my mortal. Sleep."

Paris closed his eyes, as the heaviness of healing slumber coursed through his blood. The pounding pain behind his eyes released its grip and liquid warmth spread through his limbs. When he was fast asleep, the nymph lay down next to him, wrapping her delicate arm around his shoulders. She smiled. *He'll not be mine forever, but I will love him until our time is finished.*

In the morning, Paris walked the familiar path home, anger seething through gritted teeth. His head still ached and the tender lump behind his ear throbbed with every step. He'd always known that his brothers resented him, but not to this extent. When his father's lands flanked him on either side, he scanned the road ahead. Rounding the last wide curve of the path, the house came into view. He hoped his unexpected arrival would give him an advantage over his older brothers.

Paris walked straight into the central courtyard, through a small flock of hens pecking for bugs, past the sleeping hound that barely lifted his head as Paris approached. He reached down and scratched the dog between the ears. He entered the house from a common door, careful to step lightly against the tiled floor so his brothers wouldn't hear him. As he neared the kitchen, Tymon's bold voice boomed ahead of him. He was fairly certain Lexias would be in the barn and he hoped Agelaus was out in a pasture somewhere. Paris pressed himself against the wall, peering around the corner.

"Has father selected the bulls to take to festival?" Harmon asked.

Tymon shoved a hunk of bread into his mouth. "I believe he has."

"Did he decide against the brown one? The one with the white-tipped tail?"

As Tymon began to answer, his words choked short as he was yanked backward by a quick jerk to his tunic collar. He slammed hard against the floor. He coughed and shook off the daze. "What the—" Looking up from the floor, he was surprised to find Paris looming over him. "You're home earlier than expected," he said flatly.

Trembling with rage, Paris bellowed, "Get up! By the balls of Zeus, you'll pay for what you did."

Tymon rolled onto his side away from the chair and stood, purposely putting distance between them. "It was meant only in jest, little brother. Nothing more."

Paris advanced, circling the small table, boring a hateful eye into Tymon's face.

Lexias skidded into the room. "I heard raised voices. What's happening? One of you had best speak up." When Paris took another step toward Tymon, she scolded them like boys. "Whatever you're arguing about, you'd be wiser to end it now."

Tymon turned on his mother. "We're not children for you to order about, Mother."

"You reside under my roof. You stand in my kitchen. It's enough for me to command you, grown or not."

"I'm going to beat you for what you did to me," Paris said through clenched teeth. "Apologies, Mother."

"Why is there dried blood on your tunic? Tell me, right now, what's happened?"

"They attacked my camp last night. Cracked my head with a rock. Hauled me off to some cave and left me there like some nasty beggar."

Lexias' eyes widened in horror as she turned to her eldest son for answers. "Tell me this is a falsehood, Tymon."

"He exaggerates," Tymon said. "It was in jest, Mother. Nothing more. Look, he's fine, despite his mewling like a calf over a scratch."

Paris sneered. "More than a scratch! Falsehoods fall from your lips like your arrows from your quiver!"

Tymon advanced at the insult, kicking a stool out of his way and shoving the table to the side.

Harmon jumped up from his seat, narrowly escaping being bashed by the table's corner. "Hold your anger, brother! I'm done with this war between you!"

Paris launched himself forward, reaching for Tymon's waist, and ramming him like an enraged bull. The brothers tangled their arms up, falling heavily to the floor. Lexias screamed. Paris rolled on top of Tymon and punched him square in the face. Blood splattered across the floor. Tymon reached up, grabbing a fistful of Paris' tunic and yanking him roughly to the side.

Lexias screamed again, "Stop this! Tymon! Paris!"

Tymon, blood dripping from his nostrils, quickly rolled over, pinning Paris to the ground with a sharp knee to the chest. "You fucking bastard. My father should've left you to rot on that hill—"

Tymon never saw what sent him flying across the small kitchen into the edge of the hearth. When he could finally open his eyes, he saw Agelaus standing over him with his walking staff held firmly in his grasp. "You forget yourself in my house," Agelaus' voice growled with anger and age.

"Father, I—"

Holding out a shaking fist, Agelaus fumed, "If you ever raise a hand to Paris again … disturb the peace in my house, I'll throw you out into the wilderness myself."

Lexias placed a calming hand on her husband's shoulder. "Peace, husband. They're but boys, after all."

"Boys? Aye, I see boys where men should be. I'll not tolerate this discord in my house. Do you take my meaning, Tymon? Harmon?"

Tymon dusted himself off. "Again, you elevate Paris over your own flesh and blood. It dishonors me!"

"Dishonors you?" Agelaus roared. "You ungrateful dung pile!"

"Agelaus, husband, I beg you," Lexias pleaded. "Cease fighting. Can't you see how your protection of Paris breeds frustration for them?"

"You side with them?" Agelaus asked his wife, surprise spiking his voice.

Lexias dropped her hand from her husband's shoulder. "I don't side with them. How can they know the reasons that we do?"

"I see no difference," Agelaus snapped angrily.

Paris, his head throbbing, held up a hand. "Father, don't worry. Tymon and I will reach an understanding. There'll be no more arguing between us."

"Agreed," Tymon reassured his father.

Agelaus' shoulders sagged slightly, as his initial anger calmed. He propped himself up on his walking stick, leaning against it. "My entire life has been dedicated to *all* of my sons. I protect Paris, because I must. That's all you need know. Now, get out. Out of my sight!"

The trio of brothers murmured their apologies as they jostled past their father and out into the courtyard. Once out of earshot of the house, Paris leaned close to his eldest brother, their shoulders rubbing, and whispered, "If you ever touch me again, I'll kill you. And that's a promise."

Tymon sneered. "Brave words from a bastard."

Paris turned, flashing the smile that infuriated his mother. "Indeed, they are."

ELEVEN

Paris and a dark stranger

TROY—1272 BCE

Apollo's light beat down on the gathering crowd at the bull arena. Scanning the familiar faces, Paris wiped a bead of sweat from his brow. Secretly, he longed for fame and fortune, but knew such dreams were nothing more than flights of fancy. *Yet, someday,* he vowed, *someday I will make a name for myself. Every Trojan will know my name.*

Paulinius sneered. "You think your bull superior, Paris the Pretty?"

"I don't think. I know," Paris taunted.

"Then let's put our bulls to task. Each animal proving its worth."

Leaning against the wooden railing, Paris smirked behind his hand. "You're suggesting we pit them against each other? One of them will be spoiled for sale to the temples or the dancing competitions."

"Only the loser."

Paris stepped away from the railing. "I never lose, Paulinius. It'd be unfair for me to take advantage of you and your beast. Our fathers won't approve of us fighting our bulls."

"Since when do you care what your father wishes or not?"

"When your animal loses, Paulinius, do my ears a favor and keep your whining to yourself."

Paulinius spat in the dirt at Paris' feet, his upper lip curling in a wicked grin. "Toss your insults carefully, Paris the Pretty, before you find me stuffing them back into the hole they spewed from."

Paris cocked his head and shrugged his shoulders. "The bulls must have free reign."

"Agreed."

The sleek, black hide of Paulinius' bull shimmered like pitch in Apollo's light. Its muscles bulged and flexed at its shoulders and haunches. It snorted mucus and dirt as its keeper led it to the ring.

"Look at the back on him!" an onlooker shouted. "He'll devour Paris' bull." The wagering began with fervor; men betting for or against each bull.

Jumping on the railing, Paris balanced easily on the balls of his feet. "Save your coin, my friends. This match is uneven. It wouldn't be fair if I let you lose all of your hard-earned coin just because Paulinius here has a fat contender." The excited banter turned to angry grumblings, as spectators looked from one man to the other in confusion. "What? Did you think I was serious about not wagering your coin? By the gods, lay your pieces down! Bet wisely." Paris leapt from his perch on the fence to lead his bull into the ring—although stouter than Paulinius', it was as thickly muscled with a slightly longer back. Its hide blacker than a starless sky, flashed purple and green in the sun.

Throwing their snouts into the air, the bulls each caught one another's scent. At once, they recognized the other as an enemy, a stranger with strange smells, not of the same meadows. They stomped and snorted, shaking the ground. The splendid beasts squared off face-to-face across the small arena. Paris' bull hammered its heavy hoof into the hard-caked ground, flinging clods of dirt and swirling dust into the air. Whoops of excitement and rowdy cheers went up loud enough to stir Ares from his musings.

Paulinius' bull reared its head and bellowed. It pounded both hooves hard into the ground, sending a shudder of anticipation into the crowd. Flashes of black shadow charged across the empty space at each other. The initial clash of beast against beast sounded like boulders slamming into a river. Their chests smashed together with the force of twenty armed men. Dust flew, choking the air of freshness. The mighty titans roared their fury at being in the other's presence. Hooves flew. Teeth gnashed. Wide eyed and angry, the two bulls tangled horns. The parched earth drank the blood they spilled. Another great clash and a mist of crimson sprayed the crowd. Paris licked the rim of his bottom lip, tasting the bitter iron of the bulls' blood. He almost felt sorry for Paulinius' animal. *Almost.* Although wider across the chest, Paulinius' beast lacked solid footing with too much of the wild bred out of him.

A small, steady stream of red oozed down the forehead of Paulinius' animal right between its eyes. It backed up as the blood blurred its vision. It shook its huge head, snorting blood from its nostrils. The bull stomped the ground with less power but with more determination. Paulinius frantically waved his hands, shouting curses and encouragements at his animal.

Paris, witness to bulls fighting in his father's fields, knew his champion would fight to its death. Once, he'd watched as two bulls, on their knees, continued attacking each other, biting and head butting. Agelaus' bulls were tenacious in a way that Paris hadn't observed from any other farm. His father once confided in him, telling him it was the strength they gained drinking the water from the sacred spring on their land. He'd said it fortified the bulls with Herculean might and willpower. He knew his bull would ram, bite, and tear at the other one until it was dead.

Paris' bull backed its haunches into the fencing, a thin crimson line running down its cheek, as it stomped the ground, sending up a shower of dirt. It threw its head back and roared, then charged at the enemy with its head down. Paris' animal fatally rammed Paulinius' beast. The dark creature's death scream pierced the air and everyone watched in stunned silence as Paulinius' bull hit the ground with a heavy thud.

Paulinius' stood with mouth agape, as his prized bull lay dead on the dusty arena floor, blood pooling beneath its black form. For a brief second voices rose then fell to silence again, as it slowly registered in the spectators' minds that the battle had finished so quickly. Cheers of the triumphant filled the air, overpowering the curses of the defeated.

The champion bull stood as victor with blood smeared across its head. A slight tear at the shoulder bled. The massive beast snorted loudly as it swung its heavy head from side to side, considering its next move. A dozen men clapped Paris on the back in hardy gratitude, because they'd won a pretty piece of coinage to spend as they wished, without their wives knowing or mother's questioning, while the losers would have tales to concoct about money lost.

Paulinius kicked the railing. "You killed my bull!"

"We both knew the risk, my friend," Paris said calmly. "I did try to warn you."

"You cheated me!"

"How did I manage that? I suggest you stuff your anger in your—"

"I demand compensation for my loss. It was a test of strength not to the death," Paulinius declared. "Look! Look at my bull! He's completely ruined."

"He's dead," Paris said.

"I can do nothing with him now."

Paris climbed up the fencing and bounced into the ringside of the arena. "Send his carcass to the outskirts. Feed the poor among the city."

"What trickery did you pull this time, Paris?" He scanned the crowd, desperate to garner support for his cause. "We all know how you cheated at the footrace last spring festival."

"I didn't cheat." Paris cringed at the old wound that never died. "I won that race fairly. Diodorus tripped over a rock."

"We all know that story, Paris. To hear Diodorus tell it, you shoved him in the back as you passed by."

Heat stained Paris' cheek. "I did no such thing. What need have I to stoop so low? Diodorus is stout and thick legged. Even his mother could best him in a sprint."

Diodorus had proved a bitter loser, complaining and crying foul for an entire week. The judges, however, favored Paris, calling the finish as they saw it, granting victory to him. "The judges heard both sides, as I recall, declaring me the winner. You're just angry your bull lost. Next time, think harder before you wager what you can't afford to lose."

Paulinius spat at the dirt, grinding the heel of his sandal into it. "You're nothing but a trickster by your own brothers' word." Using the toe of his sandal, he flicked the small mud clod at Paris. "That's

what your word is worth. Nothing but the shit beneath my foot."
He stormed off, still ranting and raving, leaving his dead bull in the
dust. The spectators finished exchanging and pocketing their coin,
and reluctantly walked away, shrugging their shoulders, grateful for
an afternoon's diversion, and went about their expected business.

As Paris reached for the top of the wooden arena wall, the
hackles on his neck stood on end. Behind him he heard his bull
snort, its obsidian eyes boring completely through him. *Slowly, Paris.*
Slowly. He gripped the top rail with hands of iron. The bull stomped
the ground. With a quick bounce, he swung a leg up and over, as the
victorious beast rammed into the barrier.

A voice like rolling thunder spoke. "How fortunate for you."

Paris eyed the tall man from head to foot. *He's taller than any*
man I've ever seen. "Do I know you?"

"No, not yet. But I know you."

"How can that be? I've grown up here my entire life. I know
everyone."

The stranger pushed the hood of his himation from his face,
startling Paris with his dark beauty and long, dark beard streaked
with silver. "Obviously not. Your bull won fairly."

"Victors agreed with that truth. Losers, not so much I fear."
Paris squinted at the tall man. "I'm sure I've seen you—"

The stranger's eyes shone as two polished onyx stones, set
perfectly beneath a strong, handsome brow. "No, you've not.
However, I am around more often than you realize, Paris."

Paris wiped the sweat stinging his eyes with the edge of his
chiton, and the hair on his neck prickled again. *Could it be?* "How
does a stranger speak my name with such familiarity?"

"I know all men in Troy. Some are truly more deserving than

others of my presence."

Paris pressed for an answer. "What are you known by? What is your trade?"

"I'm courage. I'm carnage. I'm the fire in the eyes of warriors."

The young herder shivered. That was no straightforward answer, and Agelaus always warned against trusting anyone who answered questions sideways.

"Are you caught without speech, young Paris?"

"How do you know my name?"

"I'm more than I appear. Your father would know my name."

"You know my father?"

"I know your *true* father, yes, quite well."

The earth beneath Paris' feet shifted. "What do you mean my *true* father?"

"Only that your father is not *who* you believe him to be."

Paris clung to the arena fencing, as his knees weakened beneath him. For a moment he believed he might collapse. "Give me your name, stranger."

"In time, you'll know me. But this isn't the day. I came only to witness the competition. Your time will come. Have no doubt, your fate is coming for you, as straight and as swift as an arrow loosed from your bow."

"What do you mean by such dark words?"

The beautiful stranger cocked his head, and slid a long finger across the railing. "I suggest you get that bull to Ares' temple priests."

"The animal is in no condition to present to the temple of any god!"

"I believe the priests in Ares temple will take the beast and deliver it to the god and send the meat to the poor."

"But the bull's already dead. It's stained with dirt, without garland, unblessed." Paris stared at the man. "I won't do something so outrageous and offensive."

"Are you quite sure you dare not to?" the man asked.

Doubt gnawed at Paris' certainty. *What the by the balls of Zeus does he mean?* Paris turned to look at the fallen bull. He knew soon it would reek of rotten blood from the heat. The carcass must be moved as quickly as possible, or the meat would sour on the tongue even if roasted to a crisp.

"I'm not sure …" Paris said, looking up. But the tall stranger had disappeared. He jumped on top of the ring fencing, balancing on one foot, and searched the streets in every direction but saw no one resembling the hooded man. How could a man of such stature lose himself in a crowd? He decided to take the man's advice. What was the worst that could happen to him? He'd be laughed at? Verbally chastised? Turned away by the priests for trying to present a defiled bull to satisfy the God of War? He resolved to do it, regardless of the outcome.

TWELVE

for a love of trees

TROY—1272 BCE

As Apollo's light dipped toward the horizon, gold and bronze bled across the expanse of blue and clouds gathered and floated quietly on the sunset sea, Paris headed for the home of his heart. The stranger's words echoed in his ears … *"Your true father."* For all of the love he'd received from his parents, the difference between himself and his older brothers pricked him with bitterness. All his life, his brothers taunted him about his black, curly hair and his blue, sparkling eyes. Their constant taunting had wedged a soft hatred between them. He knew he belonged to other parents, that whoever bore him had abandoned him. Agelaus would only tell him he stumbled upon him as a bundled child in the foothills of Mount Ida. Agelaus told the same story his entire life without variation. He loved Agelaus and Lexias. They offered him everything, except what he wanted most: *the truth.* His mind couldn't let go of the burning questions. *Who am I? Why did my parents leave me to die? I know*

Agelaus keeps something important from me. Why?

Since the brawl with Tymon and the promise he'd made his father, he'd found solace in the forest, meadows, and the rivers he traveled to herd cattle. Paris glanced up as the first star popped into the twilight sky. He and Oenone had fashioned a home within a cave hidden behind a waterfall. Paris crafted simple furniture from trees and water willows. Together, they'd collected the mountain's offerings to create their sacred space. They'd planted thick moss on the floor to pad the hard, cold dirt of the cave. Mist from the waterfall fed the living carpet. Only here, in this place, could Paris' restlessness find peace.

Paris squatted near a stream, dipping his hands in it for a drink. A cluster of moths fluttered above him. "Greetings, Oenone."

Stepping from behind a tree, she waved the moths away. "Did all go well with the bulls?"

"Yes. As expected." Paris plucked a blade of wide grass from the stream's edge. "Why is it that here with you is the only place I can find any peace?" He stood and tossed the blade of grass away in silence. It fluttered to the ground.

"Are you sad, again?"

"No," he said. *It's only half a lie.*

The nymph stepped closer and placed a cool hand on his arm. "Perhaps, you are distracted? A walk?"

"No." He looked down at her. "You're right, as always. I'm not myself. Something happened …"

"Did you not have the best bulls to offer?"

Paris watched the sparkle of blues and greens in Oenone's eyes dim. "My father's stock stood superior. It isn't that."

"Tell me what troubles you."

Questions about the mysterious stranger crowded his thoughts. "It's nothing important." *Probably a rival breeder.*

The nymph stood on her toes, pressing her lips to his. He inhaled the honeysuckle of her essence. Her lips were round and smooth against his. Paris reached his arms around her waist, as hers encircled his neck. Her lips parted, and the tip of her tongue brushed his bottom lip. His lips parted as well, and her tongue swept against his teeth. The scent of meadow flowers and wild sage filled him with the urge to cover her flesh with kisses.

Paris pulled back, taking her hands in his, turning them over so he could kiss her palms. He kissed a warm trail up one arm to her shoulder, hesitating slightly before devouring her neck. Together, they sank slowly to the grassy bank of the stream. He opened his eyes, as he laid her back. "I don't know what to do …" Her body beckoned him like a sacred mountain, calling him to begin his first ascent. Every trail, every rock, every babbling stream of her essence awaited him.

"Paris—"

"Am I hurting you? Is it unpleasant?"

Oenone pulled his head to hers, rubbing her nose against his. "No, it's very pleasant. But, I need to tell you what I've seen. If we mate, there will be consequences."

"I don't want riddles, speak plainly."

"We'll have a child … who will complicate your future and bring you great suffering."

Paris let his hand rest against her cheek. His future consisted of raising bulls; his life could use some complications. "My future is raising bulls and dancing with them. Any child of ours will bring only joy. Of that I am certain. Do you see a son for us?"

"I can't see beyond what I've said."

"So be it."

The nymph halted his kisses once again. "There is more. If you wish to take me, it will bind us forever."

"As in marriage?" Paris asked.

"Yes, as you mortals call it so."

"Then, we shall belong to one another," Paris whispered into her ear. "Forever."

Oenone relented into Paris' arms, surrendering her divine gift. As he took her, the world around them paused, the air stilled, crickets quieted, and the distant River Cebron slowed to silence. Their joining spread warmth throughout his entire body. Paris looked down into the nymph's eyes and he felt complete for the first time in his life. It didn't matter who is father was or why he'd been left to die. He filled Oenone with his passion for life, with his longing for home, with his hopes for their future. The tension within his belly grew as his cock swelled before he climaxed with a mighty roar of joy. As the shudder shook him from his shoulders to his toes, the nymph wrapped her legs around his hips, pulling him deeper into her body as she neared her release. Nature resumed its hum, busting to life at their completed consummation.

Beneath the expanse of sky, Paris became the unexpected bridegroom. "I'll never let you go, Oenone. As long as I live, I'll love no other."

Oenone's cheeks, flushed with passion, faded a bit. The smile on her lips fell to a thin line. A crystal tear slid from the corner of her eye. "You'll betray me," she whispered. "I've seen that as well."

"Why do you believe these vile things will happen? Don't I have a say in my own life? My own actions?" Paris kissed her sweetly. "I've only loved one woman my entire life, nymph. And she's beneath me at this very moment." His eagerness hardened inside of her. "I believe I'll take you again, wife."

After their second union, he rolled onto his side and plucked a cluster of tiny, pale blue flowers, handing them to Oenone. He kissed her on the cheek, then rose from their marital bed of grass. "I've cattle to look after."

"Promise me again that you'll never leave me," Oenone whispered.

He held a hand to lift her to her feet. "You've no need to worry, wife."

"Will you tell your father about us? What if he doesn't approve?"

Paris kissed each of her palms. "What's done is done. I don't need Agelaus' consent."

As oenone walked along the edge of the cool river gathering flowers and plants for healing elixirs, she stooped to pull a broad-leafed plant out by the root, and the river slowed.

"Father?" she called out.

"I am here, Oenone," a voice rumbled deeply.

She ran her hand through the stilled pool. "I have chosen my mate."

Her father, God of the Rivers, spoke through the water bubbling over smooth rocks. "He will bring you great sorrow."

Oenone jerked her hand from the water, as if burnt by fire. "I've seen it."

"A war is coming, my daughter. A war that will destroy all you hold dear."

The nymph sighed. "I'm in love, Father."

"Love changes nothing," the River God said. "Nothing."

THIRTEEN

for love of Zeus

PHTHIA—1272 BCE

NEAR THE INLET SEA

Water shimmered down Thetis' skin as she emerged from clear, dark water. A silver mist veiled her naked form as she lay on her stomach in the long grass edging the pond she called home. No other nymphs had challenged her for this small, isolated paradise she'd created. More importantly, Hera seemed not to notice her when she lingered here. Although a changeling, there was no shape shifting that could keep her safe from Hera's jealous rages.

Low hanging limbs of willow trees brushed the tips of the tall grass in the breeze. Flowering vines snaked up tree trunks and burst in perpetual color. Nymphs had no desire for the cold, crystalline luxuries and airy beauty of Olympus.

A gust of warm air passed over her body. Thetis smiled and rolled over, exposing her breasts and her triangle of tightly curled hair. She stretched her arms over her head, while the warm air licked up her center, bringing a moan of pleasure to her lips. "Zeus."

The grass swirled in a sparkling circle, as the god materialized before her. "You must stop tempting me to stray from Hera's side." His thunderous voice rippled across the grass.

Thetis covered her breasts with her hands, and sat up. "You must stop watching me."

"That's impossible."

The nymph crawled to the god's feet. He was magnificent, standing as tall as a tree with silver hair floating about his shoulders with a life of its own. "Then put us both from our miseries and take me right now. Hera can't see us or you wouldn't have come." Her body quivered with anticipation. *What would it feel like to have Zeus inside of me?*

Zeus shook his head. "It's too dangerous. She always knows." He glanced around the pond, searching for hidden enemies or spies. "Somehow … she always knows."

"Take me in a form she will not recognize."

"I can't consummate our desire until— What are you doing?" Zeus' cock jerked to life as Thetis stroked his thigh. Gently, he pushed her hands away. "Not yet."

Thetis sighed, placing her hand back on his knee.

She envied Hera. Perhaps it was the way the Thunder King gazed on her, touching her bare skin beneath her garments with only his eyes, causing her sacred parts to pulse with need. *If he would only take me in all his glory … or as a river washing over me, a flame burning across my naked breasts, or a beast ravaging me in ecstasy, I would be fulfilled.* But always the thought of Hera's retribution silenced her fantasies. Hera was a jealous goddess and rightly so.

Zeus stroked Thetis' long, dark hair. "You must also stay away from Poseidon."

Thetis shrugged. "What can I do against a god's advances?" She looked up then, eyeing him carefully, testing his truthfulness. "Am I not worthy of a god?"

"The Earth Shaker takes many women. I can't dispute that. If any god takes your prize, it will be me. Do you hope for war among the Olympians?"

"No, Zeus. How can you even ask me such a question? I was there. I saw … I've no desire to return to those times of shadow and flame." She shuddered with the memory of the mutiny against Zeus by the Others eons ago. She alone had stood by his side while the one-hundred handed beast with fifty heads kept the immortal menace at bay. *Briareus.* Its hands flailed in battle, its wicked slimy heads swirled, and each mouth frothed hungrily for divine flesh. Briareus' roars had echoed across the sky with more deafening fierceness than a hundred of Zeus' own thunder bolts. The Olympians' rebellion against their own father-brother had faded into distant memory, but she was certain no one had forgotten it. The resulting peace lay constantly on the precipice of a sword's edge. Zeus' goodwill and the Others acquiescence allowed peace, a peace that could erode into warring factions of Olympus if a lover's battle between brothers erupted over her virginity.

The Thunder King leaned his head to hers, kissing her lightly on the mouth. "You taste of salt and honey."

Leaning into his embrace, she gripped his knee with her cool hand. "I beg you take me. Extinguish the fire you ignite."

"I can't. Not yet. Promise me, you won't allow Poseidon to take what should be mine."

The nymph called after the god, "Hurry back to me."

Zeus strode off into the nearby meadow, disappearing into the thin air.

MOUNT PELION

"My Lord, if you bed the nymph, it isn't Hera you'll need to worry about. It's the child who'll come after the bedding," the centaur, Chiron, whispered into his half-brother's ear.

"What child?" Zeus countered, suspicious that Chiron had some devious scheme to take Thetis for himself. The wooly horseman had once taken a nymph, Chariclo, to wife. *Perhaps he desires another slippery beauty to satisfy his carnal lust.* The carnivals and sexual rites of centaurs were legendary, even among the gods. "You may have been granted wisdom, brother, but make certain your advice isn't to keep the nymph for yourself."

The centaur pawed the ground. "You insult me, brother. I speak of saving you from yourself."

"Speak, then."

Chiron crossed his arms across his bare chest. "Themis gave me a warning regarding Thetis. She said the nymph's son would rise to be greater than his *father*."

Zeus grimaced. "This isn't what I expected." The god paced the floor of Chiron's hall. "A son such as that could … overthrow me like I did Kronos."

"My thoughts exactly."

"No god should be allowed to take her virginity."

The centaur cantered to his cupboard. "Would you care for wine?"

"No, my mood is soured by this news."

"Here, drink this. I mixed it with ambrosia to ease your disappointment."

The god took the cup, gulping the contents. "Thetis must be married off to a mortal man. Without delay."

"There's a bit more," Chiron warned.

Zeus scowled. "Your words are less welcomed than those Hermes delivers."

"Themis *suggests* that Thetis be given to Peleus, the loyal king. Together, they'll have a son whose might will rival Ares, but not surpass it. His feet will be as swift as lightning."

"Themis suggests. So be it. Go to Phthia, then. Find the king, Peleus. Tell him he shall wed Thetis as a reward for his *loyalty*." Zeus ran his fingers through his silvery beard. "Yes, let Thetis bear a mortal son and Peleus bear the burden of a son rising in glory above him."

Chiron bowed his head, slightly. "As you desire, my lord."

INLET POND OF THETIS

Golden Hermes flew from Olympus to deliver the news to silver-footed Thetis. Delivering unwanted messages delighted him.

Thetis eyed Hermes, searching his face for a sign that he lied. *This could be a trick of Hera's.* "I've no wish to marry at all. I refuse to marry anyone." She dove into her salty pond of crystal water. When she emerged, she splashed the surface at Hermes. "You're still here? Go on. Fly away. I will not marry anyone. Not even Zeus can make me wed a mortal against my will."

Hermes knuckled his hands at his waist. "It's not your decision, nymph. The son you will bear will affect us all. So, the choice has been made for you."

"I'll speak to Zeus myself."

The winged messenger's mouth curled with a wicked smile. "You're no longer permitted such intimacy. And, if I were you, I'd let the matter rest. Hera has forbidden you for now. Zeus agrees."

"She can't exile me from Olympus! Zeus will change his mind. I am certain of it."

As he leapt aloft, he glanced over his shoulder. "It's done, Thetis."

Thetis sank to her knees in the tall grass, grief filling her. *He must change his mind. He can't abandon me like this … to a mortal.* She scanned the sky above her looking, hoping, to see a ripple in the air … a sign, any sign, that Zeus was coming to her to take it all back. But, the vast blue held only clouds and birds, nothing more. *Not to a mortal.*

For days on end, Thetis wept an ocean of bitter tears emptying right into Zeus' ears. Drinking his sacred nectar and eating the choice cuts of sacrifice gave him no pleasure. *If she should draw Hera's attention … I've no desire to experience the mayhem that would cause.* He pitied the nymph being forced to marry a mortal man. But her weeping must stop.

He flew at dawn to the edge of the nymph's glassy pond. He found her facedown in the mossy grass. "I don't think I've seen such a forlorn creature in all my days. It's unfair that fate dealt you such a disastrous plan for your son." *Mortals think we gods have the better lot, that we in all of our undying days have the superior existence. Forever is a curse, when you must watch those you care about move on without you.*

Thetis slowly lifted her head, her green eyes darkened by grief seeing Zeus standing over her. "What do you want?" she asked, miserably.

"Come to me," the god-king murmured.

"Why? Why should I? To feel you close to my heart, before you abandon me all over again?"

"Thetis, you know this isn't how I wanted our future to be. I'd hoped for … more."

The nymph stood. "You knew the dangers of pursuing me, yet you did it anyway. I was foolish enough to believe your embraces and your kisses meant more. I see now that I am like all of the others. No. It's worse for me. You're trying to rid yourself of me by marrying me to a mortal."

"You think this is easy for me? A god being denied the one thing he desires most?"

"Why? Why have you cast me aside?"

Zeus approached her, cautiously, and then took her in his arms. "It is with great pain that I do. You must believe me."

Pressing closer, Thetis asked, "Then why? If it pains you, take me here. In whatever form you desire."

Zeus steeled the quickening of his desire. Instantly, he imagined morphing into a warm rain and slowly showering down her arms and legs, running his essence in rivulets down her belly. Perhaps, enveloping her in her pond, a watery invasion of her being. But the child … he could not forget the child. Chiron's words echoed through his mind. He wouldn't risk the birth of a son who could overthrow him, turning Olympus into a battle ground. "It is impossible for us to merge."

The nymph pushed back against his embrace. "But why must I marry a mortal? A *mortal*? I'm shamed by this command." Fresh tears erupted into large, glistening drops falling as crystals down her cheeks. "You merge with mortal women without a second thought. Am I not good enough for you?"

"It's not you, Thetis." Zeus decided then that the truth might be the only way to release them both from their desires. "Chiron delivered a warning regarding the son you would bear from your first bedding."

"Chiron? What does he know? Take me here, on the grass," Thetis teased, placing his hand on her breast.

Zeus cupped the soft roundness of her flesh burning against his palm. "He knows enough, my little nymph." Reluctantly, he pulled his hand away.

"Is my son to be grotesque? An abomination?"

"No, quite the opposite. Your son is destined to be greater than his father."

Thetis paused. "That would mean—"

"Yes, that would mean war. War on Mount Olympus. We both know I can't allow that to ever happen again."

Thetis' shoulders slumped. "Then, truly there is no hope. And for me a prison on Gaia."

"Gentle Thetis, you must know it's impossible to allow you to wed any immortal. There will be no more uprisings in Olympus."

"You're right. It must not be allowed."

He rested his forehead on hers. "And if I did, it would be your fault."

"May I choose my mate?"

"I'm afraid that the matter has already been settled. The mortal has been chosen. But, I give you this, siren. He can claim you, only if he can catch you."

Thetis traced a delicate trail to his beard where she entwined her fingers into its curls. "And if not?"

The Thunder King reassured the only lover he would never have, knowing that she was the only one he would always want. "If he can't catch you, then he has no claim."

———

On the pretext of hunting stag, Peleus made his way to the secret pond Chiron not so subtly informed him of. The notion of marrying an immortal, a nymph, thrilled the king even though he knew such a match might prove perilous, if not fatal. Stories abounded of mortal men duped and discarded by jealous female deities, but he'd decided as soon as Chiron suggested the match that he'd pursue it.

He hiked in silence for most of the gloomy morning, steadily making his way across meadows and foothills, rocky trails and soggy marsh. He walked through the rising comfort of the sun and into the sweaty heat of the blazing day. His legs ached. His lungs burned. He spat out the thickened spit his parched throat refused to swallow.

Thirst forced him to stop for a handful of cool water. *I can't be far now.* As he knelt beside a pond, Peleus caught a glimpse of skin and hair skimming below the surface. By *the balls of Zeus. Is that a fish?* He scurried backwards, finding cover in a low hanging willow branch, watching the deep shadow as it emerged, to his astonishment, on the opposite side of the water.

A naked woman with skin so pale it glistened silver walked into the cover of low hanging boughs opposite him. He stalked her in silence, watching her slip into a gown of gauze so thin her curves were hardly hidden behind the tiny folds which she carefully arranged with a garland girdle. The train of her dress gathered leaves and flowers as she walked. Her movements mesmerized Peleus. His cock stiffened. *Am I hunter or prey?* Peleus willed his desire to calm.

Realizing this must be the nymph Chiron told him to find and capture, he again wondered why Zeus would sanction such a match. His past held nothing honorable enough to warrant a gift as beautiful as this nymph. He wondered, even as he stalked her, if it was the wisest action. He pushed the memory of plotting to kill his half-brother, Phocus, birthed by another nymph, from his mind. That incident preceded a long line of tragedies involving women. *Antigone …*

His memories of her limp form swinging from a slender rope still haunted him. *No, this time will be different. It has to be.* He'd been purified several times over, forgiven by the gods, and now that he'd laid eyes on Thetis, he wanted her. Determination, despite his past, focused his mind on the hunt.

Peleus employed all of the skills he'd honed for tracking illusive prey. Stay out of their range of smell, tread silently, and never take your eyes off the target. He recalled Chiron's warning, "*Thetis will resist you. It's not within an immortal's nature to be caged or trapped. She's a nymph. A changeling. She will fight with all of her might and skill. Hang on tightly no matter what form she shifts to. Do not release her, or you will lose her. Once she returns to herself, you have won. She will submit.*" Peleus thought of his travels with the Argonauts. This was a simple task compared to all that he'd overcome. All he needed to do was seize her tightly and not let go.

The hunter set his sights on the beautiful creature weeping face down beneath the tree. A gust of wind swept the tall grass, rippling the canopy of trees, and carried the nymph's sobs to his ears. Her vulnerability pricked his heart, doubling his resolve to capture her and crush her to his chest. Removing his leather sandals, he made his approach. When the nymph rolled onto her back, he instinctively crouched low in the grass like a lion, his eyes barely visible through the tall edge of verge.

The beautiful creature sat up, scanning the banks surrounding her, and Peleus chose that moment to pounce on his intended prey. His arms wrapped about her like two chains. "Nooo!" she screamed. "It's not fair! Zeus said I would be warned. Let me go!"

Peleus' arms tightened even more, wrenching the air from her lungs. Immortal instinct took over, as she morphed into an enormous hissing snake, twitched into a lion, and squirmed into a giant slimy fish. The hunter's fingers dug deeper into her flesh. "I'll never let you go, nymph."

"You bastard mortal, free me!" the fish bellowed.

"Not on my life!"

Refusing to give up, the nymph raged into a terrifying Medusa. The nest of snakes licked around her face, stretching to reach Peleus. The hunter shifted his weight back as the snakes hissed and flicked their tongues at him, but he never released his strangling grip.

"You'll never have me!" the Medusa screeched. "Never!"

"Is that the best you can do, nymph? I fear no form you can take. No matter the fangs or scales, it is you beneath the surface."

"Did Zeus send you?" the Medusa asked. "Some god has helped you, I know it."

He shook his head firmly. "It was no god, nymph. Chiron sent me here."

The snakes wilted their protest, as the nymph recognized her defeat. "Your eyes speak the truth. Although, a truth I wish I'd never seen. You'll never let me go."

"I'm committed to this venture."

Morphing to her natural form, she let her body relax slightly in the stranger's arms. "What do you want of me? A passionate exchange?"

Without releasing his grip, he pulled her eyes to his. "Your hand in marriage."

Thetis shuddered at the idea of being bound to any mortal. Her heart still burned for Zeus. "Marry you? Why should I marry one so low?"

"Low?" His laughter echoed to the sky. "You think me low?"

"All mortals rank lower than we immortal few."

He laughed again. "Do you give in then?" His grip tugged harder. "Yes or no?"

She flailed at his arms and scratched at his head, a futile last effort. "You. Are. Hurting. Me!"

"Give up, nymph. I've snared you fairly."

"Never."

"Then my kingdom will miss me. My warriors will likely follow my trail … here."

"Kingdom? Warriors? I want no more mortals treading on my sacred pond."

"Yes, my kingdom. And when they find me, they will find you locked in my arms."

The nymph's eyes rounded in horror. "What will they do with me?"

"Likely, they'll capture you and put you in a cage … at my command."

The nymph shook her head vigorously against the thought. "A cage?"

"I'll keep you displayed in the palace as my treasured pet."

"You would cage me?"

"I'd prefer a sweeter exchange. Become my queen."

"That is but another kind of cage." The nymph pressed a cool palm against Peleus' chest. "Shall we bargain?"

"Speak and I'll make it so, if it's within my power," Peleus promised.

"I'll be your queen, if I may roam freely." She gestured around the meadow. "Here in my home or peacefully at sea."

"As long as you return each evening to our bed and sleep beside me. Tell me your name."

"Thetis."

With that, Peleus released his grip on her, setting her feet gently on the ground. "It is done then. You will by my wife, the Queen of Phthia." He turned to walk away.

"Wait! Where are you going? What is your name?"

The hunter spun on his heel, strode back to face her, tilted her chin up to his, and kissed her until her mouth ached with the pressure of his lips. "Peleus. I'm called Peleus." He released her chin and walked away, leaving a trail of smashed grass behind him.

Thetis touched her swollen lips with her fingertips. "Peleus," she said. Not even Zeus had kissed her so roughly and with such passion. "Perhaps, marriage to this mortal will not be so awful."

FOURTEEN

a marriage and an apple

PHTHIA—1272 BCE

MOUNT PELION

The Olympians attended the royal wedding at the command of Zeus. They cloaked their immortal glory in human mantles, mingling freely with the mortal wedding guests from Thessaly and the nobles of Peleus' court.

Green garlands and field flowers decked the halls and towering columns of the palace. A fountain of river rocks surrounded by a ring of water drew center attention; its bottom glittered with gold and silver coins tossed as wedding bliss wishes by the guests. Bronze oil lamps blazed in every corner of the hall, bathing the room in twinkling light. At the head table Peleus beamed in triumph. His newly made queen would soon be his bedded bride.

Misfortune had followed all of his previous marriages. Someone always wound up dead. Eurythion. Antigone. Polydora. He'd been in no hurry to find another bride, saddling him with more misery. But, his advisors kept urging him to remarry, saying he needed an heir. At every turn, his advisors pushed women at him, their daughters or their granddaughters, and on one uncomfortable occasion, an acquaintance's mother. Until now, he'd abstained from the pleasures of female company, finding pleasure in the business of war, wealth, and power.

The nymph intrigued him. She craved no crown, no gold or riches. She only wanted her freedom. This Peleus found almost as tempting as her immortality and her beauty, which was unparalleled. Her skin shimmered with a pale silver light, her eyes sparkled as green as a clear pond, and her lips were round and red promising much pleasure. Her hair, the color of a raven's wing, curled down to her feet. Peleus noticed that most of his invited guests could barely keep their eyes from lingering on her. His chest swelled with jealous pride.

"Chiron!" Peleus shook the centaur's hand. "Where is …" Peleus looked behind the centaur, turning him with difficulty, "the rest of you?"

Chiron scratched at his armpit. "Cloaked for the event. I wouldn't miss this for all of the gold you could lay at my feet."

"Gratitude, my friend, for your advice. I'd never have caught her without your wise and winning words."

Chiron bowed his head. "Who'd have thought that after Eurythion, Antigone, and Polydora you'd marry again … and such a *rare* beauty at that."

"Without your help, it would never have happened. I'm in your debt."

The centaur chuckled. "I know you well enough to know you're already contemplating mating with the nymph, if you haven't bedded her by now." He rubbed at his hip. "When all is done, you may not thank me for my council."

"Thetis is finer than the widows, daughters, and granddaughters being tossed in my direction. But, your words are concerning. What do you mean?"

"There is a small matter of the son Thetis will bear."

Peleus grabbed his friend by the arm. "A son? My son? Are you certain? I'd almost given up—"

"Quite certain."

"Don't just stand there. Tell me. What about my son?"

"He will be a greater king than you. Perhaps, a better general. Likely, Peleus, he will surpass you in every measure. Which is why Zeus declined her virginity, forbidding any immortal from taking her prize."

"She was the lover of Zeus?"

Chiron shook his head. "Don't let your thoughts run wild with jealousy. He never bedded her. Didn't you hear me? Zeus couldn't risk a son … never mind. She's yours now. And so is the burden of the son sprung from her womb."

Peleus scanned the centaur's face for falsehoods. "If you're lying to me—"

"I'm offended you think so little of our long years of friendship. Do you see that man over there?"

Peleus glanced in the direction the centaur indicated. A very tall man with hair so blond it glinted silver stood in a far corner, conversing with a woman. "I don't know that man."

"No, you don't *know* him, but it many ways his charity allowed this marriage to take place."

"Charity? What does a stranger have to do with my wedding? He paid neither for the wine, the feast—"

Chiron snorted and scratched his chin. "He gave up his claim on the nymph, you imbecile."

"His claim on Thetis? Are trying to tell me that's … that's—"

"It is."

"I don't believe you. It can't be."

"Why not? You're marrying a nymph. Surely, you believe the gods are real."

"Yes, but in temples and on Olympus. Not in my palace."

"You mortals can be so tiresome at times. Look around you, my friend. Look at all of the people whose beauty beckons the eye, whose stature is head and shoulders above your own, and tell me their names."

Peleus glanced around the room again. A trio of women, in one corner, stood close together laughing and drinking wine from crystal goblets. The torchlight reflected strands of gold and silver in their hair. They stood a head taller than the tallest man. A lone man played a lyre and his music floated sweetly across the chamber. "I-I don't know some of them."

"Yet, you know all of the nobles of your kingdom …"

"Zeus wanted to marry Thetis? What about Hera?"

Chiron quickly grabbed Peleus' arm, steering him into a more private alcove. "Shah! You mortal idiot. Hera is just across the room. Zeus never intended on marrying the nymph. Just bedding her."

A thunderous roar filled the hall as the southern doors flew open. Mist spilled across the floor, curling around the approaching figure, rendering it a smudge of black amidst the grey. Slowly, the mist cleared, revealing a goddess in full Olympic glory. Her golden gown, encrusted with silver crystals and polished gems, shimmered in the flickering yellow light of the hall. Her golden hair shamed the flames. Her irises shone black as night, piercing all who looked upon her. Mortals fell into a stupor in her presence.

Thetis screamed.

Chiron muttered to himself, "Eris."

Zeus of silver-hair demanded, "What do you seek, Eris?"

Eris flashed a divine smile. "I'd hoped it a simple oversight that I was not invited, but I can see by your stunned faces that I was mistaken."

The silver-haired god cocked an eyebrow. "You aren't welcomed here, and you know why."

Eris sneered. "I'll take my leave, but not before I give the bride and groom my wedding gift." She tossed a golden orb into the assembly of wedding guests. It landed on a table, clanging loudly as it tumbled over precious glassware and silver eating utensils. Blood red wine splashed across the plates of food, across gowns and tunics, dripping onto the marble floor before it rolled and wobbled to a stop.

"You scorn me, as you would scorn the Fates who reveal a future you wish to change. You can't change the course decreed by them any more than you can change your own appetites for power and flesh." Eris gestured at the golden orb. "You're not immune to strife or grief or sorrows because you breathe the air of Olympus. You're at the same mercy as humans, when the Fates have cast their die. Brother Zeus, you know the truth of it." Eris looked into the stricken faces of each Olympian, sensing the foreboding in their eyes. "You will blame me, but it's not by my hand your fates are cast. I'm simply the messenger." She spun gracefully on her heel, her gown flowing behind her like a cloud, and retreated from the hall.

Aphrodite plucked the heavy orb from its resting place on the table. She balanced it in her palm. "It is an apple of the Hesperides. A fine gift. Pure gold. An unexpected treasure."

Athena grabbed the fruit from the Goddess of Love, inspecting it for herself. "There's writing on the side."

Hera scowled. "How did that bitch get passed the daughters of Atlas? I curse Herakles for destroying my dragon. Those ridiculous labors for Eurystheus will cost us all now. I can feel it."

Chiron elbowed a dozing Peleus. "This should be interesting. Wake up, you idiot! Look at all of the immortals among us!"

One of the king's eyes opened partially, before rolling back in his head. "What is the meaning of this—"

"Immortals have this effect on mortals, when the godly ones choose not to be seen," Chiron whispered urgently. "Shake it off, Peleus!"

"Read the message, Athena," Hera commanded.

Athena nodded obedience to her mother. "It says: *kallisti, to the fairest.*"

Aphrodite grabbed the golden apple from her sister. "Clearly, this was meant for me."

Zeus commanded, "Give that to me. It's a wedding gift for Thetis."

Hera raised a perfectly arched brow. "I suppose you believe her 'the fairest' in the room?"

"No," he answered flatly.

Hera glanced from Athena to Aphrodite, then back to her husband. "The apple is for '*the fairest*' that's clear. Certainly, Eris didn't mean that nymph, cowering in the corner. Husband, you must decide and put an end to this before it becomes … a problem for Olympia."

"How can I judge fairly between my very own wife and daughters? I will please one, angering the other two. No one will believe I chose without bias."

"True," Hera said. "Well-spoken. Diplomatic. Expected."

131

"Some other must judge, then. The winner shouldn't have to share this apple with anyone," Aphrodite said.

"Name another god, then," Athena suggested.

Zeus stepped over sleeping mortals to the center of the hall, and a hush fell on the divine. "It must be a mortal."

The Goddess of Love bristled. "How can a mortal be a better judge?"

Zeus replied, "Only a mortal can choose without bias. Only a mortal can bear the wrath of the losers on his head. I must keep all such strife far from Olympus. I'm certain you all agree."

Athena's golden helmet glittered beneath her arm. "I see the wisdom in your words. Who then?"

Ares, God of War, spoke up, "Not long ago, I encountered a boy in a bull ring. I found him to be … most *fair*. He lives on the outskirts of Troy, and is innocent of the politics of palace or temple. His blood is of royal lineage, so the injury to your pride is lessened, is it not, being judged by the secret son of King Priam?"

"His name?" Athena questioned.

"Paris. You'll find him tending cattle along the slopes of the sacred mountain."

Chiron and a sleepy Peleus watched as the wedding guests came back to life once the bargain was struck, with the wedding guests none the wiser. Soon music and laughter echoed in the hall.

"What does this mean?" Peleus asked, groggily.

The centaur scratched at his beard. "That a darkness is coming to our world."

FIFTEEN

a judgment of Paris

A bellow woke Paris, pulling him from Oenone's warm body. Stars sparkled above them. The moon, full and heavy, hung low, almost touching the ridgeline across the gorge.

Without lifting her head from the downy pillow, Oenone asked, "What is it, my mortal?"

"A bull. It's unusual for them to stir this time of night." His eyes scanned the deep purple of the sky. "This time of morning."

"Are you going to the field?" Oenone blinked sleep from her liquid eyes.

Paris knelt, running a strong hand along the line of her body, his hand lingering over each curve. He touched her between the thighs. "You make it difficult to leave, even when duty calls me."

"Is something wrong?" she asked.

"Don't worry. I'll return shortly." He leaned his head to hers, grazing her lips with his own, and whispered, "You are like wine to me."

Then, he kissed her deeply. "I drink my fill, and am impatient for more."

Oenone blushed. "I will be your wine. Night and day, my mortal." She reached her lips up to peck his with a light kiss. "Go. Be gone about your business so you may return thirsty for my ... wine."

Paris grabbed her chin in his hands, looking hard in her eyes. "I will always return." He released her face. The crisp chill of night still clung to the air, so Paris pulled his woolen cloak tighter over his chiton and tucked his sword into his wide leather belt and a dagger into a leather cuff. On his way from the camp, he grabbed his bow just to be safe. Cattle thieves were ruthless.

As he approached the place where the bellowing originated, he slowed his pace. Firelight glowed, lighting the hazy dark from beyond a row of tangled bushes. *Unexpected.* He crouched lower than the surrounding brush trying to get as close as possible to the light.

A feminine voice floated across the night, addressing him. "We won't bite you, Paris."

Paris froze at hearing his name spoken so confidently. *What trickery is this?*

"Do you think he heard you?" asked Athena, draped in golden gauze.

"Certain," said Hera the silver-haired.

"Why does he just crouch there?" asked Aphrodite.

Athena crossed her arms. "Like a scared child."

"He's little more than that, truly spoken, Athena," Hera agreed.

How do they know I'm here? Something is wrong. Paris' heart pounded fearfully in his chest.

A hand tapped Paris on the shoulder. "We're addressing you."

He jumped and spun, pulling his sword from his belt. "Show yourself!" Paris hissed, his feet firmly planted in a fighting stance, squared in the direction of the voice. He faced only the empty air. "I said show yourself!"

Feminine laughter rang as clear as temple bells behind him.

"Come, Paris, warm your flesh by our fire," Hera enticed with a beckoning finger in his direction.

Paris dared to straighten, slowly facing the golden glow of the fire to gaze fully at the women. *Tall for women. Tall even for a man*, he thought. Two of them had golden hair and the other silver. They encouraged him to draw nearer with graceful hands and pearly smiles. "Who are you and why are you here in the hills? Alone?"

"Come. Sit. We will tell you the beginning of a tale that only you can finish."

Paris eyed the elegant woman with silver hair. She clearly spoke for the trio. He approached, never taking his eyes from them. When he reached the edge of the ring around the fire, he sat. The flames warmed the chill from his shins and face.

"You are unlike any women I have ever encountered," Paris said.

"I should hope so. Most mortals are never privileged with the presence of a goddess. It's the rare few, but even then, once in a lifetime," the silver-haired Hera said.

"Goddess? Your meaning is disguised," Paris said, confused.

"It's plain, Paris. Look at us."

"You're tall. Taller than men," he offered cautiously.

The silver-haired goddess smiled. "You state the obvious. I am Hera. Wife of Zeus."

"I am Athena." The Goddess of War and Wisdom, garbed in gold, nodded her greeting.

"I am Aphrodite." The Goddess of Love nodded, as she flashed a coy smile.

"How do I know you are truly divine? Not some imaginings of a fever dream?" Paris asked.

Hera asked, "Are we not pleasant to your eye as we are?"

"Your beauty is undeniable. Maybe you're Amazons. Or some other magic."

"You think us Amazons?" Aphrodite bristled at the thought. "Amazons? How common. I think I'm insulted."

"Their height is legendary," Paris replied.

Aphrodite turned round in a circle. "Athena, sister, have I made some flawed mortal covering? Am I not perfection? Love personified?"

Athena scoffed at Aphrodite's dilemma. "You appear as you always do. Your mortal skin is as it always is."

Hera explained, "If you were to look upon our immortal selves, our true form, you would be blinded. Temporarily, of course, but blinded all the same."

"What would three goddesses want from a bull herder?" Paris asked.

"A judgment. A simple judgment," Hera said.

"Of what?" Paris asked.

"Our beauty," Hera replied.

Paris shook his head. "I'm a judge of bulls. Not women. You've found the wrong man."

Athena spread her hands in her lap. "You impressed Ares in the bull arena. He said you proved yourself a fair-minded mortal. Zeus agreed for some reason. So, now, you will judge us from our dilemma."

Aphrodite held out the golden apple. It gleamed in the blazing fire's light. She turned the orb on its side and ran her fingers over it. The engraving said *to the fairest.*

"I don't understand. What does that have to do with me?" Paris asked.

"We can't all be *the fairest* and Zeus can't be impartial. No immortal wants to live with the two who were not proclaimed *the fairest*," Athena said. "You see the predicament for Zeus."

"But, how am I to choose? If Zeus himself can't pick from among you, how am I to do so?"

Aphrodite explained, "You are the *unbiased* judge. Believe me, the thought that a mortal should choose between us repulses me. I almost dropped the apple, when Zeus proclaimed it so."

"You've hardly let go of the fucking apple since Eris threw it on the table," Athena scoffed.

Paris noted that even with a disgusted scowl, the woman calling herself Athena took his breath away. "Could this be true? You are divine?"

"Mortals," Aphrodite said, shaking her head. "Always doubting, yet always praying."

Hera clapped her graceful hands together, bringing order to the small gathering. "It's time to begin the judgment, Paris."

"What are the criteria?" Paris asked. "With cattle, it is their pedigree first."

Athena considered Paris with a nod of her head. "We'll not be judged on pedigree. We are goddesses after all."

"Bulls destined for the arena are judged by their physical structure, their stamina, their temperament," Paris said. "These qualities I can assess. Anything else, I am unworthy."

Aphrodite smiled widely. "I have the superior physical form. Shall I reveal it to you, master of bull flesh?" Without waiting for Paris' reply, she undid the clasps holding her pale green gown at her shoulders, and let is slip down the length of her body where it pooled at her feet.

Her nudity amazed Paris. Her lithe frame was perfection by any standard. Her eyes emeralds framed by delicately arched brows. Her nose straight and small, tipped up slightly at the end. Aphrodite's neck held her head with grace. Her breasts large and firm, sat high on her chest, much larger than Oenone's. The nipples, pale pink, crinkled into perfect buds. His eyes moved to her belly, then the sacred cross of her femininity. She had no body hair there or anywhere. Her sacred folds clearly visible stirred his loins with warmth. Immediately ashamed, he cast his eyes to the ground, guilt flooding him even as his body betrayed him.

"Is there something wrong, mortal?" asked Aphrodite.

"No," he lied. A battle between his head and heart raged through him. The weight of this judgment finally crushed him. *I will pay for this, one way or another. Will the losers kill me? Kill my family? Will they take revenge on Oenone?*

Aphrodite snapped her fingers. "Finish your assessment."

Against his will, he examined the tapering length of her legs, her narrow ankles and delicate feet. "You are indeed perfection to the eye. I can find no fault."

Athena followed and dropped her golden robe to the ground, exposing her naked flesh. "Paris, gaze upon me next. I am no soft mound of flesh."

Paris' eyes rounded to Athena's form. Her body was chiseled like a man's, yet decidedly feminine. Her breasts were smaller than Aphrodite's, but perfect orbs set perfectly upon her chest. She opened her arms wide, confidently encouraging him to feast his eyes on her. Her leg muscles knotted to perfection above her knees, her calves gracefully squared, and her feet were strong.

Paris shrugged, impressed by her physique. "I've never laid eyes on such a woman before."

Aphrodite hissed, "You cheat."

"Your jealousy is ugly," Athena taunted.

"I'm most definitely not jealous," Aphrodite snapped back.

Hera intervened. "Come, daughters. Peace. No final judgment has been made. One of us has yet to be evaluated." Hera disrobed, carefully stepping out of her silver gown, making sure her rounded hips swayed provocatively for Paris to gaze at.

Hera's form was much more slender than the other goddesses. Her shoulders were narrow and graceful and almost the same width as her hips. Her hair swept the ground in silky tendrils, flowing with a life of their own. His eyes scanned down her chest, taking in each heavy breast peaked with pale silver nipples. Her sacred folds lay hidden behind a triangle of curled silver hair.

"You're all beautiful beyond compare," Paris said. "Each of you bears distinctive qualities … even still I cannot distinguish who among you is the fairest."

"Wisely spoken, Paris," Athena said. "But the task has fallen to you, by will of Zeus. You must decide."

"Perhaps, the bull herder requires a more … unique standard by which to judge?" Hera offered.

"What else is there?" Aphrodite asked.

Hera smiled confidently. "We each offer Paris a gift. He must choose the gift he desires most. And in doing so, names the fairest."

Athena added, "The gift must be within the realm of power we each possess."

Aphrodite agreed. "I will give my gift last."

Athena flashed a blazing look at Aphrodite. "Sleeping with the mortal isn't what Hera meant."

Paris panicked. "I can't bed any of you. Please, forgive me—"

"None of us will bed you. I forbid it," Hera asserted, eyeing Aphrodite harshly. "There are enough bastards of Zeus among the mortals. We'll not be adding more for this contest. I'll not give my husband any reason to scorn me, despite all of his indiscretions."

"Hera, bestow your gift. I shall follow. Aphrodite shall be last," Athena said.

Hera glanced around her. "I see that you roam your land widely, yet it is limited. I will give you all of the lands north and west of Greece, and the eastern realm rich with gold and spice as yours to rule and roam for as long as you live."

"That is indeed generous, Hera," Paris said. He thought how Oenone wouldn't desire living so far from home. He had no desire to rule such a vast expanse of land. He stood without another word.

Athena sighed. "My gift is one no true warrior could resist. You're destined for great things. I can see this. I offer you unsurpassed skill in battle and warfare. Your deeds will be renown among mortals for millennia."

"I thank you, Goddess, for your deep wisdom. You gift is indeed generous." Paris again offered little to encourage the Athena. *I've no desire for war or legend.*

Aphrodite stepped forward. "Paris, I can see you're a cautious man. Thoughtful to the last. I can't offer more than my realm, as the Hera has decreed. So, I can offer you love. Love is my gift."

Paris smiled. "That is a gift I bear already."

The Goddess of Love clasped her hands in front of her. "But not from the most beautiful woman in the world."

Athena shot up from her seat on the log. "There was to be no mating between you and Paris."

"Your dullness bores me, Athena! I said *woman*, not goddess," Aphrodite laughed. "I wasn't offering myself."

"I want no other woman," Paris said, quietly. "I love Oenone."

"There is a mortal whose beauty will rival that of your nymph. And I proclaim her love … yours."

Hera shook her head. "What game are you playing, Aphrodite? What an odd gift. I know of no human whose beauty rivals the heavens."

"You mean yours," Athena spat.

"Watch your words with me. I afford you a position on Olympus, as a daughter of Zeus. But you're no child of mine. We both know—"

"Peace, Hera. I speak of a woman who has yet to be born," Aphrodite said.

Paris nodded. "You offer me a woman who hasn't seen the light of our world?"

"She will," Aphrodite promised. "Trust me, she will."

Paris considered his life. Since the cave incident, he'd chosen to live most of his days peacefully with Oenone. Their marriage he considered a sacred bond. She'd revealed to him the gentle ways a woman loves a man, coaxing him, encouraging him to rise to ecstatic heights. His body never felt such pleasure. He'd no desire to leave the nymph for realm, war, or another love. Yet, he understood that he must judge. *If I choose Hera, I'll have to leave Oenone. If I choose Athena, I'll become someone who I'm not. War brings misery. If I choose Aphrodite, my life will be my own for years to come. Perhaps, she will forget in time, or let me refuse in the future.*

"I've made my decision," Paris said. "I choose … Aphrodite's gift."

"What? What did he say?" Hera asked, genuinely confused.

"Typical mortal man, choosing by what dangles between his thighs," Athena screamed, yanking her golden robe up to her shoulders and fastening the clasps. "I should unveil my full glory at you, bastard herder. Blind you for your puny efforts."

Hera was equally distraught. "Did you say Aphrodite's gift served you best? You actually chose an unborn female to the world being laid at your feet? I agree with you, daughter." Hera picked up her gown, draped it over her arms, stomping several steps into the woods, before disappearing from sight.

"You will pay for the insult, Paris. On that you may count." Athena followed Hera's path and she too disappeared into nothing.

Aphrodite picked up the golden apple lying innocently on the ground. She gleefully tossed it into the air. "It's mine. I am the fairest."

"Congratulations, Goddess," Paris said.

"When the moment presents itself, *she* will be sent to you," Aphrodite promised.

Paris bowed his head in deference. "I thank you, Goddess." When he looked up, only a dying fire was before him. Breathing a sigh of relief, he decided it was best not to say anything to Oenone. She'd only worry. *There is time yet for all of this to fade to nothing.*

───────

Although the wedding feast ended on a sour note, the wedding night proved a sweet and vigorous affair. Thetis lay sleeping in the curve of Peleus' side. The nymph's cool skin was as smooth as silk against his coarse hairiness. He'd thought his heart immune to love, but with each mating the iron heart in his chest softened. He'd satisfied the nymph from every possible angle until she collapsed into the linen, both of them smiling in the dark. Sleep had eluded him the entire night. Usually, sex satiated him into a deep slumber. He blamed the wine. He'd drunk enough of it to fell a wild boar.

Thetis stirred in the crook of his arm. Her long, black hair spilled across his shoulders and pillows, tangling between their entwined legs. Peleus watched her sleep-filled eyes flicker back and forth beneath their lids. Her peaceful smile put him as ease. He brushed the side of her face with his hand and gently kissed her forehead. He marveled that even in sleep the nymph's beauty surpassed any female he'd ever laid eyes on. Pulling her closer to him, he wrapped his arm tighter around her. He wanted to protect her forever, keep her to himself. When he promised her freedom, he had no idea that her presence would compel him to want her more. Keeping his promise would prove more difficult than he originally believed.

The morning sun lit the edges of the curtains brightening the chamber with the coming of Apollo's glory. Thetis opened her eyes to find her new husband gazing down at her.

Thetis reached a hand to her husband's sleep-matted honey brown hair, her fingers curling through his long locks. "Do you find me as pleasing in Apollo's light, as in the darkness?" she cooed.

The very sound of her voice set his desire burning. "You please, nymph. In every way a man can be pleased." He rolled onto his side, facing her, kissing her above each eye.

The nymph blushed. "I, too, am well satisfied. I didn't think a mortal man capable of igniting such a fire within me." Thetis smiled up into Peleus' large, blue eyes. She stroked his coarse beard, and brushed a stray honey gold curl from his forehead. "Did you find the wedding gifts pleasing as well?"

"I was surprised by Poseidon's gift of Balius and Xanthus. They will be the finest horses in my stables. I never imagined such a thing truly existed."

"And Chiron's spear?" Thetis asked.

"Never gripped a finer balanced shaft and blade," Peleus assured her. "Chiron said the blade was forged by Hephaestus himself." He leaned his head down to kiss her. "Our marriage is only one day long and already the gifts exceed what any mortal deserves."

Thetis' liquid eyes darkened with seriousness. "There is one other gift left to give, my husband. Although, it's rather small now, it will increase as the days pass. I hope it will please you."

Peleus' brow wrinkled. "What do you speak of? I know of no other gifts."

"It's my gift, Peleus, to you."

"There's nothing you could offer that would displease me," Peleus said his voice rough with passion.

Thetis pressed her naked body closer to his, pressing her hot center into his hard thigh. "Your seed has taken hold in my belly."

Peleus rolled onto his back and stared at the ceiling of their marital chamber. His face revealed nothing.

"There's more."

"Speak the words," he said softly.

"It's a son. He'll be golden like his father and blessed like his mother."

Peleus' eyes found hers. In that moment, his tormented heart found wholeness. "With your blood running through him, he'll be the mightiest warrior the Myrmidons have ever followed."

"Then, you're pleased?"

Peleus grabbed his wife playfully and pulled her on top of him. He placed both hands on either side of her sweet, soft hips, positioning her legs so she straddled him. He growled, "Ride me, nymph. Ride me until I can take no more." For the first time in years, he felt sure that the unfortunate marriages of his past couldn't touch his love for the Thetis.

Thetis grinned down into his joyful face. "As you wish."

PART TWO

Destiny and Doom

Sing, Muse, sing of Phthia's queen
blue flames circling
destiny's dark descending

Sing of Mycenae's queen
black smoke rising
red rivers roaring

Sing of Sparta's daughter
emerald eyes glittering
ruby rage ruining

Sing of Troy's defender
and her Forgotten Prince
one for love
and one for doom

Sing, Muse, sing the song of princes …

SIXTEEN
flames of immortality
PHTHIA—1270 BCE

I don't want to think of your death at all. Ever. My pleas to Zeus have all gone unanswered, little one. He hides from me. Thetis cradled a sleeping Achilles against her bare breast. Looking down into his face framed by golden hair, she traced the strong jawline he'd inherited from Peleus with her finger. "Surely, you will be the most beautiful mortal man who's ever lived." For the past year her love for Achilles consumed her waking moments, for a terrible darkness chased the sea nymph's joy for her young son. A second prophesy revealed by Themis threatened her son's very life. *I don't want to lose him to war.* She brushed a golden curl from his cheek.

Achilles' blue eyes, as bright as lapis lazuli, blinked and he looked up into his mother's face. The child smiled widely at her. Thetis returned the loving gaze and bent her head to kiss his forehead. His small hand grabbed her naked breast, pulling her nipple into his mouth. "You are forever hungry, Achilles." She hugged the weight of him closer to her chest. Soon, he fell back to quiet slumber, nursing softly, even as his arms and legs hung slack across her lap.

The words of Themis haunted her. *"Your son's renown shall surpass his father's, but his future is not sealed in that honor. A great war is coming and in it he must choose from a double fate. If he refuses to go to battle, he shall rule after his father and die forgotten without glory. If he chooses battle, he will become the greatest warrior the world has ever known. His name will be sung on the lips of generations to come, long after the gods themselves have been forgotten."*

"I have no choice but to perform the ritual, little one," she whispered softly, crystal tears splashing against the tiled floor.

"My lady?"

Thetis turned, lifting a finger to her lips. "The prince sleeps. What is it, Chara?"

"The king awaits you, my queen."

"Tell him I'll be there shortly. The baby …" Chara nodded, backing out of the chamber. Thetis cradled Achilles, careful not to wake him as she stood. After laying him in his cradle, she tucked a linen blanket around him. She bent to kiss his cheek and sighed. *Yes,* she thought, *tonight I will begin the ritual.*

The deep hours of night pulled Thetis from her bed, that and the ache of breasts engorged with milk. Peleus lay snoring in sated slumber. Thetis exhausted him with hours of vigorous sex and a small concoction in his drink. Slipping quietly from the bed coverings, her feet found the floor and she walked silently across the cool stone floor to Achilles' bed. He'd kicked his linens off, so she gently wrapped the soft blanket around him as she scooped him up in her arms. The baby nuzzled his face into her warmth without waking, as she opened the chamber door just enough so a sliver of light from the hall lit her face.

Satisfied that the household slept, Thetis slipped through the door, balancing Achilles' weight in her free arm.

Making her way into the great hall, she moved in the shadows of the red marble columns until she reached the entrance to the lower levels of Peleus' hall. Thetis removed a torch from a heavy iron sconce and descended into the darkness. The stairs wound deep beneath the palace, leading to the king's private temple dedicated to all of the gods. Servants were forbidden in this sacred room so she had little concern for interruption. Achilles stirred in her arms as she quickly made her way deep into the tunnel. When she reached the chamber, she placed the torch in an iron bracket set into the wall. Shrugging out of her chiton, she bunched it into a pile with her feet. She placed Achilles on the mound of clothing while she prepared the silver basin for the sacred fire.

Thetis removed a wooden box from an alcove and opened it. The pungent aroma of holy herbs wafted into the still air. Frankincense. Ambrosia. Herb of Moria. Medusa grass. And the rare prize of a few strands of Zeus' silver hair. Thetis pulled out the frankincense and set it in the bottom of the wide rimmed basin with kindling. Taking a thin reed from the box, she used it to catch a small flame from the torch. She knelt before the basin and lit the dry matter until it smoked and caught fire. Then she added the other elements except for the hair of Zeus and the ambrosia.

Achilles whimpered in his makeshift bed. Thetis rose to gather him to herself. He clung to her in the dimly lit unfamiliar room and found her engorged naked breast. He latched on hungrily, gulping his mother's milk. The nymph sat before the flames that licked the rim of the silver bowl, her precious son comfortably cradled in her lap. Reaching into the box, she pulled out the vial of ambrosia. As

Achilles suckled, she undid his blanket, exposing his bare skin, and poured the ambrosia elixir on her son, rubbing every inch of his skin with it. When she rubbed the soles of his feet, Achilles kicked at her hand and bit down on her nipple with his front teeth.

Putting a finger in his mouth, she broke the latch he had on her breast and switched him to the opposite side. "Sorry, little one. I must cover you completely, if I'm to save you at all." She continued to massage the god's golden nectar into his skin. When she was satisfied with the ambrosia, she placed the hair of Zeus into the fire. Blue then red flames licked around the silver basin until thin fingers of silver rose from the heat. Thetis pulled Achilles from her breast. He squalled. "Hush, my golden boy. This will be quickly over."

She held him over the dancing flames that reached for his feet and curled around his ankles. Achilles wailed loudly, squeezing his eyes shut against the searing pain. Tears filled Thetis' eyes as she waited for Achilles' mortality to burn away.

"What the fuck are you doing to my son?" roared Peleus behind her. A handful of royal guards followed him. "I knew you were hiding something from me. But, I never thought you'd stoop so low as this."

Startled, Thetis jerked a dangling Achilles from the fire. Words failed her.

"Answer me, you witch! What treachery do you perform? Roasting my son to death like an animal?"

Thetis stood, hugging Achilles to her naked breast. "You don't understand, Peleus. I am—"

Peleus took three long strides toward his wife. "I don't give a blasted shit why you wish to burn my son." He ripped the child from her embrace.

Thetis stumbled backwards. "I love Achilles. You know that's the truth. I do him no harm! Give me my son!"

Reeling from what he'd witnessed with his own eyes, he shook his head. "He's *my* son. I curse the gods for giving me yet another wicked woman. And you, Thetis, you've broken my trust for good. Get out! Get out of my palace, nymph!"

Thetis watched in horror as the enchanting flames cooled to embers in the bowl. Her heart sank knowing the ritual hadn't been completed. She'd never have another chance to gather strands of Zeus' hair. The duality of Achilles' fate, foretold by Themis, was now sealed. "You have no idea what you've done, Peleus. You've set our son on the path of doom."

"He's safe from harm as far as I can tell. His destiny to surpass me is no small task. And I shall see his fate to the bitter end without your meddling craft."

Thetis noted the angry twitch of her husband's jaw. How could she explain that the physical pain the child endured now, would be but a flash compared to immortality?

"Get out of my sight, nymph. Go back to your pond," the king seethed.

Thetis picked up her garment from the floor and slipped it over her head. "Let me at least kiss my son."

Peleus stepped back from her reach. "You'll never lay a hand on Achilles ever again."

Disgraced, Thetis fled with her grief back up to the main hall and out of the palace gate. Her feet carried her to the inlet pond where she threw herself on the grass and wept bitterly for her son. She wept for his dark future. She wept because she knew her husband would keep her precious joy from her. She wept because her love for Peleus was now broken. She despaired because she knew this time even Zeus wouldn't help her.

SEVENTEEN

sacrifice of Cassandra

TROY—1270 BCE

Hecuba arranged her daughter's long, dark tresses into braids beaded with gold and tied with silver cords. She'd known this day would arrive and rip the fragile joy from her heart. *I am losing another child to Apollo …* "Stand my sweet girl."

"Mother?"

"Yes?" Hecuba said, as she wrapped the golden belt of coins around her daughter's hips, arranging the soft pleats to perfection.

Placing a soft hand on her mother's, she squeezed her fingers gently. "Were you thinking of *him* just now?"

Hecuba's hands never stopped arranging Cassandra's gown. "Who, my dear?"

"Mother, you know who I mean."

Without meeting her daughter's inquiring gaze, Hecuba stood.

"The *Forgotten Prince*," Cassandra spoke aloud the only name she knew for the brother she'd never known.

Hecuba's regal bearing straightened. "No."

"Mother, I can feel your sadness."

Sighing in defeat, the queen's shoulders relaxed. "Apollo's snake made you too wise for one so young." Recalling the sight of her beautiful twins entwined with a giant snake licking at their ears, Hecuba shuddered. As horrified as she was, it was more frightening to think that now she would have to turn her daughter over to the god. The union with the snake had sealed their fates as seers. There was no turning back. Apollo had spoken.

"I will pray that the god answers your prayers," Cassandra said.

"What prayers can bring the dead to life? Not even the gods have that power. The dead are to dust and their souls to Hades."

"I will pray that your sadness is lifted. That you will smile and be happy."

Hecuba shook her head. "Pray for no such thing, daughter. Grief is the only way left for me to love him. My heart aches for the loss of that sweet face." Clutching at her breasts, a tear slid down her cheek. "These still ache because I only briefly suckled him. No, dearest daughter, don't pray that my grief is lifted. I need it to survive."

"As you wish it, Mother."

"This morning is your day. No more unhappy words. Let's rejoice in your joining the order of the god. Are you frightened?"

"A little," Cassandra admitted.

Hecuba embraced her daughter. She inhaled the sweet essence of her hair and the gentle shoulders of a girl not yet a woman. Tears stung the queen's heavily kohl-lined eyes, clinging stubbornly to her lower lashes. She pulled back, holding her daughter's shoulders in each hand. "I've never been more proud of you than this day. I think I have not loved you so much as this moment."

"I'm glad I make you proud, Mother."

The queen took her daughter's face between her hands and met her eyes. "No matter where the god leads you, where this journey takes you, I will always remember my little Cassandra splashing in the fountain, giggling with me at noon naps, and her sweet, gentle kisses on my cheek. Know this, my love. And forget it not. Forget me not."

"I'll remember. I promise."

The cool morning light gave way to the warm afternoon as the procession to Apollo's temple wound through the maze of the stone paved streets of Troy. Throngs of citizens watched as the Princess Cassandra made her pilgrimage to the god. Flower petals like soft rain fell about her head; their honeyed fragrance filled the air. The people rejoiced that a royal daughter would serve the most revered god and by default serve them with her beauty and influence.

Cassandra counted each step with growing anticipation and fear. There were exactly seven platforms of seven stairs each leading to the main entrance between seven rows of enormous pillars. Once inside, attendants led the princess to a dimly lit private chamber. Inside, a bowl of flames licked the air at the feet of an enormous golden statue of the god.

"Remove your clothing," the high priestess commanded.

Cassandra's heart raced. Her tongue nervously passed over her lips. "Why?"

The high priestess pressed her lips tightly together. Her face a wrinkled mask of disdain? Anger? "The god commands it of us all," she replied evenly.

The princess reached up and unfastened the golden pins holding her gown at the shoulders. It floated silently to the floor. Embarrassed, she wrapped her arms across her bare breasts and squeezed her thighs closer together in a futile effort to conceal the dark patch of hair from the high priestess. "What do I do now?" Cassandra asked.

"Lay on your back before the god."

Cassandra looked down at her feet. "There's no covering or rug? I'm to lie on the bare floor?"

"Nothing of this world shall touch your flesh, only the hands of the god. After you're confirmed."

"Confirmed?"

"For your virginity."

Cassandra's eyes widened. "I am a virgin. I swear. I—"

"All young women make such proclamations. Who would admit their defilement at the feet of the god? Now, lie down before him."

Cassandra's knees shook as she knelt on the cold marble, never once taking her arms from her breasts. She lay down as commanded. The high priestess placed a warm palm on her lower belly and used her other hand to spread Cassandra's legs. Tears of humiliation burned behind the princess' closed eyes. The elder woman's fingers pressed into her privates with difficulty, before she felt a slight sting and a burning sensation. The woman withdrew her hand and wiped a small amount of blood on a piece of linen.

"Apollo will be pleased. You are intact and smaller than most initiates." She took the cloth smeared with Cassandra's blood and placed it in the bowl of fire at Apollo's feet. The flames hissed and spewed white smoke into the air.

The soft-falling footsteps of the high priestess disappeared, leaving the Princess of Troy alone. Cassandra allowed her tears to slide down her cheeks where they pooled in her ears. Her entire body shivered, as the dark marble floor chilled her bare skin. Time passed slowly and she drifted to hazy sleep to escape the unknown.

A warm breath blew across her shoulder, startling her. She tried to sit up, but a heavy, hot hand pressed her shoulder back down. A masculine voice whispered gently into her ear, "Close your eyes. Don't open them unless I command."

Cassandra's eyelids obeyed the command. She tried to cover her privates with her hands, but her body no longer responded to her wishes. *What is happening? He can see me. Mama, what's happening? Why did you bring me here?* Even though she couldn't see him, the heat of his observation burned her skin.

"You are confirmed?" the voice asked.

With a quivering voice, Cassandra replied, "Yes."

"I am pleased."

"You are Apollo?"

"Who else would I be?" Apollo said. "Don't talk. I want to look at my offering. Make certain it pleases me."

Apollo's warm touch slid over every inch of her. He ran his fingers across her breasts, cupping each one. "Satisfactory." Apollo slipped his hand between her thighs, pressing his fingers into her opening, testing her virginity. Cassandra squirmed against Apollo's intimate probing. "You're … not ready to accommodate a god."

Cassandra squeezed heavy tears from her eyes. "Apologies." Her voice vanished into the vast chamber.

The god moved over her naked body like a wave of hot air. "No need for such mortal expressions to me." Tiny tongues of flame swirled across her skin, burning and enticing her to writhe against them. Her body vibrated with the heat. She fought to keep her eyes shut. She fought to stifle a scream. Terror filled her. For the first time, she realized that being taken by a god would not be what the weaving women spoke of. There would be no gentleness or caressing her to shaking legs.

The marble beneath her shook and slowly her body rose from the floor. Her head fell back, suspended by nothingness. Her hair tumbled like a waterfall spilling onto the marble. Burning hands grabbed her thighs and spread them forcefully apart. Her arms were useless to help her. They weighed as two anchors at her sides. The heat of Apollo moved between her open legs. He slowly pushed a searing flame into her sacred cross. Cassandra howled with agony. Her body twitched and arched in protest of Apollo's invasion of her most intimate places. When he was finished, she felt the hot liquid of their union seeping from her and pooling beneath her bare buttocks.

"Your reaction is most displeasing." Apollo's disappointment echoed in the chamber.

The god's hold on her released, so Cassandra pulled her legs closed and sat painfully upright. The marble floor beneath her had risen into a large altar.

"Open your eyes."

Cassandra obeyed, but kept her focus directed away from the direction of Apollo.

"Look upon the magnificence you spurn with your mortal fear."

Her eyes traced a path along the floor toward the sound of Apollo's voice. She glanced up and beheld the most beautiful creature she'd ever seen leaning casually against his own statue. He stood unashamedly naked and taller than any man she'd ever known—even Hektor himself would be dwarfed by such size. She averted her gaze from his fiery member. The god's skin shimmered like liquid gold. His eyes burned bright blue and orange. His hair curled perfection of honeyed crystal veined with silver.

Cassandra met his gaze. "I'm sorry I haven't pleased you." *Thank the other gods. Now, I can go home. I want my mother.*

"Dry your eyes. I have no pity for mortal fear. What do I care for your sentiments? I don't. I take what is owed me. I take what I want. Sometimes, I'm satisfied. This time, unfortunately for you, I am not."

"Am I to be rejected?"

Apollo stroked his chiseled chin with long elegant fingers. "No. No. No, you will serve me, simple mortal. I grant you the foresight you desire."

Cassandra bowed her head. "I'm grateful." The words burned her in the back of her throat.

"You may not be, considering your words will always fall upon deaf ears."

"Why do you hand your blessing with a curse?"

"It will make the games … much more interesting."

"The games?"

"Mortals," the god sighed in exasperation. "You intrigue from afar, yet up close you tend to bore. Your prayers and supplications are our greatest entertainment, and I admit, a source of competition."

Understanding dawned on Cassandra. "We are nothing but pawns to you? Our lives … meaningless to you?"

"Now, by the balls of Zeus, she sees."

"What's to become of me?"

"You'll be trained, here, in my temple. Serve me. Obey me.

Submit to me without question."

Tears stung her eyes. "And if I refuse?"

Apollo's laughter rang sweetly through the chamber. "You're one to question. There's no right of refusal, unless you wish a plague or two to sweep the citadel."

Cassandra realized reasoning with Apollo would be futile. She knew submission must come. She couldn't bear it if her disgust and disillusionment for Apollo should bring harm to Troy. *I'll protect Troy no matter what he commands.* Serving the god would not be the joyful serenity she believed it would be. "I accept your blessing, Apollo." She lowered her head. "I give my full obedience to the god."

"There it is! My docile mortal has finally figured out the game. You may end up pleasing the god … in time."

When Cassandra looked up, he was gone. She glanced about the chamber. The fire was out. The light had dimmed and she felt suddenly chilled. Within moments the high priestess entered, followed by three young female attendants. The first carried a bowl, the second a towel, and the last a fresh chiton. They looked so young, younger than she. Had they also been subjected to Apollo's assault? She shuddered at the thought.

"Step down, Cassandra. You must be cleansed," the high priestess commanded.

Cassandra slid from the altar. "Is it always this way? With Apollo?"

"Only the chosen are bound to Apollo as you now are. The rest serve in peace."

"What do you mean … serve in peace?"

"Spread your legs so you may be washed clean of your blood and the god's flow."

She looked down at her thighs and saw her blood mingled with pale silver liquid—the contrast a beautiful mess, smearing her legs with the visible evidence of how the god raped her and stole her virginity. A single thought horrified her. "I will not conceive a child from this, will I?"

"Only if the god wishes it."

As the maids busied themselves bathing and dressing her, tears once again welled and spilled down Cassandra's cheeks. Her life was no longer her own. Her body was no longer her own. Her mind would no longer be her own. Apollo would be life and torment for her. She would curse and serve him until her death.

EIGHTEEN

a brother's love

TROY—1270 BCE

C assandra woke with a start. The dream of the giant snake licking at her ears had awakened her every night since she'd been cruelly initiated into Apollo's service. Hot tears slid down her face in the dark. She curled into a ball on her bed, pulling the coverlet tight around her.

"Sister, are you awake?"

Cassandra propped herself up on one elbow. "Helenus, why are you here … again.?"

"Why are you crying … *again?*"

"I can't tell you."

"You've told me everything since we were children. What happened in the temple? What did the god do to you? Did it hurt? Was it with a snake?"

"I said I can't talk about it. Any of it."

Helenus walked to her sister's bedside. She flinched when he tried to stroke her cheek. "You can't hide your pain from me, Cassi." He knelt beside her. "You never could."

Cassandra wiped a fresh tear from her face. There was no one in the world she trusted more than her twin brother. Growing up, they'd always been able to read one another's minds, finish each other's words. They were two, yet one. "It was … not what I expected."

"Did Apollo reveal himself to you?"

"Yes."

Her brother's eyes rounded in awe. "You're truly blessed, sister. The god doesn't reveal himself to just anyone."

Cassandra frowned. "He cursed me, Helenus."

"What are you talking about? Why would he curse you?" A pale moon beam lit his face, revealing a horrified grimace. "You were a … virgin, weren't you?"

"I was," Cassandra said, miserably.

Helenus turned his sister's face to his. "What did he do to you?"

"Raped me. The god raped me."

Tears stung Helenus' eyes. He whispered, "Raped …" into the close space between them. "What did he have to gain?"

"Pleasure at his games."

Helenus' hand flew to his mouth as some new horror filled his racing mind. "Did he curse you with a child? By the balls of—"

"Hush, brother. He may hear us. But no. There is no child."

"What other pain did he inflict? Surely, I see something more in your eyes. I hear more in your cries while you dream."

"He has given me the seer's sight, but my words will never be believed."

"I don't believe it."

Cassandra' smiled wanly. "You see? It's already begun."

Helenus frowned. "I'll always believe you, Cassi. Never doubt that. Did you tell Mother?"

Cassandra sat up and grabbed her brother by the arm, her fingers digging deep into his flesh. "Promise me you'll never tell her anything."

"But—"

"No. Never. Now, promise me. She'll be disappointed that I've dishonored our family. Besides, what can she do? Ask Father to seek retribution against … *him?*"

Helenus chewed at his bottom lip and shook his head. "I suppose there's nothing we can do about it, in truth." He reached for his sister's hands wrapped in the coverlet. "If I can protect you from now on, I will. I swear it."

"I keep praying to the other gods that *he* will forget I exist."

"I'll add my voice to your prayers as well."

Cassandra smiled up at her brother. "I don't know what I'd do without you."

"Don't worry about what will never happen."

NINETEEN

Clytemnestra wakes

PALACE OF MYCENAE—1270 BCE

Clytemnestra wept in horror as thin fingers of bitter smoke crept beneath the barricaded door. Loud crashing, men barking orders, and random screaming filled her with even more dread. She'd never heard a man scream before tonight. War had always been something that happened far away from her, regaled in stories and songs around late night hearth fires.

"Shah, little one." The princess pressed her crying baby to her chest and opened her gown so he could latch on to her breast. He quickly took her nipple in his mouth and suckled himself calm. *Where is Tantalus? I beg you, Gods of Olympus, let my husband live.* Tantalus had given her strict orders to remain unseen and hidden in this unused maid's room, hoping, she was certain, that no one would recognize her as his wife if the palace should fall to Agamemnon and his invasion force. She stroked her son's brow and cheek as he nursed, the babe oblivious now to the danger moving through the palace.

When her husband told her that word had reached the palace that her father, Tyndareus of Sparta, had sided with Agamemnon against King Thyestes of Mycenae, her husband's father and her father-in-law, she hadn't believed it. Clytemnestra had argued that her father would never send such a force against Mycenae because he'd already pledged his loyalty to Thyestes through their marriage. Tantalus had no answer for her but the truth, she realized now, as she sat in fear waiting for Tantalus to return.

A loud, bellicose voice shouted, "Where is she?!" The question bounced through the stone hall. Clytemnestra closed her eyes against her worst fears. She recognized the voice. *Agamemnon.* More crashing filled the hall, followed by the shuffling feet of heavily armed warriors.

"There is no one here," a low voice spoke.

"Next!" another subordinate voice yelled.

Then, the banging began on the door to her room. She knew within moments she and her son would be prisoners of the exiled prince come to reclaim his throne.

With each bash against the wood, she shuddered. Within moments, the wood splintered and the enemy spilled through the opening like a flood. Clytemnestra screamed. Agamemnon pushed his way through his men dragging a body.

"Tantalus?!" she shrieked. The fist of the exiled prince wrapped so tightly in her husband's hair that his swollen bloody eyes were stretched to slits in his face. The parts of his exposed flesh were smeared with dark red streaks and blotches. Had it not been for his royal armor she would not have known the identity of the captive being dragged before her. The contents of her stomach soured and choked her. She turned her head and vomited onto the floor.

"Ah! You couldn't even keep your woman safe!" Agamemnon laughed. His men followed suit laughing at her wretchedness.

"You're a cruel man!" she spat out weakly. The baby at her breast began to whimper.

"Shut that squalling brat up."

Clytemnestra gently bounced her son in her arms to calm him. Tantalus reached an arm in her direction.

"Look at this fucking fool!" the exiled king bellowed. "Look upon her while you can usurper. May the horror in her eyes haunt you in the Underworld."

Clytemnestra's eyes rounded in fear at his words. The giant man hovered over Tantalus, his blade arched and glinting in the air. With a tremendous force, he drove the blade point deep through her husband's chest. Blood spurted from the wound and gushed down the corners of his mouth. His eyes wide with shock found his wife's. His unintelligible words gurgled through the blood pooling in his mouth, and then he collapsed in an unmoving heap at his murderer's feet.

"Give me the child," Agamemnon roared.

Clytemnestra wept, pressing her baby closer. "Please, he's only a babe. Still nursing from my breast." Her body shook. *He's going to kill us. Why, Father? Why?*

"Do you think I give one shit for a bastard son of Tantalus? The usurper's son?" Agamemnon sneered at her. "Retrieve the child," he said icily to his men.

A nameless, dull-eyed soldier reluctantly stepped forward. He glanced at Clytemnestra clinging to her child, then back to his king. "My lord—"

"Take that fucking child!" Agamemnon roared.

The soldier pried the screaming child from his mother. The

princess lurched forward in a futile effort to stop him.

"Take hold of her," Agamemnon ordered. "Give me that bastard's child."

"He's also my son, my lord! Please, let him live! He'll cause you no harm," Clytemnestra pleaded. "I'll take him back to Sparta. Raise him without claim." Tears burned her eyes and blurred her vision. Mucus ran from her nose and into her mouth. "Please, I beg you …" Her son's wails ripped her heart from her chest. "Please …"

Agamemnon stopped for a brief moment, as if considering her request, and then he lifted the child up by both feet and swung him overhead before bashing its body into the floor.

Clytemnestra howled, turning her head before the dull thud of her son hit the hard ground. A thin shower of wetness sprayed her cheek. She resisted the urge to wipe the damp away, knowing it was blood, but wishing not to see it on her hands. The chamber fell silent, except for Agamemnon's breathing and her sobbing. She dared not look in his direction.

Agamemnon tossed the broken body to a startled soldier. "Throw this piece of meat to the dogs."

Clytemnestra heaved uncontrollably, spasms shaking her entire body. She wailed, "My father will make you pay for what you have done to me. The gods will surely curse you." She turned and retched what was left in her stomach onto the floor.

"You're wrong, Princess of Sparta. I paid for this … for *you*."

She forced herself to meet his gaze, carefully avoiding the bloodied mess on the floor at his feet. "Paid for me?"

"Why else do you think I would spare your life? I have no love for you."

"I'll not be your slave! I'd kill myself first!" she screeched. "My father would never agree to barter me into slavery! Never!"

"He didn't." Agamemnon sneered, letting his words sink in. He smirked watching the truth slowly dawning on her face.

Clytemnestra shook her head vigorously. "I will *never* marry you, you fucking murderer!" Spittle spewed from her mouth as she continued screaming. "You killed my husband. Made me a widow!" Anger and grief wracked her entire body with jerking spasms. "My son …" She hung her head and her shoulders slumped with her loss. A tiny moment of silence filled the chamber, then Clytemnestra leapt to her feet and reached for the nearest soldier, grabbing clumsily for his sword. Her effort was easily subdued by a pair of strong hands.

"Tie her up securely. I can't have my bride trying to kill me in my sleep or escaping into the Underworld after the gold I've paid her father. Set watch on her for the entire cycle of Apollo."

"Yes, my king," answered a young warrior in bloodied armor.

"Send an envoy to Sparta. Inform King Tyndareus his daughter is safe. The marriage will take place as we arranged. Send this usurper's body to the meat carver. I'll feed him to my uncle as my father did once before."

Horrified, Clytemnestra shrieked, "I will never submit to you! Never!"

Agamemnon crossed the space between them in two heavy strides. He seized her roughly by the chin. A whimper of pain passed her smashed lips. "You *will* do as I tell you, bitch. You have no options now." He released her from his grasp and turned and walked away, barking orders as he passed down the hall.

Three men escorted the princess to her chamber and tied her securely to a chair. Two stood outside of her door, while one remained in the room.

"What happens now?" she asked her guard. He remained silent. "For love of Zeus!" Clytemnestra resigned herself to waiting. Waiting for what, she had no idea. Behind her eyes, she saw her beloved Tantalus on their wedding night, his hands shaking with desire. He'd come to her gently, softly not wishing to frighten her. He'd coaxed her love with sweet words and tender caresses. She tilted her head back and howled her anguish. *My son, my sweet son.* The front of her gown was wet against her engorged breasts. Her son would've nursed hours ago. And now, she couldn't even wrap her arms around herself for comfort. She wanted to lie on the floor, hugging her knees to her chest and weep a river, but she was pinned to a hard chair. Images of her battered husband and her innocent baby flashed behind her eyes, forcing fresh tears to fall. She didn't care anymore what happened to her. Everything she loved had been taken. Nothing remained to anchor her to this world. She prayed silently for death to claim her, as she closed her eyes, sobbing quietly until sleep took her to another realm.

"Wake up, Princess," a woman's gentle voice coaxed Clytemnestra through a fog of memory and dreams. "Wake up, Princess."

Slowly, Clytemnestra's mind focused, her eyes blinking slowly open. A pair of unfamiliar dark eyes stared down at her. "Who are you? Where am I?" she asked, sitting up.

"You are in the lord's bed, my lady." The older woman fussed about the linen covers as if the morning greeting was ritual.

Clytemnestra shook her head. "Where?"

"My lady, you are in the lord's chambers in Mycenae. Does the lady not remember?"

"How long have I been sleeping?"

The maid stopped smoothing the coverlets. "For three days, my lady."

"Three days? That's impossible. Just yesterday …" She tried to recall the events, but they came only as blurred images. "Yesterday …" The princess looked at the old woman.

"The past is gone, my lady." Her eyes didn't waver. Their steady gaze discouraged questions. "Come, you must bathe and make yourself presentable."

"For what purpose?"

"To meet your future husband, of course."

Clytemnestra froze. "Agamemnon."

"Who else, my lady?" Her eyes again warned of speaking too much.

"I cannot."

The elder maid leaned close enough to her face that Clytemnestra could smell the mixture of honey and mint on her breath. "If you wish to keep the breath the gods grant you." She gripped the princess' fingers. "Agamemnon is not kind, my lady. He is a man of war. Your tears mean nothing. Your pain means nothing. Only the wealth your family provides means anything to him. Forgive me for speaking so bluntly."

The princess considered the maid. "What do they call you?

"Neola, my lady."

Clytemnestra raised an eyebrow. "Full of youth?"

"There was a time." Neola smiled slightly. "Some of us have years long enough to remember the Old Ones."

"The Titans?" The princess partially stifled a small laugh. "Mirthful is a name that would have suited you fine, I think."

"Come, my lady. We must get you up and ready."

The reality of her situation crashed in on her again and Clytemnestra dropped her thin smile. It was no fault of Neola's that she found herself in this predicament. Politics, coin, and greed were to blame … and the loss of the gods' favor in her regard.

"Neola?"

"Yes, my lady?"

"What happened to …to the king?"

"The usurper Thyestes has been exiled to Cythera."

"Mercy. Granted mercy?"

Neola arranged the folds of her mistress' dress, carefully layering the soft pleats beneath the golden belt. "It is no mercy to live in isolation from all you love. To grieve over the loss of one's son. Better Agamemnon had killed him."

Clytemnestra stiffened.

Neola bowed her head and backed away. "Apologies, my lady."

Clytemnestra reached a gentle hand toward Neola. "Please, you meant no harshness on my account."

"I spoke without thought. It will not happen twice."

"You may be the only kindness I will find here now."

"You will find joy again, my lady."

"All that was happiness has abandoned me."

The maid folded her arms across her chest. "While you live, hope exists. It's only hidden beneath your pain."

"How do I forgive what he has done?"

"If I could answer that, my lady, I would be called *oracle*."

Clytemnestra laughed quietly. "Truly, you possess a humorous quality."

"I may have some welcome words, my lady."

"Speak them."

"Your family arrives soon. Perhaps, your mother can comfort you?"

"Yes. That is welcomed news." Clytemnestra headed for the door. She knew her way around the palace of Thyestes, now returned to the House of Atreus and Agamemnon.

TWENTY

the ravishing of Leda

PALACE OF MYCENAE—1270 BCE

"I'll be fine! Quit fussing. It's a short walk from the palace. What harm can come to me here?" Queen Leda insisted.

"Mother. Take your maids at least," Clytemnestra pleaded.

Leda stared into her daughter's lovely face, noticing her swollen eyes and slightly sunken cheeks. She sighed. "The truth, my darling, is I rather enjoy my solitude. All of these guests arriving. The commotion. I require a few moments when someone or other is not calling out for my approval or opinion." Queen Leda didn't miss the furrowed brow on her daughter's forehead. "Don't fret, Clytemnestra. Everything will be set right … in time."

"There are more guests than I expected," the princess admitted, casting her eyes downward. "Mother, I don't want to marry Agamemnon."

"I asked your father to reconsider. He refused to budge." Leda took her daughter's face between her soft palms, looking her directly in the eyes. "Daughter, we women are all pawns of the men we wed.

Men such as your father and Agamemnon, they have business that reaches passed our feminine understanding. Be certain of one thing, when they engage in the politics of power, it is we who pay the price." The queen pulled the faded green himation over her head, concealing her identity, and walked out the garden gate.

Leda enjoyed walking in solitude. The quiet gave her calm to endure the loud and constant clamoring of palace halls. In the palace, the constant flow of visitors daily required her attention to hospitality. The butchers, the bakers, and the kitchen work never ended and always necessitated her final approval. How many goats to kill? Which stores of wine to serve? How much bread should be prepared? So many questions and calls on her name wearied her.

"I wish the sun would stand still for one day and let me have peace," Leda murmured to herself. She walked on in silence until she came to the edge of the clearing leading to the pond. Letting her head covering slide to her shoulders, she breathed the air deeply like someone who'd been imprisoned in a stale chamber. Only now did she allow herself to think of her daughter's circumstance. What Agamemnon had done was unforgivable. And Tyndareus forcing Clytemnestra to play the cornerstone of their plan by marrying her to the very man whose hand took the life of Tantalus was more than cruel. *Their greed has no end.* She'd never held much love for Tyndareus, but she adored their children. Tyndareus' affections for her had cooled early in the marriage after he discovered Pollux was sired by Zeus. It garnered him no honor that the mighty Olympian had invaded her body against her will. From his discovery on, her husband had spurned her affections, seeking solace elsewhere, far from her bed except on the drunken occasion when he felt he must reclaim what the divine intrusion had taken. Being at the mercy of men, be they mortal or not, soured Leda on intimacy entirely. The unintended effect was the distance she kept from the children she loved, in order to protect them from Hera's wrath, and Zeus himself.

Leda took in the sight of the deep green water ahead. "Finally." As she approached the pond, she caught sight of a pair of snow swans swimming across the glassy water with their downy grey cygnets. She laughed as the babies bobbed and crisscrossed behind their parents, feeding and clumsily navigating the water. The graceful parents trumpeted back and forth.

The queen's thoughts turned again to the marriage her husband had negotiated for their elder daughter. Agamemnon impressed her as a shrewd man, an intelligent man … and quite used to having all manners of his life strictly controlled. He possessed an outward appearance of civility, but she sensed something dark ran beneath his cool presence. Leda startled at a loud collision behind her. She turned, expecting to find a bandit or worse.

A lone black swan with wings slightly open, chest heaving met her surprised gaze. Far above an eagle screeched its fury. Leda squinted into the sky, catching sight of the golden bird of prey circling high over head. "Seems you've escaped the clutches of certain death and dinner," the queen said. The swan folded its wings, making no move to retreat. Leda held out her hand. "Come then, bird. Come. I'll not hurt you." As if in understanding, the dark beauty approached. The queen stood still, not wishing to frighten the exquisite creature. When it finally stood at her feet, its elegant neck and head reached almost to her shoulder. "What a magnificent bird you are." The swan nuzzled its head against her breast. Leda took a step backward with the unexpected force of the swan's presence. "Strong for a—"

"God," a voice echoed in her ear.

Confused, Leda backed away from the advancing bird.

"You will not escape me, Queen of Sparta."

Leda froze. "You! You speak?"

"Why look so surprised, Leda?"

"Zeus?" she questioned, horrified.

"Again, I come to you."

Leda recalled the pain of coupling with Zeus. The agony of it rendered her ill for days. "No, please. No more. You promised you wouldn't violate me a second time, if I bore your offspring. I gave you a son. Please—"

"You will bend to my desire. I am bound by no promises to mortals," the feathered Zeus said. "If I cannot have the nymph, I will have you. No mortal can keep me from what I want." The black swan pressed toward her and Leda scrambled backwards, stumbling on the hem of her gown. She fell hard against the ground. The swan flapped its wings as if taking off in flight, but instead launched itself at her, landing heavily on her belly, pressing her firmly against the wet grass. Pain seared through her sacred parts as the dark-feathered beast shook its body into hers; its wings opened wide above her in triumph of its act.

The sunlight dimmed as the bird waddled toward the brush. It shimmered darkly, its form stretching its length and shape into the silver god-king of Olympus. Leda lay ruined and bleeding on the ground as Zeus disappeared into the verge and from her sight. The queen placed a shaking hand on her stomach. She knew he'd left her with child once again. Tyndareus would not be pleased. She wept, wondering what would happen next. The rape exhausted her and she collapsed on the ground unable to rise.

After a long time, she slowly stood to her feet. *Zeus will not defeat me. No man, be he a god or no, will ever defeat me.* Disheveled and dirty, Queen Leda made her way back to the palace, hoping no one would see her before she could cleanse her body of the despicable act.

TWENTY ONE

vows in blood

PALACE OF MYCENAE—1270 BCE

Clytemnestra sat quietly as her maid arranged her hair, her heart thudding heavily in her chest. Knowing that her father had arranged this tragedy only deepened the wound. She sighed, resigned to her fate, but unwilling to accept it. She would find some way to survive this marriage. Even as her maid fussed over her, she planned her escape. She would run for anywhere else and when an opportunity presented itself she would travel as far away as she could. There was nothing to keep her here anymore.

The door opened followed quickly by her mother in a flowing red gown and a sheer golden himation wrapped around her shoulders. "My darling." Smiling, she leaned to kiss Clytemnestra on the cheek. "You're a most stunning bride."

"I don't care how I look for that murderer," Clytemnestra seethed.

"You'll drop such treasonous talk, immediately. You may be the future queen of Mycenae, but you're yet young. You're not above being slapped for your impudence by your mother." Leda turned, speaking sharply to the chamber maid, "Leave us." The queen waited until the room was empty before she softened. She stretched both hands out to Clytemnestra in apology. "My sweet child. My poor child. Do you think I wish you to marry this bastard after what he has done to you? Your family?"

"You confuse me, Mother."

"Do you know that maid?" Leda asked.

Clytemnestra thought for a moment, realizing she'd never seen her before that morning. "No."

"Do you think Agamemnon will not have you watched? Not wait for a sign you are disloyal? Do you think he would not turn his rage against you once he has achieved his purpose?"

"What is his purpose, Mother?"

"To make Mycenae the richest kingdom of the Three Seas."

"You would have me continue as if he's done nothing? Even Thyestes received greater mercy than I am expected to endure. Agamemnon killed my husband. My son. Your grandson. Does this mean nothing to you?"

Leda took her daughter roughly by the shoulders, shaking her words into the young woman between clenched teeth. "You stupid girl! Have you not learned already? Do you think men the only creatures who go to war? The only ones who gird themselves in armor? You think there's more bravery in hacking a man in two than the plight of women, who pass by the horror, slipping on the blood and shit of strangers to find their men? Bring them home.

Stitch their gaping holes, praying to the gods for their healing all the while knowing death drags them to the Underworld? Every step you take, every word you utter is a strategy in a war for control of your world. Agamemnon has won the first battle." Tears slid down her daughter's cheek, and Leda gentled her tone. "Gird yourself, my darling, with your words, your plans. Don't let him win the war."

The princess wiped the tears from her eyes and stiffened her jaw. "I will rule my world."

"Now, you sound the true Spartan princess."

Clytemnestra stood, smoothing her gown. Leda admired her daughter. "So young, my darling. Yet, none more beautiful … save the goddesses of Olympia." A brief flutter in her womb startled her.

"What's wrong, Mother?"

Leda placed a hand over her lower belly. "Nothing. I'll be fine." Her womb was already budding with new life. *Not yet, not yet …* She silently cursed Zeus. A knock sounded on the door. Leda stepped to open it, pushing all other concerns aside. Neola stood in the doorway.

"Let her in, Mother." Clytemnestra smiled at the elderly woman she'd met days ago. "*She* is trustworthy."

Neola nodded to her mistress and the queen. "My lady, it's time. They await you in the great hall."

"Tell my Lord Agamemnon that I am on my way."

Neola nodded, bowed, and left the chamber.

"Remember my words," Leda warned.

"I will not soon forget any of this, Mother."

Clytemnestra had smiled sweetly but stiffly through the ceremony, even as her heart screamed for bloody vengeance. She sat unmoving on Agamemnon's bed, the bed recently belonging to Thyestes the exiled king, and waited for her new husband. *I hope he chokes on a bone and dies.* She passed the time examining the chamber. It looked much as it did before the son of Atreus returned to violently reclaim his throne. Her eyes scanned the bright colored frescos and mosaics, all of them beautiful. *I will have them chiseled away and redone. I will make this chamber my own. I will claim my rights as Queen of Mycenae.*

Time passed too slowly. She had watched Agamemnon drink his fill of wine at the wedding feast, so she hoped that his marital rights would be over quickly. *I've never lain with any other man except Tantalus.* The memory of his gentleness beat as a dull agony in her chest. *Bury it. Bury it deep, Princess of Sparta.* She knew the love she bore her dead husband would not find its equal on this earth. Spreading her legs for Agamemnon would be a maneuver to secure her position and gain power for herself, gain control over as much of her realm as possible. Her mother was right. It was all a game to her father and newly-made husband. She would play the game and win Mycenae for herself. Then, a thought occurred. A thought so alarming she hadn't even dared allow its full materialization until this very moment. *Children. His seed might take hold.* Clytemnestra squeezed her eyes shut against the brutal image. That memory would only ruin her newfound resolve. Any children from this distasteful marriage would be innocents she could use to anchor her position. *Yes*, she thought, *I will need children.*

In the sweet and silent darkness of a foreign bed chamber, Leda slumbered soundly. From the abyss of dreamers' sleep, a hand softly shook her shoulder until her eyes fluttered open and she startled at the silver shimmering light of a goddess.

"Shah, Leda. It is I," the silver goddess whispered.

"Aphrodite!" Leda exclaimed. She sat up, pressing her back against the wall behind her.

The goddess laughed. "Fear me not, Leda. I am here to deliver wondrous words to you."

"I am your servant," Leda spoke, the words cracking with uncertainty.

"Calm your fears, daughter. I know about the child you carry."

Leda's hand moved protectively to her belly. The slight mound beneath her hand gave her some comfort. "Child?"

"You think my father would not bless you this second time?"

The Spartan Queen remained silent, petrified at what Aphrodite might divulge. When gods mixed with mortals it was never peaceful.

"Perhaps, you find dissatisfaction with his act?"

"No. I am pleased. I am only surprised," Leda said quietly, pushing her rage at her violation by Zeus aside.

"I have come to bless the child," the goddess informed.

The life in Leda's womb fluttered again. "It is far too early to feel the child …" She looked to Aphrodite for answers.

"Not for the mortal children of Zeus. You should know."

"He will be mortal then?" She found relief in the goddess' words.

"Of course, mortal. It is to be a girl this time."

"A girl child?"

"You mortals and your questions. Yes, your child is a girl. And I bless her with great beauty. I mean to make her the most beautiful woman who ever graced mortal life. You *will* call her Helen."

"Many thanks, Goddess. Forever I am in your debt for such a blessing," Leda said. Even as the words whispered passed her lips, she knew the blessing would be a curse for any mortal woman. How much turmoil would such an existence cause their family? For Sparta? Would this child turn the eye of jealous Hera in their direction?

Aphrodite nodded at the mortal queen and her light faded into nothing, leaving Leda staring into the dark. The silence, once a comfort, now filled her with an eerie sense of doom and disaster. She contemplated the news. There was nothing she could do now, only time would reveal the fate of her unborn daughter, Helen of Sparta.

TWENTY TWO

a reluctant prince

PALACE OF PRIAM—1269 BCE

Hektor twisted the golden belt about his waist, shifting too much fabric to one side. "She's too young, Mother."

Hecuba signaled a servant to rearrange the pleats. "You'll not bed her until she's sixteen. Her parents have agreed, as did your father." She walked behind her son, admiring the fine cloth. "She's already highly skilled at weaving. I'm not certain I could've weft and warped a finer cloth."

Hektor faced his mother, placing both hands on her shoulders. "I don't care about her loom and threads."

"What do you care about, then?" Hecuba took a glass of ruby wine from a servant. "She's said to be a great beauty already. Eyes of silver-blue. Dark hair as wavy as the sea. Skin as bronze as a polished shield."

The Prince of Troy sighed, walking to the balcony. "I remember Shavash, slightly. It was years ago."

The queen laughed. "You could hardly stop talking about your horse."

"What boy doesn't talk of his first love to everyone he meets?"

"You and Ares were inseparable, true. Perhaps, that's what will happen between you and the Princess of Pedasus?"

"What if there is nothing between us?"

"It's a profitable and peaceful arrangement for Troy. Pedasus is a solid ally in the south and very wealthy." Hecuba met her son at the balcony, placing a hand over his. "We do what we must for Troy." She swept her free hand before them both. "The people and the land depend on us to honor our duty, to provide and protect them."

Hektor looked down into his mother's sad eyes. "No one understands that more than you."

The queen's face blanked of all expression, before shifting her gaze once again to the blue expanse beyond the citadel to the dark sea. "It would've been a blessing from the gods if time truly served to soften heartbreak. But it's a curse, isn't it? The more time passes, the more keenly we feel our losses carved into our very soul, even as the memories fade around the edges."

"You saved the city by letting go."

Hecuba bristled, jerking her hand from her son's. "Saved the city from what? Where were the dangers threatening our shores? Our *great* wall?"

"Apologies, Mother. I didn't mean—"

Gathering her anger, she bowed her head. "It's not your fault, Hektor. I stand here speaking of sacrifice and honor, but I didn't let go … I've never let go. If your father hadn't pried the babe from my arms, he'd still be here. Prophecy be damned. Who am I to stand here advising you with false wisdom?" Hecuba lifted her gaze. "I would never have let him go, not even for the city."

Hektor looked out on the city he'd grown to love. "Do you think I'll be a good king?"

"I'm certain of few things, as the years pass, but of that I have no doubt. Songs will be written about you and the great deeds you'll accomplish. If you're fortunate, perhaps, a song of love."

Briseus fussed with her gown. "I don't like the color, Mother." She scratched at the golden belt.

"It brings out the pale of your eyes. It's a fine blue dye. Very costly. Your father searched high and low for such a treasure." Shavash cupped her daughter's cheek. "I've dreamt of this day since I carried you beneath my heart."

"I don't care about Chryseis' prophecy. I don't want to marry a warrior."

"A prince, Briseis. Hektor is the Prince of Troy. There is no more worthy man than he."

"He's old."

"Wise."

Briseis wrinkled her nose. "Old. Wise. What if he's hairy? Stinks of horse?"

Shavash laughed. "Daughter, you needn't worry about such matters. He's said to be most handsome. He was a lovely boy, as I recall."

"If you say so." Briseis gave a final tug at her gown. "Can we get this over with?"

"Smile."

"I don't want to smile."

Shavash sighed heavily. Moving to her daughter's side, she grabbed Briseis firmly by the chin. "Marriage isn't about what we want as women. It's about what we provide to our husbands and our cities. The men plant their seeds in our bodies and we bear the fruit of their legacy." She squeezed tighter. "It's the way of our world. If you're blessed with a kind and handsome husband, bear him many children, consider yourself blessed by the gods. Fight this, and you will surely be cursed and not just by the gods, but by your father ... and your mother."

The young Princess of Pedasus stared into her mother's hard eyes. Her chin quivered in her mother's tight grasp. Her lips moved awkwardly as she said, "I obey."

Shavash released her grip, returning once again to the doting mother. "Good. See, you're more ready to be a wife than you realized."

———

Tender olive branches and flowers decorated the courtyard, filling the air with the pungent aromas of a fresh spring. Colorful ribbons and banners fluttered gently in the warm breeze. Musicians plucked a melodic tune with lyres and flutes. All eyes turned toward Briseis clinging to her mother's hand, as she followed behind her father, King Briseus, into the midst of the joyful gathering anticipating a betrothal of the Prince of Troy to the Princess of Pedasus. They stopped before the king and queen seated across the way.

King Briseus bowed his head, Queen Shavash elbowed Briseis

to follow suit. The princess kept her eyes downcast, afraid to look up and find the man her parents intended her to marry staring at her.

Queen Hecuba spoke with a soft command. "Raise your face to me, child. Let me see for myself this great beauty, not yet in full bloom."

Briseis lifted her head, leveling her eyes to the queen's. She squirmed under Hecuba's intense scrutiny.

"It's true, you do have an enchanting face." Signaling across the courtyard, Hecuba caught Hektor's attention. "You should meet my son, Prince Hektor."

As the queen finished speaking, a tall, dark-skinned man came to stand beside her. His shoulders were so wide that he blocked the afternoon light. Briseis blinked and her heart pounded.

Shavash smiled widely at the man. "Hektor? You've grown so much I can scarce see the boy you used to be."

"Queen Shavash, I am honored you remember me at all."

"How could I forget the boy who could think of nothing else but his warhorse? Do you still have him?"

Hektor smiled, showing all of his teeth. "He's a fine animal. The prize of the royal stables."

"As it should be," Shavash replied.

Briseis picked at her palm with a fingernail. *He's so old and hairy.* Sweat trickled down the center of her back. *I don't want to marry him. I don't want to marry anybody.*

Queen Shavash put her hand gently behind her daughter's back, pushing her slightly forward. "Prince Hektor, this is my daughter, the Princess Briseis."

Briseis glanced up to see Hektor's expectant face. In the corner of her eye, she could see her father standing there beaming with pride and hope, and a young woman staring at her with eyes of ice.

She bowed her head. "I-I am …"

Hektor laughed. "Am I so ugly, then?"

Giggling nervously, Briseis squeaked, "No." *Just hairy.* Crimson heat crept to her cheeks.

"That's good to hear. It would be awkward if my future wife found me undesirable."

A voice said, "She will never marry you, brother."

All heads turned toward the woman with the icy glare. Briseis shivered.

King Priam's face flattened with impatience, as he snapped, "Keep your ill words to yourself, Cassandra. It's her destiny to marry the greatest warrior. She will marry Hektor, if he will have her."

The Trojan princess' face turned as white as ash from a dead fire. "There will be smoke and fire when *he* arrives. And *he* will take her as his prize."

Horrified faces turned toward Briseis. Tears spilled over her bottom lashes. *What does she mean? What smoke and fire?*

Prince Hektor ignored his sister's words. "Would you care to see the stables, Princess Briseis?"

Still shaken, Briseis whispered, "Yes, if my mother will allow it."

Queen Hecuba waved a hand and a royal guard gently escorted the strange woman away. "Of course, she will. She'll recall the way to the Hektor's heart is through the stable."

As Hektor extended a warm hand, Briseis smiled for the first time in days. *Maybe he isn't too hairy after all.*

Hektor walked with long, confident strides and Briseis practically ran to keep up with him. He talked of Troy, his brothers, his training and none of it made any sense to her. Her mind was bent on the future, a future where this stranger would be her husband.

"My father was right. A horse was just what I needed. Briseis, you're not afraid of horses, are you?"

Startled from thought, Briseis shook her head. "No."

"Good, Ares is bigger than most. He's hot-blooded, and may not allow you to touch him. He will choose."

Briseis nodded. "Will he bite me?"

"I don't think so." Hektor winked, as the princess' eyes widened in fear. "Pay no mind to my sister's warning. She's touched by Apollo."

The princess nodded again. They walked down a long row of stalls. Horses whinnied and snorted as they passed.

"It smells of horse and earth," Briseis said.

Hektor laughed. "And so it does."

Stopping in front of a stall larger than the others, Hektor whistled softly. Briseis heard straw rustling and a loud snort before the biggest, blackest horse she'd ever seen filled the stall opening. It met Hektor's eyes, as the prince reached to stroke the mighty jaw of his warhorse. "This is Ares. Ares, this is the young princess I am to wed someday." Ares stomped a hoof against the ground, and shook his head back and forth before looking down at the girl.

"Go ahead, you can touch him. He won't bite you, not as long as I am here."

"That isn't very reassuring," Briseis said, looking up at the horse. "He's beautiful and big."

"Aye, he is that. Aren't you, Ares?"

Briseis reach a trembling hand out to Ares' cheek. The horse nudged into her open palm and sniffed. She jerked her hand back slightly, but kept reaching until it pressed warmly against the horse's face. "He's softer than I thought."

"He's the prince of the stables here. Nothing is too good for you, Ares." Hektor looked down at the girl beside him. "It must be strange to be promised to a man as old as I am. I remember when I was thirteen. Marriage was the furthest thing from my thoughts."

Briseis dared a glace. "What did you think of?"

"War and horses."

The princess giggled. "I think of my loom patterns and playing under the trees."

Hektor smiled. "You'll have years yet to play. Marriage is a long way off for both of us."

TWENTY THREE

three princesses

PALACE OF SPARTA—1268 BCE
HELEN

Gray clouds swept swiftly across the sky, dimming Apollo's light to a dreary gray. Caster looked into the sky. "We've seen more dismal days lately, than all last year combined."

Pollux shrugged. "The gods are always angry about one thing or another."

Seated on a large boulder, the brothers watched as Helen toddled about in the grass with her nursemaid close behind. Caster crossed his arms over his chest. "Do you believe the rumors are true?"

"About Helen?"

"Yes. Don't you think it odd our mother is rarely with her?"

Pollux rubbed the dark stubble on his chin, as he eyed his little golden-haired sister giggling and running about. "She's well cared for." How could he explain to his brother that he knew the truth, because he too was fathered by Zeus? The god's blood coursed colder in his veins, and anytime his eyes met Leda's the secret passed between them. "Our mother isn't the warmest woman in our lives."

Caster laughed. "No, that's a certainty. But, I know that pretty nursemaid is."

"You've bedded Helen's nurse?"

"Don't look so shocked, brother. What's not to admire?"

"She suckles our little sister."

"Come now, Pollux, don't tell me you've never bedded a woman with milk in her tits?"

A heavy drop of rain hit Pollux on the forehead. He stood. "Let's get back to the palace before it rains."

"That's not an answer."

"It wasn't meant to be."

Caster signaled to the nursemaid, who smiled coyly back at him. "What do you think will happen to Helen when she comes of age, if she's truly the daughter of—"

Pollux bristled at the implication. He knew the truth all too well. He knew his truth. He knew silence was the best protection. "Best to keep such thoughts to yourself. Whatever her fate is, it won't be an easy one."

HYPOPLOKIA THEBE
ANDROMACHE

Hektor smiled at his hosts, King Eetion and Queen Mira of Thebe, who'd feasted him for three days straight. Maintaining a strong alliance in the south was of vital importance to Troy, but he tired of the noise and commotion. Hektor's head ached from too much wine. The king had sent a number of beautiful women to his chamber every evening, yet tonight, he dreaded more of the same, preferring solitude. Nodding to his host, he stood and dismissed himself.

Instead of walking to his chamber, the prince made his way to the gardens. *Peace.* Near the center, a fountain trickled water over a large basin. He found a nearby stone bench and sat. His back still ached from the long ride south. The sweet tones of flutes and lyres from the great hall carried softly on the night air. *Aye, peace at last.* A footstep crunched on the gravel behind him. The hairs on Hektor's neck prickled. Placing his hand on the hilt of his short sword, he said calmly over his shoulder, "Approach and show yourself."

"Apologies, my lord, I thought I was alone."

Hektor turned where he sat. "What are you doing by yourself, here in the dark?"

The woman stepped from the shadows into the light of the stars. She wore a purple himation wrapped closely about her body and her dark hair spilled over her shoulders. "I could ask the same of you, stranger."

"I'm a guest of the king."

"The king is kind. He turns away no beggars."

Hektor bristled. "I'm no beggar, my lady."

The woman took a tentative step forward. "No. I can see now that you're not."

"I'm Prince Hektor."

"Shouldn't you be in the hall? Isn't the feast in your honor?"

"It is. Feasts are tiresome. I'd much rather be with horses or training. But, come. Sit. Speak with me. Tell me your name."

She approached, uncertain. "Horses are magnificent creatures."

The prince looked more closely at her. "Yes, they are." She was ordinary compared to Briseis, but there was something about her. Her eyes spoke to him. Her voice music in his ear. "Forgive me for speaking plainly, my lady, but I find I can't take my eyes from you."

The woman hugged her himation closer. The light in her face dimmed. "I'm no great beauty, my lord. It's unkind to mock me."

Hektor shook his head. "I speak in all sincerity, my lady. You captivate me. I beg of you, tell me your name."

Tilting her chin up, she revealed, "I'm Andromache, daughter of King Eetion."

Hektor stood; horrified that he'd been so bold. "Forgive me, Princess."

"There's nothing to forgive, my lord." Andromache turned to leave.

"Don't go, Andromache. Stay and speak with me. The night is yet young."

Andromache glanced at her feet. "My father wouldn't approve of such a meeting with a man betrothed to someone else."

"I give you my word, my intentions are virtuous."

"Is that not what all men say?" She smiled shyly. "Goodnight, Hektor, Prince of Troy. Breaker of Horses."

Hektor watched the Theban princess fade into the darkness. His heart was still pounding against his chest. He knew in that moment what he must do. As soon as Apollo's light broke a new morning, Hektor sped on Ares for Troy. He took no proper leave of King Eetion, as his mind was bent on convincing his father to break the betrothal contract with King Briseus. For if he could not, Hektor knew he'd be a miserable man the rest of his life.

PEDASUS
BRISEIS

Briseis picked at her fingers, waiting for her betrothed to enter the great hall. *Why is he here? Will he take me away, before my time?* She dreaded marriage almost as much as she dreaded the blood that would finally make her a woman. The heavy doors across the hall scrapped open and the Prince of Troy entered with an entourage carrying wooden chests and baskets brimming with fine linens. Briseis' stomach churned in fear.

Hektor approached the royal family, bowing deeply at the waist. He waited.

King Briseus signaled the prince to look up. "We're happy to receive you, Prince Hektor. Although, we're a bit surprised at your timing."

"My apologies for not sending word, but what I wish to discuss should be done face-to-face."

Queen Shavash nudged Briseis, who stood rigid and silent at her elbow.

"Greetings, Hektor," Briseis said softly.

Hektor bowed deeply to the young girl. "Princess."

Briseis looked up hearing her name, finding a pair of warm brown eyes gazing at her. A smile escaped her lips, which she immediately reined in. *How did he get to be so handsome?* Now, her stomach fluttered. *Has a year flown by so quickly to change everything? How did I think he was hairy and disgusting?*

King Briseus rose from his chair. "Come, let us walk. Bring the wine."

As Briseis watched her father and betrothed leave the hall with a gaggle of servants behind them, she glanced at her mother. "Why do you look so worried, Mother?"

"A prince doesn't arrive unannounced and bearing gifts, when the tidings are good."

TWENTY FOUR

death of a dream

LYRNESSUS—1267 BCE

Queen Shavash wept bitterly into her hands. "How could the prophecy have been wrong?"

"It's a good match. Mynes will be king after his father. Lyrnessus is a wealthy city, or have you not noticed?"

"But the prophecy!"

King Briseus comforted his wife. "There was no name given. How do we know it wasn't Mynes all along?"

Shavash squinted. "Because he's not the greatest warrior who ever lived. Apollo was clear."

"Mynes is young yet. There's time for his song to be sung."

"You believe Mynes superior to Hektor?" Shavash shook her head. "Why? Why did you release Hektor from his word?"

Briseus took his wife's hand in his. "Would you wish your only daughter to wed a man who loved another?"

"He would forget the other woman in time."

"And then there was the waiting. Priam is still producing sons from his harem, and Hektor believes he must begin producing heirs of his own. He refuses to bed Briseis before her woman's blood is upon her." Briseus took his wife's hand in his. "Besides, I think you underestimate a man's desire, when a woman has stolen his heart."

Shavash glanced up at her husband with red-swollen eyes. She wiped a fresh tear with an elegant finger. "What do you mean?"

"Have you never guessed, woman?" He kissed her tenderly on her soft, but wrinkled cheek. "Even though the years have left their marks on us," Briseus tilted her chin up, "when I look at you, I beg the gods for a long life. Only immortality would give me time enough to spend with you."

Shavash's eyes sparkled with unshed tears. "But—"

The king kissed her lips. "Shah, my love. Mynes is a prince and will give our daughter a life she deserves. If the gods truly favor her, they will give her a love like the love I bear her mother."

Servants moved about the feasting tables like bees buzzing among flowers. Sweet wine flowed freely in stemmed golden cups. Platters brimming with honeyed figs stuffed with almond paste, hot crusty flat loaves of bread, and roasted goat and beef lined the trestle tables. Bowls of fresh cured olives and soft goat cheese were nestled between the larger dishes.

Briseis picked at several olives on her tray. Being discarded by

Hektor had humiliated her, and now, having to endure yet another betrothal feast stung worse than the original rejection. *The gods are cruel.* From the corner of her eye, she saw Prince Mynes laughing with her father's advisor. She ate an olive and washed it down with her wine, grimacing at the bitter combination.

"Is your wine not to your liking?" Mynes asked, as he tore a hunk of flat bread.

"It was the olive brine. It didn't flavor well."

He offered a piece of bread with goat cheese to her. "This will make the wine sweet again."

Briseis looked at her betrothed under her lashes, taking the morsel. She ate it and then sipped at her wine. She smiled despite her misgivings. "That is much better."

Mynes returned her smile, popping a sticky fig into his mouth. "These make the wine even sweeter." He licked the honey from his fingers. "How old are you, Briseis?"

"I've seen fifteen winters."

The prince grinned. "I must seem old to you."

The princess' eyes widened. "I hadn't thought—"

"When I was fifteen, I would've thought so."

"My mother says you sing."

Mynes laughed, showing all his teeth. "Not as good as I swing a sword."

Briseis nodded, thinking about the prophecy. *Perhaps, he is the one.*

"I hope in time, you will learn to love Lyrnessus as your home."

"The gods place us where they will for a reason."

The prince held up his cup. "To my princess." He sipped it, offering the shared vessel to Briseis. She took it and drank. "May the gods bless us with good fortune and long lives."

TWENTY FIVE

Peleus' revenge

PALACE OF PELEUS—1266 BCE

"That wretched bitch deserves death." Peleus paced the great hall. Chiron's news weighed heavily on Peleus' mind. Years ago he would have welcomed the opportunity to wage war against the city of Iolcus and Queen Astydamia.

Chiron pawed the floor with a hoof. "There's no better time to strike than now, Peleus. The king is dead and she is weak."

"I'll never forgive her for her part in Antigone's death."

Chiron crossed his arms over his chest. "Most unfortunate, indeed."

"She lied, Chiron. Lied! Pushed my wife to …" Antigone's limp body hanging from a noose flashed through his mind. "She didn't deserve such an end."

"No, she didn't."

"That sack of lies told Antigone, I was going to cast her aside and marry her daughter."

"Which was only a half-truth," the centaur mused.

"Wishing to bed a woman is not a proposal of marriage." The king sharply eyed his friend. "I regret that."

"I'm certain you do, Peleus. I know all too well the temptations stirred by the soft flesh of a woman."

Peleus continued pacing. "When that bitch Astydamia told her husband, the man who purified me for killing my father-in-law … accidently mind you—"

Chiron rubbed his chin thoughtfully. "Yes, the unfortunate boar incident."

The king whipped around, facing the centaur. "Do you doubt me?"

"On the contrary. I would say Artemis had her hand in the entire affair. Continue," Chiron encouraged.

"Not long after news of Antigone's death reached me, Astydamia tried to give herself to me, but I wouldn't have her."

"That would have been difficult for any man to resist. You are to be commended, my friend. I'm not quite certain I would've been so … off-putting."

"After the pain she caused? I couldn't have been more repulsed than if she'd been smeared in shit. She told her husband I tried to seduce her. Can you believe that? I tried to seduce her?!"

"Lies. All lies," Chiron agreed. "And after the accusations, King Acastus abandoned you in the woods of Mount Pelion."

"I can hardly forget that. If you hadn't come to my aid—"

"My centaur brothers would have killed you," Chiron finished with an understanding sigh.

Peleus stopped pacing and rubbed his thin beard. "If I attack her now—"

"You would have your revenge and gather to your coffers great wealth."

"True. Sea raids only bring so much gold. Sacking Iolcus would bring slaves as well." Peleus nodded his head. "There is always need for gold and slaves."

"Slave girls," Chiron laughed.

"The mind of a centaur, even one so blessed with knowledge, is always on the rut." King Peleus stopped in the center of the chamber. "But what of Achilles? He's young, yet."

"Send him to me. I'll train him, as I did you."

"Then it's settled. I'll assemble the Myrmidons. Head for Iolcus." A wicked grin crept across Peleus' face as he thought of war and retribution. "That bitch will wish she'd never laid eyes on me."

Chiron twitched his tail. "I almost pity her. *Almost.*"

Achilles kicked the ground. "I don't want to go, Father."

Peleus placed a firm hand on his son's head. He was already taller than any other boy his age. "It's only for a time. It's not forever."

"But I don't like the centaur. He's mean."

Peleus laughed at Achilles' worried face. "You're only five. Your opinion isn't surprising, my son. He seeks only to make you grow strong in mind and body."

Achilles exhaled defeat. "I won't like it."

"No, I suppose you won't. In time, I promise you'll appreciate the gifts he gives."

"What gifts?" Achilles asked, mildly intrigued. He hadn't thought he'd be receiving anything of value from the shaggy man-horse. "A sword? A shield?"

"Knowledge, Achilles."

Disappointment filled his voice. "Oh."

The king admonished, "Close your mouth or flies—"

"Will put worms in my belly. I know." Achilles closed his mouth, but remained disappointed.

TWENTY SIX

blessings and curses

PALACE OF MYCENAE—1266 BCE

Neola eyed the swell of her mistress's middle. "It's close to your time," she said knowingly.

"It's different this time, yet the same," replied Queen Clytemnestra. She placed her hand beneath her heavy belly, lifting the pressure for a moment. "This child is quieter than …" Her voice trailed off into silence. *My son. I'll never forget you.* In her heart, she buried her grief and anger at his cruel death, but she would never forget or forgive her husband.

"The king will be pleased that you are well."

"That he should care so deeply, I am grateful." Clytemnestra smiled through her response.

The maid nodded her understanding. "My lady, forgive my

boldness …"

"Go on, Neola. Your honesty is a gift to me."

Neola lowered her eyes. "If you find some joy in this child, it takes nothing from your memory."

"You may go," Clytemnestra said. She waited until the door shut quietly, before walking to the open balcony. She stood gazing out over the sea. Over the years, she'd heard so many tales about warriors setting out for war and adventures over this expanse of blue. The wine dark sea some called it. Sometimes, she wished Poseidon would rise up as a huge sea beast and swallow her whole. *Like the Trojan maiden. I hate Mycenae.* The sun glinted on the water's surface as she prayed silently for death to claim her. As her grief crept through her like a sickness, the child kicked her roughly in the ribs. It was enough to bring her back to the world. "Don't worry. I'm here."

"Where else would you be?" a deep voice inquired behind her.

"My Lord Agamemnon," the queen said. She quickly wiped a stray tear with an elegant finger and turned to flash her husband a brilliant smile. "I speak only to comfort this child."

Agamemnon reached between them and placed his hands on either side of her belly. "Our child, my love. My son." Since she'd revealed her pregnancy to him, he'd softened and become quite loving. Although his affection sickened her, she promised herself she would endure it not just for her own sake, but for her children, the heirs to the Mycenaean throne. She'd rule her world and the kingdom, for that much she'd swore to the gods of Olympus in the quiet of her heart.

"We can only hope, my lord." She could never bring herself to return his affectionate greeting. It turned her stomach to hear him speak with love's tongue to her. *Never*, she thought, *never will I love you.* "Has word come yet from Sparta?"

"It has. Your mother and her entourage arrive within the week."

"And the child? The girl?" she asked.

Agamemnon grimaced. "The girl child comes with her."

"Helen," murmured the queen. "I shall like to meet my youngest sister."

"Unfortunately, the rumors proceed her." Agamemnon scowled.

Clytemnestra playfully slapped his arm. "She's but a baby yet. Surely, you hold no grudge against such an innocent?" She remembered all too well how he regarded the innocence of youth not at all. To soften the chastisement, she reached up to kiss his rough cheek.

The king smiled as he shook his head. "How you lead me by the cock woman."

"Is there any other way to lead a man, my lord?"

"Woman …" Agamemnon whisked her up in his arms. "You'll pay for that remark."

Clytemnestra laughed sweetly. "As you wish."

The king laid her gently on the bed. She watched him disrobe, revealing his huge, muscled chest covered in dark curls of hair. She couldn't help but compare him to her love, the husband of her heart, Tantalus. He'd been smooth with little body hair and smelled of salt and honey.

Agamemnon lifted her gown, exposing her bare stomach and naked flesh. She closed her eyes and conjured up the face of Tantalus, as Agamemnon pressed firmly into her wet flesh. With her dead husband's dark eyes looking down at her, behind the veil of her eyelids, she endured the act … and found her body more willing with child. She climaxed quickly and Agamemnon rammed her until he shook with his own release and collapsed next to her.

———

Clytemnestra rose tired and achy from her bed, her husband had left before the dawn. She rubbed the dull ache in her back with a knuckled hand. "Neola!"

As if from air, her maid appeared. "My lady?"

"Draw a hot bath."

Neola eyed her queen suspiciously. "How long has your back pained you?"

"All night. After Agamemnon and I … he left and I have been unable to settle comfortably."

Neola clapped her hands together. "My lady, have you not guessed?"

"At what?" the queen asked, irritated. "Guessed at what?"

"Perhaps, your labor has begun."

Clytemnestra blinked and shook her head. "No. That's not possible."

"Why not?"

"It … I-I'm not ready," she said. Memory of the pain and work of childbirth filled her with dread. "I'm not ready."

"My lady, perhaps the child is? You're strong. Delivered a healthy babe once before …" Neola's voice trailed into silence. She sighed slowly. "Apologies. I intended no—"

Again a reminder of the past. The heartache of losing her young son ripped open the tender scar she bore in silence to keep him always with her. "I know. It's the truth." Suddenly, it occurred to her that she hadn't considered she might lose this child before it was born, or that she herself might lose her life. *Death would not be so horrible*, she thought. *I could escape this wretched place.*

A sharp pain low under her belly pulled her from her morbid thoughts. "Neola, you're perceptive. The child *is* coming."

The maid clapped her hands again in excitement. "To your bed then, my queen. I'll fetch the women to ready your chamber and inform the king."

Clytemnestra obeyed. "I trust in your hands, Neola."

The maid bowed her head. "Your praise is too good for me."

"It most certainly is not. Go, now, fetch your women."

Neola left quickly and returned before Clytemnestra had settled into the bed. The gaggle of concerned women followed the queen's personal maid. Two male servants carried in the birthing chair and promptly left the sacred work of delivering the heir of Mycenae to the women. The birth attendants shook freshly bleached linens open, refolded them across the foot of the bed. They poured water into waiting basins and stoked the hearth fire in the chamber.

"Neola, I am too warm already. Please, put the fire out."

"My lady, soon enough you will shiver with cold and pain and ask for flames. We must keep the fire stoked and the water warm. For the child." Neola pulled the coverlet down and folded it neatly at her queen's feet. "Mira, come." A rounded woman with kind dark eyes appeared at the bedside. She motioned the woman toward Clytemnestra. "How much longer will the queen labor?"

Mira looked into her queen's eyes, nodded deference. "Forgive any discomfort this may cause. I will be as gentle as I can." A painful spasm took Clytemnestra by surprise. She sat up as the sharpness increased, pulling a tight ring of pain beneath her navel. The queen screamed out her agony. The mid-wife pressed her hand gently against the queen's abdomen and inside of her once the pain passed.

"I can feel the child's head. It will not be much longer if the goddess Eleithyia wills it." Another woman rushed to the mid-wife's side with a basin of water, so she could wash her hands clean of the birthing muck.

A few short hours passed before Clytemnestra felt the urge to push the child to the light. The pressure built and her eyes flew wide open with surprise and exhaustion. She grabbed Neola's arm in fright. "It's time!" The mid-wife and her attendants rushed to the queen's side and helped her to the edge of the bed. Neola assisted Clytemnestra the short steps to the birthing chair. The mid-wife shifted the queen's gown up over her waist. Another searing pain ripped down the queen's back and her thighs. She grunted with the urge to push the child to the light. A small gush of water mixed with blood splashed on the tile. The queen threw her head back and cried tears of exhaustion. "I cannot!"

"You can, my queen … and you will," Neola assured her.

"I'm so tired—" Another overwhelming urge gripped her body. Her legs shook with the effort to birth the baby.

"The head! You're close, little one!" the mid-wife cried aloud, then quietly prayed, "Eleithyia, beloved goddess, bring him swiftly if it pleases you."

Just then, the hearth flames flickered. The women turned to witness a breeze fluttering through the curtain at the balcony window. A pale dusty ray of light spilled into a circle on the floor in the center of the chamber. The women ceased all movement and bowed down in awe as the goddess materialized before them. She towered over them. Her gown shimmered silver and bronze in the folds. Stars flashed at the hem as she walked toward the queen. The women whispered her name in awe, "Eleithyia …" Clytemnestra's eyes met the goddess' gaze.

"My daughter," the Goddess of Childbirth's honeyed voice soothed the laboring queen, "you have suffered long with this pain." She knelt before Clytemnestra and placed her cool hand on the queen's arm. "You have suffered much in silence. I've been watching you. Rest easy, daughter. I'll finish the work for you." The gleaming goddess reached her hands inside of the queen, and without pain or crying out, Clytemnestra delivered the baby into the welcoming arms of Eleithyia. The goddess extended a long, pale arm toward the astounded maids. "Bring me the blade and the linen," she commanded in a hushed voice. Neola scrambled to obey. Eleithyia cooed softly to the babe as she cut its life-cord and wrapped it securely. The goddess looked up, smiling, "It's a girl."

"May I see her?" Clytemnestra asked.

Eleithyia laid the swaddled babe into her mother's eager arms. A joy so deep filled Clytemnestra that she cried and smiled. She didn't believe it possible that her broken heart could ever love anyone or anything again. Her ruined soul rejoiced in the little hand griping her finger. She undid the covering to kiss the baby's tiny toes and fingers.

Neola wept to see her queen so obviously filled with happiness. "Praise Eleithyia," she whispered.

Clytemnestra looked up at Neola. "She's perfect, is she not?"

"She is, my lady. What will you call her?"

"Iphigenia," she said. "My strong little one."

Eleithyia walked to the balcony and paused. Turning around, she said solemnly, "She's yours … for a time. Treasure your days with her."

TWENTY SEVEN

a mother's comfort

TROY—1265 BCE

"K ing Eetion has accepted the last payment," Hektor said. Hecuba continued weaving. She let a moment pass as if she hadn't heard the announcement. Out of the corner of her eye, she watched her grown son toe the floor with the tip of his sandal. Smiling to herself, she pulled the blue weft thread through the width of the warp threads, then combed it tightly against the others. Without stopping her work, she said, "My son has decided on a wife. You're certain you wish to break the betrothal to Briseis?"

Hektor nodded. "I didn't intend to love another, but I have. I knew Andromache was my destiny the moment I saw her."

The queen, still pulling her delicate threads, asked, "Your father has given his blessing?"

"He has. But it's your blessing that matters to most to me."

Hecuba's hands deftly pulled a purple weft thread through the warp. "Briseis is more beautiful."

"Andromache captured my heart. Her family brings an equally strong region into alliance with Troy."

The queen put down her work and turned to her eldest son. Tears glistened in her eyes. Her smile was sad. "Where has all of my time flown? I sit here weaving and time steals my world from me. My son, my Golden Warrior, was it only yesterday that you sat next to me telling me that one day you'd take a wife?"

Hektor took a seat next to his mother on her bench, taking her hand in his. "Many years have passed, Mother. Don't be sad. I don't wish my joy to bring you sorrow."

"Then, you're truly happy?" Hecuba asked.

Hektor looked at his mother sitting at her weaving, as she'd done since he was a boy. "I can't imagine my world without her. There was a time I didn't know Andromache existed and my life was full. I laughed. I fought. I broke horses and many bones." He paused, kissing his mother on the cheek. "Now, I feel as if I've been looking my entire life for her. Only her."

Hecuba squeezed Hektor's hand. "Don't mistake my tears as displeasure. On the contrary. I'm quite pleased." She looked Hektor in the face. "It's no easy task letting go … One day, if the gods are on your side, you'll experience the ache of releasing your own children to a life of their own. Then, you'll know my sadness is mingled with pride and joy."

"You'll not be hurt that I wish my own household?" Hektor asked.

"On that account, yes, I'll be hurt," she answered truthfully.

"I've come to rely on your strength against the storms that darken my heart." She cupped his cheek. "You've been the light that pulls me through, and now that strength belongs to another. It's the way of our world." Hecuba pulled her hand gently away from her son's face, resuming her weaving. "It's natural to desire your own dwelling. Raise your family apart from the palace."

"Then, it's settled. You give me your blessing?" he asked.

"You have it. Now, go and leave me to my loom. This is a difficult pattern. I would work in silence."

Hecuba watched as her son walked from the chamber. When she was certain he was gone and wouldn't return, she let her tears fall freely. She'd never let him know that his presence had saved her all these years and kept her grief from consuming her even after so many years had passed.

MYCENAE

Clytemnestra held her daughter close as the babe suckled for comfort. Iphigenia's chubby fingers wrapped around one of her mother's long, elegant ones. The queen brought their entwined hands to her lips, kissing her daughter's tiny hand. "You'll grow strong, my little one." The baby's bright eyes looked into her mother's, and she smiled without breaking the suckling latch. "I wouldn't trade these moments for anything, Neola."

The old woman, packing extra linens into a chest, struggled to stand. "I'm glad you have found happiness, my lady."

"Yes, I believe I have." She smoothed Iphigenia's coverings. "It's been a little over four years."

"As the years pass, hurts fade."

Clytemnestra looked up at that. "Faded, but not forgotten."

Iphigenia bit down on her mother's nipple. "Ouch. No." Clytemnestra put a finger in between her daughter's lips and her nipple, forcing the latch to break. She switched the little princess to the other side. "Do not look so surprised, Neola."

The chamber door swung open and Agamemnon stepped in followed by a handful of advisors.

Clytemnestra hastily covered her bare breasts. "You should give me privacy."

Agamemnon dismissed his entourage with a gesture. "You should have a wet nurse."

"Prepare me stuffed dates and figs, Neola."

The servant nodded and exited, leaving the queen and king alone in the nursery.

When she heard the door close, Clytemnestra removed the covering, exposing her bare breasts, heavy yet with milk for her husband to gawk at. *Yes, I will have control of my world, you fool.*

The king fairly growled, "You tempt me to make another child, woman."

Clytemnestra bowed her head slightly. "I will always do my duty for the kingdom." Then, glancing up, she shot Agamemnon a more inviting stare. "And for its king."

Agamemnon paced. "How much longer will the child take the tit?"

The queen rested a graceful hand on her daughter's back, pulling her close the way a warrior hugs his shield to his chest in battle. "A while yet. Although, she has begun to bite, so I'm told soon she can begin with mashed fruits and grains."

"Good. You're fertile, but it was a long time planting that row before the seed took hold."

The queen's jaw twitched. "My lord, these things take time. But, we've a healthy daughter."

Agamemnon approached his wife, and staring down at her, reached a hand to her other breast. He cupped it like a handful of gold coins. "I need a son."

Iphigenia's bare foot kicked at Agamemnon's hairy arm. When the king scowled, the babe smiled at him with her mother's nipple still in her mouth. The king softened. "I don't know anything about raising daughters."

Clytemnestra gathered Iphigenia's feet to her. "I do, my lord. Don't worry. We'll have sons to keep our daughter company, soon enough." The queen shifted her weight in her seat. "Have you no other warm comforts, while you wait for the nursing period to end?"

The king resumed pacing. "They grow tiresome." He eyed his wife, a tall beauty with dark hair flowing freely about her shoulders. "And I want no bastards in my palace." His cock jerked to life with his desire for his queen. "Make it soon." Abruptly, he turned and left.

The queen gazed lovingly down into her daughter's eyes. "You will win him over, my little princess." She patted Iphigenia's swaddled bottom. "This is our world now." Clytemnestra smiled to herself. "Ours."

TWENTY EIGHT

Hektor's bride

HYPOLAKIA THEBE—1265 BCE

King Eetion smashed his bronze kylix on the table, splashing wine everywhere, sending platters clattering, and shaking the nerves of those seated near him. "I've something to say!" he bellowed. The conversation and laughter died down—the eyes of all of the royal guests turned toward the king. "When pale dawn pierces the morning sky, we make for Troy. The city of brick and gold. The city where men are breakers of fine horses. The palace where I'll leave my daughter, Andromache, forever." The king held his cup high. "King Priam and I have struck the bargain for her hand. Troy has paid a fine tribute for our princess. She'll be well received. If I'm not mistaken, she's already won the heart of Prince Hektor." The assembly cheered and clapped their free hands to their thighs.

He swayed slightly as he stood. Several groans sounded from the guests. "What? What's this? Tired of an old man speaking for his daughter? Disgraceful!" A few voices mumbled. "Daughter, may your new life bring you as much joy as your mother has brought me." The king winked at his wife, who shook her head in mild embarrassment. "True! We've had troubling years. Quit your gossip!" His grin widened, knowing that rumors of their tempestuous relationship had certainly reached the ears of everyone assembled for the farewell. "There's none as fair in form or heart than my Andromache. I would've agreed to nothing less than a royal prince for her." The feasting throng cheered again. "It's time to make your offerings, my girl."

Andromache shyly stepped forward. Such a large and noisy gathering on her behalf unnerved her. She longed for a simpler life. A quiet life. She'd hoped to serve the goddess Artemis, or even the god Apollo, but she'd not been selected. The high priestess of Apollo informed her parents that her fate would lead her elsewhere and to a more public existence. When her father came to her, telling of Prince Hektor's wish to marry her, she resisted at first. Her father had reminded her that a daughter's duty was to obey and contribute to her family's honor. Andromache acquiesced to his request to marry a man she'd seen only by the dim silver light along a chance garden path.

When the Trojan prince arrived with the first gifts of betrothal, she'd barely spoken to him. He was a tall, intimidating man. Dark, curly hair hung to his shoulders, framing a perfectly chiseled jaw and his blue eyes sparkled like midnight stars. His skin was darkened from years of training under Apollo's heat. He had a wide, honest smile that reached his eyes. And it was that which made Andromache think she might be able to trust this man, perhaps even love him.

"I'm ready, Father."

She laid a small hand loom and a pair of her maiden sandals at the feet of the household shrine to Hera. "I apologize they are so worn," she whispered. The princess pulled her himation over her head and spoke silently to the goddess. *I've never lived on my own. And I'm frightened. Help me to be a steadfast wife.*

As she knelt before a similar shrine to Artemis, a servant girl came up next to her carrying a small sharp knife on a bronze platter. Andromache took the blade in her hands and took a thin lock of her long, black hair between her fingers. She cut the lock off mid-length and placed it at the painted wooden feet of Artemis' statue. *Help me to put aside my childish thoughts and become a woman my husband will respect and, if I don't ask for too much, that he will love me. Goddess, he will be my all in Troy. I'll have no family, no friends except the ones I am able to make. Guide me in this passage from woman to wife.* She pulled her himation closer over her head and remained in supplication. In the background, she could hear her family talking and the wagons being loaded below. *Artemis, I'm frightened of marriage. That it will hurt. I can't tell my father or my mother. Their hopes are great that I'll be a good wife, perhaps queen one day. Troy is … a great city. How will the nobles accept me? I have no desire to leave my family. I'll be alone in Troy …*

A warm, comforting hand weighed on her shoulder. Andromache tried to open her eyes and turn to see who had approached her, but found her eyes and body would not obey.

"Young daughter," a golden honey voice sounded in her ear. "Calm your fears. Win the queen's heart."

"What if I am unable? I am just a girl," Andromache whispered out loud.

"The way will come to you."

The pressure on her shoulder released. The presence vanished. Andromache stood on shaky legs. *Artemis*. The goddess had spoken to her. She rubbed her shoulder where the goddess's hand had rested. It ached fiercely. She'd share her fears with no one. She did worry about Queen Hecuba. It was widely rumored she was a cold woman since the loss of the Forgotten Prince. She'd no idea how she would gain the acceptance of the queen, but the goddess had made it clear that was the path she must follow.

"Good! I see you are finished praying to Artemis," her mother said behind her.

Andromache turned and flung herself into her mother's soft bosom and loving arms. "I will miss you, Mother."

Mira, a gentle woman, kissed the top of her daughter's head and held her close. "Not as much as I'll miss you, my sweet child."

"Must I go?" Andromache couldn't help but say the words.

Her mother nodded. "All women must go to their husband. But you, my little dove, go to the most handsome man in the Troad. He's beyond compare, is he not?"

"He's old," she said.

Her mother laughed. "Yes. Yes, to you he must seem old. He's a man, no mere boy."

"What if he will not love me?"

"Daughter, you're a young flower, eighteen winters have you blossomed in this household. Have you not caught a glimpse of yourself? Have you not earned the love and respect of your family?"

"But what—"

"Andromache, listen to me. Hektor's just a man. He'll be helpless at your feet soon enough. He'll protect you. If I'm not mistaken, he'll love you, if he doesn't already. Come, child, stop this worrying. The carts are loaded. We wait only for the bride." Her mother patted her cheek playfully. "You know your father hates waiting."

TROY

Hektor looked out from one of the south facing balconies, down into the streets of Troy. Women carried water to the walkways and steps lining the central plaza to wash the dust from the stone. Garlands of flowers and elegant greenery hung from balconies and adorned the main passage to the center of the citadel. His servant had sent word that the wedding entourage from Hypoplakia Thebe had arrived within the upper gates of the citadel and soon the gamos, the day of his wedding, would begin.

His stomach knotted as he watched the first wagon pull up to the palace entrance below.

"It's a fine day to take a wife," Hecuba said behind him.

Without turning, Hektor replied, "Do you think I'll make a good husband?"

"Such a question, my Golden Prince. Of course. You'll be the finest."

The morning sun splashed the streets with golden light as the last wagon pulled into the crowded mess of new comers. A heavily veiled figure stepped from a sheltered cart.

"That's her most likely," Hektor whispered to his mother.

"Yes."

"Do you think I've made a wise choice, Mother?"

"If you've chosen with your heart, yes."

"I know not all brides love their husbands. I intend to make her love me."

"My sweet Hektor. You can't force a woman's heart. She must give it freely or it means little. If you woo her, Hektor, with gentle words and your fidelity, you'll win her."

Mother and son watched as the guests entered through the palace doors below and fell from their sight.

"And so it begins, my son," Hecuba said.

———

The maids stripped Andromache of her gown and wrapped her in a soft linen towel. The ritual bathing tub had been moved into the chamber, and placed in the center of the room. Her mother and their female attendants gathered, chatting softly awaiting the sacred water bearer. The bride stood silently apart from the assembly. Women's voices raised in song filled the air.

A giddy servant blurted out, "They're here!" Within moments the chamber door swung wide as women bearing jars of water carried from the nearest river filed through into the room. One by one they emptied their clay jugs into the bath. Cassandra, priestess of Apollo and Hektor's sister, carried and poured the final vessel. Andromache squeezed her hands together, as Cassandra's eyes lingered overlong on her face before indicating she step into the ritual bath.

The bride dropped her covering to the floor and stepped into the chilly water. Her skin prickled with the cold. Andromache lowered her body into the water and shivered. Cassandra dipped a small jar into the water, pouring it over the bride, completely drenching her. With the next pour, Andromache closed her eyes and spat out a mouthful of water.

The crash of pottery startled everyone in the room. Andromache's eyes flew open. She turned her head to see Cassandra's horrified face staring at her with eyes wide open and glassy.

Hektor's bride stood from the bath, while a maid scurried to wrap her in a drying towel. With a trembling voice, Andromache asked, "What is it, priestess? Why do you stand so amazed? Speak, you're frightening me."

Apollo's priestess shook her head, but continued to stare unfazed. "Words are of no use. You'll not hear me."

"I hear you," Andromache said with fear rising from her gut, worming its way to her chest.

Cassandra nodded. Her hand rose with a shaking finger pointed at her. "You'll be led in chains before the ships," she warned, tears streaking her face.

"Before what ships?" Andromache asked, terrified.

"The ships from Achaea."

"There are no ships from Achaea here," a strong female voice echoed through the chamber.

Andromache turned to see a tall, elegant woman wearing a golden circlet on her head. Her dark hair was curled and arranged so that it spiraled through the golden ring and spilled down her shoulders and back. Her gown was pale blue and sheer. She appeared as a goddess among the assembled females. *Hecuba. She must be Hecuba.*

"The son of the greatest warrior will lead you in chains from the ruins." With that pronouncement, the god's fever left and Cassandra visibly slumped.

"The son of the greatest warrior shall take her away? Hektor? Why should our new daughter have fear of her own husband or

227

son? Cassandra, your visions are always askew. Look at what you've done. Frightened the bride with useless prattle."

Queen Hecuba addressed Andromache, "My dear, the greatest warrior is my son, your husband, Hektor. Any son of his would be your own. You need never fear from Hektor. Put her words from your mind and be at ease. She speaks in riddles and provokes fright."

Andromache's lips twitched slightly when she tried to smile at the queen.

Hecuba clapped her hands. "Bring the wedding gown."

Andromache's mother nodded to the servants to obey the queen. The gown was presented to Hecuba who draped it herself over Andromache's head and fastened the shoulder broaches. The queen stood back, admiring the shimmering saffron folds. "Your mother's work is stunning." She smiled. "You're a most fetching creature, Andromache of Hypoplakia Thebe."

"I thank you, Queen Hecuba."

Hecuba laughed quietly. "You may call me mother as Hektor does. You'll be as my own."

"As you wish, Mother."

"Are you ready to make the journey to Aphrodite's temple? Hektor is already waiting."

Andromache pulled her veil over her head. "I am, Mother."

Queen Hecuba motioned the doors be opened. The throng of women spilled quickly from the room with gowns flowing behind them as if a breeze blew against them. Spectators tossing flower petals and sweet herbs before the procession lined the path to the temple. Andromache kept her eyes down, watching one foot then the other peek from beneath the hem of her dress. Questions about her future rose up and fell away. *Will I bear fine sons? Goddess, let him be kind, please. Let him love me.*

As the procession made its way up the glistening white steps to the entrance of Aphrodite's temple, Andromache's stomach clenched so tightly she thought she'd be ill. *It's too late to turn back.* She remembered the conversation Hektor had with her father when he'd brought the final payment for her hand. She'd spied him from the shadows of the hall. She'd thought he looked older than when she saw him in the garden that night two years ago. *I don't even know what it is to love a man.* Andromache squeezed her eyes shut, recalling the images conjured up by her mother's explanation of what a wife must do.

The procession halted and Andromache stumbled. Queen Hecuba caught her elbow, leading her forward to the side of a man she knew was Hektor. Daring to look up, she could see her father and a man she assumed to be King Priam waiting near the altar.

The Prince of Troy took her hand and led her to the altar before Aphrodite's marble image. He reached for a simple clay jar of wine and poured it into a bowl before the goddess's feet. After taking a sharp blade from his belt, he grabbed Andromache's hand. Instinctively, she withdrew it, letting out a small gasp.

"It only stings for a moment. The goddess demands our blood in exchange for her blessing," Hektor spoke quietly to her, reassuring her that the pain would be slight and quick.

"I'm sorry, my lord," Andromache murmured.

"Give me your hand."

The young bride held out her trembling palm. Hektor took it more gently this time. He drew the blade deftly across the soft skin, leaving a thin red line. He held it over the bowl of wine until a drop fell, breaking the surface tension. Releasing her, he then performed the rite on his own hand.

Hektor prayed the required words. "Goddess, we ask that you bring us many healthy children."

Andromache remained at his side with her hand elevated, unsure of what to do about the thin wound. She had nothing to wipe the blood away.

Hektor took her delicate hand in his own and pulled a corner of his chiton free to wipe the hurt. "It will heal over quickly. It's not so deep." With that, he turned with Andromache at his side and faced their families. Cheers and applause echoed through the chamber.

King Priam stepped forward, embracing his son warmly. Andromache could see the pride in his eyes for Hektor. "I'm most happy for you, my son."

"Thank you, Father. I'm famished!"

"Yes! To the great hall! We've a feast to devour!" The king's voice boomed against the stone walls and columns.

Golden light from hundreds of oil lamps flooded the great hall of Priam's palace. Garlands of tender olive branches and draping pines adorned walls and tables. Wild flowers and rosemary springs strewn across the floor sent spicy aromas into the air as the guests crushed the stems with their feet. The tall columns were wrapped with ivy and delicate white flowers. Tables were laden with platters of roasted boar and beef, trays of fish and foul, and bowls of sweet plums and figs stuffed with honeyed goat cheese.

Flanked by a pair of Apollo's priestesses, Hektor and Andromache were escorted to the statue of the god erected for the reception. His golden figure was adorned with flowers and ivy and his head crowned with sacred laurel. The bride and groom offered food and wine before the deity. Cheers rose from the assembled guests.

King Priam stretched his arms wide before the company in the hall. All voices hushed.

"Family and friends, honored guests. Be seated. Celebrate with me and my queen, the marriage of the Prince of Troy and his bride, Andromache of Hypoplakia Thebe." A great noise of chatter and applause rose, filling the massive chamber with joy as the assembly took their seats. Hektor was positioned at the king's right hand and Andromache at her father's side. Very quickly, servants appeared carrying kylikes of wine. Drinking bowls were filled and passed between guests. The clanking of platters and pottery signaled the feasting and merriment had begun.

As wine flowed and men's bellies filled to bursting, a handsome singer stepped forward with his lyre and a simple stool. He set it down, taking position with his instrument on his knee. His fingers plucked the strings and sweet music filled the air. The guests hushed, anticipating the wedding song. Hektor hoped his new bride would be pleased with the commission.

As the minstrel sang, Andromache's father stood, signaling his daughter, as her patriarch for the final time, to stand. She placed her hand in her father's and he led her before Hektor. The guests clapped their hands to their thighs. Men and women cheered their young prince. Hektor stood, acknowledging their presence.

Hektor walked around the heavy wooden table to stand by his bride's side. He grabbed her by the waist with a firm hand, while King Eetion feigned resistance. Then Andromache's father spoke the binding words, "Gathered together are the witnesses who will confirm that on this eve I give my daughter, Andromache, to Hektor the Prince of Troy, to have as wife. May you both be blessed with an abundance of children." With tears in his eyes, King Eetion lifted the veil from his daughter's face, handing her over to her husband. With a small step, the Princess of Hypoplakia Thebe leapt into her new life.

"You're as beautiful as I remember," Hektor said just loud enough for his new wife to hear.

"Thank you, my lord."

The Prince of Troy whisked her from her feet and carried her from the hall to the happy sound of more cheering and laughter. He carried her all of the way to the wedding cart that would take them to the house he'd prepared for her, for their life together away from the palace.

Andromache's mother along with the female relatives and servants began the marital procession, weeping and wailing, as Hektor tugged on the oxen's reins and the heavy beasts lumbered the cart away. A baker's boy, adorned with a crown of slender olive branches, had been chosen to carry the bread basket before the cart. He handed bread to the wedding guests and spectators as he walked with the bride's family to the nuptial home. Some of the women waved torches about to scare the bad spirits away from Andromache and Hektor on their wedding night. Others carried fruit and wild field violets and sweet smelling roses to bring good fortune, occasionally throwing some at the bride and groom. Several flute players blew happy melodies while the procession meandered through streets.

"Hold!" Hektor called out. The throng of merry-makers halted. Hektor nimbly jumped from the cart, reaching up to assist Andromache down.

Hecuba handed Andromache the ritual torch. Several servants emptied the wagon of the few possessions being towed in the cart, carrying them into the house.

"Clear the wagon!" Hektor commanded. Everyone stood back as the bride held the flame to the wagon's axle.

As flames and smoke spiraled into the dusky night, Queen Hecuba spoke. "Don't look back, Andromache, for you are now home."

The prince then lifted his bride, quite by surprise, in his arms and carried her into the house, shutting the door with his foot, sealing them in and alone for the first time. He carried her directly to their bed chamber.

Andromache trembled as he set her down in the center of the room. Hektor, realizing his young bride must be nervous, poured them a kylix of wine.

"Drink. It'll calm you."

Andromache took the cup and sipped at the contents. "It smells of cinnamon and honey."

Hektor watched the pulse beating wildly through the vein in her neck. "I meant drink the entire bowl." It sounded more of a command than he intended.

His young wife drank the wine, until only a drop remained on her bottom lip. The prince kissed it gently from her mouth. Her lips parted slightly, and he wrapped his arms around her, kissing her deeper than before. Hektor tasted the spiced wine on her tongue, as his own swept through her mouth with urgency. Andromache's body softened. He smiled as her hand shyly explored his lower back. Her touch intoxicated him.

Finally, he slipped his fingers beneath the shoulder fastenings of her gown and swept the delicate cloth from her shoulders, exposing her breasts. Andromache visibly shook under his gaze. "You're beautiful. You've nothing to fear from me."

Andromache dropped her head as nervous tears filled her eyes. Hektor tilted her chin up so their faces could meet. He kissed her forehead, before lifting her in his arms. When she pressed her face against his chest, he was certain she'd feel his heart pounding as he carried her to their marital bed. Gently, he set her down on the linens and furs.

Leaning back against the pillows, Andromache brought an arm up to cover her bare breasts. Hektor lay beside her and kissed her with great tenderness. He wished to raise a fire in her heart for him, he wished her to burn for his kisses, his touches, his lovemaking. Slowly, her arm relaxed and she turned on her side, wrapping it around his neck and pulled him closer.

When her body arched toward his, he knew she was ready for the necessary consummation of their marriage. Untangling her arm from his neck, he sat up, unbuckling his waist belt, and then pulled his tunic over his head.

He caressed his wife's cheek flushed with embarrassment at his nudity. He helped her slip her gown from her body, and then lay her back. He kissed her slowly as he entered her. She arched and cried out as he pressed his full length into her body.

"I'm sorry," he whispered against her ear. "The hurt is momentary." Hektor moved slowly, not wishing to injure her. Andromache's body soon eased into the lovemaking. He smiled into their kiss, as her legs shook and her fingers dug into his shoulders. Only then did he release his passion, hoping his seed would take hold and plant a son in her womb.

TWENTY NINE

something long forgotten

TROY—1265 BCE

The blush of dawn lit the sky as Hektor and Andromache woke to the song of women outside of their new home.

His words brushed lightly against her ear. "How is my wife this morning?"

"I'm … tender," she said shyly.

"I don't think that can be helped," he replied, tucking a stray lock of hair behind her ear. "You move me, Andromache. As I've not been moved before."

"Then, we are the same, my husband."

Hektor's smile widened. "Then you won't mind if I …" his fingers traced a trail to her thighs, "take you once more before we're forced by that singing to leave our bed."

They made love with deliberate slowness, extending their newfound pleasure and joy in one another. When they finished, Andromache lay atop him and confessed in a quiet voice, "I thought you old."

He snorted laughter and slapped her bottom. "I'm not so old now?"

She dipped her head against his shoulder. "No."

"Perhaps, I need to prove my stamina once more."

Andromache giggled into his chest. "I'm willing."

***

Paris watched from across the arena as King Priam welcomed the Prince of Troy with open arms as he took his place with the new princess. Queen Hecuba sat separate from the king, looking sad to him even at this distance. It was said not all mothers take their son's marriages with grace. Perhaps, she didn't like losing her eldest son to his new wife. He also took note of the woman draped in white standing apart from the royal family. *That must be the oracle princess.* The tall, proud sons of Priam stood randomly around the king facing the games.

Loud, excited banter filled the air as the crowd's anticipation of the public ceremony consecrating Prince Hektor's union with Thebe. The entire city had been waiting to celebrate the marriage of its prince to his princess. The bull dancing arena was decked in laurel garlands and flowers for the final day of the royal wedding celebration. Paris hoped to win the prize of gold coin to take to Agelaus and Lexias. He'd grown taller and stronger than his older brothers in the last year. He knew his skills with the bulls had also grown superior to almost any of his competitors, so he told himself that he had as good a chance as any to take the prize. The royal family settled into their seats and Priam signaled the games to begin by raising his right arm and bringing it sharply down across his chest.

Cassandra eyed the man with dark, curly hair jumping elegantly over the decorated bull. Her blood cooled and slowed and her eyes glassed over before rolling back, revealing only the blind whites of her eye balls. She saw a baby wrapped in royal linen being nursed by a silver bear … an older boy caught between bulls in a corral … her own mother weeping endlessly in a dark corner of the palace. When the vision passed, she stared hard at the man who had prompted her vision.

Helenus took her hand. "What is it, Cassandra? What did you see?"

"How could I miss him? He *is* Hektor, but not."

"Who? What are you talking about?"

A faded memory of her mother weeping pushed forward, clouding her mind more than Apollo's sight. *The Forgotten Prince. He's the Forgotten Prince. My brother. The doom of Troy. He must die. He must die.* The priestess raised her arm, the sleeve of her chiton hanging to the ground, and pointed an accusing finger at the bull dancer. She whispered hoarsely, "The Forgotten Prince." The crowd's roar nearly drowned out her words.

"You must be quiet before father hears," Helenus warned.

Queen Hecuba turned her head to Cassandra. "What did you say, daughter?"

The priestess of Apollo stared at the man leaping over the bulls and spoke again. "He is the doom of Troy," she hissed, and then she shouted in desperation, "*He is the doom of Troy!*"

Cassandra's words rose above the din this time, pricking King Priam's ears. "What's this? What treason are you spewing now, insane girl? Keep your tongue civil. Better yet, keep it silent. We don't want your prattling nonsense ruining Hektor's celebration."

Cassandra ignored her father. "He is the Forgotten Prince."

Hecuba stood up, going to the railing. Her shawl slipped from her shoulders and fell to the ground. Priam gazed across the ring, his interest now purposed, as he studied the tall figure of the man facing the bull that was stabbing at the dirt. The beast's heavy hooves sent showers of dust into the air, before it charged. The dancer sprinted with the wind at his back, launching himself forward, as he gracefully grabbed the bull's horns. The force of their collision propelled the man into the air, but he never released his hold on the horns. Priam watched as the young man's body cleared the dangerous horns and whipped around, his back parallel to the bull's but never touching only to land safely on the ground making his leap appear an easy task. The crowd cheered the dancer's skill and elegance.

Priam looked to his wife. Hecuba's knuckles whitened as her grip on the railing tightened. The blood had drained from her face. He moved to her side.

Hecuba's voice shook with hope and fear. "Do you think it possible? I can't take my eyes from him."

"The dead cannot rise and walk among us," King Priam said quietly, regretfully.

Hecuba's grip released the railing. "No, they can't," she murmured, her hope already fading.

The king reached for her hand, but she pulled it to her side before he could. "I'm sorry. Truly." In all their years together, since they'd lost their second son, he'd never been able to reach her heart, or comfort her. "Drop your arm, Cassandra."

Cassandra refused to quiet. "It's him, Father. Look closely."

His daughter's insistence annoyed him. But, he couldn't resist her words, so he looked harder, squinting his old eyes. The dark, curly hair. The towering height. His gait. In fact, from this distance, he might be mistaken for Hektor. "It can't be …"

"It is," Cassandra said simply, lowering her arm.

"Bring me that damned cattle herder, Agelaus," the king yelled to his guard. "Bring him to me straight away."

"Where will I find him?" a guardsman asked.

"He'll be down there." The king pointed toward the pens under the arena. "He'll be with the bulls no doubt." Priam didn't even look as the men scurried away. He sat down heavily in his chair. The young bull leaper had disappeared. Another had entered the grounds with a fresh bull. His mind raced with thoughts of the day he'd handed his squalling son to Agelaus, who'd sent the gruesome evidence of his deed. He dared a sideways glance at Hecuba. She sat staring straight ahead, a single tear streaking down her pale cheek.

Hektor's words pierced Priam's thoughts. "Are you well, Father?"

"I don't know. In all honesty, I don't know."

"Does it have to do with Cassandra's warning?" Hektor asked, his concern for his father rising.

Priam looked at his eldest son, and then at his many other children gathered for this special occasion. Of them all, the king knew only Hektor remembered. He'd been all of five summers old when his brother was lost to them. "Her words…impossible. If it's so, I'm the king who banished him." He swallowed hard. "Worse, I'm the father who sent him to die."

"Cassandra's always spilling some mystery which amounts to nothing."

"Only one man can provide the answer. I've already sent for him."

"Then we'll hear what he has to say," Hektor said.

They didn't have to wait much longer, as the guards returned. King Priam signaled Agelaus to approach. The bull herder knelt before his king.

King Priam stood, making no indication his subject should get up. "Agelaus, years ago I made a terrible request of you. Do you recall?"

"I can never forget that day," Agelaus said, his voice cracking.

"Good. Tell me what happened to that child." Beside him, Hecuba gasp.

The bull herder twisted uncomfortably as he knelt. "In front of the queen?"

"She has a right to hear the truth," King Priam said.

Agelaus swallowed hard under the hot gaze of the royal family. "I cut out his tongue and left him to die, as you commanded."

Hecuba fell back into her chair. Andromache stepped to her new mother's side. Cassandra wept.

The king pressed him further. "Who's the young bull dancer resembling my sons?"

Agelaus prostrated himself before Priam. "My king, please forgive me. Please forgive me."

Priam stiffened with equal measures of hope and horror. "You did as you were commanded. I find no fault in you. Get up."

Agelaus' lips brushed the stone. "If I'd only done as you requested …"

"What riddle is this, Agelaus? What have you done?"

"I-I … couldn't, my king. I just couldn't let the child die. I went back for him. He survived."

Priam sank into his chair beside Hecuba. "Where is my son? What have you done with my son?" he demanded.

Agelaus confessed, face down to the stone before his king's feet, "The bull dancer, my lord. He's the bull dancer."

"There can be no mistakes, herder, or that you will pay for with your life."

"It's true. And certain. I raised him myself."

Hecuba's hand flew to her mouth, stifling a cry.

Priam commanded, "Bring him to me."

———————

Despite his aching bones, Agelaus quickly stood. "Yes, my king." He bolted from the royal compartments, making straight for the stable holdings. As he rushed to obey his king, his mind whirled with worry about the future of his family. What would Lexias say? How would she take the news? What punishment would the king give him? He'd stolen the prince from him … he reasoned against the latter as his own fear. Priam said it was no fault of his own.

He spotted Paris talking with some men. "Paris!"

His tall, handsome son turned. "Father! Did you see that last pass with the bull? I may have won with that leap."

"I did. And perhaps it was enough."

"Perhaps?" Paris asked incredulously.

"Paris, there's no time to talk about bull dancing."

Paris threw his head back, laughing. "The heat is making you mad. No time for bull—"

241

Agelaus grabbed Paris roughly by the elbow, pulling him close. He pressed his mouth next to Paris's ear. "I barely have time to tell you what you need to know. All will change for you I fear."

"Concerning what, Father? The purse is not so large."

"Everything."

"You make no sense, Father."

"Paris, you know I love you. Lexias loves you as if you were our own."

Paris pulled his arm from his father's grip. "Now, you cause concern. Why are you speaking as if you are about to punish me?"

"Have you never wondered about your true parents?"

"Often, yes, and you've failed to speak regarding the matter."

"I'm ready to speak. I must speak."

"Father, what's happened? Why now? Has someone threatened you?"

"It's none of that. But your real father has seen you and wishes you to come to him."

Paris snorted disbelief, a wave of unexpected anger rising to his chest. "My *father?*" He turned and grabbed the post of the pen behind him to steady himself. "I'd hoped one day I might find my true parents, but I gave that up years ago. Now, you tell me *he* is here? That he desires to meet me?"

"Yes, that's what I am saying."

"What if I don't wish it? I've a wife and work your land … What would a new father wish of me? I see no reason."

"Paris, my dear son, you've no choice."

"What do you mean, I've no choice? I have a fucking choice and I choose not to visit this man."

"Paris, trust me. If you don't go, he'll find me and run a sword through me without a doubt."

"No one has the power to compel you or me to do what's against our wills."

"Paris, it's the king. King Priam."

Paris dropped his hands to his sides, and turned to look Agelaus in the eyes. "You're a crazy fool. By the balls of Zeus, what are you talking about? I'm no king's son. I'm no prince." He shook his head. "Why are you doing this? Why would you jest regarding such a thing?"

Agelaus spoke, "It is no jest, Paris. You're the Forgotten Prince."

Paris recalled the story. A prince born years ago who the king had put out to die. It was rumored the queen never forgave the king. "What has this to do with me? Nothing. I was an abandoned and unwanted child. You found me and raised me."

"Paris, I was the servant chosen to leave the prince, you, in the wild. I left you there. For days I couldn't sleep. The gods sent me nightmares, so I went back. Found a silver-bear feeding you. Artemis I suppose. You were dirty, but your cheeks were rosy. I brought you home. We raised you as our own. Paris, I took you directly from the hands of Priam himself. I've no reason to speak untruth."

Two armored guards appeared behind Agelaus, alarming him, and his urgency grew to desperation. "You must come with me to meet the king, your true father."

Paris sized up the guards and considered his father's words. He knew deep within that his father, the only father he'd ever known, was speaking the truth, yet the words refused to take root in his mind. He'd wanted to know the truth for so long, and now after finally hearing it, the truth sounded foreign in his ear, not at all the welcomed news he'd thought it would be. To be a prince would change everything about the life he'd come to love.

One guard stepped up. "Are you Agelaus?"

"Yes, yes I am," the bull herder acknowledged.

"The king orders you return with the bull leaper."

Agelaus looked to Paris and said, "We're coming presently."

The guards escorted Paris and Agelaus straight to the royal compartments. As Paris approached he caught the eyes of several younger princes and princesses. They looked curiously at him. Then, he caught the image of a man a few years older than himself whose visage was almost a silvered mirror's reflection of his own. His fingers touched the dip in his chin. The king rose to greet him.

"You are …" Priam glanced at Hektor, then back to Paris. "You are him. I see the blood of my fathers in your face, now that I can see you closely." The king smiled broadly, tears filling his eyes. "You are him."

Paris bowed his head. "I don't know who I am, my lord."

"Agelaus tells me he's raised you as his own?"

"Yes, he has been father to me my entire life," Paris said.

"He has told you, then, how you came to his household?"

"Only recently has he told me a tale I can't believe."

Priam nodded. "It's hard to hear the unbelievable and believe," the king sighed. "Yet, it's true what he tells you."

Paris grew angry. "Why?" He looked to the faces staring coldly and disbelievingly at him. Paris gestured at the royal family. "Why was I cast aside from among your jewels? What wrong had I done? You can't be my father."

"I'm your father. You'd done no wrong. My seer gave a warning prophecy that your birth would bring destruction to Troy. So you were sent away—"

"Sent to die, you mean."

"My decision was only to protect Troy."

Paris stepped away from the king, placing distance between the dawning truth and the world he yearned to keep. "Yet the city stands, as do I. Perhaps your seer was more practiced in deception than truth."

"The seer must've misread the signs and the gods intervened through Agelaus to save you."

Hecuba stepped forward without saying a word. She raised a hand gently to Paris' cheek. Her large, brown eyes softened with fresh tears and joy. "You're my son. I'd know this face anywhere; even in the depth and fire of Hades I'd know this face. My son … the Forgotten Prince to all, save me. You've lived in my grieving heart my entire life." The queen embraced a surprised Paris and held him tightly to her, as she wept quietly. Slowly, Paris brought his arms around the weeping woman.

Watching his mother embrace the stranger, Hektor smiled for her joy and release of pain. He pulled his new wife to his side and whispered in her ear, "This will change everything for her."

Andromache whispered back, "You're happy then?"

"Yes, yes I'm glad. Her heart has suffered long enough."

"You hold no jealousy or ill will toward him?"

"None. Curiosity, perhaps."

"Then you're more generous than Deiphobus. His face holds more hate than curiosity."

Hektor noted his younger brother's squinting eyes and slight sneer. "Jealousy serves no purpose here. If he's the Forgotten Prince, it's his right to return and claim his rank after me." Andromache nodded agreement and nestled closer into Hektor's embrace. The appearance of the man would seem joyous, but a shiver ran through her, a foreboding of things to come.

While the queen wept and chatted with the bull leaper, Priam pulled Agelaus aside to ask him a question in confidence. "What of the tongue you sent me, years ago?"

Agelaus cast his eyes to the ground and replied, "It was a dog's tongue, sire."

Cassandra wept in the dark room. She wept for her mother. She wept for her father. She wept for Troy. *No one believes me.*

The door opened quietly and Helenus entered on tiptoe. "Cassi? Are you awake?"

"Yes, but leave me alone."

Helenus tripped on the edge of a carpet. "By the balls of Zeus, light your lamps, sister."

"I prefer the dark."

Reaching out his hands, Helenus found the back of a chair. Feeling his way around it, he sat. "It wasn't your fault, you know."

"He'll bring the fall of our city. I've seen it."

Helenus inhaled, and then let his shoulders relax. "Sister, the time of the prophecy is past. He's a grown man. His birth didn't bring any danger to Troy at all."

"He lives, so it's enough. The prophecy is yet to come."

"I want to believe you, Cassandra, truly I do. But what do you suggest now? Murder? It's one thing to expose an infant, and quite another to kill a grown man."

Cassandra leaned forward in the dark, a hand reaching out to grip Helenus by the knee. "Is it?" Her fingers dug deeper.

"Ouch, you're hurting me."

She released her grip. "It must be done, or Troy will fall."

"Have you not thought that our brother's return is the will of the gods? Allowing him to return could be a god-sign heralding a new prophecy."

"Or the beginning of our doom."

Helenus stood. "I'll send a servant to light your lamps, sister. You spend far too much time in the shadows. More light will ease your mind."

Cassandra shrugged. "As you wish."

As her brother walked through the door, she knew a thousand oil lamps couldn't release her mind from the darkness Apollo cursed her with. Even though she hoped with each new vision to be heard, she found nothing but scorn and anger. Helenus, with his promises to believe her, was gentler in his disbelief than most. *I'm alone. As Apollo intended. Cursed.*

THIRTY

son no more

TROY—1265 BCE

"What? Do you jest at my expense?" Lexias screamed. He ducked as a clay plate whizzed past his ear. "There was nothing I could do to stop the king," Agelaus defended himself.

"You could've lied! Isn't that what we've been doing all these years? Who'd know?"

"The priestess, Lexias, she singled him from the crowd. Called him the Forgotten Prince. She wouldn't be silenced."

Lexias dropped the cup from her hands and it cracked to pieces on the tile floor. "A lunatic girl rants and you give up our son? He's *our* son." She pulled her bare breast from her chiton. "I suckled him with my own tit! He's mine!"

Agelaus, judging it safe to approach his wife, moved to comfort her. He knew her heated words only covered her hurt and betrayal. She'd loved Paris, as he did. "Lexi, he's a Prince of Troy. Priam's second son. You've always known the truth of it. One day he may even rise to become King of Troy, the gods forbid Hektor should fall."

"Do you remember when he'd talk to the cows? The chickens? He believed he could get them to lay more eggs …" Lexias cried freely now. "I know what you say is true, Aggie. But my heart refuses to give him up."

"We must. For his sake, we must allow him to take his rightful place."

Paris gazed out at the green meadow lined with slender pines. He shielded his eyes from the sun, when from the corner of his sight he caught a flash of gold and silver. A shadow formed in the distance, landing on the ground as gracefully as a bird, making straight for him. Paris recognized the form he'd seen before, years ago, so long ago he'd almost forgotten the encounter and the judgment.

"Aphrodite. It's been as a lifetime," Paris greeted the goddess with the appropriate deference.

"I'm pleased you remember," she said.

"One does not simply forget … Aphrodite."

"Careful and as charming as I recall."

"What brings you to the mortal realm, Goddess? Another contest?" Paris asked.

The goddess closed the small gap between them. "You've grown quite pleasing to the eye with the passing years. I hadn't noticed how much so, until now."

Dread knotted the back of his neck. There was nothing he could offer a goddess that she couldn't take for herself. "An undeserved compliment, Aphrodite."

"I understand your true bloodline has been revealed to you? That you are a son of Priam?"

"Apparently, it is so."

"You don't sound so pleased with this discovery. Apollo and Artemis played their parts well."

"What has Apollo to do with me? And Artemis?"

"It was Apollo's curse upon Priam for Hesione's … shall we say, departure from Troy that led to your circumstance. It was Artemis who suckled you as a she-bear until the herder returned for you."

"So, Agelaus was right … about the shining bear," Paris said.

"Enough talk of the mundane. I bring you news of the beauty that will one day belong to you, as I promised years ago."

Paris didn't want to hear the news. He'd hope that the goddess would forget the promise being pleased with her title of being the fairest. "What news, Goddess?"

"She's been born, Paris. She'll be the most fair of mortal women. And she'll be yours."

"I'm thankful you've remembered the promise of such a gift on my behalf, but I have a wife I'm pleased with. I desire no other."

Aphrodite laughed at Paris' thin rebuff of her gift. "Men don't refuse the will of the immortals."

"I meant no insult, Goddess."

Aphrodite smiled. "I take none. You needn't have any immediate concern. Helen is yet a child of two winters. I'll not deliver her up, until she has bled as a woman."

"Where is she from? What city?" Paris asked.

"Why do you fret so? Don't worry. When the season is upon you, I'll provide the way to her."

"So I have time yet?"

"Time for what, mortal?"

"To make my home in Troy."

"Take your place among the princes," the goddess said. "I'll return." Without further discussion, the goddess shimmered into thin air, leaving Paris unsettled. He didn't want a different wife. He loved Oenone. Betraying her would be like betraying himself. His thoughts troubled him all of the way back to the home he shared with the nymph.

"There you are, my love. The evening meal is almost cold," Oenone said. Paris sat at the table without returning her greeting. "Is something the matter?" the nymph asked. Again, her husband didn't answer. "Are you thinking about Troy again?"

Paris lied, "I can think of nothing else."

Oenone sat next to him. "I wish there was some comfort I could give. But I'm afraid I've more heaviness to add to your burden."

Paris looked at his wife. "What is it?"

"I've had a disturbing vision of our future, my love. One that pains me greatly."

"Speak, then."

The nymph folded her hands in her lap. "I've seen that you will abandon me for another. One who is golden and fair from across the sea."

Paris thought of Aphrodite's promise. *Helen. It must be this Helen she speaks of* …"I'll never leave you, Oenone. I couldn't forsake you for another; it'd be as if I cut off a part of my flesh. No, I'll not leave you."

Oenone remained silent.

"There's more?" Paris asked. *By the balls of Zeus, bad news is all around.*

"War will come to Troy. And you'll be wounded … grievously. I'll be able to heal you. But only me, no one else."

"War? In Troy? I can't believe that. The walls are impossible to breech. The world knows this. Who'd start a war they couldn't win?"

"That wasn't revealed. Only that the war will come." She grabbed Paris' hand. "Promise me, that if this comes to pass, you'll send for me. Let me heal your wounds, so you aren't lost to me forever."

"Oenone, nothing's going to happen to me."

"Promise?"

"I see you won't be deterred." He kissed her forehead. "I promise."

"Promise you'll always love me," she said quietly.

"Shah, Oenone. I'll love you, always." Paris kissed her sweetly on the mouth and rested his forehead against hers. "But I must take my place among my true family."

"When will you go?"

"When Apollo rises."

Oenone took his hand. "Let's not waste any time with words."

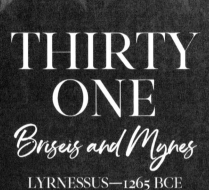

THIRTY ONE

Briseis and Mynes

LYRNESSUS—1265 BCE

Tendrils of sacred smoke curled in the air as Briseis climbed the steps within Aphrodite's temple, making her way to her way to her bridegroom. She leaned heavily on her father's arm. Beneath the edge of her veil, she watched her feet peeking from the hem of her gown. She always thought this day would take her to Troy, but she'd been wrong. Briseis tried not to let disappointment sour her mood. *Mynes has been kind.* She smiled despite herself. *Mother lied about his singing.* Her father squeezed her hand, as he stopped at the final step.

"Mynes is waiting." He kissed her through the gauzy veil. "You've made me proud. No father could ask for better."

Briseis' foot hovered slightly on the last step, before she made for

Mynes' side. As she neared, he reached for her hand. His calloused palm reassured her of his strength. And when he lifted her veil, his smile reassured her of his kindness.

Walking Briseis to the foot of Aphrodite's statue, he whispered for her ears only, "Are you ready?"

"Will it hurt?"

"A slight sting," Mynes said, taking her hand and lifting it above the bowl of wine the priests had set before the goddess' image. Pulling a sharp blade from his belt, Mynes quickly drew blood across Briseis' palm. She winced slightly as he steadied her hand and a single drop of blood plopped into the bowl. He then passed the blade over his own palm. Their blood now mingled with the wine, a sacrifice to the Goddess of Love. "We are one, Princess."

The small gathering of royals and family cheered the sacred union, before making the procession back to the palace for the wedding feast.

As they lay naked and entwined in their marital bed, Briseis shivered with chill and fear. Mynes' body, covered in dark, curly hair, scratched at her soft skin. His cock pulsed and pressed against her thigh. *What's he doing? Why's he waiting? Doesn't he want to take me as his wife?*

Mynes kissed her forehead. His lips brushed her cheek as he said, "I see so many questions in your eyes."

"I'm sorry, my lord."

Mynes placed a finger to her lips. "You've nothing to apologize for, Briseis."

"Are you displeased with me, Mynes?" She dared to look him directly in the face. "You haven't taken me …"

The Prince of Lyrnessus chuckled, brushing a thumb across her lips. "Are you so eager?"

"I … don't know. I only thought … My mother told me …"

He propped himself up on an elbow. "May I speak plainly?"

Briseis nodded against his shoulder.

"Not all husbands and wives have love between them, but I'm certain love will blossom between us in time."

"I understand."

Mynes' eyes searched hers. "I've no wish to damage the fragile thread that binds us by taking you before you're ready."

"How will I know … if I'm ready?"

Mynes bent his head to kiss her mouth, his voice husky with controlled passion. "Will you allow me to try and please you?"

"Yes," Briseis whispered, shaking.

Taking her chin in his hand, Mynes pulled her mouth to his and kissed her deeply. His tongue passed her teeth, tangling with hers. Wrapping his free arm around her waist, he pulled her body toward his. His lips brushed her cheeks, traveling down her neck. Every downy hair on Briseis' body rose in song as if Mynes had plucked a melody from a lyre. "You're trembling."

By the gods, he smells of spice. "Yes …"

Mynes tenderly swept his hand down her side, sliding around her hip to her lower back. He let his fingers trace up her spine, before he kissed her again. His fingers stroked the nape of her neck, as his mouth placed tiny kisses at her ears, chin, and down her neck. Briseis moaned, her body softening against his.

The heat building in her belly urged her to return his passion.

What's happening to me? I need him, but how? She wrapped a leg over Mynes' hip and his swollen cock slipped to the space between them, dancing and seeking a home. His kisses burned her skin. "I'm ready," she whispered. "I'm ready."

Her husband pulled her beneath his body, spreading her knees with his thighs. "It will hurt at first."

"The heat … can you end it?"

Mynes reached a hand to guide his cock into her wet center, pressing the tip of it inside of her.

Briseis cried out, but her hands grabbed his buttocks, pulling him closer. "More."

His restraint, now unbound at his wife's urging, flooded into their union, as he pushed his entire length into her body.

Briseis' eyes flew open and she gasped. "I feel you in me."

"Move with me," Mynes said.

Briseis wildly rocked her hips against his body, clawing at his shoulders. She wanted to stop the growing urge; it was uncomfortable and pleasurable all at once.

Placing a hand on her hip, he said, "Slowly, woman, or you'll not shake before I spill my seed."

Mynes made love to her, slowly and deliberately, penetrating as deep as he could, and pulling from her as far as he could without breaking their bond. Then, he rolled her on top of his hips and she stopped.

Embarrassment stained Briseis' cheeks. "I don't know what to do."

"Just move your hips against mine. It'll come to you."

Briseis rocked shyly at first, as the fire built again at her center. Mynes placed his hands at her hips, helping her move up and down, as she lost herself in their passion. As her breathing became louder, he slipped a hand to her sacred flesh and rubbed at the swollen bud crowning their union. Quickly, Briseis' entire body shook, a loud cry of fulfillment echoed across the bed chamber. Then, she collapsed against his chest.

Mynes rolled her to her back, without pulling his still throbbing cock from her body. As she lay beneath him, biting at her bottom lip and moaning, he gently thrust into her. His mouth caught a budded nipple and he suckled at it, while his own pleasure spilled into her. Together, they lay sweating and tangled before the gods.

In the dimming light, Briseis kissed her husband's shoulder. "Is this how a husband and wife blossom?"

He smiled against her hair. "It is."

"How long does it take? For love, I mean?"

Mynes pulled her closer in the crook of his arm. "Not long at all."

THIRTY TWO

the king of wine

LEMNOS—1264 BCE

The winds of Aeolus slept, so the last leg of the journey to Lemnos was slow and uneventful, and hot and muggy. The rowers pulled hard at their oars in the still air. Mynes stood at the prow of the ship, one hand on the rail and the other at Briseis' waist.

"I must warn you, my sweet wife, about King Euneus."

Briseis reached for her husband's hand with hers. "I fear nothing, so long as you're with me."

Mynes smiled down at her. "But who will protect me from your charms?"

"I suppose nobody. You're my prisoner forever."

"Torturous."

Briseis leaned her head back against his broad chest. "Why do the old women rant against love, when it's such a sweet existence?"

Mynes shrugged, pulling her closer. "I don't know. Men often council to hold off marriage, but I find I quite enjoy it." One hand slid down to squeeze his wife's buttock.

"What did you want to say about King Euneus?"

"His … enjoyments tend to the depraved. He may try to entice you and I into—"

"What?"

"Don't worry, I will refuse any offers."

"Then why do we go to his court?"

"Because his wine is unsurpassed."

Briseis turned in Mynes' arms, tiptoeing to kiss his chin. "Tell me something this king has done that counts as depraved."

Mynes narrowed his eyes. "I can't speak of such things to my wife."

"But can you *show* her?"

"Woman, do your appetites have no limits?"

"No, thanks to you. I can't be satisfied."

Mynes laughed into the slight breeze, as he took Briseis' hand. "Get below, wife. I'll see you *satisfied* before we dock at Lemnos."

Briseis giggled and followed, while the crew rowed and held the course.

COURT OF KING EUNEUS

King Euneus swept into the hall in fine robes, golden cuffs at his wrists, and a head of dark curled hair with beard to match. The servants scurried at his late arrival, as his royal guests were already seated and feasting. He sat in his chair positioned between Mynes and Briseis.

He nodded at Mynes. "I'm pleased you've made the journey unmolested by pirates, or pesky Greeks."

"As am I."

"It seems the coast along the Troad is never truly safe, since Herakles sacked Troy and murdered King Laomedon nearly forty years ago."

Mynes nodded seriously. "True. Marauders have been emboldened ever since that atrocity, despite King Priam's efforts."

Briseis plucked a fat fig from her tray. "Wasn't your father, Jason, a Greek?"

King Euneus' brown eyes glittered as he turned his attention to her. "Princess Briseis." He kissed Briseis' hand with the fig still between her fingers. "He was. But, shall we speak of more pleasant matters?"

"I apologize, I meant no offense, my lord."

The king smiled disarmingly, his teeth pearly perfection. "I've taken none, my lady." He turned again to Prince Mynes. "Are you here for trade, or …"

Mynes shifted uncomfortably in his seat. "Wine. Your vineyards are renowned."

The king laughed. "So they are." He shoved a chunk of lamb in his mouth. "If you change your mind, I've a new shipment of slaves, if you're interested. Those for the field and the *house* variety. I've a few with rare talents I could part with for a sum."

Briseis' eyes rounded at the offer. "You mean female slaves?"

Without making eye contact, King Euneus nodded. "There's great profit turning flesh and bone to coin."

Mynes intervened. "No slaves this time. Just the wine."

The banter and music continued, as self-doubt crept into Briseis' mind. *Why would he offer women to Mynes? He said, 'this time.' Is there some arrangement?* Her husband's expert maneuvers about her body were surely honed somewhere. *But slaves? Right under my nose? I've been a fool to think no other women know him as intimately as I.* "Mynes, my lord, will you excuse me? I'm feeling unwell."

King Euneus nodded. "Of course." He signaled a servant. "See the princess safely to her chambers. Remain without until her husband joins her."

———

Late into the night, Mynes entered the room on unsteady feet. He tripped over an edge of carpeting, knocking an oil lamp from a table as he caught himself. "By the balls of Zeus!" he hoarsely cursed into the dark.

His robes dropped to the floor with a soft thump, before he slid beneath the linen next to Briseis. He pressed his face into her hair, whispering, "My turn for satisfaction." As his hand reached for her, she stiffened.

"How many others have there been?"

"What?"

Briseis turned, facing her husband. The outline of his face was barely visible in the half-light. "How many women have you lain with?"

Mynes' passion cooled and he rolled to his back. "Why do wives ask such questions?"

"What does that mean?"

"Do you truly wish a number? Would your amorous feelings ignite knowing there were ten, twenty, fifty women before I married?"

Tears pricked Briseis' eyes. "So many?" she whispered.

"Briseis, isn't it enough to know I've lain with no others since taking you to wife?"

"How can I know for certain?"

"Do you not feel the truth between us?"

"I don't know …"

Mynes brushed her cheek with the back of his hand. "No other woman compares to you."

"Is that all I am to you, Mynes? A woman to satisfy your *urges?*"

"When did my wanton wife become so shy? What more do you wish from me, besides my cock?"

"Love."

"Love?"

Briseis bit her lower lip, trying in vain to stop the hot tears falling down her cheeks.

Mynes leaned over her face in the shadowy light between them. "My lady, don't cry if it's my love you desire. You've had that since the first night I held you in my arms." He bent his head to hers and softly kissed her lips. "I've only ever loved one woman. And she's here with me."

Briseis wrapped her arms about his neck, returning the kiss. She pulled away. "But King Euneus said—"

"Shah. No more fretting about what has passed." Mynes pulled her close, kissing his wife deeply now. "Why is this gown between us?"

No sooner had Briseis slipped it over her head, then Mynes' mouth was at her breasts. His tongue suckled each nipple to a tight bud. Briseis closed her eyes to the familiar hunger building within her belly.

Mynes made love to her slowly, deliberately. "Let there be no more doubts."

THIRTY THIRIEE

Agamemnon's son

MYCENAE—1263 BCE

"H e's a fine son," Agamemnon beamed. "The gods bless us."

Neola rolled her eyes, as she fussed about the queen's fresh bed linens. *They should curse you, except that would harm my queen.*

Clytemnestra leaned back into the pillows of her bed, the bundled newborn cradled against her breast. "Would you care to hold the Prince of Mycenae?"

"I … I don't know anything about—"

"Hand the king his son."

Neola stopped tucking in a blanket. Glancing sideways at Clytemnestra, she found her queen staring at her expectantly. Sighing slightly, she came around the bed and gathered the sleeping baby. "As you wish, my Lady."

Agamemnon stood with his arms crossed tightly over his wide chest. When Neola held the prince out to him, he took a small step backward.

"Just support his head. You can't break him—" *Yes, yes, he can break a child.*

The king slowly opened his big, hairy arms, carefully cradling his son. "He weighs no more than a dagger."

Clytemnestra laughed softly. "What did you expect, my dear? But see how perfect his fingers and toes are? He does resemble you. Furrowed brow and all."

Agamemnon fumbled with the bunting. "How do you undo this? He's wrapped tighter than a goat for slaughter."

"My Lord, allow me." Neola stepped forward, expertly unwrapping the lower half of the swaddling cloth, exposing the baby's tiny feet.

Agamemnon took his son's small foot in his hand. "They are wrinkled like an old man's."

"All babies are wrinkled like old men." Clytemnestra smiled wanly. "It's been nearly three weeks, Agamemnon. And our son still has no name."

The king examined the baby from head to toe. "He appears strong … Orestes. His name shall be Orestes."

Nodding in agreement, Clytemnestra said, "Fitting. To conquer mountains."

"The heir to Mycenae should have a strong name." At Agamemnon's pronouncement, the child's face screwed up awkwardly and he began to wail.

Clytemnestra held out her arms. "He's hungry."

Neola took the squalling bundle from the king, returning the babe to his mother. She did not miss the gleam in Agamemnon's eye when the queen pulled a swollen breast from her chiton for the baby to suckle.

"There, now, little Orestes." The newborn's mouth swiped against the large nipple, before latching on and sucking hungrily. Clytemnestra pulled her son snug against her body. "See, soon he'll be satisfied and sound asleep."

Agamemnon approached the bed, gazing down lustfully at his wife. He bent to kiss her cheek and slipped a hand beneath her gown, pinching the unoccupied nipple between his fingers. Lifting them to the tip of his tongue, he tasted the wetness. "Sweet."

Clytemnestra made no protest, as her husband pulled her chiton open, exposing her other breast.

"Leave us, Neola," Agamemnon commanded.

With a worried look at her queen, the servant reluctantly left the chamber. The door thudded shut behind her.

"Your breasts delight me, wife."

Clytemnestra narrowed her eyes. "I'd prefer you let our son eat in peace."

"That is not what I'd prefer." He knelt beside the bed, leaning his head to her breast. It was steadily leaking milk, wetting the front of her clothes. "You forced me to wait too long when Iphigenia was born. I won't be as patient this time."

He licked her nipple, circling his tongue over it, until it tightened into a nub. He sucked gently at first, and the nectar filled his mouth. Agamemnon swallowed. "You taste like summer wine."

Leaning her head back against the pillows, Clytemnestra closed her eyes. Orestes was now fast asleep cradled in the crook of her arm. "It is not *unpleasant.*"

Agamemnon smiled wickedly. "Only you could be so cold and wanton all at once." His cock twitched to life beneath his robe. "I may not be able to lay with you, but you can pleasure me in other ways."

"Now?" Clytemnestra asked, surprised.

"Now."

"What would you have from me?"

He placed her hand beneath his chiton. "Stroke the seed from me, as I drink from you."

Clytemnestra laid Orestes behind her on the bed, stuffing a blanket roll around his little body. She made room for her husband on the mattress. "Come, then."

Agamemnon lay alongside his wife, suckling at the same breast he'd tasted just a moment before. The milk streamed into his mouth, warm and honeyed. Clytemnestra reached to slowly stroke her husband. He sucked harder. She stroked faster. Agamemnon groaned.

To Clytemnestra's surprise, her body grew ... *warm*. Since any flow from childbirth had ceased, she allowed her free hand to move toward the sensitive bud crowning her sacred opening. Her fingers quickly found the soft flesh and she rubbed at it. "Harder," she whispered, urgently.

Agamemnon took so much of her breast into his mouth, milk dribbled down his chin. He reached for her other breast, kneading the nipple between his fingers.

"By the gods," Clytemnestra moaned.

Agamemnon placed his hand on hers, as she slid her fingers over her sacred folds of flesh. When her hips convulsed with her pleasure, he let his seed erupt over her hand.

With the act completed, they looked each other in the eye,

saying nothing. Clytemnestra released her grip on him, wiping her hand on the front of her already ruined chiton.

"You're satisfied?" she asked.

"For now." Agamemnon stood. "I will come to you again." He grinned. "Tomorrow."

Clytemnestra forced a smile. "Tomorrow, then."

After her husband left the chamber, she got up from the bed to wash herself. Placing the wet sponge between her legs, she wiped the smell of sex away. But, she couldn't cleanse the memory of the act from her mind. It troubled her that she'd found such an intense release in what they'd done together. *At least he can't get me with child in this manner.* Even if her body betrayed her on occasion, she was determined not to lose sight of her ultimate goal. She would be master of her world, not Agamemnon.

THIRTY FOUR

love conquers all

LYRNESSUS—1262 BCE

"Your kingdom someday, little one." Briseis rested her hands beneath her round belly, as the child stretched against her ribs. Leaning to the side, she attempted to avoid the uncomfortable tightness building at her lower back. The ache eased and she breathed easy again. Standing from the reclining couch, Briseis walked to the balcony overlooking Lyrnessus' fields. If she squint her eyes, she could just make out the pale blue of the horizon across the Bay of Edremit. Much farther to the north, she knew Troy stood as the shining citadel of the East. "In another time, that would've been yours. I'd thought it mine, before—" Another pain doubled her and she gripped the banister. "By the balls of Zeus! What's happening?"

Your daughter seeks the light …

Briseis looked around the chamber. "Who's there?"

Have no fear, daughter, I am with you.

Another pain, this time much sharper and stronger, ripped across her belly and a gush of bloody water splashed at her feet. "Bree! Come quickly! Bree!"

The princess' chamber door flew open, as the maid servant took in the scene before her. "My lady! By the gods, it's your time!"

Briseis' eyes widened in fear. "So soon? I'm not ready. I have—" Her knees buckled.

"My lady!" Bree swept to Briseis' side, lifting the princess to her feet, half carrying her to the chamber bed.

"The pain. By the … balls of … Zeus. I.can.scarce.breathe."

There is glory in your pain, Briseis.

"Bree, who else is here?"

"No one, yet," she said, tucking a sheet about the princess. Bree ran to the door, yelling down the cavernous hall for the midwife. Within moments a gaggle of women flew through the door clucking about the impending royal birth.

Briseis' scream startled them all. The midwife was at the princess' side in the blink of an eye, pulling back the privacy sheet. Her hands firmly palpated Briseis' belly. Without a word, she pushed Briseis' thighs apart. Her eyes widened.

"What's wrong?" Briseis asked, tears spilling down her hot cheeks.

The midwife pressed her lips together in a grim line. "My lady, this will be a difficult birth. I must put my hand inside of you to confirm my suspicions."

"Do it!" Briseis screamed as another pain wracked her body. She groaned in agony as the midwife's hand pressed into her. "By the gods …"

Bree pressed a cool cloth to her lady's forehead and cheek.

"The child is breech," the midwife pronounced, wiping her hands on a towel. A hush settled around the chamber. They all knew it was likely a death sentence to mother, child, or both.

Briseis wept. "No. No. By the gods, no!" Another pain tore through her.

Bree dipped the cooling cloth in the water basin again. "Can nothing be done? Can you save Princess Briseis?"

Briseis rolled back against the cushions. "Save my child, please."

If that is your wish …

Yes, save my child. "Save my child. Take me instead."

Bree's face whitened. "What's she saying?"

The midwife answered, "What all women say, when faced with such a choice."

A dusty swirl of air blew into the chamber, snuffing out the oil lamps. The women froze, as a tall, glittering woman emerged from the small storm. Her gown flashed silver and gold. They fell to their knees, heads bowed, the goddess' name on their lips … *Eleithyia.*

The goddess glided to Briseis' side, stars blinking along the hem of her gown as she moved. She reached out a pale, cool hand to Briseis' forehead. "Calm yourself, daughter. I'm here."

Briseis smiled weakly. "Gratitude, Goddess."

Eleithyia signaled to Bree. "You appear a strong maid. Help me set her onto her knees and place her hands on your shoulders." She looked to the midwife. "Watch. Learn."

The midwife nodded, as Briseis was placed into position.

The goddess moved her hands on either side of Briseis' hard belly, running her palms flat against the lower abdomen. "Now, push your daughter to the light. Push like a warrior afield. Push for your life and for hers."

Briseis cried out in agony, her limbs shaking with effort. Blood spilled as the child's buttocks crowned.

"Hold your lady tightly." Eleithyia's voice was steady, as her hands worked calmly. Gently, she pulled each leg to length. "Push, Briseis." The goddess, holding the babe with both hands, slightly turned the torso, releasing a shoulder blade and freeing the arm. Then, repeated the same for the other arm. The women gasped as the child hung half-suspended, face down, from Briseis' body. Eleithyia positioned one hand on the baby's chest, while the fingers of her other hand cradled the neck and head. "One last push, Briseis. Victory is yours with this battle."

Briseis' fingers dug into Bree's shoulders. She screamed with her final effort, as the goddess guided the slippery child to the light. The princess collapsed against her maid, weeping with her exertions and aching body. Gently, Bree lay Briseis down.

Eleithyia handed the limp newborn to the midwife. "Rub the baby with clean linen, until she cries." Turning to Briseis, she said, "You've won this battle, but you'll lose the war."

"What do you mean? What war?"

The goddess stood to her full height, sparkling in the dimly lit room. "The one inside of your heart, daughter." With the ominous words still hanging in the air, Eleithyia's image shimmered to nothing.

The midwife stared at the spot the goddess had stood. "By all that is sacred, I never thought in all my days to witness this. Blessed be our princess and her child."

"Bring me my daughter," Briseis said, proudly. Once the weight of her baby was settled in her arms, she smiled and joyful tears filled her eyes. "Phila, for *love* conquers all."

THIRTY
FIVE
Achilles' lessons

MOUNT PELION—1261 BCE

"Hold the lyre like this, Achilles," Chiron admonished. "It's to be stroked, not pawed at."

"I hate music lessons," Achilles groaned. "Can't we train with sword and shield?"

"You're impossible, imp!"

Achilles bristled. "I'm no imp! You … you horse man!"

Chiron threw his head back and roared with laughter. "Horse man? That's the extent of your youthful wit? You call me a *horse man?*" He laughed, until he could laugh no more.

Achilles stood fuming with his fists dug into his hips.

"Little Achilles, perhaps we should train. You'll drop that sour face, will you not?"

Achilles brightened. "I will."

"Grab your weapons. Meet me at the sand pit."

The young warrior thrust his arm triumphantly in the air. "I love fighting!"

Chiron twitched his tail, narrowing his eyes as Achilles ran off to gather his weapons. "Exactly what I'm afraid of. Too much fighting, not enough reasoning."

Late into the afternoon, the centaur clashed wooden sword to wooden sword with his ambitious pupil. "Keep your shield up, young Master! Up I say!" Chiron landed a heavy blow to Achilles' shield and the boy stumbled backwards.

"Ha! You'll not unbalance me twice!" Achilles charged at Chiron, who rose up on his hind legs, avoiding the onslaught. "You can't do that!"

"I just did."

"It's not fair," Achilles said, lowering his sword and shield slightly.

Pushing forward, Chiron used the tip of his wooden blade to press his ward to the hot sand at the exposed shoulder. "Nothing is fair in battle, Achilles. Best to remember that."

Achilles rubbed his shoulder, wincing slightly. "Yes, I'll remember." He stood and spun, slamming his sword into Chiron's furry shin bone. The centaur reared up in pain. "I'll remember to never trust a centaur!" Achilles laughed at landing the trickster blow.

Chiron landed heavily, sending a shower of sand into the air. As Achilles shielded his eyes, the centaur reached for the boy's shoulders just as he was backing away. "You'll pay for that, young master."

"I was hoping so!" Achilles jeered. "Now, fight me again!" Achilles spun from under his teacher's grasp and quickly took his attack stance.

Chiron's smile lifted on one side, revealing a straight bridge of teeth. "As you wish."

Wooden blades clashed and splintered in the hot sun. Master and student fought until they were both drenched in sweat. Dried salt tipped the ends of Chiron's curly tufts below his chest. The centaur thrust his weapon at the young warrior who blocked the practice blade with his shield. When Achilles found himself backed against the sand pit wall, he knew he had to do the unexpected. He dove beneath the centaur's legs, tucked into a roll, and sprung back to fighting form before his master could turn around.

"Clever!" Chiron shouted and lowered guard. "I believe we're finished for this day."

"You're tired? I've energy yet."

Chiron snorted. "Go run then. Take the hounds. Run until you've exhausted yourself. If that is even possible. I have matters requiring my attention."

Achilles dropped his practice armor into the sand. "If you say so, Chiron."

"Stay out of trouble this time. And by the balls of my brother, Zeus, stay away from the other centaurs. They'd just as soon roast you like a plump lamb and stuff you with dates than endure further harassment at your hands."

Achilles promised … sort of. "I'll *try* to stay out of their way. But if one should cross my path, especially that Batilamus, I might have to—"

Crossing his arms over his broad chest, Chiron cocked his head. "I'll roast you myself, young Master."

"You take my joy, Chiron."

"My intent exactly." His hoof dug into the sand. "Off with you." He watched the Golden Warrior scamper off and twitched his tail. "There'll be no taming that one."

Achilles returned drenched in sweat just after the light of Apollo had slipped from the sky. He peeled his damp chiton over his shoulders and tossed it carelessly on the floor.

From the dark, Chiron's voice echoed through the chamber. "Have I not told you about strewing your clothes about the floor?"

Achilles, his nerves steeled to startling, shrugged. "Why do you hide in the dark?"

Chiron emerged partially into the dim light of the cave hall. "You answer my question with a question?"

"You're always sneaking away into the dark."

"I'm not sneaking away. I'm … *resting*."

"Why do you need so much rest? Aren't you an immortal beast? Insatiable."

"Once upon a time, I was."

"Then, you're not immortal?"

"No. Not any longer."

Achilles narrowed his eyes. "Why does everyone say that you are?"

"Immortality can be a curse, young Master. It came to be so for me. Quite by accident, but nonetheless, there it is."

"Tell me how it happened? Did it hurt? I mean, losing your immortal soul?"

Chiron stomped a hoof against the stone floor. "There's not

much to tell."

Achilles perched on a hard stone bench. "I'll listen, if you'll tell it."

The centaur's hooves clicked against the floor as he entered the main chamber. Achilles could see that he was limping. "Is your leg bothering you again?"

"You've yet to pick up the filthy garment. And you expect a tale?"

"Chiron, you steal my joy," Achilles said, as he scooted from the bench and retrieved his clothing. "There. I've done as you asked." He sat back down still clutching his rumpled chiton.

"Very well, then. I suppose you know of my … origin?"

"I only know you call yourself brother to Zeus."

"Because he is. His father and mine are the same. My mother was sea nymph, like yours. Taken unwillingly by Cronus."

"What was her name? Does she know of my mother?"

"Philyra," he said. His mouth formed the sound of her name like a foreign word slipping from his tongue. "It's likely they've met, I suppose."

"But how did you turn out to be a centaur?" Achilles' eyes rounded. He ran his hand against his rump. "Will I become a centaur?"

Chiron's laughter rang through the cave hall. "That's what you fear? Turning centaur?"

"Our mothers were both nymphs, I thought—"

"That's irrelevant, young Master. My form comes from my mother's attempt to escape Cronus' grasp. She morphed into a mare trying to flee. She was … unsuccessful, and Cronus took her as a horse. So, I am thus." Chiron held his arms wide. "I was born a centaur and granted immortality."

Achilles' eyes rounded. "What happened?"

"Apollo raised me, for neither my mother nor father wanted to do so."

"And you're immortal so they couldn't just kill you," Achilles blurted out.

Chiron folded his arms. "True enough." He twitched his tail. "Apollo was generous with his gifts."

"Is that why you know so much about the world? From the god?"

"It is."

"How did you lose your immortal power?"

"Herakles."

"What did he do to you?"

"So many questions. One of his poisoned arrows grazed my arm. The poison bound my body with great pain. Although I couldn't die, I wished to. It was a rather terrible experience. Herakles, feeling guilty I suppose, petitioned the gods to free me of my immortality. He exchanged my gift for Prometheus' freedom. The pain, although not as unbearable as it was, continues until I pass to the Underworld."

"That's why you require rest?"

"Yes, young Master."

"You knew Herakles?" Achilles asked, awestruck.

"Quite a knack for getting into trouble. Not unlike another boy I know," Chiron hinted with a smirk.

"Shah! You don't mean me, do you?"

"Achilles, I've never known anyone to wind up in more predicaments than you."

The young prince hung his head, slightly shamed. "I'm not so bad, am I?"

The centaur cantered to his young pupil and ruffled his matted golden hair. "Make no mistake … I rather enjoy your company, even if my fur begins to streak with silver."

THIRTY
SIX

matchmakers

MYCENAE—1260 BCE

With hands clasped behind his wide back, King Agamemnon paced the great hall of his palace. "Do you think the dowry is enough?"

Queen Clytemnestra poured her husband a cup of deep ruby-colored wine. "Drink this, my lord, and put your fears at ease."

Agamemnon took the cup and drained it nearly dry. He grimaced. "It's bitter."

"King Peleus prefers libations that bite the tongue. All of their wine is bitter. Their northern grapes are inferior to ours."

The king smiled slyly at his wife. "You've planned ahead. Thoughtful. It pleases me you approve of this match."

"You'll have your northern allies, and our daughter will someday have a kingdom to rule." She brushed her fingers across the marble table between them. "Although, Phthia is a rough and rugged land." She glanced up. "With bitter wine."

The king resumed pacing. "It's a fair offer. What could be keeping him? It's not that far from the main gate to here."

From the hall's southern entrance, the King of Phthia entered with servants towing chests behind him.

Agamemnon raised a hand in greeting. "My lord, Peleus. Welcome to Mycenae."

Peleus bowed his head. "I'm honored."

The queen signaled a slave to pour their guest some wine. "Your throat must be parched after such a long, dusty journey."

Taking the proffered drink, Peleus signaled his servants to bring forward the chests. "Tokens of good faith."

The queen knelt before the chest nearest her. "May I?" It was richly carved wood and inlaid with gold and silver. She ran her hands along the top. "The chest itself is exquisite."

With a glittering eye, Peleus encouraged, "Open it."

Clytemnestra undid the silver latches on the sides and pulled the lid off. She glanced up at her guest. "You honor our daughter." Pulling a wide piece of blue cloth from the bolt within, she held it up to the light. "Magnificent. I've never seen this color of blue before. It shimmers as if weft with silver."

"Achilles' mother dyed the wool herself, from Poseidon's wedding gift. He'd told her the snail ink was mixed with the god's ambrosia. You'll find more of that in the other chests."

Closing the trunk, the queen scanned the entourage. "Truly one of a kind, my lord. And your women are skilled at the loom. Has Achilles' mother come with you?"

Peleus shifted his feet, slightly. "She returned to her home after our son was born."

"I heard whispers you drove her from the palace."

Peleus' shoulders stiffened. "It's a complicated matter."

Eager to get to the politics of the meeting, Agamemnon cleared his throat. "A table has been prepared for us in the main courtyard. Perhaps, more wine and food are in order as we discuss the matter between us?" Slaves hurried to stow the chests, as they walked across the hall and outside.

A tented pavilion shaded a table laden with trays of fresh baked bread, sticky dates filled with soft goat cheese, and ripe figs and grapes. There were steaming bowls of fish and roasted goat. And more northern wine.

As Peleus sat, he admired the royal spread. "Your hospitality is well known. But truly, my lord, Agamemnon, you've exceeded expectation."

They sat as slaves served them. The queen picked at the food on her plate, while sipping the bitter wine. "I'm curious, Peleus, why not choose Helen as a match?"

"How can I answer you, my lady, without rudeness?"

"With honesty."

Peleus glanced nervously at Agamemnon. "You've heard those *whispers*, I'm certain."

Clytemnestra bit into a date. "Regarding?"

King Agamemnon signaled for more wine. As he caught his wife's eye, he realized she wasn't as amicable about the proposal as she'd led him to believe. "Enough talk of Helen."

King Peleus sat back in his chair. "I'll answer your queen. It's said that Helen is a wild girl. Undisciplined. Too beautiful. Such a woman would not be suitable for my son."

"Why not?" the queen asked, leaning forward.

"Achilles is strong-willed and blessed by his mother's immortal blood. He'll need a wife who'll bend to his will, not test it."

Clytemnestra's jaw twitched ever so slightly. "An honorable husband can make any wife bow to his will. Is the boy still training with the centaur?"

"He is."

"Do you believe he'll make a good king, one day, when you're gone from this world?"

"My lady, Achilles will be the finest king who ever sat on the throne of Phthia."

Agamemnon thumped the table with his hand. "It's settled then. For the price we agreed on."

Peleus lifted his wine cup. "May the gods bless the union of Achilles and Iphigenia, when they come of age."

"Yes." Clytemnestra lifted her cup, but did not drink. A shiver ran through her. "Iphigenia."

THIRTY
SEVEN
swift Achilles

MOUNT PELION—1259 BCE

Trails lined the foothills of Mt. Pelion where Chiron trained Achilles. "Run! Run as the wind, young Master!" the centaur shouted over his shoulder at the young man keeping pace behind him. Chiron burst into full gallop with Achilles hard on his heel. They ran full force until they reached the edge of the plain. The centaur pulled up the pace.

Achilles grabbed his sides and took a few deep breaths. "I could've overtaken you, you know."

Chiron noted the absence of sweat. "Interesting."

"What?" the prince asked.

"I believe you may be telling the truth."

"I never lie to you." Achilles straightened up. "Well, mostly."

"That was an honest statement. Your lack of sweat tells me you did indeed hold back."

Achilles grinned mischievously. He pointed across the level plain stretching out before them. "Care to wager which of us can make it across there first?"

Chiron glanced across the lengthy course. "What is the wager?"

"You carry me back to the cave."

The centaur laughed. "You're heavy, young Master. I'll agree if you make the wager even."

Achilles sputtered a drink of water. "Carry you back? You weigh like a rock!"

"I suggest you win, then." Chiron pawed at the ground. "Ready, young Master?"

Achilles tossed his water pouch aside, taking position next to his mentor. "Get ready to carry me all the way back."

Chiron reared up and shouted, "Catch me if you're able!" The centaur pounded the ground with heavy hooves, sending showers of dirt and sand in Achilles' direction.

They ran with the wind at their backs, Achilles matching stride with the great beast. Chiron glanced over his shoulder. "Run!" he shouted. "Run!"

Achilles needed no more encouragement than that. He kicked his heels higher so that his feet barely touched down on the ground. He ran as if inspired by fleet footed Hermes. The edge of the plain neared and Achilles finally pulled away from Chiron, touching the edge of the plain in triumph.

The centaur pulled up his hooves to break his speed, needing to catch his breath before speaking. "You're the first! Never has a man beat me in a foot race. Never."

"It's your training that gives me advantage." Achilles grinned. "I'm glad I won, because it's a long way back home."

Chiron heaved a heavy, tired sigh. "Climb up, young Master. We best begin." He held his arm out to pull Achilles up.

"Tell me about Herakles," Achilles said.

"What would you like to know?"

"Did you know him when he defended Hesione, the Trojan princess?"

"Yes, I did. That's a good tale, young Master. Would you like to hear it?"

"Leave nothing out."

Chiron's eyes twinkled. "Hesione was a beautiful woman. Perhaps, the most beautiful woman to ever grace the city of Troy."

"You should know I suppose," Achilles said.

"Young Master, I'm chaste … for a centaur," he laughed. "I thought you asleep when—" Chiron stopped. "Were you awake every time?"

"Every single time," Achilles confirmed with a lopsided smirk.

Chiron glanced over his shoulder, narrowing his eyes. "You're a roguish one."

Wishing to draw attention away from his many misdeeds as quickly as possible, Achilles said, "I've been admonished often enough on that account. Continue the tale, please."

"Very well. King Laomedon's daughter, Hesione, *was* a very well-respected Trojan. Let's see, how does it go? Ah. The king had commissioned Apollo and Poseidon to assist Aeacus, your grandfather, in building the great wall around the city. The summer heat got the better of the king, or so many would like to think, but I believe Ares had a hand in it … regardless, the king refused to pay the gods. Apollo, of course, sent the usual plague, but Poseidon sent a creature never before seen by mortals, one that he awoke from the bottom of the sea. Plague and death spread throughout Troy, and when the sea monster appeared King Laomedon believed his city doomed. And well he should've believed it. Really, what did he think would come of defying the gods?" Chiron asked aloud.

Achilles was completely under the centaur's spell. "He's fortunate Troy didn't crumble beneath his feet."

The centaur agreed. "True. I've often wondered why the gods didn't destroy the city. The king consulted the oracles, who told him that if he sacrificed his daughter, Hesione, to the sea monster the city would be saved. She was stripped of her garments and chained to the rocks facing the sea. Imagine her humiliation. Stripped and chained by her very own father. Pitiful really. As it so happened, Herakles came through the city on his return from campaigning against the Amazons. Herakles offered to save the princess if King Laomedon would give him the horses he'd inherited from King Tros. The horses were from Zeus. The king agreed. Herakles waited for the sea monster, and when it appeared all gnashing teeth and flailing tail, whipping the waves into a frenzy, it swallowed Herakles in one gulp."

Achilles gasped. "How did he get out?"

Chiron scratched at chin. "He had to battle the beast from within. It took him three straight days to hack his way out of its belly, but he did save Hesione. Laomedon refused to give up the horses. So, Herakles killed the king and all of his sons, except for Priam. Herakles was so disgusted by the king's lack of propriety, he refused to take the princess as compensation for the slight. He gave Hesione as scraps to Telamon and Priam became king of Troy."

"Priam just let his sister be taken away as a captive bride? Without a fight on her behalf?" Achilles asked incredulously.

"Didn't even lift a finger. Priam's an old man, now, clinging to his Trojan throne. Zeus knows his sons enough to retire to a life of ease in the country somewhere. His eldest, Hektor, is quite capable. But, Priam chooses not to step aside. And by the balls of my brother, Zeus, the man has an appetite for women rivaling that of my own kind! There must be thirty or more sons claiming the king's paternity."

"You almost sound envious, Master."

"No, I envy no man, young Achilles."

"I've heard that Hektor is the greatest warrior that ever lived."

"You'll give him competition when you reach majority."

Achilles nodded. "Yes, I think I shall. Tell me, what became of Hesione?"

"She had two sons by Telamon. Both half-brothers to Ajax. And your half-cousins."

―――――――――

Achilles rested against the rock looking up at the stars. "Chiron?"

"Yes?"

"I hope that when I am dead I'll have achieved something worth recounting in song."

"I've no doubt you'll be among the greatest."

Achilles turned his head to face his mentor. "Truly? Or do you jest at my expense?"

Chiron nicked a few small pieces from the wooden horse he was carving. "I don't jest." He tossed the wooden horse to Achilles. "You'll be legendary."

"How? What will I do?"

"I've seen that one day you'll take the immortal horses of Peleus into battle. You'll conquer cities by the dozen and crush thousands."

"Where? When?" Achilles sat up. "Tell me."

"I can't see that far. Besides, it's not for man to know the total of his life before it happens, or what would be the point of living? The game of it would be without purpose."

Achilles resumed scanning the stars. "What if I became a constellation?"

Chiron snorted. "Shall I call you Narcissus?"

"Shah. I'm only talking to you."

"The gods hear you. To wish one's form be cast among the jewels of night is wishing for immortality. Humans best steer from such thoughts, or risk invoking divine anger."

Achilles sat up again. He strained his ear toward the dark. "Did you hear that?" he whispered harshly.

The centaur put a finger to his lips, as he backed away from the fire, shrouding himself in shadows. He motioned for Achilles to follow suit.

The distant voices grew more distinct. "This would be far easier if I could *see* where we are going."

"It would've been better had you avoided any contact with that whore."

"She lied! How was I to know he held any affection for her?"

"It can't be far now."

The two men emerged at the edge of the fire's light. The taller one halted the horses.

The one with bandaged eyes asked, "Why are we stopping, Peleus?"

"Shah! You idiot!" Peleus spat between clenched teeth. "You

wish to be bludgeoned to death by wild brutes?"

The brush opposite the odd pair rustled. Peleus slid slowly from his horse, landing silently on the ground. "Show your self!" he commanded, sword at the ready.

Chiron's immense figure burst into the circle of light, startling Peleus. "Hold, friend! It's only me. Chiron."

Peleus stepped back, sheathing his sword. "Chiron! I'm glad we found you. I was beginning to think I'd forgotten the way."

The centaur reached down to embrace the king, his former pupil and his friend. "You're a long way from the palace."

"I wouldn't have made this trek had it not been for Phoenix here. Blinded by his own fucking father."

"A woman's doing?" Chiron asked.

"A man's troubles can usually be traced back to a woman," the king replied.

The centaur nodded in agreement. "The ones without virtue can easily lead a man astray by his—"

"I'm innocent! How many times must I tell this tale in my own defense?" Phoenix asked angrily. "I'm the one blinded. By the balls of Zeus, I'm fucking blind!"

"Ah!" Chiron said. "Now, I understand why you've risked traveling through the hills of Pelion in the dark. Achilles!" he called. "All is well. It's only your father, Peleus."

From the shadows, a young man emerged. The yellow light of the dying fire flickered shadows across his form. He stood almost as tall as a man. His limbs were uncovered and finely muscled. His golden hair fell in a messy frame about his face and shoulders. The gods' favor touched Achilles. "Son."

Achilles approached warily. It'd been years since he'd laid eyes on Peleus. The passing of time had stolen his affection for his father. The king was a stranger to him now. "Father."

Peleus reached to embrace him. Achilles allowed it. "A rather cold greeting, my son."

Achilles looked to Chiron for guidance. Chiron nodded. Achilles spoke, his voice deep and melodic. "Apologies, I meant no slight or disrespect, Father."

"Chiron, I think it may be time for Achilles to return. Take his rightful place at my side. It seems he has forgotten why he's being tutored by you."

Phoenix interrupted. "I hate to break up a family quarrel, but remember why we came here in the first place?"

Peleus nodded. "We can discuss my son later. For now, Chiron, I need your assistance if you will?"

"Let us return to my cave. Any medicines I require will be there."

Once back in the centaur's cave hall, Chiron had Phoenix lay on an examining bed. He pulled the bandages from his eye sockets, and examined the dried, bloody depressions that had once held his eyeballs. "I can't tell if the damage is permanent. If his body accepts the treatment and the gods are willing, he may see again."

"If I had eyes, I would weep at that statement," Phoenix said flatly.

Peleus chuckled. "Your sense of humor is intact, at least."

"Fuck my sense of humor."

"Maybe you should have fucked the whore instead."

"I swear by Zeus, Peleus, if you were not the king, I'd pay to have you whipped."

Chiron pulled fresh strips of linen from a basket. "Achilles, bring me the amphora marked with black figures circling a fire."

Achilles retrieved the vessel. "What medicine is this?"

"A mixture only the gods can provide. Dust of Gaia and blood of the immortals." Chiron proceeded to pour the dry earth from the amphora into a flattened bowl. He poured wine into it and mixed a thick paste. "This will hurt, Phoenix. Beyond any pain you have experienced. Peleus, hold his arms. Achilles, hold his legs. Don't release him until I say it's safe." The centaur placed a dagger hilt in Phoenix's mouth. "Bite this."

Chiron set to work. He took a fine, thin bladed knife and reopened the dried eyelids. Phoenix moaned, arching in agony. Fresh blood spilled down his cheeks. Chiron looked at both men assisting him and nodded. "Now, don't let go." He pulled open the first eye and filled the gory socket with the muddy paste. Muffled screams passed the dagger's hilt in Phoenix's mouth and he clawed at the bed beneath him. His body writhed in agony. Chiron filled the second socket and again Phoenix thrashed in pain, his screams passing the dagger's hilt and echoing around the chamber. Sweat drenched his body as he twisted and clawed through the torturous remedy. His chest heaved greatly. His limbs convulsed. The dagger fell from his mouth, clanging loudly on the stone. Foam leaked from the corners of his mouth. Peleus and Achilles held him firmly as directed. Many long moments passed before Phoenix's body relaxed, twitching only now and again. Then, he was completely stilled.

"What's happening, Chiron? Why isn't he moving?" Achilles asked.

"His body's healing. This was undoubtedly more painful than losing the eyes in the first place. He should be fine. You may release him." Chiron wiped his brow. "Shall we have some wine, then?"

THIRTY EIGHT

Phila's Dream

LYRNESSUS—1259 BCE

Briseis held the cool cloth against her daughter's rosy cheek. A hot tear slid from the corner of her eye. The fever swept quickly through the city, striking the wealthy and the poor alike. Her daughter struggled against the linen.

With eyes closed, Phila cried out, "Mama! Mama! Where are you?"

Briseis stifled a sob. "I'm here, sweet girl. I'm here."

Phila settled at the sound of her mother's voice. Briseis dipped the cloth in the basin, wringing out the excess water before dabbing it gently at her daughter's cheeks and neck. The oil lamps flickered in a breeze from the window. Briseis turned her head, but no one was there. *Why do you punish her? How could she have offended any of you?* "How? Tell me!"

Bree placed a hand on her shoulder. "My lady, the gods give and take from us all. You must rest. Take some bread and wine."

Briseis shook her head. "I can't leave her. What if she wakes and I'm not here? What if she's frightened once again, who'll calm her?"

The nursemaid's hand tightened with reassurance. "Not long, just a brief rest. Keep up your strength for when she awakens. She's a busy child, as you know."

Briseis smiled despite her exhaustion. "Phila is that." Lifting her daughter's tiny hand to her lips, she kissed it softly. She pressed it to her own cheek. "Even her hands are hot. It's been three days. By all the gods, how much longer must she suffer?" Briseis wept again. *Is this the war I'm to lose?*

"My lady, please, you must rest."

"I can't leave her, Bree. I can't."

Bree nodded. "Let me bring you a tray. Eat while you keep watch."

"Yes. That will do."

As the nursemaid closed the chamber door behind her, Briseis climbed into the small bed beside Phila. Her daughter's body radiated unnatural heat without sweat to cool her. Briseis laid her head next to her little girl's. "Just a moment to rest my eyes. Just … a …"

"Mama, why do you weep?"

Briseis slowly opened her eyes, as her daughter's small hand stroked her forehead. Behind Phila, Apollo's light filled her vision. She blinked back the brightness. "How long was I asleep?" Shielding her eyes with her arm, she chided, "You should be in bed."

Phila flashed a smile so brilliant, Briseis was forced to squint. "I'm well now, Mama."

Confused, Briseis reached for her daughter. "The fever … you've been ill for days."

"But no more. I love you, Mama." Phila turned and walked away, glancing one last time behind her. "Farewell, Mama." The light surrounding Phila dimmed and her image faded to darkness.

Briseis sat bolt upright. She glanced around the chamber. The oil lamps burned low and a tray of bread and figs sat on the table, untouched. Bree. Yes, she let me sleep. She reached for her daughter's hand. It was cool. "The fever has broken." Relief washed over her. Briseis touched the little girl's cheek. It was cool and growing cooler. Relief turned to panic. Phila's voice rang in her ears. "I'm well now, Mama."

"No. No … no!" She whisked the linens from Phila's body, feeling her daughter's arms and legs. "No, not now." Briseis pulled Phila's lifeless body to her breast. "My girl. My girl." Disbelief mingled with the first wave of grief. "I can't lose you."

Briseis recalled the day they chased the orange and blue dragonflies in a field. Phila's laughter ringing sweetly in the air. "My girl." She rocked Phila's body, as another memory stung through the denial. The day they picked flowers for the old women in the palace. "My sweet girl." Grief filled her chest with the weight of the heavens, and the wail of loss filled the bed chamber, echoing down the hall and into the courtyard below. As she rocked and wept into Phila's hair, she was certain joy would never touch her life again.

The mournful sound of a flute floated through the street as Briseis led the woman, garbed in drab colors, bare armed and bared necked, through the lower gate to the royal tombs below the city. She walked mindlessly, one foot in front of the other, a veiled shade passing over land. The scent of Phila's skin, washed with rose water and anointed with frankincense oil, still filled her nostrils. It had been an agony washing her cold, small body in preparation for burial. With every stroke of the damp cloth, memories had flooded her heart. When Phila's body lay for a day of viewing, Briseis barely left her side. No food passed her lips. No wine. Nothing. Everything tasted foul and bitter. The bare spot on her head where she'd pulled out a tuft of hair in her grief throbbed beneath her veil. She rubbed at the tender wound without flinching. *How will I remember her in days to come?* Briseis stumbled on a rock.

Shavash caught her daughter's hand, keeping her from falling completely to the ground. She pulled Briseis to her side, kissing her cheek through the black veil. "We'll get through this, my lovely girl."

"I'll never get through this," Briseis whispered hoarsely. "Not even if I lived an immortal life."

Shavash patted her daughter's hand in hers. "There are no words of comfort." The two women, mother and daughter, walked on in silence with the mourning singers trailing behind them like the delicate train of a gown. Their voices cracked the air with songs of sorrow.

Ahead of the women and the litter carrying Phila's body, the grandfathers and father of the princess rode their horses. Their armor glinted in the morning light of Apollo. The procession crawled over the narrow road, leading to the tomb of Mynes' family. The late morning stretched to mid-day when the procession finally stopped. Servants rushed to move the stone blocking entry to the burial chamber. Then, one by one, they moved the funerary gifts inside.

Mynes took Briseis' hand, and together they disappeared first into the dark opening, followed by the rest of the family. Walking by torchlight, they passed skeletal remains of long dead ancestors.

Briseis choked on the putrid smell of death. Panicking, she gripped Mynes' arm. "We can't leave her here. In this place."

Mynes took her hand in his. "We must, Briseis."

"It's dreadful. It frightens me."

"It's not a place for the living. We trespass only because we must."

When they came to the slab where Phila lay, Briseis wept as the household servants set bowls of carnelian, amethyst, and golden beads around her daughter. A simple wreath of laurel leaves hammered out of gold circled Phila's brow. The flickering light cast an ethereal glow over Phila's pale skin.

"She almost looks alive," Shavash said, quietly.

"My sweet, sweet girl," Briseis mumbled, miserably.

Mynes put an arm around his wife. "We will have others. In time, we will find joy again."

Briseis stiffened in his arms. "I can't imagine that at all." She looked into her husband's eyes in the dim light and saw the confusion and hurt there. "Perhaps, in time." But, in that moment, her love for Mynes diminished ever so slightly. He was a prince, handsome in face, and brave. But, he'd never understand what she'd lost as a mother. Nothing replaces the joy of a daughter's gift of love. Phila loved her unconditionally, not because of gold or position, but because she was simply her mother. She was Briseis' whole world, and she'd lost it forever.

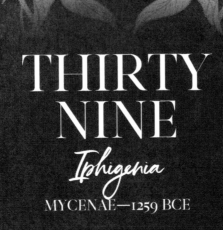

THIRTY NINE

Iphigenia

MYCENAE—1259 BCE

Agamemnon sucked the sweet juice from a stalk of a yellow field flower. "Here, Iphigenia, try this one." He handed a freshly picked flower to his daughter, as they walked along the shaded path.

Iphigenia stopped short of putting the stem in her mouth. "Is it good?"

The king laughed. "Would I make you taste something bitter?"

"No, I don't think so."

"Go on, then. Chew the stem first."

Iphigenia bit the slender stalk, crunching it between her new front teeth. The sweet nectar touched her tongue. "You're right, Father." She sucked at the stalk. "How have I never tasted this before?"

Agamemnon took his eldest daughter's hand in his own. "It's a soldier's secret. When there's no food to eat, you can find fields of these almost anywhere. It's better than starving."

"I see."

"Do you know why I like them so much?"

"Because they're sweet?"

"No." He bent to pluck another flower, snapping the stem shorter, and placed it behind Iphigenia's ear. "Because yellow is the perfect color for my perfect girl."

Iphigenia beamed under Agamemnon's compliment, and hugged his hairy arm to her cheek. "You are the best father."

Agamemnon knew his core was brutal and vicious, far from perfect, but this little girl had carved out a space in his heart where only darkness had dwelt. "When I married your mother, I hoped she'd give me a son."

Iphigenia's smile faded and her shoulders slumped. "All fathers wish for sons before daughters. We aren't very important, especially to kings."

Lifting Iphigenia up in his arms, Agamemnon's heavy beard scratched her smooth chin. "But, when the midwife laid you in my arms, I forgot all about sons and princes. Because of you, I fell in love with your mother."

Iphigenia's smile returned, brighter than before. "So, truly, you love me, too?"

The Great King rubbed his nose to his daughter's. "I loved you first." He set her down. "Come, let's return home."

"Can I pick more flowers before we go?"

"Certainly." He watched his daughter carefully selecting certain stalks, passing over others. *One day, I'll make her a marriage to bring her glory. A mighty warrior with a mighty heart. A kingdom to rule as queen. Nothing less for my sweet Iphigenia.*

FORTY

Thetis' plea

MOUNT PELION—1257 BCE

Achilles crept in the dark along the edge of the field. He piled stocks of dried wheat, and then pulled the flint from a small leather pouch on his waist. The dried wheat smoked and turned red with tender flames. Pleased with himself, he smiled and piled more dry stacks and twigs on the growing fire. A gentle breeze swirled tiny glowing embers into the air. Achilles added more fuel to his fire. The breeze stiffened, blowing larger embers higher and farther than before.

Another breeze whipped a flame far into the tall parched stalks of an adjoining field. He blinked and the far field was a flame. Achilles panicked and ran. He ran into the forest and back up the mountain to the safety of Chiron's cave hall.

"Where have you been, young Master?" his teacher asked, pawing the ground impatiently.

"Wandering."

"With soot on your face? You reek of smoke."

"I built a fire to keep warm."

Chiron set his scroll down, considering Achilles with all his attention. "What have you done this time?"

"Nothing."

"Achilles, we've been at this game before. I know that sheepish look about you. Answer me truthfully."

Achilles exhaled, hanging his head in defeat. "I think I caught a farm on fire."

"You think? You're impossible, Achilles." Chiron twitched his tail. "I've taught you all I can. You're unwilling to learn more. You're impetuous. I'm sending you back to Phthia and Peleus, before all my coat falls out."

"Apologies, Chiron. I was only—"

"What you always do. I'll hear no more. You've done quite enough for one day."

PHTHIA
PALACE OF PELEUS

"Achilles!" Phoenix yelled. "Achilles!" Phoenix grabbed a nervous servant by the sleeve. "Where is he? I know you've seen him."

"Master, I … I—"

"Spit it out, man!" Phoenix was in no mood to be chasing after Achilles again.

"He's to the stables, my lord."

Phoenix released the man who scurried off and out of sight. "I should beat that boy," he mumbled to himself.

"You'd first have to catch him. And that, dear friend, would be near impossible as far as I can tell," Peleus said.

Startled, Phoenix turned his head. He'd no wish for Peleus to think him inept at his duty, but the present circumstance only revealed his fear, the truth. "Surely, *you* can compel him to his studies."

"I've been at war enough times to recognize a losing battle. Achilles will do as he pleases. If Chiron can't curb his will, then we certainly will not," Peleus said.

"As young men, we obeyed our fathers without question. Our tutors."

"Achilles is not entirely mortal. His will is stronger than most. Obedience is not everything. As men, we throw off the word, except to the gods make our obeisance."

The nervous servant reentered the chamber.

"What is it now?" the king asked.

"A man, my lord. He c-claims … h-he claims …" he stammered.

Peleus looked him in the eye, reading the fear. He put his hands on his hips, tilting his head back in disbelief. "How old was his daughter?"

"Widowed," the servant answered.

"He chooses the older ones every time." Peleus looked to his friend. "Why is it that with age we desire the slender flesh of youth, tender breasts that have never milked a child … and he, strapping youth, who causes any female in his wake to wet her thighs, chooses the older women weighed down by children and sagging breasts?"

Phoenix laughed. "We're old. That's your answer. The young ones lay beneath us quietly. Let us heave our business and roll away. The older ones are more … vigorous."

Peleus addressed the servant. "What does the man ask for in compensation? Does his daughter make complaint?"

"No, my lord … sh-she claims—" he stammered again.

"Out! Out with it!"

"She claims she carries his child," the words tumbled out, as the servant shrank back in fear of being beaten for bringing such unwanted news.

Phoenix laughed out loud. "Peleus! Maybe you *should* send him back to Chiron."

"I can't have a fucking peasant woman wandering around the city claiming to carry the child of Achilles. Agamemnon won't stand for bastards running around threatening his daughter's legitimate heirs," Peleus roared in frustration. "I'll send her away. Far away. Her entire fucking family will have to be sent. I'll have to compensate them for their trouble and their silence, of course."

"My lord, there's more."

"What more can there be? What could be worse than this shit?"

"Thetis has arrived and asks audience." The nervous servant, already on his knees, hunched like a turtle, backed up even more. Peleus' wrath was legend among the servants and the slaves.

"Thetis?" he asked. "Thetis." His eyes narrowed to angry slits. "That bitch dares to step on these grounds after what she did?"

"She'll not be moved, my lord."

"Of course she will not be moved."

"She says she has urgent news regarding your son."

The king acquiesced. Where his son was concerned, he would hear her. Achilles was a weakness of sorts for him. He loved the boy. "Grant her audience."

Within moments, Thetis appeared in the hall. Long years had passed since he'd seen her. She stood silently waiting for his greeting.

"You have not changed with the years," he finally said. Her beauty had power over him still, and until this moment, he hadn't realized it.

"You have more silver in your hair than I recall," Thetis replied.

"Always the observant one."

"It's a gift."

"You didn't leave your pond to spar words with me. What do you want?" Peleus asked, his annoyance audible beneath the calm.

"Achilles has returned from Chiron's protection?"

"I should've guessed the reason. You wish to see the child you so carelessly tossed in a fire? Or have you forgotten you tried to kill my son?"

Thetis took several steps toward Peleus. "Is that what you think of me, truly? That I would bring harm to my only son? My only child? *Our* only child?"

Phoenix cleared his throat. "I'll take my leave, friend. You've family matters to attend to."

"No. Don't leave. This nymph will be gone momentarily."

"Peleus, my dear husband. Will you not hear me out after all of these years?"

The king considered her request, as her beauty began its intoxicating effect on him. *She left me to my own decisions regarding the boy*, he reasoned. "Speak, then."

"Those long years passed, when Achilles was new in the world. I was filled with great joy." Thetis took several more steps toward Peleus. "I'd never known more sweetness in all of my days than the day he first suckled at my breast." The nymph pressed closer to the king. "I loved him."

Peleus gruffly responded, "What of it?"

Thetis smiled disarmingly. "I was trying to protect him, Peleus. Achilles' birth came with a price."

The king recalled Chiron's warning that Achilles would be greater than his father, but he failed to see the connection. "What do you mean 'a price'?"

"A prophecy had been revealed to me."

"Nymph, you're trying my patience." Peleus crossed his heavy arms across his broad chest, building a wall between them. He was determined that she wouldn't move him.

Thetis reached a slender hand out, touching his arm. "Peleus." She came closer. "Husband."

The king shifted his feet. He grumbled, "Speak already. What do you know?"

"Our son will die in battle."

"Your words bring no revelation. Warriors die in battle."

"He will die in battle against the Trojans ... and he will die young."

"No state quarrels with Troy. Who'd dare attack the Great Walled City? It is impregnable. Your oracle lies."

"It's true. The war has not come, but it will. And with it, we will lose our son. There will be none to take your place as king in Phthia."

Peleus ran his fingers over his lips. He thought of the bastard grandchild he was exiling. *True, there will be no heir worthy enough to succeed me.* "I considered he'd die in battle perhaps when he was a man with wife ... and children." He stabbed Phoenix with a warning glance to keep his silence. "You've come with some remedy?"

"May I explain what you saw years ago? That now it may make some sense to you?"

Peleus relaxed his shoulders slightly, his guard dipping lower.

Thetis squeezed his forearm slightly. "Achilles has a choice to make regarding Troy. If he goes, he'll die. If he stays, he'll live to be an old man."

"Again, nymph, your words offer no revelation. It's hard to die in a battle if you're not in it."

"You misunderstand, Peleus. If he goes to war, he will die but his fame and glory will be infinite. Songs will be sung. Stories will be told. He will be equal to the gods by immortality of his deeds. He'll make this choice and you know it. He's been trained to make this choice. Yet, it will leave you without a son and future king."

The king nodded. "I agree. He'll choose war. He won't believe that he'll die a young man. No one has bested him in practice. He'll not foresee that anyone could. Besides, the young never think of death."

"We agree then. He won't believe our warning. It's why I was preparing him for immortality as a babe."

Peleus whipped his head toward Thetis. "What? What are you talking about?"

"I was burning him, preparing him with ambrosia invoking his immortal blood as protection against this very fate. If he'd become immortal, it wouldn't matter if he went to war or not. My son ... *our* son would live."

"Thetis, you know it's impossible to outwit the Fates. We're all doomed by those harsh goddesses."

"But he has a choice, Peleus. It's a rare gift. One that most mortals don't receive. Keep him from Troy and he'll live."

"How do we do that?"

"Send him to Skyros."

FORTY ONE

a son for Paris

TROY—1257 BCE

P aris cradled the tiny baby in his arms. "I'd all but given up hope we'd have a child."

"Our son," Oenone said. "He's beautiful, isn't he?"

"Yes. Smaller than I imagined. Much smaller than the calves."

The nymph laughed softly. "Much smaller than a calf. He carries your blood, my love. Dark curls already."

Paris gently thumbed his newborn son's chin. "The dip. I didn't realize it such a prominent feature."

"A handsome one," Oenone sighed, contentment coursing through her at the sight of her husband and child together.

"What shall we call him?"

"Corythus," Oenone replied.

"A good, strong name." Paris tucked the edge of the swaddling cloth under his son's tiny dimpled chin. "Someday, you'll see the world from atop the Great Wall. You'll see the land of your father and grandfathers. It's a sight, little one."

"You're not going to take him from me, are you?" Fear rose in Oenone's heart like a dark cloud. "You can't take him from me."

Paris returned the squirming child to his mother. "Peace, Oenone. He belongs with you. But someday he'll see the palace and the world of Troy."

Oenone opened her chiton so Corythus could take her breast. "Paris, I've seen an awful image in my mind."

"What was it?"

"I'm afraid to speak it aloud. It's all smoke and fire."

"Tell me. I'm not afraid to hear it," Paris said.

A silver tear slid from Oenone's eye, turning to crystal as it fell. "A great warrior is coming to Troy. He'll carry a sacred spear of Pelian ash. And he'll lay your city to dust."

"You sound like Cassandra with all of her ill tidings. No one can bring Troy to its knees. The city is well guarded. Fortified by a wall built by the gods themselves. Our Hittite allies and all of the other cities stand behind us."

The smell of smoke filled her nostrils. She knew the end would bring more pain than she could bear ... than any survivors could bear. Knowing, also, that her beloved would forsake her before the end stole the joy she should be having. But that knowledge she held close to her chest, like her son, fearful that should she unleash the words a storm might sweep her away in its misery. Oenone pushed the dreadful image of Troy in ruin aside, forcing her vision into the deepest, darkest part of her mind. *Maybe I'm wrong. I pray to the gods that I'm wrong.*

She watched as Paris kissed his son's little hand with his fingers wrapped around his father's thumb. *Oh, my father, let me be wrong.*

FORTY TWO

talk of bastards

"It's time we find you a wife," Agamemnon said, casually stuffing a chunk of roasted lamb in his mouth. The greasy fat dripped into his thick beard. He wiped the back of his hand across his lips. "You can't keep bedding all of my slave women."

Clytemnestra sipped her wine. "One of them is ... with *child*." The queen enjoyed watching her brother-in-law squirm in his chair. "Unless you're prepared for a brood of bastards, you might consider my husband's advice."

Orestes, who'd been content to push his food around his plate, perked up. "What's a bastard?"

Iphigenia kicked him under the table.

"Mother, Iphigenia is kicking me."

Clytemnestra silenced their bickering by raising an eyebrow.

"Which slave claims I've fathered her child?" Menelaus' face reddened in his defense.

"The one with flaxen hair. Last week, she vomited into a basket, when she was selecting my wardrobe. When it happened a second time, I demanded she tell me who'd fathered the child she was carrying. The fear in her eyes told me all I needed to know. I set a watch on you."

Menelaus shouted, "You overstep your place!"

The queen leaned back in her chair. Glancing at Agamemnon, then back to her brother-in-law, she said, "You believe I would do such a thing without first consulting my husband?"

Menelaus glared at her.

The queen pressed her point. "Can you deny you've visited Fabia—her name is Fabia, in case you didn't know—every evening since you've been a guest in our home?"

"I'm not a *guest*. I'm *family*."

"You're skirting the question, brother. Answer it."

Scowling, Menelaus pushed his plate away. "I'm entitled to seek my pleasure."

The king's cold laughter echoed across the hall. "Entitled? Entitled to *what*? Breed your bastards under my roof?

"The slave makes a claim. What of it? She lies."

Clytemnestra leaned forward. Eyes shining like polished onyx, her lovely mouth curled in a wicked grin. "Fabia's protruding belly is *no* claim, Menelaus. It's truth. Do you need to wait until my halls are filled with red-haired bastards to believe?"

Orestes plucked an apple from a platter of fruit. "Am I to have a cousin, Uncle Menelaus?"

Iphigenia slapped her brother's arm. "No."

"Ouch," Orestes hissed. "Stop it."

Clytemnestra shook her head. "Even your niece understands the … delicate situation you've placed our family in."

Menelaus blustered. "But, I-I couldn't have—"

Agamemnon slammed a hand on the table, jolting everyone to silence. "My slaves are wise enough to know they don't breed with each other without my permission. I control how many people this household can sustain. You took your pleasure and spilled your seed. Now, she's with child."

"What do you want me to do about it?" Menelaus asked.

"That's exactly the point, isn't it? What *are* you going to do about it? You've no land of your own. I'll have to send her away. At great loss to me. You know full well the dangers of illegitimate children."

Menelaus' shoulders slumped. He let out an exasperated sigh. "Only too well."

Agamemnon drained his cup of wine. "As I said, it's time we find you a wife."

Sitting next to Clytemnestra, little Elektra yawned. The queen scooped her daughter into her arms. "Elektra is tired. It's late. I'm going to take her to bed."

Agamemnon smiled slyly. "Send for her nurse."

"I'd rather see to her myself."

"As you wish. Perhaps, I will visit you later, wife."

As Clytemnestra left the hall with Elektra in her arms, she almost laughed to herself. *Men are easily led to conclusions they believe are their own, if you feed their hungry cocks.*

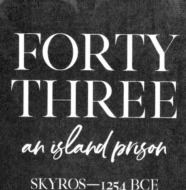

FORTY THREE

an island prison

Achilles dug his heels into the sides of his horse, spurring him on through the surf. The beast's heavy hooves pounded into the wet sand and its silver mane whipped across Achilles' face as he leaned over its powerful neck. The moon lit a narrow rippled path across the water like an arrow aimed at the dark horizon. A cloudless sky passed over rider and horse as the darkness grew. Since arriving in Skyros years ago, he's been forced to hide among the women, wearing women's clothing as a guise keeping his existence a secret from the outside world. His mother had insisted, she'd wept, and she'd begged him to do her bidding without question. He'd obeyed. Riding under night's cloak was the only time Achilles could cast the falsehood aside without breaking his oath to his mother.

He rode until he came to a cave partially hidden by an outcropping of rocks along the shore. The horse knew the way into the cavern without prodding. Achilles dismounted into the soft sand.

"Easy." After wrapping the reigns around a tall standing rock, he pulled a bright red apple from his side pouch. "Your favorite." The horse nipped at the fruit before grabbing it between its teeth. Achilles scratched his mount between the eyes.

Achilles stretched his back and shoulders. "Time to put muscle and bone to use, Melias." The horse stomped a hoof. He retrieved his sword and shield from their hiding place. The practice weapons were not of good quality, but heavy enough to train with while he waited for his mother to release him from this prison. He never expected to be in Skyros this long. The years had dragged on and now he found himself itching for a reason to leave. Most days he thought of little else. Hefting the shield on his left arm, he picked up the sword with the right and sliced the blade through the air at an imagined foe. He danced with imagined enemies until his skin glistened with sweat and his blood pounded in his ears. The night stretched to almost morning before he rested.

"Truth, Melias … I long for war. What good is all of this practice if there is no war? What adventure is here in Skyros? None."

The horse shook its mane.

"You're right. There's Deidamia. She's been pleasant enough. Beautiful." Achilles grinned, slapping his thigh. "And she's willing." From his seat on a rock, he watched the sky push from purple to pale watered wine. "Time to return to the palace."

After replacing the weapons in their hiding spot, he mounted his horse. Melias shook his neck nervously. Achilles placed a steady hand on his stead's wide neck. "Calm, boy, calm."

A light sea mist floated into the cave and Melias stomped his hooves, forcing Achilles to look down. The sandy floor of the cave was now covered with a thin layer of water. "Mother?"

Thetis rose up from the mist. "Yes, it's me."

Achilles dismounted and warmly embraced his mother.

"I've missed you, Achilles."

"And I, you," he said.

"How do you fare, here, in Skyros? In the court? All is well?" Theists asked, smoothing a stray lock of hair from his face.

"I'm well, Mother. Life at court is … boring, but I suspect you know that already. Is it time to leave this place? My hands itch for real opponents. Battle! It's time to tell me why I must hide who I am."

The goddess took in her son's massive frame. "It must be difficult to hide your form beneath the folds of a woman's gown."

Achilles laughed. "I'm told I make a most fetching woman."

Thetis sighed deeply. "Oh, my sweet son. How do I tell you why you're here? I fear I know your decision even before I've voiced the alternative fates you've been given."

"Mother, you must tell me. I can't stay on this island much longer. The very air suffocates me."

The nymph's eyes glistened with tears. "Then, I'll speak. You were born with a dual nature. The blood of immortals and mortals flows through you. Because of this, you've been granted a rare choice … to steer the direction of your star." Thetis watched Achilles' eye narrow and his brow wrinkle. "In the days to come, the Greeks will bring war to the Great Wall of Troy. It's there that death will claim you. You'll not return to the house of your father."

"Is this war to happen in my old age? Dying an old man swinging my sword … I can think of no better way to end my days."

"No, Achilles. The war is not far away. It's why I've hidden you from the world. I've no wish for death to swallow up your youth."

"That's a dark premonition indeed," Achilles said. "To die young and have wasted years here, on this island? That's a cruel trick to play with my life."

"There's more. Your early death will bring you great renown. Your glory will have no end."

"The silver beneath the dark. But you spoke of two fates."

The goddess touched his shoulder. "If you stay, refuse to go to war, you'll live a long life. Longer than any mortal because my blood runs through you. You'll prosper and fall into obscurity, as is the fate of all mortals. To be forgotten when memory fades."

"Obscurity," Achilles muttered the word. "A darker fate than early death."

"I only ask that you not make the choice in haste, for once you begin down either path you set your destiny in motion. There can be no going back."

Achilles nodded his understanding. "I promise to consider all."

"That is all I can ask," the goddess said. "I must go. The sea calls me home."

"Mother?"

"Yes?"

"Will you ever return to him? Peleus, I mean?"

She smiled, but gave no answer before disappearing into the rising fog.

Achilles remounted his steed. Together, he and Melias flew above the cold surf crashing on the shore, splashing sea and sand behind them.

"Play the song again, Achilles," Deidamia pleaded. "It was beautiful."

"If you wish." He leaned over the pillow. "Kiss me first."

Deidamia turned her face from her lover. "You ask that of all of my sisters."

"What? You know I love you, don't you?"

"You address them all with similar affection. You don't truly love me."

Achilles wrinkled his nose. "With you it's from my heart."

The princess looked up at him through thick dark lashes, her eyes moist with unshed tears. "Do you speak sincerely?"

Achilles knew a part of him meant the words, but the wildness pulsing through his veins cried out for freedom and blood and bronze. He recalled Chiron's words that one day he'd ride his father's immortal steeds, Xanthus and Balius, into battle sacking cities and cutting his enemies low. He realized this must be the war with Troy his mother warned him about. Domestic life had no hold over him, yet an early death wasn't a desirable option either. But to fall into obscurity meant his name would be forgotten and no deed accomplished by his own hand would be worthy of mention. That was unacceptable. *I must be more than an old man with children circling my knees.*

Achilles looked into Deidamia's face and wasn't sure he'd ever love just one woman. He loved them all too much. Peleus had often chastised him for doing so. He certainly couldn't remain in Skyros forever. "I mean the words as much as I can."

Deidamia's smile fell from her face. Her tears spilled down her cheeks.

"You know I'm here only until I am released by my mother."

"I know. I'd hoped … that you'd stay."

"Nothing can keep me here forever," he said.

"What if you had family … here, in Skyros?" Deidamia asked shyly.

"I've no family here. I've already spent too many years from my rightful home. I long to fight real battles. Go to war. One day I'll follow my father and rule Phthia. Who'd respect me if I'm untried at warfare?"

"But, what if you did? Have family, I mean," she asked again.

"My father would never leave Phthia. My mother would not be confined within walls when the water is her true home. And I've no children."

Deidamia's cheeks flamed. "You will," she whispered.

Achilles sat back. "You're with child?"

The words fairly choked her. "Yes. I'm carrying your child."

He hadn't expected this but realized, now, that he should have. "Have you told your father?"

"No."

"We'll tell him together then." His honor would allow nothing less.

Deidamia flung her arms around his neck and cried. "Gratitude, Achilles. I thought you might be displeased. Cast me aside. Not want me, or our child."

He pulled her close to comfort her. "All will be fine, Deidamia. It'll be fine." He spoke the words to comfort himself, as much as her. His mother's warning still swam about his head.

Achilles watched king Lycomedes pacing in front of his grand chair like a caged lion. He feared no physical reprisal from him, but he had concern for Deidamia. He'd taken the princess without the king's consent or knowledge, producing a child. Achilles knew he'd violated the sacred understanding of hospitality granted him in Skyros.

The king finally spoke. "I granted your mother's and your father's wish to secret you away among my family … to hide you among the very treasures I hold dearest. And you repay my kindness by stealing my daughter's virtue?"

"I've no excuse for my actions under your hospitality. I offer my apology."

"You should beg my forgiveness before you feel the weight of my blade on your neck."

"Death would be too harsh a punishment for a son of Peleus."

"You threaten me with your father's name? Isn't that a noble move!" Lycomedes laughed out loud. "You disrespect me, and then have nerve to threaten me?"

"I meant only that death would be too harsh a punishment. I took your daughter out of love."

Lycomedes stopped his pacing. "What are you proposing, Achilles? Marriage? Marriage without your father's consent? Now, that would be an offense I've no inclination of explaining at the point of a blade. Everyone knows you're promised to the daughter of Agamemnon."

"My father would be more outraged by my death, and more accepting of an alternate marriage. He'll be pleased with both my choice of bride and the child."

Lycomedes considered Achilles' words, his sincerity. "How many summers do you have?"

"Seventeen, my lord."

The king crossed his arms over his belly. "You're young for a husband. I would've preferred an older, wiser man for my daughter. The deed is done, however." He resumed pacing. "Fine, we shall have a wedding. This very night, we shall have a wedding."

"So be it," Achilles said. His mother's words echoed in the back of his mind. *If I take her to wife, am I consigning myself to a life of nothingness? No glory?* He worried that this marriage could set in motion a fate he didn't truly want. But, if he refused to marry the princess, he just might meet an earlier death than prophesied.

The king clapped his hands. A thin servant woman appeared. "Fetch Deidamia to me. At once." The servant disappeared. "Off with you, Achilles. I've much to do."

"My lord." Achilles nodded. "I'll see you when I come to claim my wife." With that, the Golden Warrior departed, lost in his own concern for the future.

FORTY FOUR

a bride for Theseus

SPARTA—1254 BCE

Theseus spied the girl dancing in the temple of Artemis. Rumors of the beauty and grace of Tyndareus' youngest daughter had spread far beyond the kingdom of Sparta. It was widely whispered that Tyndareus was not the girl's father, that Zeus himself had sired her. Now that he'd seen her with his own eyes, he'd no doubt that this lovely creature carried immortal blood. Everything about her moved as perfection. Her hands and arms graceful, her golden hair hung loosely to her hips, her bare feet stepping to the music moved with unnatural grace. His loins stirred with heated desire. *I must have her. I deserve her after all of the shit the gods have put me through.* It galled him that as king of Athens he hadn't a proper queen, and now, seeing Helen with his own eyes, he knew he'd steal her for his queen, if he must. *I It's honorable*, he reasoned, *to steal a bride ... especially one whose father was surely Zeus.*

"Well, what do you think?" Pirithous asked.

"That I have found my wife. None is as fair as that Helen."

Pirithous shook his head. "You're an old man. She's barely on the edge of womanhood by the glance. Why not chose the elder girl there?"

"I want who I want." Theseus narrowed his eyes at his friend. "And this is fine talk from a man who wishes Persephone as a bride. You imagine sneaking off with her an easier task?"

"You've a plan, then?"

Theseus was already plotting strategy. "Tyndareus will follow hospitality. He'll invite us to dine and sleep in the palace as his guests. We must make certain he drinks plenty of wine."

"Easily done, if the rumors of his wine stores are true. Where will you take her? You can't settle her in Athens."

"My mother's house in Aphidnae will be safe enough," Theseus said.

"It's settled. A daughter of Zeus for us both."

"Sit! Let us eat and drink until we fall on our faces!" Tyndareus laughed, as he welcomed his guests with a feast fit for kings. Lamp light and torches burned brilliantly in the dimming light of day. Mounds of meat and cheese filled platters on long tables. Amphorae of wine had been brought up from cool cellars and stood ready like infantry to attack the guests with merriment and forgetfulness. "You remember my sons, Pollux and Castor?"

"They've grown to men since last I saw them," Theseus answered.

By the balls of Zeus! They're warriors. Sweat pricked the back of his neck, trickling down the center of his back. He and Pirithous would have to stay clear of them for they most certainly kept watchful eyes upon their sister. "Lady Leda, it is an honor to be in your presence once again." Theseus purposefully ignored Helen, although her beauty stung his peripheral sight.

"Has it been so long, Lord Theseus?"

"It has."

Queen Leda sipped her wine. "I hear you've been an adventurer of late."

"There have been many stories, my lady. Best you … believe them all." Theseus' eyes twinkled, recalling his mischief and mayhem.

The queen nodded knowingly. "I'm certain I shall. Perhaps, our singer will regale us with a poem or two about the great King Theseus."

"I've no need to call attention to my deeds. I'm afraid not all are pleased to hear the tales."

Pirithous chimed in, "No they're not. Those—"

"Enough … storytelling on my account," Theseus interrupted. If he was to succeed tonight, it was better that his hosts not think of him as a threat.

The queen nodded. "As you wish, but we require some entertainment." The musicians played and the small company lost itself in drink and song.

Helen and her maid walked through the courtyard talking quietly, their shoulders occasionally bumping together as they whispered. Theseus and his accomplice spied the pair from behind manicured shrubs and an oversized potted olive tree. As the girls came closer, Pirithous reached for his dagger. Theseus grabbed Pirithous' hand, shoving it down. "Not now, you idiot!" he spat between clenched teeth. "They haven't seen us."

"It's only a precaution," Pirithous whispered angrily. "You remember what happened last—"

"If you speak again, I swear by the balls of Zeus I'll kill you myself."

Helen and her maid were about to pass into the darkness edging the courtyard, when the spies startled them from behind. Theseus seized Helen, stifling her cry for help with a heavy hand over her mouth. The princess struggled against the iron grip around her waist, but she was no match for her attacker's strength.

"Easy, girl. I'll bring no harm to you," Theseus whispered against her ear.

Helen tried in vain to pull her body free, but the man held her hard against his chest. She bit the side of his hand covering her mouth, but her attacker didn't flinch. Within moments, her body heaved in exhaustion and she ceased her muffled cries.

"I won't harm you or your family if you come away without calling attention to yourself. If you scream and bring the guards or your twin brothers, I swear by Zeus I'll slit your family's throats one by one. Do you understand?"

Helen peered into the visage shrouded by cloak and cover of night. "King Theseus? Is that you?" she asked, honeyed innocence dripping from every word. Her captor tightened his iron grip around her waist, until she couldn't find her breath and the world swam before her.

Helen slumped in Theseus' arms, while the maidservant still struggled against Pirithous. The Athenian king hefted Helen under an arm, took two heavy steps toward his accomplice, and then clobbered the girl behind her head with his free hand. She slid quietly from Pirithous' hold to a messy heap on the ground.

"I could've done that," Pirithous said.

"What were you waiting for?"

"Nothing." Pirithous shook his head. "No dagger. Use a dagger. Kill. Not yet. Make up your fucking mind, Theseus. You change it like a woman changes hers upon dressing."

"Shut your mouth, Pirithous. Did you make the ship ready? Keep it secret?"

"Aye, captain, I did," Pirithous mocked his friend. "We need to move before the guards realize something's amiss, or her damn brothers come after us."

The two kidnappers ran into the darkness with their captive. Helen's limp body jostled roughly as Theseus dodged low hanging tree limbs and thick brush. He feared she'd wake, but couldn't slow his pace. They mounted the horses where Theseus laid the yet unmoving Helen across the beast's back. He dug his heels into the horse's ribs and into the night they flew at breakneck speed toward the ship that would wing them all the way to Athens where they'd be forced to travel by road to safety in Aphidnae and his mother to the north.

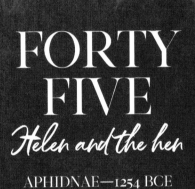

FORTY
FIVE
Helen and the hen

APHIDNAE—1254 BCE

Aethra shook her head in disbelief, half mortified and half impressed with her son. "A daughter of Sparta, you say? That's quite a feat."

"A daughter of Zeus."

"Even more impressive."

"She's captive for now. Bride soon enough," said Theseus.

"By the look of her, she should bleed soon."

"And when she does, I'll take what I am owed by the gods! She must remain hidden until then. If her family discovers her here …" He stepped closer to his mother. "They'll raze the city to the ground. No one will be safe."

Aethra's eyes widened. "Aren't you returning to Athens? Haven't you been absent long enough? Had adventure enough?"

"You may be mother to me, but you've no right to pelt me with questions," Theseus replied sharply.

"My concern is only for my son. For Athens."

"I've a promise to keep on Pirithous' account. His sight's set on even more deadly prey than this slip of a girl."

"Who's more challenging than this creature?" Aethra asked.

Moving closer still, Theseus pressed his lips to her ear. "The wife of Hades."

His mother gasped. "How does he expect to pluck a prisoner of the Underworld right from under the god's nose?"

"We've not yet considered all aspects."

"You don't have a plan? A strategy?" Aethra stepped back into a chair and collapsed. "Truly you must cease all of this trespassing across the world. There are consequences for disrupting the course of the things, for trying to dislodge what is, for what you desire."

"Mother, you worry needlessly. We'll distract Hades and pull Persephone back to the world she belongs to."

"So many things can go wrong. If he catches you. If you fail to convince her. Make no mistake, Hades will kill you both, or worse."

"Perhaps. Perhaps not. Have you considered that mayhap Hades is tired of a woman nagging him through the course of the day?"

"There are times it pains me to listen to your thoughts. These misguided notions of yours will be your demise. Mark my words."

Theseus kissed his mother's cheek. "There is nothing to worry about."

"There's always something to worry about. Life isn't so easy. The gods see to that."

"Take care of the girl until I return. She can help you with the chores."

Aethra laughed. "Unlikely. I doubt the girl's ever seen the inside of a cooking pot."

"Mother," Theseus chided.

"I jest, my son. Yes, yes I'll keep her under watchful eye. If that's what you desire."

"It is."

"Consider it done, then." Aethra approached the girl. "Come, child. You have no need to fear me." She extended her hand to Helen. She watched as the captive bride looked from the ground to her outstretched palm. Helen's glare revealed defiance, not fear.

"Where do you take me?" Helen asked cautiously.

"To a bath. You reek of sweat and horse."

In the morning, Helen woke in a strange bed tangled in linen. She propped herself up and surveyed the room. She expected the mother of a king to be well-tended, and was surprised to find she lived modestly rather than lavishly. Theseus' mother was still asleep in the larger bed across the room, so Helen quietly slipped out of hers. She walked to the window and looked out on mountains and hills that seemed familiar, yet she knew they were foreign to her. *Please, Aphrodite, help me. Artemis guard me. Athena defend me.* Helen wiped her finger across the window's narrow ledge and wrinkled her nose at the fine dust and dirt that stuck to her skin. "She needs a maid servant."

"That's what you're for, young miss," said a voice behind her.

Helen's back stiffened. To be made queen unwillingly was one thing, but to be made to serve this old hag was quite another. "I'm afraid I'll disappoint you, mother of Theseus the kidnapper." Helen's venom sounded sweet enough, but the words struck their mark as she intended.

The old woman flew across the room faster than Helen had anticipated and stood over her with hand raised to strike her insolence.

"Your speed belies your age, old woman," Helen laughed. "You'd do best not to strike a princess of Sparta."

"You're nobody here in this house except my maid servant. You'd do best to keep your wicked little tongue inside of your mouth."

Helen smiled. "I believe I'll speak as I wish. Lay a hand to me and—"

Aethra swiped a heavy hand across Helen's cheek. "And what will you do? You best learn your place."

Helen stood amazed that the old woman had nerve enough to actually land the strike, and was surprised at the sting, but remained unmoved and undeterred. She seethed at the rough treatment and it hardened her resolve to stay strong and not give in to these cretins of Athens. She knew her father and brothers would be searching for her and would eventually find her.

"Get to the kitchen. I'll show you how to prepare the morning meal."

"I don't cook."

"You will if you intend to eat, girl."

"Helen. My name is Helen."

Aethra grabbed Helen's chin, squeezing her cheeks together so roughly that her mouth contorted and her lips burned. "You'll not utter that name again in this house. When my son gives the order, you'll be claimed. Until then, you remain silent about who you are and where you came from. Or I'll slit your throat myself."

Helen stared hatefully, but nodded understanding. *Aphrodite, grant me vengeance on this old hag.* She followed the old woman to the kitchen.

Aethra handed Helen small basket. "Go gather the eggs."

"Gather eggs?"

"Are you deaf, child?"

"No. I don't know how to gather … eggs." The thought of putting her hands next to filthy hens disgusted her. She shuddered.

"Erika!" Aethra hollered. In moments a middle-aged woman stood in the entryway. "Take this girl out to the hens. See she learns how to gather eggs. If she gives any trouble, you've my permission to hit her. She hasn't quite learned her place."

"Yes, my lady." Erika glanced at Helen with a small measure of compassion. "Let's go, child."

"I'm no child," Helen said tersely.

"Good. You'll learn quickly then. Come." Erika led the way across the court and down a narrow dirt trail to a small field settled with a large wooden hutch. Helen watched as a few hens pecked the hard ground while others nestled quietly in the grass. Brown and mottled hens flapped about and in and out of the hutch.

"Where do they put their eggs?" Helen asked.

Erika laughed. "They don't put them anywhere. They lay them." She pointed to the hutch. "There, or sometimes they nest about in the field if they feel safe enough."

"That should make gathering their eggs easy."

"Mostly. Strange you haven't knowledge of a farm."

"True, I don't."

"You've been a household slave then?" Erika asked pleasantly.

Helen glared at the maid. "I've never been a slave to anyone."

Erika shrugged. "Well, young miss, you're now in the service of the queen mother."

Helen spat on the ground. "Yes, I've had taste of her mastery."

"I wouldn't let Lady Aethra hear you speak in that tone. She'll beat you. Mind me now. She'll beat you and have no remorse."

"I'm not afraid of her."

"You should be, young miss," Erika warned. "We'd best gather the eggs. Lady Aethra will want her breakfast soon." Erika entered the hutch carrying the basket. Helen followed on her heel. It was dark and musty.

Helen wrinkled her nose. "It smells of shit and old hay."

"You'll get used to it. Here, watch me." Erika put her hand into a pile of dried hay and pulled three dark brown eggs. "Now, you get that nest there."

Helen put her hand just under the piled straw and pulled an egg out. "There's bird shit on it." Her stomach heaved, and she wiped her fingers on her apron. "I'll never eat another egg as long as I live."

"You're a strange child. Yes, you will, if you're hungry enough."

"I'll never be that hungry."

"How can you be so unfamiliar with— Oh no. Not again."

"What's the matter?" Helen asked, keeping her arms close to her sides.

"That hen there. She's trying to hatch her eggs again."

"That's not her purpose? To hatch eggs by sitting on them? That much I've heard."

"How do you not know about hens? I suppose you know very little about any of this."

"Nothing would be more accurate." Helen leaned too close to

the stubbornly nested hen and it growled and clucked at her. Helen aimed to strike the bird.

"No! Don't!" yelled Erika.

As Helen brought her hand down, the hen flapped its wings at her, growling and pecking at her hand and arm. Helen screeched. All of the hens startled, flapping about in the hutch. Feathers and dust flew. Helen screamed louder and batted at the frantic birds failing to achieve flight. Erika laughed so hard tears streamed down her cheeks. She managed to push Helen from the hutch, still laughing.

"You're a pretty one, even with tangles and feathers in your hair." Erika's wide smile threatened to burst into laughter again.

Helen fumed. "Don't mock me, peasant."

The insult sucked the air from Erika's amusement. "Peasant? I'd be careful, young miss, who I called a peasant in this house." Erika closed the space between them and slapped Helen so hard a red imprint of her hand stained Helen's cheek. "Not all of us began so low."

The slap stung Helen's face and her pride. No one had ever dared strike her in her life, and this made the second time in a single day. She put her hand to her cheek. "Don't ever touch me again."

"Speak no more insults and I'll have no need." Erika turned on her heel and walked back to the main house, leaving Helen standing there to make her own way.

FORTY SIX

Caster and Pollux

ATHENS, KINGDOM OF THESEUS—1254 BCE

An entire moon had passed since Helen disappeared. And now Pollux and Castor, followed by an army of angry Spartans, waited impatiently outside of the city of Athens. Clouds darkened the sky as they looked for the messenger's return.

"Why does the man leave us lingering? They must have an answer by now. It's either yes or no," Pollux said, as he reined his horse in to calm it.

Caster shrugged indifference. "They have much to consider, brother. Either we burn this fucking city to the ground now … or later. They have knowledge of Helen's whereabouts. Of that I'm certain."

"Lies have fallen from every lip trailing Theseus," Pollux added.

"Truth. Why these imbeciles gather behind him astounds me.

Clearly, his youthful glory has passed into a reckless old age."

Pollux pointed toward the road. "Look, there. A rider approaches."

The messenger pulled his horse up at a short distance from the brothers. "I bring you word from the city. Your sister is not within."

"Your response is late. Why not say so from the beginning?" Pollux asked.

"I'm the messenger. It's not my place to answer for the Council."

"And where is your king?" Castor asked.

The messenger squirmed under the questioning. "Theseus has been long absent from Athens."

The brothers consulted each other with their eyes, confirming neither believed a word. Pollux crossed his arms across his armored chest. "That's troublesome news." Urging his mount forward, he added, "We know Theseus took our sister. You leave us very little choice."

"Please, the Council assures you that Helen is not here."

Castor sneered. "You don't have her, you say. You don't know where your king is, you say. What polis doesn't know the whereabouts of its king and commander?"

"If Helen was within, the Council would return her with deepest apology. She's not within. That's all I know."

The brothers looked to each other and nodded.

Pollux raised his eyes to the wide-eyed messenger. "Prepare for war."

The man wasted no time turning his horse and riding off, dirt flying like rain behind his horse.

Castor roared after him, "We'll burn Athens to the ground!"

Pollux shrugged. "We best prepare the men for a short fight."

"No battle is ever short, brother."

Most of Athens lay in a ruin of ash and smoke while the brothers reassembled their army. The Athenian defense was stronger than expected from a bunch of farmers and potters, but no match in the end for Spartans.

Castor wiped the grime and sweat from his eyes. "We should rest for the night. Feed the men."

"Agreed." Pollux twisted on his horse, trying to see his back. "A fucking arrow nicked my shoulder. Can't believe those bastards actually hit me! Fucking Athenians."

"See yourself to the healers. Get that shit cleaned and tended."

"I'll see you after," Pollux said, as he rode off.

Castor made it to his tent and dismounted, handing the reins to a waiting slave. "Make sure the horse is rubbed down properly and fed. We begin again at first light." The slave nodded silently. Stepping through the opening, he glanced at the lavish dinner set on a low table, inhaling the welcomed smell of roasted meat and honeyed fruits. Castor sat down and a serving woman poured his wine. *A full belly and a warm woman to fuck ... a good diversion from the killing I've done this day.*

"You're unknown to me. What do they call you?" Caster asked.

Startled at being addressed directly, the woman spilled the wine on the table. "Apologies, my lord." She quickly wiped the mistake into her apron.

"There's none necessary," he said, as she stepped into the shadows. "You haven't answered my question."

"Reah, my lord."

"Reah. Come into the light." The woman approached cautiously.

Castor caught a glimpse of her form in the corner of his eye. "Come closer." Reah obeyed. "How long have you been in service to my family?"

"Recently, my lord."

Castor stuffed a glazed date in his mouth. "You're not from Sparta? Speak up, woman."

"No."

"Then …"

"I'm from Athens. Newly brought to camp."

Castor nodded, sitting back slightly in his chair. He eyed her, as he would any prize of war. Smiling, he took in the curve of her breasts and hips. *She'll make fine company for me this night.* "It's good you were spared. We won't stop, until our sister is safe in care." The prince returned his attention to his meal.

Reah stood, shifting her weight nervously. "My lord, may I speak?"

"Yes. And pour more wine."

As Reah poured, she said, "There's one man in Athens who might know where your sister has been taken."

Just then the tent flap flew open, as Pollux rushed in. "I'm famished! Look at you, brother. Eating without me!" He sat down heavily on a bench, grabbed a hunk of meat from a platter, took an enormous bite, and spoke with his mouth full. "Tomorrow, we raze what remains of this fucking polis to the ground!" He lifted his empty cup to the shadow. "Wine! I need some fucking wine!"

Reah stepped forward to pour.

Pollux captured her wrist in his free hand. "And who's this nymph?"

Reah froze.

Castor gulped his wine and plopped another sticky sweet date in his mouth. "She's from Athens. New to camp."

Pollux slapped his thigh and laughed loudly. "You've already claimed this tempting morsel for yourself, I see."

"I've said nothing."

"We're brothers! I can see in your eyes that you want her. Take her, she's yours." Pollux grabbed Reah's buttocks. "She'll be a hearty field to plow. More wine, woman!"

"How's your shoulder?" Castor asked, taking the conversation in a different direction.

Pollux rotated his arm in a circle. "As if it were never injured. The physician said it was just a scratch. No poison, thank the gods. He did suggest I pray to Apollo for certain healing."

"Then you'd do well to follow his advice," Castor said. "I've word there's someone in Athens who may aid us in recovering Helen."

"Well, spill the news," Pollux said, again shoving meat and bread in his mouth, washing it down with a hearty gulp of wine. "Speak."

Castor motioned Reah to the table. "Tell us what you know."

Reah ran her tongue over her dry lips. "I don't know for certain if he will know. But if anyone were to possess the knowledge, it would be Academus. He's always privy to secrets within the polis."

"Then, we'll summon him," Pollux said. "Titus!"

Immediately, a stout bearded man entered the tent. "Yes, my lord?"

"Find the man Academus from Athens and bring the secret monger to us. We would have words with him about Helen."

Titus nodded and slipped from sight into the night. Reah retreated into the shadows, just outside the vision of the brothers, but within earshot.

The hours passed into early evening, the brothers reveling in their war exploits, before the messenger returned with the wanted man. Titus shoved Academus into the dimming fire light of the princes' tent. "Here's your man, my lords."

Rubbing his hands together, Pollux stood. "Quick work, Titus. I knew we could count on you."

"My lord." Titus bowed his head. "I'll take my leave. I await your word outside." Titus again slipped from sight.

Academus stood of average height, the portrait of a wise man with his thinning hair and graying beard. "What do you want from me?"

"We want our sister returned. Nothing more," said Pollux.

"You've been told she's not within the city."

"We have," Pollux said, as he walked around the table separating himself from Academus. "But we've been informed that you may know the truth of the matter. The truth that lies beneath the surface of these lies you tell."

Castor reminded their captured guest why he should comply. "You'll have heard Menestheus has been appointed king ... by us. Your fucking Athenian Council be damned."

Academus' eyes widened with fear. "I'd heard such news, but I didn't know if the rumor was true."

Castor shrugged. "We only wish to see our sister rightfully returned to us."

The old man worried his hands together. "We've been told Helen wishes to be free of Spartan control. Even though she is young. Theseus is rescuer, not thief."

Pollux pounded a weighty fist on the table, causing random items to bounce and clang together. "She's been taken against her will by the balls of Zeus! You'd do well to hand her over or give her up. We'll annihilate every polis in this fucking region until we discover her. Is your secret worth all that?"

Now, Castor stood. "To us, our sister is worth all of the blood we must spill. And righteously so."

Academus looked from one brother to the other. Their eyes held the hard truth. They would not give up. "You'll return to Sparta if you have your sister?"

"We will," the brothers spoke in unison.

Academus hung his head. "I love Athens more than I love the king who absents the throne. If I speak falsely, may Father Zeus strike me down." He glanced awkwardly around the tent, as if expecting a bolt of lightning to end his life at that moment. "Helen is being held by the queen mother in the north. Aphidnae."

Pollux smiled mischievously, "That wasn't so bad, was it? Titus!"

The messenger reappeared. "We ride to Aphidnae in the north at first light. Prepare the men."

Titus bowed deeply and quickly. "Yes, my lord." And he left to follow his orders.

Castor summoned reah to his bed. "Why did you give up Academus to us?"

"You're destroying my home for a woman I don't even know. I'd have you stop before Athens passes into legend ... or worse, darkness."

"You love Athens that much?"

"I do."

"There's more. You're holding back something of importance. Speak."

Reah squirmed under Caster's intense scrutiny. "I've a husband."

"Ah. I see your dilemma. You hope to be returned to him, do you not?"

A tear slipped down Reah's cheek.

"Since you've been moved to help us, as much as yourself, I may grant what you desire. Providing your personal offering is given with … enthusiasm."

"My lord," Reah asked, shifting her feet nervously, heat flaming her cheeks at the implication, "what offering do you require?"

"I'll not sleep alone," Castor said, holding out his hand. "Come. I know how to please a woman."

FORTY SEVEN

Helen Triumphant

APHIDNAE—1254 BCE

Aethra stood from her loom, dropping her shuttle and thread, when she heard Erika shouting through the courtyard. In moments the frantic servant burst into the weaving room, her eyes wide and darting around the chamber searching for safety. The queen mother grabbed her servant by the shoulders and shook her. "Who. Is. Here?" she demanded. "Who?"

Erika pointed a shaking finger at Helen. "Her. They're coming for her! Why did King Theseus bring *her* here?"

The queen mother raised her eyebrow. "That girl?"

Erika shouted loud enough for the secret to break. "She's the lost princess of Sparta! Helen! She's Helen!" From within the household, Aethra heard various accidents occurring—pots dropping and platters clanging followed by dead silence.

Helen's laughter filled the silence. "I warned you, you old hag, that my brothers wouldn't rest until they found me."

Aethra spat at Helen. "You've been nothing but trouble since my son brought you here. Curses follow your beauty. You'll chase peace, but it'll always elude you."

"Spartans have no need of peace, old woman," Helen replied.

"A day will come when you'll regret such words," the queen mother warned. "As for now, we'll greet these brothers of yours. Hand you over without argument from me."

———

Pollux and Castor held their troops at the entrance of Aphidnae, continuing into the city with a small contingent of men to the house of Aethra. The eerie stillness of the streets was broken only by the occasional barking dog or crying child. They rode for a short while, before an old man crossed their path.

"You there!" Pollux shouted.

The old man startled and missed his step. He turned to find the Spartan brothers pressing toward him. Picking himself up, he broke into a run, but age betrayed him. He was no match for them.

Castor pulled his horse up in front of the man. "There'll be no escape for you, friend."

The old man's voice shook as he said, "You're no friend to this polis, any more than you were to Athens." He shoved his balled up fist at the young princes. "You'll be cursed for what you have done to innocents."

Pollux laughed sarcastically. "We've nothing to fear. Our

retribution was brought about by Theseus' treachery. Lay your threats at his feet. Athens' punishment was just."

The old man was defiant. "Have you come to do the same to us?"

"Not if Helen is returned before Apollo's light fades to darkness."

Castor spoke up, "Where's the queen mother's residence? We were told it sits in the south."

The old man nodded agreement. "That is so."

"You know this house?" Castor inquired.

"All of the polis knows of Aethra's household."

"Lead us there," Pollux demanded.

The old man considered the jar in his hands and put it down. "Come, then." He led the brothers down several deserted streets. Finally, the man stopped before an unassuming door in a high wall surrounding a courtyard. "Here."

Castor tossed a silver coin at the man's feet. "For your services, we thank you."

The coin bounced on the ground. The old man looked at it and spat. "I'll take no silver from the likes of you." He walked away, disappearing down a nearby side alley.

Castor motioned a guard, who pounded the wooden door with a heavy fist. After a brief wait, the door cracked open slightly. The brothers pushed their way through mounted on their fully dressed war horses, hooves clattering loudly on the stone. A few servants scattered like rats.

"Helen!" Pollux bellowed. "Helen!"

An elegant older woman appeared. She walked without haste toward the uninvited guests. "I am Aethra, Queen Mother. Matron of Aphidnae."

"Where's our sister, Helen? We know you hold her against her will," Castor said.

"She's within and well cared for."

"How can you speak to her welfare? She's held as a captive, stolen from her family."

Aethra ignored Castor and continued with pleasantries. "Refreshments after such a long journey? The day is hot."

"You extend hospitality as if you've done no injury to us. I'd no more drink water in your household, than I'd piss in my own cup. Bring Helen at once."

Aethra nodded. "Bring the girl."

Castor and Pollux dismounted. After a brief wait, Helen burst in to the courtyard running straight for her brothers. "I knew you'd come! I knew it!" She threw her arms around Castor, then Pollux.

Pollux picked her up, swinging her around like he did when she was a babe. "Little sister! Apologies it took this long. Are you well?"

"I am," she said. "No thanks to this old hag."

Pollux set her down, kneeling in front of her. "I see. What satisfaction do you require, Princess of Sparta?"

"I would have her for my slave." Helen smiled slyly, as she eyed Aethra over her brother's shoulder.

"Done," Pollux said. "Bind the woman," he commanded.

Three soldiers came forward, making for Aethra, who screamed, "You can't take me! You can't!"

"The way your son couldn't take our sister? Let Theseus retrieve you if he ever returns," Castor said.

Aethra resisted the soldiers. "But my house!"

Pollux took two long steps to the woman, grabbing her roughly by the arms. "You no longer have a house. You're no longer queen of anything. You'll serve our sister, as she commands, and if you don't

… I'll beat you myself. You're fortunate I don't beat you now." He shoved her and she lost her footing, stumbled back, and fell hard to the ground.

As Aethra struggled to get up, Helen came to her side, smiling like a lioness over her kill. "Let's see how you fare in Sparta."

FORTY EIGHT

princes no more

SPARTA—1254 BCE

yndareus shook his head in disbelief. "Theseus has been my friend since we were young. I didn't believe him capable of treachery against me. Had it not fallen from my own sons' lips, I wouldn't believe it still."

"What's to be done then, Father?" Castor asked.

The king's shoulders slumped, as he shrugged in resignation. "She must wed. We can't risk that another guest may slip away with her. To us, she's simply Helen. But to the world beyond us, she holds some mystery. The rumors ..." Tyndareus looked his sons square in the eye. "It'll only worsen as she blossoms to womanhood."

"Agreed." Castor nodded.

Pollux rubbed the stubble of his beard. "Only one question

remains. Who will you invite to marry Helen? She's sharp tongued. Strong willed. Not the picture of a docile wife."

Castor agreed. "She'll require a firm hand. A very firm hand."

Tyndareus paced the floor. "There are but two men with will enough to subdue your wildcat sister—Prince Odysseus of Ithaka or Menelaus, brother to Agamemnon."

"Both fine choices. But how to convince them?" Castor mused.

Pollux shrugged his shoulders. "I'd be more worried war may come to us, if there's no opportunity for all eligible suitors to seek her hand. Helen's surely the most prized princess in all of Greece."

"You speak truth, my son. But, if all of the potential suitors descended on this house, our hospitality might be spread thin. We'd have to control the situation. Control the outcome."

"Yes, send word out that when Helen reaches womanhood, a feast will be held and the best husband will be chosen from among the guests. Hold contests, if you will," Castor said.

Pollux clapped his hands together. "That's an excellent suggestion. Likely many gifts will flow into Sparta and our treasury."

Tyndareus signaled for a servant to fill his wine cup. "A contest would prove entertaining, yet perhaps won't yield the best man for Helen. What if Odysseus or Menelaus don't win?"

"That's a dilemma," Castor said.

"We've seen that Helen's presence can undo a man. Imagine a hundred … Has there truly been no word from Theseus?" Tyndareus asked.

Pollux shook his head. "None. Although, the whispers are that … well, they're too preposterous to be the truth."

"Speak. What've you heard?"

"He's taken the road to Hades to steal away Persephone. He and

Pirithous. They've been taken prisoner by the god himself. Forced to forget this life among mortals."

Castor chuckled. "His balls must rival Zeus. If ever I faced Hades, I would hope to forget the experience as well. Father, what of Helen? Let Theseus rot wherever he may be."

Pollux added, "Perhaps, you can fix the events so *your* choices for her husband have advantage? Odysseus excels with a bow. I'll wager none can beat him in such a challenge. Menelaus, well, perhaps a contest of ass licking?"

Castor spit out a mouth of wine. "A contest he'd win with no doubt."

The king sat on a couch between his sons. "My thoughts dwell on Helen's security. On Sparta's security. We must align ourselves carefully. Plan the competitions carefully. Odysseus comes from afar. He's earned a fair reputation for strategy. But I fear he'll refuse Helen, because he'll not risk the safety of Ithaka to rivals. He's capable of handling your sister, but I think the man too practical."

"Menelaus then?" Castor asked.

Tyndareus twisted the wide gold cuff on his wrist. "He's a boastful man. Not as hard as his brother, your brother-in-law. I think he'll risk the match, as he has no kingdom of his own to worry about."

Pollux narrowed his eyes at this. "If she takes a man without a kingdom of his own, where do you propose they take up residence?"

The king stood, then paced under the burning scrutiny of his son's eyes. "Think of Sparta. How much would you sacrifice for her?"

"You mean both of us quite literally?" Pollux asked, looking at Castor.

"Helen will only be safe if she remains in Sparta, as a Spartan princess … and one day its queen."

Pollux tossed his kylix on the floor. It clanged and rolled to a stop just short of his father's feet. "There it is! Usurped by that fucking red-headed Mycenaean ass licker!"

Castor was troubled as well. "What of my brother and I? Where shall we go? Do you suppose Menelaus will tolerate his rivals beneath his nose?"

"You'll have to abdicate publicly. Take an oath before the polis supporting Helen's husband," Tyndareus said. "You both must think of Sparta before yourselves."

"If you believe this the wisest course, then we'll support you," Castor said, looking to his brother. "As always."

Pollux shoved a chair across the room. "Fuck Mycenae!" And he stormed out of the hall.

Tyndareus, exhausted by worry, slumped in his chair. "It's for the best," he said quietly. "For Sparta."

"Pollux will come around, Father. It's a bitter potion you asked us to swallow ... even for Sparta's sake."

"Your honesty is appreciated, my son. But, the time for choosing is a long way off. We have a few years perhaps? I must plan this wisely. Chose Menelaus without appearing to *choose Menelaus*."

"Best start with Agamemnon."

"Yes. Yes, start with the king of Mycenae. I will send word of my intent. He'll keep the secret for fear of losing a kingdom for his brother."

Beneath the shade of an apple tree, Helen and her cousin, Penelope, wove little mats from tall blades of grass. Castor and Pollux, out of earshot, sat watching and alert for intruders.

Helen tossed a handful of grass weaving aside. "My father told me I must marry soon."

Penelope lay her weaving in her lap and tucked a stray hair behind her ear. "Surely, not too soon?"

"He's worried I'll be kidnapped again," she said, pointing at her brothers standing guard. "I can hardly relieve myself with any privacy anymore."

"Were you frightened?"

Helen shrugged. "I suppose." She plucked a blade of grass, eyeing it for weaving value. "I knew *they* would come."

Penelope marveled at her cousin's bravery. "I would've been."

"I was attacked by a chicken," Helen said, casually.

Penelope giggled. "A chicken?"

"I swatted it. Feathers went everywhere—"

"A chicken?" Penelope laughed so hard she couldn't speak. The thought of Helen batting at a chicken was too much. Her laughter was contagious. Before long, Helen was laughing, too. The girls, on the precipice of womanhood and marriage, fell back into the warm grass giggling uncontrollably.

Sunshine pierced through the branches above them, speckling them in golden light. The humor faded as they stared up into the leaves and unripe fruit. Penelope turned to watch her cousin twirling the blade of grass between her fingers. *She's much prettier than I'll ever be.*

Helen sighed. "Do you ever wonder what life would be like if we never had to marry?"

Penelope's brow wrinkled. "How would our father's legacies continue, if we didn't have children?"

"I'm not sure I want to be a mother."

Sitting up on her elbows, Penelope chided Helen. "You can't mean that! You'll have strong Spartan boys and girls. The boys, you'll have to send away, of course, but the girls will be with you until they're women. You'll never be alone."

"What if I wish to be alone?" Her eyes shifted in the direction of her brothers. "I'm never alone now. I hate it. I long to be somewhere I can walk freely about *without* being spied on."

Penelope hadn't considered that. "But what about your father's legacy?"

"He has three other children for that."

"I want an entire hall filled with children."

Helen placed a hand on Penelope's hand. "I hope you get your wish, cousin … but I know you're really thinking about *making* the babies."

They giggled again, as the day lazily passed above them.

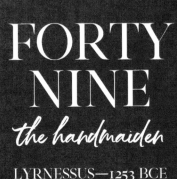

FORTY NINE
the handmaiden

LYRNESSUS—1253 BCE

Mynes paced before the chamber hearth, its heat doing nothing to warm the chill in the air. "I don't know how you can refuse. It's been years since Phila …"

Briseis whispered, "Died."

"We've lain together a thousand times since then, and—"

"Only disappointment."

"Not once has my seed taken hold."

"And you fear I'm barren. What good is a wife who can't conceive an heir?"

"The midwife advised that Phila's birth likely damaged your womb. I see no evidence she's wrong."

"Neither do I."

Mynes sat beside his wife. "I don't ask this of you to hurt you. I ask for my city, our city. I must have an heir."

"You promised me, years ago, you'd take no other women."

"I still have not."

"How is this different?"

"A handmaiden will carry the child. You and I will raise him as our own."

Briseis eyed her husband. "The trip you made recently to Lemnos without me …"

Mynes looked away, studying the dying hearth fire. "I've already purchased the woman. She's been proven fertile."

"So, it's done, then."

"Not entirely."

"What else can you expect from me? You don't require my permission. You've already consulted with the council."

"I want you with me. The handmaiden is only the vessel to carry the seed; you're the only woman who can encourage the desire to release it."

"You ask too much."

"If you refuse, then an audience will be forced to watch, including the queen. There must be at least one witness that the act was finished. There can be no doubt of fatherhood." He ran his fingers through his hair. "I'd prefer my mother wasn't forced to watch." When Briseis didn't respond, he added, "Have no doubt it's you who holds my heart. Coupling with this woman is a necessity, not a desire."

Squeezing her fingers tightly together in her lap, overwhelmed by her inability to provide an heir, Briseis nodded. "Very well."

Briseis clenched her jaw, willing her eyes dry for this ritual coupling. She knew it was for the good of Lyrnessus, but the deed tested her love for Mynes and her dignity. Beside her the chosen handmaiden lay serenely, too at ease with what was about to happen. They'd both been stripped and bathed and put to the bed to await Prince Mynes.

When he entered, he was also naked. He'd been scraped and rubbed with scented oils from head to foot. Briseis braced herself, as her husband came around to her side of the bed. Without a word, and deliberately avoiding eye contact with the woman next to her, Mynes pulled the linens, exposing his wife's nudity. She saw his cock twitch, before she closed her eyes against him. Her husband lay beside her, his hands caressing her sides and thighs. His cock now stiffened completely as it pressed against the soft flesh of her thigh.

Mynes pulled Briseis beneath him, plunging his entire length into her. He leaned close to her ear. "I'm sorry." His mouth covered hers, as he pumped rigorously to bring her pleasure without releasing his seed.

Briseis' body, familiar with his rhythms, met his thrusts with a vigor she hadn't intended. She wrapped her arms around his neck, a small sigh escaping her lips. As her husband pleasured her, she realized his hand was caressing between the handmaiden's thighs. An unfamiliar hand squeezed her breast, teasing her nipple. Briseis moaned. Then, the hand slid down her body, and rubbed at the throbbing flesh. Mynes thrust harder and Briseis moaned loudly. In a flash of heat, she shuddered, crying and clinging to her husband.

As her breathing calmed, Mynes slid from their sacred union to mount the handmaiden beside her. Briseis stole a glance as her husband pressed into the other woman. The handmaiden arched her back into Mynes' thrusts. She wanted to look away, but found she couldn't. Jealousy and curiosity encouraged Briseis to reach a shaking hand to the handmaiden's breast, cupping it from the side. Mynes dipped his head to kiss the other woman. A heat filled Briseis' sacred flesh, and she moved closer to her husband as he plowed the woman who would carry his child. She leaned her head to catch the woman's nipple in her mouth. Instantly, it crinkled to a peak on her tongue. She suckled it, shyly, then with deliberate purpose. The handmaiden moaned, wrapping a hand in Briseis' hair. Then, Briseis reached a hand to the union her husband made with the woman. She rubbed at the woman's soft, wet flesh as had been done to her. The handmaiden's hips slammed into Mynes, as she clawed and cried out with pleasure. Briseis left her hand deliberately between them as her husband spilled his seed into the chosen vessel.

FIFTY

maiden no more

SKYROS—1253 BCE

Achilles looked out across the churning blue ocean at his feet and beyond to the horizon. The birth of Neoptolemus had pleased him, yet the thought that his fate would end on this island gnawed at his gut. His spirit yearned for the clash of sword on sword, shield against shield. He couldn't believe that his purpose was nothing more than to sit upon a throne and decide which crops to plant, which orchards to trim, or which vines would yield the best wine. "This cannot be all," he said to the sea. The tide washed up at his feet, and then pulled back, sucking the sand out from under him as he stood lost in thought. "I have always had an affinity for the sea," he spoke into the breeze. "My fate must be out there, not here on the rocks and sand of Skyros."

The sun blazed overhead. And then he heard the sign—an eagle's screech from high above. He shielded his eyes from Apollo's light and spotted the bird, a mere speck against the blinding blue.

Again the eagle screeched. Satisfied, Achilles turned from the beach to head back to the palace. As he walked, he stripped the woman's clothes from his back. He tired of the disguise. He was impatient to take the first steps from his prison into the world of war he knew, now, would find him.

———

Achilles made his way to the chamber he shared with Deidamia. He heard his son crying before he reached the door and pushed it quietly open. He smiled at his wife cooing and comforting their son.

"Shaaaahhhh, Neoptolemus. Shaaah," she whispered, holding her breast to the baby's searching mouth. He latched on and suckled hungrily, placing his little hands on either side of his mother's swollen breasts.

Achilles laughed, startling his wife, but not the child. "He has much the same mind as I do."

"Shah! Husband you are of *singular* mind," Deidamia chided.

Achilles brushed her long dark tresses from her shoulder and kissed her neck. "Do you make complaint?"

Deidamia sighed and smiled. "I will never make complaint of your hands upon me."

He reached his hand to cup one of his wife's heavy breasts. "I should hope not."

She slapped his hand away. "Your son requires my attention."

Achilles withdrew his hand. "After then."

"As you command, husband."

PART THREE

Three Brides

Sing, Muse, sing of the Warrior King
and his cunning bride
above all else
… always her

Sing, Muse, sing of the Forgotten Prince
and his doomed bride
above all else
… always her

Sing, Muse, sing of the Golden Warrior
and his bloody bride
above all else
… always her

Sing, Muse, sing of the shining Olympians
thieves of hope …

FIFTY ONE

gambling debts

GYTHIUM—1252 BCE

Patrokles stared at his hands in disbelief. Blood ran in thin streams of spider webs through his strong fingers, staining his skin. "What have I done? What have I done?"

Las lay lifeless on his back with Patrokles' dagger plunged to the hilt, angling oddly from his chest.

"I only meant to defend …" Patrokles scanned the stunned faces staring back at him—some horrified, some surprised, some blank. "It … it was a mistake. An unfortunate slip of my blade." Patrokles knew no words would bring Las back to life, for surely his soul was winging its way to the Underworld, even as he knelt in stunned disbelief.

Demius pulled Patrokles to his feet, avoiding the bloody mess of his hands. "You should flee this place, Pax. No one here will believe you acted in self-defense. They'll put you on trial. Find you guilty of murder. His family founded this pitiful port. You'll find no friends here. None to vouch for you."

Patrokles stood on shaky legs, wiping his hands absentmindedly on his tunic. "I should return to Phthia."

"Why? Head to Sparta. If you win that beauty's hand, this," he indicated with a flourish of his hand, "will be a trifle long forgotten. If you leave now, you can make it to Sparta, and then back to Phthia if the worst should come. Stand here much longer and surely you'll be discovered. Your face betrays your shock and guilt."

Patrokles considered the advice. "I hear nearly a hundred men have found their way to this feast for Helen's hand. I'll be one of many. My offerings will be meager compared to most."

Demius hooked his fingers through his belt. "But few can claim a face as handsome as yours. If she is like other women, you stand a better chance than most."

Patrokles smirked. "True." Stooping, he pulled his dagger from the dead man's chest. "Sorry, Las. You deserved better." He wiped the blade on his chiton, before sheathing it at his waist and mounting his horse. "It was to be a short venture regardless. If Tyndareus' hospitality measures with rumor, I can resupply food and wine before heading to Phthia."

"May the gods speed you on your way. Hurry, get out of here. Go!"

"To better days, old friend."

"Find a stream before you enter Sparta. Better yet, a river. You're filthy," Demius laughed.

"A river, aye!" Patrokles replied, his voice falling short as he rode off with a dust storm rising behind him.

Demius watched Patrokles shrink into a speck on the horizon, before he turned his attention to the bloody corpse at his feet. "Now, to make you disappear." He gave the evil eye to the remaining gawkers. "Go on! Get back to whatever business is yours!" Demius groaned as he hoisted the limp body over the back of his horse and headed for a pond he knew of—one where large animals were known to prey on unsuspecting guests from time to time. "If the gods are with us, they'll send a bear or pack of wolves to feast on you. I do apologize. Someone should've warned you about cheating Patrokles. He loses his temper when he gambles. Especially, if you try to cheat him."

FIFTY TWO

a feast for beauty

SPARTA—1252 BCE

S uitors descended like rabid dogs on the house of Tyndareus, when word winged its way across Hellas that the lovely Helen was to be married off to the most agreeable man. Every unmarried king and prince from every Greek kingdom, large and small, near and far, from every island across every sea arrived at Sparta hoping to win Helen's hand.

From the balcony, Pollux surveyed the growing throng of warrior kings and princes in the courtyard. Odysseus, Prince of Ithaka. Thoas, King of Pleuron and Calydon; Antilochus, son of Nestor from Pylos; Patrokles, son of Menoetius from Phthia; Teucer of Salamis, son of Telemon and the Trojan Princess, Hesione; and Ajax the Elder of Salamis. His knuckles whitened as he gripped the wooden railing. "I hope our father's plan works. A gathering such as this can easily become a small army within."

"His plan is solid. The execution of it may yet prove dangerous," Castor said.

"How will he choose the man without the losers crying foul?"

Castor clapped his brother on the back. "I think he means to stage a false contest, allowing the red beard to win."

Pollux scowled. "These events encourage men to brag. Look at this bunch of strutting peacocks. I'd rather strangle that Mycenaean coward, Menelaus, than bow down to him."

"He's no better man than us, but we do it for Sparta."

Pollux smashed his fist against the railing. "He's not worthy of Helen or Sparta. Mark my words, he'll bring us to ruin before the end."

Castor nodded silently. "That may be true. You've seen the men below and noted their origins. How else could father have dealt with this? I see no other way."

King Tyndareus leaned against a column, searching the ocean of suitors for the Mycenaean prince. He stretched his neck to see beyond those positioned nearest his vantage point. So intent on spying was he, that he didn't hear the Prince of Ithaka approach him from behind.

"Are you well, my lord?" asked Odysseus.

Tyndareus repeated the words. "Am I well?"

Odysseus met the king's eyes. "What troubles you, King Tyndareus? Surely, you're worried. The creases in your brow number more than those belted at your waist."

"Are you so quick to judge me?"

"I'm an observer, nothing more."

Irritated, Tyndareus waved his hand at Odysseus. "It's true enough. Look at all of these men. Do you believe they'll leave my kingdom in peace, when a suitor is chosen for Helen? You believe they won't claim there was some treachery afoot? Rip Sparta to shreds in a frenzy at not being chosen?"

"A thought of that has crossed my mind, as well. Helen did stir them—"

The king shook his head. "After I forbid her to show herself and stay sequestered with the woman. Rumor enough can stir restless men."

Odysseus nodded in understanding. "Helen's no easy woman to control, I see. My lord, if I may speak freely?"

"You may, Prince of Ithaka. Your head for strategy proceeds you."

"Use the past to aid the present."

Tyndareus narrowed his eyes at Odysseus. "To what end? How so?"

"It's widely known that Helen was kidnapped, because her beauty intoxicated Theseus beyond reason. Use this knowledge to force the men into a binding oath to protect her and her future husband. For, if rumors are true, marriage will not protect men from her beauty's affect."

Tyndareus stroked his beard. "Continue."

"Allow Helen to choose her husband. None can claim foul play, if she chooses."

"Let a woman choose? That's preposterous. Dangerous," Tyndareus said, even as he considered the logic.

"The men will believe they stand an equal chance to win her admiration and her hand." Odysseus leaned closer to the king. "But, you've chosen already, haven't you?"

Tyndareus shrugged. "Why do you ask this?"

"If Helen were my daughter, I would have."

The king grabbed Odysseus by the elbow, pulling him aside. "For Helen's safety, she must remain in Sparta. There is only *one* choice."

Odysseus narrowed his eyes. "A man without a kingdom of his own. You mean to marry her to … *Menelaus*."

"It's a sacrifice that must be made."

"What of Castor and Pollux? Your sons are in agreement?"

"Castor rests easier than Pollux with the situation."

Odysseus placed a hand on the king's shoulder. "Will they support the match? That's all that matters."

"I have their word."

"Then it's done. Announce to the suitors your intention and inform Helen who she must choose."

The king's laughter rang hollow. "If you were Helen, would you choose Menelaus?"

"I see your point. He's neither the strongest, the handsomest, nor the brightest among us."

"I fear Helen's rejection due to his lack of fine features most. I have but one question, Odysseus."

"What's that?"

"Why are you so willing to give up claim to Helen, when the others will surely protest?"

Odysseus fingered a fold in his chiton. "There's another I find more beautiful than Helen. It's her I favor."

"I should've known your assistance would come with a price."

"I've asked none," the prince protested.

"But it's on the tip of your tongue. That much I can see with my old eyes."

Odysseus' black eyes glittered. "I'd have Penelope, daughter of Ikarus, as my wife."

King Tyndareus placed both hands on his hips, considering Odysseus' request. "You've earned your reputation, Odysseus. The negotiator, the strategist."

"That's a yes, then, my lord?"

"I'll speak to Ikarus. I'll make certain he won't reject your offer."

Helen wrinkled her nose at the thought of the big, red-bearded prince bedding her. "Theseus would've been preferable."

Queen Leda clasped her hands in her lap. "Daughter, if there were some other way … We can't risk a war on your behalf. Men will clamor for the right to claim you. What happened with Theseus will likely happen, again if you aren't closely guarded. Who better to keep you safe than Menelaus? Where better to keep you safe than Sparta?"

"But he is old and fat."

The queen pressed her lips into a thin line of resignation. There was no way to oppose the king's will, even though she agreed with her daughter entirely regarding her husband's choice. "There's Sparta to consider. Mycenae will be a powerful ally."

"What if I refuse to choose him? Or any of them? What then?"

"If you vowed celibacy to serve the gods, I believe your father would marry you off regardless."

"Truly?" Helen asked.

"Daughter, you know what we are to men. Our value is between our legs and in our ability to bind two families together for greater good. Think of the bargain your father made at your sister's expense. Forced to marry the murderer of her world. All for power. For gold. You believe he'll allow you freedom? No. He'll seek to control Sparta and you, until his last breath."

Helen motioned a slave girl to clasp her jeweled necklace around her neck. "Then I'll choose Menelaus to please my father." She knew her mother was right; she'd rebel in her own way.

Leda hugged her youngest child. "You were blessed by the goddess, my child. For eighteen summers, you've brought me great joy. I'm afraid your path was never meant to be paved with ease."

Helen admired her image in the polished silver plate. *I will take a lover ... maybe two.*

Tyndareus held his hands high, quieting the rumblings of the hundred men seated around the hall.

Ajax, son of Telemon, called out, "You'll allow a woman to choose?" Grumblings of disapproval flooded the hall.

"My lords and princes!" Tyndareus cried out. "Give me your ear!" Again the king held his hands high signaling peace.

Odysseus stood and shouted over the assembly. "Good men of Hellas! Give the king a chance to speak in his own hall. He must have reason for granting Helen the right of refusal." The clamor calmed at his words. The Prince of Ithaka threw open his arms. "You see, Tyndareus? We await your reasoning with eager ears."

The king nodded his thanks to his discreet accomplice. "My lords! How can you expect me to decide among you? Who would be pleased by my refusal of his hand to match my daughter's? I would make enemies of states I regard as friend and ally." The suitors mumbled in agreement at his logic. "If Helen chooses, then I cannot be blamed for making one man's life a misery."

Laughter filled the hall. A voice rang out, "Look at poor Theseus! Vanished to the Underworld!" More laughter followed.

Tyndareus winced at the reminder of Helen's abduction. "That leads me to my request." The men focused their attention on him. "Each of you must bow before me and take an oath supporting Helen's choice. Promise to serve her chosen husband with military aid, if ever she's abducted again from her home." The men quietly sized each other up. "Then, we're in concord."

The king walked to the head of the hall, where a pair of priests held a magnificent horse at bay. On his signal, one priest stepped forward, slicing the great beast's neck. The animal staggered, falling to its knees while a third priest held a silver hammered bowl beneath the stream of hot blood. An agonized gasp escaped the horse's throat before it fell silent. Tyndareus took the bowl of sacred blood. "Swear your oath to me by blood. Then, Helen will dance for all, and choose the one."

The men lined up broad shoulder behind broad shoulder, dipping their fingers in the sticky crimson before kneeling to the King of Sparta. They all spoke the words of promise and protection on behalf of Helen's unnamed choice, each believing himself a viable candidate for her consideration. As the oath taking stretched on, fresh platters of steaming meat and hot bread were set on the tables. Wine spiced with cinnamon and sweetened with honey was poured into every drinking vessel. Once again, laughter and goodwill filled the air.

Finally, with all oaths properly given and accepted, the suitors began to bang their fists impatiently on the tables, slowly at first, building to a great crescendo of muscle on wood and silver against clay. The cue given, the musicians picked up their instruments. Soothing sounds of lyre strings being plucked and flute chambers emptying floated across the air, and the suitors sat, awaiting the event like hungry hounds.

From the southern entrance, Helen entered heavily veiled in golden silk with her train floating behind her. Her feet were bare and her hands graceful. As she twirled and swayed, the men caught glimpses of her porcelain skin and pale-honey colored hair. Her eyes, heavily lined with black kohl, flashed like polished emeralds glittering in the sun. The music increased in tempo and Helen moved her body to match the speed, her hips shaking, her undulations mesmerizing the suitors who strained to catch sight of her. Some reached out their hands to touch her clothes and inhaled the sweet, spicy scent of her in the air as she whirled by. Cocks throbbed beneath tunics, straining against intimate bindings with carnal desire to take her there in the hall. Lust rose in the spaces between the suitors, hands itched to rub their desire against their own legs …

Breathless, they watched, captivated as she collapsed into a heaving pile of veils as the music abruptly ended. The suitors sat in stunned silence watching Helen as she slowly rose to her feet. She removed her veil and tossed it at Menelaus' feet.

The men looked to one another in confusion as Menelaus picked up her veil. Helen's voice rang clearly for all to hear. "I have chosen."

Menelaus surveyed the crowd, a smug smile on his face. The suitors pressed for a better glimpse of Helen to see what they were being denied forever.

King Tyndareus approached Menelaus. "Will you accept my daughter's choice of your hand? You may deny, if you wish." Tyndareus knew he wouldn't, but it was a small gesture he offered in part to appease all of the disappointed men.

Menelaus' smile nearly split his face with greedy joy. "I accept the offer, my lord."

The king took Menelaus' hand in his own and joined it to Helen's. "It is done. Helen has chosen. I call on you all to remember you to honor the blood oath you've taken. Honor it and may your days be long. May peace reign across your lands. May the gods bless all in your possession and care. Come, Castor and Pollux, and pay your fealty to the next King of Sparta."

The brothers approached, shoulder to shoulder, marching like two hoplites into battle, and faced the red-bearded future king of their polis. They knelt before the would-be-king, offering their swords in times of peace or war. In unison they spoke, "For the safety of our father's lands and the true bloodline of Sparta, we give our public pledge to protect and serve you both."

Helen lifted her brothers to their feet. "Only out of love for a sister shall either of you ever serve me." She kissed them on the cheek. "I accept your protection."

A rowdy cheer ascended toward the heavens, ushering in a new era for Sparta, a future era tangling the world with oaths and gold and blood.

FIFTY THREE

race for love

Icarius held Penelope's hand in his own hand. "Daughter, are you certain of your choice?"

Shyly, Penelope answered, "As certain as a maid can be."

"Your Uncle Tyndareus encourages the match."

Penelope knew Helen had intervened on her behalf, as well. "Then, you're agreeable to Odysseus' troth?"

Her father sighed deeply, as if the matter plagued him. "He has a kingdom."

"Yes," she replied, barely able to contain her grin. "I shall be a queen, like Helen."

Icarius gently dropped his daughter's hands. "A far away kingdom."

Penelope smoothed a pleat on her gown, feigning to fuss at a snag. "Not that far away."

Icarius looked his daughter in the eye. "Once you leave, you'll forget about your home and your family here, in Sparta."

"How can I forget my family? As queen, I can visit when I please."

Penelope's father shook his head reluctantly. "Very well. But, I have one condition."

"Which is?"

"He must win you in a foot race against your other suitors."

Penelope bit her bottom lip. "The other suitors?"

"Some of Helen's suitors remain. They've expressed their desire to settle for her cousin."

"Me?"

"It's an honor to fall second to Helen. I've also enticed a few Spartan noblemen to compete in the contest."

"It's all arranged?"

Icarius opened his arms to Penelope. "Come, come. No tears. Your Odysseus might win you yet. If he doesn't, then surely a better man will. I leave the matter of your husband to the gods." He hugged his daughter and released her. "Pick out your best gown. Prepare yourself."

Penelope bowed her head, hiding her disappointment and fear. She had no idea if Odysseus was swift-footed. *What if he loses and I'm forced to marry another? I must get word to him. If he doesn't win me …* She choked on the thought of some other man bedding her. *He must win. By all the gods, I will run away if another man takes me as a prize.*

Odysseus worried after Penelope's secret messenger informed him of Icarius' terms. What could Icarius have against him? Why not agree to the betrothal and dowry? His daughter would be queen. *Why is that not enough?* If he lost, Penelope would belong to another man. *I must make certain I take the prize as my bride.* Suspecting his competition would be chosen from among the losing stragglers of Helen's suitors, he made his way to the outer courtyard where he knew they camped. Hospitality dictated they could remain for a fortnight, or longer.

Teucer waved him over. "Odysseus! Come! Join us!"

Nodding, the sly young king smiled and took a seat at the crowded table. "I was hoping to find someone awake," he said, whisking an amphora from the table. "And drinking." He feigned a hearty gulp from the tall jar.

"Yes, join us for the most *delicious* wine. I believe old Tyndareus has hidden his best stores from us," Patrokles slurred slightly, as he drank deeply from his wide-brimmed cup. "But it won't stop me from drinking it."

The men laughed. Odysseus sized them up around the table. *Teucer has heavy legs.* He feigned another gulp, wiping his mouth on the back of his hand. *Patrokles is already drunk, but he's swift as the wind. That could be a problem … if he shakes free of the heavy head he's sure to wake with.* "Patrokles, you're cup is near empty!"

Patrokles laughed, eyeballing his cup at an odd angle. "So it is." He reached for an amphora and shook it, before tossing it to the ground where it shattered into a dozen pieces.

Odysseus held out the jar in his hands. "Allow me, my friend." He filled Patrokles' cup to the rim.

"Gratitude, Odysseus … *generous* Odysseus. I heard it was you who put the oath idea in Tyndareus' head."

Shrugging, Odysseus said, "Tyndareus keeps his own council. Perhaps, it was Diomedes?"

Diomedes spat out a mouthful of wine. "Look what you made me do. Still can't believe I took that damned oath." Swigging another gulp, he stood and stretched his limbs. "But *my* consolation will be the lovely Penelope."

Odysseus clenched his jaw tightly. *Athena!* Diomedes was carved like a god, tall and wide. *He barely has a man's beard. And too arrogant.* He watched his competition's muscles ripple like a mountain stream. *By the gods, he's probably hung like a centaur. If he wins, he'll … to Penelope …* Odysseus couldn't even finish the thought. "You'll have to win the race first."

Drunken laughter sounded around the table. Diomedes laughed loudest, and then finished his wine. "I'm for sleep. I have a race to win tomorrow, as our lord Odysseus has reminded me."

"So soon?" Odysseus goaded. "You're the youngest here. Will you let it be said a bunch of old men can drink more than the giant Diomedes?"

More drunken laughter.

Diomedes scoffed at the idea. "Pour the wine, *old* man."

Odysseus poured Diomedes a generous cup, feigning another heavy draft for himself. "Tyndareus is definitely keeping the best of his stores from us. Who else has entered the race for Icarius' daughter?"

Teucer grinned. "I'd take Icarius' daughter any night … in any way."

Diomedes laughed. "Do Trojans even know how to keep a woman satisfied?"

"I'm as Greek as any of you bastards. The Trojans can rot behind their high walls. And trust me, I can make any woman wrap her legs around my thighs."

A short, stout man named Eumelus nodded. "I won't pass it up. I'm not likely to win, but who knows who the gods will favor?"

Teucer said, "There's the sharp truth of the matter."

Clytius, the eldest of the gathered men, added, "The gods love to cut us with their truths. We, busy with suffering, bleed for their amusement."

Patrokles nodded. "The gods bend us over every chance they get."

"Not all of us," Eumelus said. "You should be wary of speaking such things aloud, Patrokles. You suppose the gods can't hear you?"

Patrokles looked up into the night, twinkling with silver jewels. "Are you listening up there? If I've offended you, strike me down."

Everyone held their breath, expecting Patrokles to be struck down by a lightning bolt, or spear, or plague. But nothing happened in the silence.

"They sleep," Patrokles said, reaching to pull the wax plug from a fresh amphora. "Wine?"

All of the men held their cups out as Patrokles clumsily poured another round.

Odysseus smiled to himself. *Good. Keep drinking. Drink until dark oblivion forces you all to bed.* "I was sorry to hear about your brother, Clytius."

The old man's eyes watered. "It was a bitter end for Iphitus. He deserved better than what Herakles did to him. Do you still have the bow he gave you?"

Odysseus nodded. "It hangs in the great hall. That was my first real adventure."

"And led to Iphitus' last."

Odysseus lifted his empty cup in a toast. "To Iphitus."

All cups raised and wine was drained. When dawn's rosy fingers crept across the sky, Penelope's suitors straggled off to bed. Drunk and wobbly. As Odysseus watched the last man stumble away, he chuckled. "Just as I'd hoped." He hurried to his bed to catch a few precious hours of rest before the race.

In the bright light of late morning, the list of contestants was thinner than Icarius had hoped. Patrokles was nowhere to be found. Diomedes looked like he'd risen from the Underworld. Teucer was vomiting into a potted olive tree. Eumelus stood no chance, even against the compromised runners. Icarius warily eyed Odysseus, who stood poised and fresh.

Icarius signaled for the contestants to line up. "Whoever brings back the first apple from the king's orchard will win my daughter's hand."

Diomedes protested, "That's outside the city gates!"

Icarius shrugged unapologetically. "I'm not forcing you to compete, Diomedes."

After some mumbling and groaning, Penelope's suitors lined up. Teucer. Diomedes. Eumelus. Nireus. Prothous. And Odysseus.

Odysseus stole a glance at Penelope. She stood stoically by her father's side. Her face was pale. He'd done everything in his power to sweeten the odds in his favor. He'd even begged Athena to intervene. It was up to the gods now … and his swift, sober feet.

When Penelope's father gave the signal, the suitors sped from the starting line, kicking up a storm of dust. Their feet hardly touched the ground as they practically flew like a flock of birds toward the orchard. In the blink of an eye, they dropped down the first hill and from the onlookers' sights.

Odysseus' chest burned as he ran as fast as he'd ever run before. His legs grew heavy, but he pressed on right behind Diomedes' heels. He caught a whiff of stale wine. Certain Diomedes was still drunk, he silently cursed the man's youthful powers of recuperation. He pushed passed the pain, until …

I am here, Odysseus.

Athena?

Run, my son, run like the wind. Prove you are worthy of loyal Penelope.

A surge of heat ran through Odysseus' limbs and his legs kicked up higher and faster. A cloud of dust and small pebbles hit Diomedes in the face. When he reached the orchard, Odysseus plucked the nearest apple. Turning, he shot past the other runners before they'd even reached the trees. *Thank you, Athena.*

The crowd waited expectantly for the first man to appear. Hands shielding eyes. Necks craning. "There!" someone yelled. People pointed.

"Teucer!"

"No, Diomedes!"

"It's Odysseus!"

"Yes, Odysseus!"

"The King of Ithaka!"

Odysseus ran with Athena at his side until he crossed the finish line and handed Icarius the apple. Panting, he leaned over, resting his hands on his thighs to catch his breath, but not before he caught a glimpse of Penelope's broad smile.

Well done, my Odysseus.

Whatever you ask of me, I will obey. You've given me my heart's desire.

Victory is sweet, until it isn't.

Icarius tossed the apple back to Odysseus. "You've won my Penelope, though I expect not without a god's help."

The King of Ithaka only smiled. "I couldn't lose her. She was never my second choice. She is my destiny."

Within days, Penelope had packed her entire life into wooden boxes. Her father had wagons loaded with dowry gifts to follow his daughter and son-in-law to far off Ithaka. As she scanned the chamber she'd called her own, she glanced at her new husband still in bed. She blushed knowing that beneath the linen draped across his middle he wore nothing. Not a stitch of clothing.

With his eyes shut, Odysseus asked, "Have you never seen a naked man before?"

Penelope's chest burned with embarrassment. "I … Not until last night."

He lifted the linen covering, inviting his wife back to bed. "Woman, quit gawking and come here."

Penelope gasped glimpsing his nakedness in broad daylight … and his readiness to consummate their union. "It's morning." Her voice cracked. "You'll see everything."

Odysseus laughed softly. "Exactly."

"But the carts. My father."

"They can wait. All of them. But I cannot."

Penelope bit her bottom lip, swallowing hard. She walked to the edge of the bed.

Odysseus sat up, pulling the covers completely off, exposing every inch of his naked body. He reached out a hand to his new wife.

"Come here, woman."

Penelope climbed onto the bed and knelt before her husband. Her heart pounded. She unpinned one shoulder broach, but held the fabric against her bare breast. Odysseus leaned over and deftly unpinned the other broach, gently taking both of her hands in his. The delicate fabric slid down to her waist. She saw the desire in his eyes.

Odysseus leaned back, taking her with him. "I've waited my entire life for a woman such as you." His hands swept down her sides, smoothing over her curves, cupping her buttocks. "No woman is as beautiful as my love."

"Not even—"

"No one."

As Apollo's light reached its zenith, Odysseus and Penelope's entourage of servants and carts laden with dowry offerings began the long westward journey to Ithaka. A giant dust cloud rose behind them. Leading the way in his chariot, Odysseus held the reins in one hand, while the other was wrapped tightly around his bride's shoulders.

"Penelope!" a voice cried from behind.

Odysseus turned, squinting through the haze to see who called out to his wife. "Who can that be?"

A dark figure emerged. "Penelope!" the man cried out again.

"It is my father," Penelope said, quietly.

Odysseus held up his hand, signally for the entourage to stop. "Are you certain?"

"I am."

"Then, we will hear what he has to say."

Within moments of bringing the caravan to a grinding halt, Icarius made his way to his daughter. "I can't let you go to Ithaka. It's too far. You're too young."

Penelope, gentleness guiding each word, said, "Father, Ithaka isn't so far. And many women are already mothers at my age. Surely, you don't wish to deny me the glory of bearing princes?"

Icarius wept openly. "But, you can give him up. It's not too late. Stay with me in Sparta."

Odysseus ground his teeth. "You seek to stop me from taking my wife home? You stage a race, hoping to keep me from your daughter. Now, you follow me, begging her to return with you, forsaking me?"

Penelope placed a steady hand on her husband's arm. "Father, I have made my choice. I have obeyed your will to marry the victor of a race of your making. I can't undo what has been done. It would heap dishonor on me and on my husband."

"What will become of me? Who will look after an old man?"

Odysseus spoke tersely, "That isn't my wife's concern." He glanced down at Penelope, noting the tears in her eyes. His irritation softened. "If you wish to stay—"

"No." Penelope pulled her himation up around her head, turning her back on her father. "I belong to you now."

Smiling, Odysseus signaled for the caravan to pull away. "Only by Athena's grace are you by my side. By her will, we belong to each other."

FIFTY FOUR

reclaiming the past

TROY—1251 BCE

A crisp breeze swept across the balcony, a clear sign that Persephone once again prepared her journey to the Underworld. Priam pulled the heavy wool robe tighter across his chest, returning to his seat near the hearth. *Is this what happens when men get old? We sit, unraveling our regrets from the tapestry of our lives.* He sank back heavily into the chair, staring with watery eyes into the dancing flames. *Hesione.*

"Father?"

Startled from his thoughts, the king straightened in his seat and stood. "You've come. Good." He signaled his servant to pour their wine. "We've much to discuss, Paris."

The second son of Troy glanced at his feet. "Is this about

Oenone? I've told you she'll not live in a city of stone. Corythus is happy with his mother."

Priam held up his hand. "This has nothing to do with the nymph or your son."

"I've heard the rumors. You're worried about your legacy … and the safety of Troy, because Andromache has yet to produce an heir."

Taking the proffered wine from his servant, Priam then commanded, "Leave us." Once alone, the king handed Paris the cup brimming with heady wine. "Sit. I have a delicate matter requiring my attention. I believe you're the one to help me."

Paris swirled the wine before taking a healthy swig, resting the cup on his knee. "Don't you usually request Hektor for such things?"

The king sized up his second son. Paris was nearly Hektor's height. His jaw a bit wider and squarer, his nose perfection, and his eyes twin azure flames. *No wonder the women swoon as he passes by.* "Don't be jealous of Hektor's place at my side. He's the first born. It is his right."

"I am not envious of my brother." Paris sipped his wine, wincing at its bitter bite. "Except for his sword work. On that account, he has no equal. Had I not be raised by a shepherd—"

"I'm aware of the life you would've had, if you'd been raised as my son. But the gods had other plans for us, didn't they?"

"Is that why you've called me here? To talk about the life divine plans stole from me?"

Priam leaned forward in his chair, gazing intently into his son's eyes. "That is precisely what I wish to speak of." He sat back into his chair again, staring again in to the flames. "Have you heard the story of Hesione?"

"The princess taken by Herakles after the Invasion of Troy?"

"Yes. That's the one."

"Only she left Troy and never returned."

"That part is true enough, but there is more to it than that. Laomedon, my father and your grandfather, dishonored the gods."

Paris scoffed at the notion. "I find it difficult to believe."

"Do you? Have you ever wondered how I was able to abandon you, after you were born? Why I didn't try to keep you?"

"A man obeys the gods. Even if they're wrong … as they were regarding me. My birth didn't bring the doom you feared so much."

Priam's finger picked at the silver pommel of the dagger at his waist. "It's far more complicated, Paris. I fear the circumstances of your birth reach back many years."

Paris squeezed the stem of his kylix tighter. "What are you talking about?"

"Laomedon, my father … your grandfather, wasn't the most honest man. He changed his mind like the winds of Aeolus, making promises one day and breaking them the next."

"What does his changeable mind have to do with me?"

"Everything, my son. There was a time, not so long ago, that sections of the wall around our city were in ruin and in some places, unfinished. Laomedon hired two skilled stonemasons to refortify it. They worked for an entire year restoring the wall, making it what it is now. When they demanded their payment, Laomedon refused."

Paris shot a surprised glance at his father. "Why would he dishonor his word?"

Priam shrugged. "Who can say? But what happened next … was a nightmare. The men left the city, angry at being cheated. Within days a plague swept through the city, bringing death to every family in Troy." The king closed his eyes to the hearth light. "And the immortal power of Gaia was unleashed on the city."

"That's just an old wives' tale to scare children."

"I assure you it was real. Very real. The beast rose from the sea. It had the giant head of some ancient Egyptian crocodile. Scaled and vicious. Its roar fell on the city like a thunderous storm. In the dead of night, it slithered and crawled across the hills, consuming beast and mortal alike. By the light of Apollo, it would slink back into the sea, so the men couldn't kill it. The priests told my father the only way to appease its voracious hunger was to offer it a sacrifice. And not just any sacrifice, but a virgin princess. My sister, Hesione." Priam paced before the dying fire. "My father wasted no time chaining Hesione to the rocks as a sacrifice for the city."

"I thought she went west? How did she escape?"

"Herakles."

Paris whispered, "Herakles."

"In an agreement with my father, he slew the beast, claiming Hesione as his prize. When Herakles tried to claim her and take her west, my father once again dishonored his word."

"What happened then?"

"Herakles sailed home and my father sent me southeast to Phrygia. In my absence, Herakles returned with a small fleet and sacked the city, killing my entire family, except for Hesione. I returned in time to confront Herakles, but I was young … too inexperienced against such a warrior. I became king because of my cowardice. And he took Hesione, while I watched from the ramparts."

"What has any of this to do with me?"

Priam took Paris by the hand, pulling him from his chair. "Come." The king walked his son to the veranda. "Do you see the entire city below and beyond?"

Paris nodded. "I do, but—"

"As the king, all that your eyes can see is your responsibility. The people. The land. What you desire most is always second to *her*. And every time I contemplate this story, I can't help but think something more sinister is at work. Some unknown curse or plague is drawing two sides together for a terrible purpose." He grabbed Paris' hand with iron fingers. "Who sent that sea monster? What god created it? Why Troy? I can't help but think the wall and the beast are joined in some way."

"Is that why you sent me away? Because you feared the creature would return?"

"That or worse."

Paris placed a warm hand over his father's wrinkled one. "Troy is safe, Father. I've returned and no harm befell the citadel. All is peaceful."

"True. For now. But there's more. The day I consulted Apollo regarding your mother's vision about your birth, the priestess mentioned Hesione. Asking if I was satisfied a daughter of Troy lived among the Greeks. Until last night, I didn't understand what I must do. Aphrodite has sent me a vision that you would bring a woman from across the Aegean. I know in my bones it must be Hesione."

Paris flinched at the mention of Aphrodite, dropping his hands to his sides. "You wish me to bring Hesione back, don't you?"

Priam wiped a tear from his eye. "That's exactly what I want. I should've never let her leave. She didn't want to go. But I could do nothing at the time. I had to secure the walls first, so Troy couldn't be sacked twice by the likes of Herakles. Some years passed before I sent Antenor to bring Hesione home. But Telemon, friend to Herakles, had taken her to wife and refused to release her."

"Where is she now?"

"She remains in Salamis as wife to that fucking Greek pirate."

"You wish me to kidnap another man's wife? And bring her to Troy?"

"She's a *daughter* of Troy. Hesione belongs among her own people."

"Oenone will not like that I'm leaving."

"You're a prince of Troy now. What's best for the city is what matters most. Hesione must return."

"When do I sail?"

"A ship is being readied even now."

Paris sighed, setting his cup on a nearby table. "I'll go, Father, but I must say farewell to Oenone and my son."

"Go, then. Say your good-byes and bring Hesione back where she belongs." The king embraced his son warmly. "The gods' ways aren't always easy for us."

Paris nodded. "No, they aren't. I'll do my best to make you proud."

Priam smiled. "What father wouldn't be proud of a son such as you?"

———————

Hecuba found Priam sitting alone in the darkened chamber. "I heard Paris is to leave. Sail west at your command."

"Yes," Priam said solemnly.

"Why was I not consulted?"

Priam turned his attention to his wife. "I don't require your permission to send any of my sons on a mission."

Hecuba bristled. "It's Paris … he is different."

"No, he isn't. He must earn the respect of the people and this task will ensure that happens."

"So, it's true then. You're sending him to Salamis for Hesione."

"Whispers travel faster than the wind in my palace."

The queen shrugged. "Our son will always be my concern. Why send Paris? He's but newly welcomed in Troy."

"He has yet to accomplish anything of merit in the eyes of the people. If he can bring home a lost daughter of Troy, he'd be elevated in their eyes. He would be truly accepted as a Prince of Troy, as he should have always been."

"You've been absent from my side for almost an entire moon. Has all thought of us fled your memory?" Oenone cast her eyes to the ground.

Paris stiffened. "No. You and our son are always on my mind."

"Why the delay home?"

"Much has happened, Oenone."

Aphrodite's voice echoed through his mind. *It is time, Paris, it is time* … He didn't want it to be time. He feared what was to come.

Oenone held her hand out to her husband. "Come, my love, let's walk and talk. Tell me everything."

But Paris didn't take her hand—instead, he walked alongside her careful, to stay half a step in front.

"My father has asked me to travel to Salamis. To negotiate the return of his sister, my aunt, Hesione."

Oenone plucked a long blade of grass brushing against her hand. "She's been hostage long enough to call Salamis home. Doesn't she have sons? Greek sons? What if she has no desire to return to Troy?"

"She belongs in Troy. She was taken as a prisoner. Why would she wish to remain among foreigners?"

Oenone shrugged in silence.

Paris stopped and faced Oenone. "Are you happy with this life?"

"We've lived in peace for many seasons. The River flows. Our son thrives."

"And you've no wish to live in Troy? Ever?" Paris asked in earnest.

"None. You've always known this. I belong here, in my world. And you with us."

They came to the sacred tree where they took their vows and Paris stopped. The truth stuck in his throat like a lump of bread too dry to swallow without aid of wine. "Oenone, I …" Clouds filled the sky, casting shadows on the green hills as they passed overhead; the gloomy light a foreboding of the murky future shrouded by dreams.

Paris dared to look into his wife's face. "The ship's already prepared. They wait only for my return to set sail. I must go. You know this," he said quietly.

"Will you return? To us?"

The birds ceased their songs. The wind riders with delicate wings of thin gossamer dropped like autumn leaves around the meadow. The nymph searched her husband's face for comfort. Tears spilled. "I can't live without you."

Without answering her, Paris let his lips fall to hers. He clung to her as a wave of grief and foreboding washed over him. *She's been my home, my heart.* He knew he must collect Aphrodite's gift, or risk offending the goddess. Paris knew it was no coincidence that Priam's command and Aphrodite's words collided. He would obey his father, King Priam, and the goddess. *How can I tell her I will bring home another woman?* She tried to warn me years ago

"There is no wind," he said, holding her close for a final kiss.

"My love, soon the men will call for you to join them," Oenone said, as a silver crystal slid down her cheek.

Paris brushed his thumb across his wife's soft lips. "I'm afraid."

Just then, a gentle breeze stirred the air.

Paris broke from her embrace. "You're right. The crew will be waiting. They'll want to catch the fair winds to cross the sea." He turned, and without looking back, made the long return journey to the dock and his waiting crew.

From afar, Oenone watched the bright blue sail of Paris' ship billow in the breeze. The oarsmen dug deep and swift into the cold cobalt water, white foam churning with every stroke. Only now did Oenone allow herself to weep. She clung to a thread of hope that Paris' love would sustain this distance, this test of faith. She prayed her premonitions false.

"Nereids of the sea," she whispered in prayer, "bring him back safely to me." The salty air whipped her hair across her face. "Bring his love back to us."

Cassandra stood on the rampart of the great wall of Troy next to Hecuba watching the ship carrying Paris to far distant Greece. Moved by Apollo's curse, she spoke, "He'll bring the doom of Troy."

Hecuba crossed her arms tightly across her chest. "You speak of evils long since proven false. He brings not doom, but renewed hope for Troy."

The two women remained side by side watching the ship until

it fell from sight behind the sea and sky.

Cassandra wiped a tear from her cheek. "I speak the truth, but you'll not hear me."

"I lost Paris when he was just a babe. I won't let the gods frighten me with their riddles and false dreams again."

FIFTY FIVE
the lost princess

SALAMIS, PALACE OF TELEMON—1251 BCE

Paris stood in awe of the great hall in Telemon's palace. For such a small island as a kingdom, he'd expected a cruder structure, not bright frescoes and finely carved columns. Sheer drapes swirled in the warm breeze sweeping across the hall from the west. A servant handed him an alabaster cup trimmed with gold filled to the brim with a heady wine. The spicy aroma of cinnamon and honey warmed over his tongue. *What is taking so long? Perhaps, Hesione refuses to speak with me?* He took a seat on a long couch near the open hallway.

As Paris drank his second cup of wine, a door in the middle of a garden fresco on the wall across from him opened. A tall, elegant older woman entered, followed by a retinue of servants. The woman's dark hair was streaked with silver and coiffed in delicate curls caught up behind her head. Her pale blue gown fluttered about her feet as she walked across the chamber.

Paris stood and set down his wine.

Standing before her guest, Hesione hesitated for a moment. "It's been many years since a Trojan stepped foot in Salamis."

"Your brother, my father, sends his most sincere greetings."

"Which of his concubines is your mother?"

"My mother is Queen Hecuba."

Hesione narrowed her eyes in disbelief. "I know of only Hektor. The world knows of Hektor. However, the tales of my brother breeding bastards reach us."

Paris stiffened. "I assure you, I am Hecuba's son."

Hesione motioned to the man who'd entered beside her. "Shall we sit?" Slaves scurried to stage three low reclining couches near the central hearth.

As they eased back into their seats, the servants set up trays of soft cheese, olives, and sticky dates. An odd silence settled between them.

"I suppose Podarces … no wait, they call him Priam now, wants me to return to Troy."

Paris nearly choked on a date. "Yes, he feels … guilty for letting you go all of those years ago."

"Did you know that my own father chained me to a rock as a sacrifice?"

"So I was told."

Hesione sipped her wine. "Well, at least he told you that."

"My father thinks you'd be happier if you returned to Troy and took your rightful place as a princess in your own country."

"My father had many faults, but he was the rightful king.

Podarces—Priam—was the youngest. He should never have become king."

Paris scanned the wall behind his aunt. The fresco depicted a ship on stormy seas, white foam against a wooden hull. Yellow sails billowed in the wind. And behind the ship a great sea monster roared. He noted for the first time a figure at the bow. Long, flowing blue gown and veil. *It's her.* A brightly painted sun broke the clouds against a soft blue sky. *It's her story on the wall.*

Hesione turned to see what captured Paris' attention. Facing him, she said, "Yes, that's how I came to Salamis."

"I hadn't believed my father about the beast."

"Sent by the gods, surely. I pray the world never sees the likes of it again."

Sitting up, Paris leaned forward. "How can you be happy here? Far from the lands you came from?"

"You believe it was all joy for me?" Hesione laughed dryly. "Women survive the lives handed them by men. Has my brother not thought of the hardship I've endured carving out a place for myself, my son, here in Salamis? Did he suppose Telemon's first wife would embrace me, a war prize, with open arms?"

Oenone's face flashed behind Paris' eyes. He'd left her without telling her the truth. But her eyes. *She knows the truth. Hesione is right.* "Our lives are only ours, so long as the gods will it."

"Our lives are never ours. Have you not learned that yet?"

"Then, you are content to remain, here, in Salamis? There is nothing I can do to persuade you?"

"I am old, Paris. I have lost the sound of Troy from my tongue. I will die a Greek, thanks to my brother's cowardice." She clapped her hands and the trays were cleared. "Come. Let's talk of more pleasant things. Tell me about yourself, nephew."

Hesione led Paris to a secluded beach with a pebbled shore. Apollo's light waned as they walked. Black and white sea birds cried overhead. The soft crunch of the beach beneath their feet filled the space between them.

Hesione asked, "So, you were raised by a bull herder?"

Clasping his hands behind his back, Paris nodded. "I learned much from Agelaus."

"Do you see him often now that you live in the citadel?"

"No. That life belongs to another man."

"I understand what it is to leave one life, for another." Hesione patted Paris on the shoulder. "It seems you've also been forced into a life not of you're own making." She hugged her himation closer to her chest. "You will find peace … *eventually.*" They walked on a bit farther. Hesione stopped. "Isn't the sun glorious this time of day?"

The golden light caught in his aunt's hair and softened the years on her face. "It is."

"When I was younger, I dreamt of marriage and children. Now that I'm old, all I can think about is freedom from the responsibilities of both. I had a vision of you, Paris."

"Do I want to hear it? Visions and prophesies have never offered me good tidings."

"I couldn't say if it was one way or the other. Perhaps, you'll know the meaning?"

Paris rubbed his chin, the shadow of a day already evident. "What did you see?"

"I saw a ship on a stormy sea. And a woman's voice carried on the wind."

"What did the voice say?"

Hesione met Paris' gaze. "In Sparta, you will find her."

Paris ran his hand through his hair. "*She* will be in Sparta."

"Does that hold meaning for you?"

"Aye. A dark meaning."

"Then, your journey here wasn't entirely in vain."

Go to Sparta, Paris. Take her. She's yours.

"I will leave in the morning."

"I'll see your ship is resupplied." Hesione touched Paris' arm. "I'm sorry you'll return empty handed, as did Antenor."

"When Troy lost you to these Greeks, it lost a treasure."

Hesione shrugged. "Perhaps, someday I'll send my son, Teucer, to see his grandfather's kingdom."

Paris smiled broadly, using the charm that disarmed Lexias time and time again. He liked his estranged aunt. "He will be welcomed in Troy."

FIFTY
SIX

the handmaiden's moon

LYRNESSUS—1251 BCE

Across the courtyard, Briseis caught a glimpse of the handmaiden's belly rounded like a full moon. The sting of resentment resurfaced. *Why did they take my darling Phila and leave me barren? What offense have I committed?* She found herself silently questioning and cursing the gods since Mynes informed her that the handmaiden had finally conceived. Briseis had secretly prayed, until that moment, that the gods bless her own womb just one last time. But, her flow returned month after month. After the first ritual union, she'd demanded the chosen woman not touch her. She also removed herself from the bed once Mynes was on the verge of spilling his seed, and turned her back as her husband coupled with the handmaiden. Hearing the woman's moaning was torture, and sometimes, she caught Mynes' own suppressed roar of pleasure. And after those evenings, her heart ached for days afterward.

The handmaiden was laughing with another servant woman. Briseis stood from the bench and walked in the opposite direction, but not before she spied the handmaiden protectively rubbing her protruding belly.

"My lady!" a voice called to her.

Briseis stopped mid-step. It was the handmaiden. *She dares address me?* Shame for what they'd done the first union and jealousy for the rest stained her cheeks crimson. She turned, forcing a blank stare.

"My lady, I've good news."

"You may speak." Briseis' jaw clicked tightly.

"The midwife tells me I will deliver the prince any day."

"Then the gods bless Prince Mynes."

"Yes, he's been most generous to me."

All of the resolve Briseis built to isolate herself from the inevitable, tumbled to the ground. "How so?"

"He's promised to provide for me and our son as long as I live."

Briseis' lips pressed to a tight line. *Don't ask anything. Turn and walk away.* "You won't have anything to do with *our* son … or daughter, when the child's born. You're simply the vessel. Not even important enough for a name."

The handmaiden smiled slowly, like a thief pulling a hidden blade. "My lord, Prince Mynes, calls me by my name when he visits my chambers."

"Your chambers?"

"How else do you think me rounded so quickly with his love? You believe those few times of coupling in your presence would plant his seed so quickly?"

A red anger flashed behind Briseis' eyes and her hand flew out, striking the handmaiden hard on the cheek. "He gives you his seed. Nothing more."

The handmaiden ran from her, crying and holding her hand to her burning cheek.

A single oil lamp cast a dim glow about the royal chamber. Mynes allowed his eyes to adjust before entering. To his surprise, Briseis was still awake and staring into the shadows. "Are you unwell?" he asked.

"No."

Unbuckling his belt, Mynes dropped it to the floor. "Good." He stripped his chiton, tossing it to the ground as well. Naked, he walked to his wife. "Come to bed."

"Have you been with *her*?"

"Her?"

Briseis gripped the carved wood of the hand rests on her chair. "The handmaiden."

"Malina."

"Did you, just now, come from her chamber?"

Mynes hesitated. "Yes."

Briseis stood. "Why? Why was I not enough for you?"

"This is different, Briseis. She carries the heir to Lyrnessus. I thought we had an understanding."

"We did, but you have gone around it."

"Would you have me be cruel to her … as you have been?"

"I didn't intend to strike her." Briseis averted her eyes. Her chin quivered and tears threatened to spill. "I'm incomplete. Worthless, because she can do what I cannot. All of the world witnesses my shame."

"Briseis," Mynes sighed, "I've only ensured that she would get with child. I have no love for her."

"You take pleasure in lying with her. I've heard you. Your sounds when you …"

"For seed to spill, a man must feel the joy of the moment. It passes quickly. Briseis, I *fuck* her because I must. I find pleasure in it, true. But, it isn't love. I don't linger with her."

"But she said—"

"Malina is a slave. Nothing more."

"She said you'd provide for her after."

"She will be nurse maid, as well. What of it?"

"I wish her gone."

Mynes took Briseis in his arms; her body stiffened against his. "In time, she will be sent away. If that is what you wish."

Briseis wept bitterly. "I'm not strong enough to endure this."

"Yes, you are. Once our son arrives, joy will find your heart again."

"I want our world the way it was."

"We are too old for such wishes. It's the way of gods to make us suffer and learn our place. If the gods showed favor to kings and queens, they'd never have taken Phila—"

Briseis' old grief broke through and she slumped against her husband's bare chest. Bitter tears now emerged. "Why did they take her from us? She was perfect."

Mynes kissed her forehead. "She shone as a bright star in the darkest night." He swept his wife into his arms and carried her to their bed. As he lay her down, he kissed her tear-stained cheeks. The salt of her grief wet his tongue. "We'll not forget her." He kissed down Briseis' neck. "I haven't forgotten us, my love. My heart belongs only to you. Until death steals me to the Underworld, I'm yours."

"Swear it."

"By all the gods of Olympus, I swear it."

"Make love to me, Mynes, make love to me so that my doubts disappear."

"As you wish, wife."

Apollo rose in the sky, dragging the golden light behind his chariot, when Mynes finally finished loving Briseis. As his wife slept, he watched her eyes flutter. He wished their life were simpler. He wished their daughter had never died. He wished for a hundred years to love her. His beautiful Briseis.

FIFTY SEVEN

a Trojan guest

SPARTA, PALACE OF MENELAUS & HELEN—1251 BCE

Helen handed the baby to the wet nurse. "I believe the child is hungry. She pushes her face to my breast."

The wet nurse took the baby and cooed at its soft fussing. "There, little Hermione, little princess." She opened her gown and the babe hungrily latched on to the large nipple and quickly calmed.

Helen watched her daughter suckle at the other woman's breast. She'd hoped a child would bring her happiness with Menelaus, but she'd been wrong. The young queen sighed heavily and looked out her window to the hills beyond the palace. She yearned for a different life. Sparta was more prison than home, since her marriage. When Menelaus took the crown as king, the freedom she'd enjoyed since childhood shrank to the palace grounds. Now, her days were marked with endless thoughts of escape to live a life of her choosing, not one the king dictated.

"I'm told we have guests this evening, my lady," the wet nurse said.

The queen leaned against the ledge. "We do. I hear a Prince of Troy has arrived with horses as gifts for my husband."

The wet nurse rocked the child in her arms as she nursed it. Her experienced hand swept the baby's forehead to lull the tiny princess to sleep as her royal belly filled. "Aye. I hear the horses are almost as magnificent as the prince himself."

Helen's eyes narrowed. "The horses merit such praise?"

"Aye. So I've heard."

"I should see them for myself. Perhaps, one will be a suitable match for Hermione." Helen adjusted her hair in the polished silver mirror and smiled. "You have care of the princess."

"Aye, my lady."

Helen swept through the door. "See that Aethra has the hall properly prepared."

With her mistress gone, the wet nurse kissed Hermione's soft pink cheek. "You're too young for a horse, sweet face. Too young. If I know your mother ... wells, no mind then."

———

paris brushed the tawny hide of the mare until the silver undertone shimmered. "You're a pretty girl." He gently patted the horse's neck.

"She is," a voice behind him sounded as music in his ears.

The prince turned to find a woman with eyes the color of a pale green staring at him. "She's for the queen. Queen Helen."

"Interesting. I'd not heard you'd be bringing gifts to the house of Menelaus. You were headed to … Salamis was it not? To rescue the dusty crone, Hesione."

Guilt at his failure forced his eyes to the dirt and straw beneath his feet. "She's family, my lady. I've failed in my aunt's regard. And when I return to Troy, I'll have to face the reflection of that failure in my father's eyes."

"I see. Family is … *important* for many reasons."

Paris couldn't help but notice the golden highlights of the woman's hair. The perfection of her skin. "Family is all things relevant to life."

"There's a feast in your honor this evening. Hospitality demands nothing less than a feast for a Prince of Troy."

"Will I see you there?" Paris asked.

Helen walked to the horse and ran her hand down the mare's elegant neck. "She's a fine beast." The horse nuzzled Helen's shoulder, bringing a coy smile to the queen's lips. "The queen will be pleased."

Men laughed. Women laughed. The silver strings of lyres and joyful song floated on the air. Paris was into his second bowl of wine, when the herald announced the queen's entrance. All festivity ceased. His eyes fell on the golden beauty from the stables. He nodded to her. *Of course. How could she not be the famous wife of Menelaus?* Merriment resumed as she entered, taking her place between her husband, King Menelaus, and the guest of honor.

Paris lifted a hammered silver bowl to his lips, as a voice whispered seductively, "*She's yours. Take her.*" The hair on Paris' arm stood on end. He knew the voice. "Aphrodite?" Her name was barely audible as it passed over his lips.

"*It is.*"

"I can't," he said.

"*You can.*"

Menelaus asked, "What can't you do?"

"Drink more wine!" Paris laughed.

"Of course you can!" Menelaus clapped Paris on the shoulder. "Let's drink until we fall where we stand!"

Again, Aphrodite taunted, "*She's yours. Take her.*"

Helen took the shared vessel between herself and Paris, raising it to her lips. "We meet again."

"It was an unfair advantage, my queen. I didn't know who you were."

"Do I sense disappointment?"

"Only that I hoped the woman I met was unattached. Now, I see that you most clearly are. I would've put you from my mind, if I'd known."

"You've been thinking of me? I'm flattered, Prince of Troy." Helen reached a hand to his. "You're most noble."

Paris slid his hand from hers. "I've spoiled your surprise. My apologies, Queen Helen."

Helen's finger traced the rim of their shared bowl. "The mare."

Paris swallowed hard, secretly annoyed that his cock twitched against his thigh. "Yes, the mare."

"She's a most lovely creature. The most handsome addition to the royal stables, I'm certain." Helen took another sip of wine, before proffering it to Paris. "Will you take me to her?"

Paris took the bowl. "You mean, now?"

The queen nodded. "That's what I mean." She put a hand on her husband's shoulder. He turned to face her. "Did you arrange for this gift? The horse from Troy?" Before Menelaus could utter a word, she kissed his cheek. He flushed more ruddy than he was by nature. "You're the most adoring husband a wife could ask the gods for."

The king gripped her hand in his. "You're pleased, then?"

Helen batted her eyes under his heavy attention. "I am."

Menelaus' fingers dug into her thigh. "You may thank me later."

Helen looked down at the greasy hand smear on her gown, hiding her disgust. "May I visit her now? At the stables? I barely caught a glimpse of her earlier. I should like to thoroughly inspect my gift now that I know she's mine to keep."

"Go! Go, my love. Take the guards with you." Menelaus swiped his hand against the air. "Go! Enjoy the gift."

"I should like the Trojan Prince to accompany us. He knows the horse better than anyone. I would hear all about this mare."

Menelaus, the wine filling him with warmth and his wife's kiss filling him with promise of a heated night in the dark, felt generous. "Yes, by all means. If the prince doesn't mind leaving such a festive hall behind?"

Paris twisted the golden cuff at his wrist. "I'd be honored."

As they walked to the stables, Helen pulled her himation closer about her shoulders. "The chill is unexpected on a night like tonight. Stars blazing against a clear black sky."

Paris removed his own cloak from his shoulders and wrapped it around Helen. "I'm used to the chill. I've spent many nights under such stars." He was highly aware of the three guards shadowing them, so was careful not to look into her eyes. Once at the stable, she commanded the guards to wait outside. They obeyed their queen.

The tawny mare with a silver mane whinnied at the sight of

Paris. "There now, girl." Putting his hand to the horse's nose, he stroked it softly and scratched her behind the ears.

Helen held out her hand to the horse and followed Paris' lead. She let her fingers brush against his as she stroked the horse.

Paris pulled his hand to his side and stepped back. "What are you doing?"

Helen pressed closer to him, dropping her himation and his cloak to the ground. "This is what you want, isn't it?" She rested a soft hand on his chest.

"I-I … No, we can't," he gently rebuffed her advance. "I have a wife."

Helen laughed quietly. "And I, a husband. A wife matters not to me. She's not here, is she? How will she know, unless you speak the words to her?"

"But Menelaus …" Paris leaned closer, warming to the overture. Aphrodite's words sang in his head. "*Take her, she's yours …*"

"He'll never know. Not a single word from my lips, Paris, Prince of Troy."

"I can't deny that you're more beautiful than—"

Helen gently touched his cheek, letting her fingers trace the line of his jaw and the side of his neck. As she pulled his head down to hers, she asked, "Are you thirsty, Paris, Prince of Troy?"

Paris' dark eyes bored into hers with a hunger so palpable her heart raced with anticipation.

The prince bent his head to kiss her full, waiting lips.

"*Take him. Own him …*" a woman's voice spoke near Helen's ear, instantly sparking a desire deep within her belly for Paris. Desire turned to burning flame beneath his kisses. The fierceness of her need of this stranger shocked her. "I want you inside of me."

Paris lifted her silken gown over her hips and slipped his

hand between her thighs, sliding his fingers into her sacred cross. Exquisite moans escaped her lips. Helen spread her thighs so he could reach deeper inside of her. "More. I beg you more."

Paris picked her up, so she straddled his hips. Balancing with her thighs resting on his, he pressed her back into a nearby wooden beam. Holding her with one arm, he released his cock with his free hand.

Helen felt the heat of the tip pressing into her inner thigh. "Why do you pause?" she whispered into his neck. "Take me. I must have you, or I will die."

Paris plunged his lust inside of her. He rammed her with hard, hungry thrusts. Helen grabbed at his shoulders, digging her nails into his skin. She wrapped her legs tightly around his waist. Each thrust reached deeper, until the heat inside of her reached its peak. Paris covered her mouth with his to stifle her cries as she reached a shaking climax. He followed quickly after, spilling his passion deep inside of her. When the madness passed, he gently set her on her feet. They stood panting and holding each other like long lost lovers.

Helen broke the silence between them. "I feel as if I've only now discovered home."

"In this, you're not alone." Paris buried his face in her neck, covering her porcelain skin with kisses.

"Take me with you," Helen whispered into his ear.

Paris abruptly ceased the onslaught of his lips, lifting his head to meet her gaze. "You wish to go to Troy?"

"I can't be parted from you. Not now."

As he kissed her, any thought of Oenone fluttered away. "Nor I from you. Helen …"

The world around Helen faded as his warm mouth descended on hers again. She tasted the wine and honey on his tongue. He smelled of the sea and stars. His kiss deepened. Helen's knees weakened, and he pulled her closer, kissing her harder. The tang of blood on her bottom lip excited her. In that moment she lost all desire to be queen of Sparta. Since marrying Menelaus, she'd seduced many men in her quest for love, but none had awakened her passions until now. All of her life she'd built walls around her heart. Now, with a stranger's kiss, all of her defenses tumbled to dust at her feet. Her heart lay exposed for the first time in her life. Paris was pulling her love to the surface and it frightened her. This prince from Troy was unlocking the gates guarding her very soul, one by one, with each kiss, with each caress and she was helpless to stop him. What frightened her most was that deep down, in the secret recesses of her heart, she wanted him to possess her, every part of her. She wanted to become a part of his very soul, a part of him that he couldn't live without. For the first time, she longed for a cage, a prison, a dungeon … any walls at all that would bind them together forever.

Paris broke the spell. "We should go. Your husband will be suspicious if we don't return soon."

"Let the polis and Menelaus be swallowed up by Poseidon's raging sea. I don't care. Let the sea swallow me as well, if I can't be with you."

Paris pulled her tightly against his chest. "What you ask is impossible. I can't deny that I desire it. But it can't be done."

A tear slid down Helen's cheek. "I'll die if I can't be with you."

Paris wiped the tear away with his thumb. His guilt slowly returned him to his senses. "Apollo's glory will rise each day after I've sailed for home. In time, this feeling will fade into a pleasant memory … for us both."

"I think you're mistaken, Paris. I've been imprisoned here in

Sparta my entire life. Guarded and protected like a delicate treasure. I long for freedom. For love. I've none of those things here. Take me with you or I'll surely die of a broken heart and broken spirit."

"I don't see how it can be done," Paris said. "What of your child?"

"Hermione must remain in Sparta. She's the rightful heir," Helen replied.

"Can you live without your daughter?" Thoughts of Hecuba's grief came to mind. He wondered if Helen truly knew what she was sacrificing. Then it occurred to him, the plain truth of this easily professed love. They were both under Aphrodite's influence. Helen knew nothing of the judgment, yet she was the promised treasure. Would her love fade if she knew her place as pawn for the Goddess of Love's triumph as the fairest? The pull of wanting Helen was as the moon upon the sea. He knew that it was happening, yet could not … *No*, he thought, didn't want to halt the ebb and flow between them.

Helen's eyes filled with tears. "No sacrifice is without pain."

Paris shook his head. "I still say it is impossible."

"If I show you the way, will you consider my offer?"

Paris didn't answer immediately, but then, "Yes."

Helen embraced her new lover. "What a life we shall have, you and I." She smoothed her gown and re-pinned tendrils of her hair that had escaped during their lovemaking. "Then, we should go."

After Paris returned safely to his private chambers, the words of Aphrodite echoed in his head. *How can it be done, Goddess? You've gifted me the impossible. I have a wife. I can't steal the wife of another.* Paris conjured up Oenone's face. *I can't …*

The goddess's words floated overhead. *"Yes you can, Paris … and you will. It is your destiny to love her and herald the doom of Troy."*

He couldn't live without the woman. A stranger. A foreigner. He would let Oenone go. *But what of Troy? Am I truly the curse?* Paris wept.

The golden glow of Apollo's light flooded the queen's chamber. Helen opened her eyes and smiled remembering the lovemaking she shared with Paris. She imagined herself as a princess of Troy. It was told that the women of Asia were highly regarded by their men and families and not treated as mere chattel. *My life will be more glorious in Troy. I'll be free.* A knock sounded at her door. Helen kicked the coverlets off. "What hour is it?"

Through the door Aethra called out, "My lady, it's approaching the midday meal."

Helen walked to the door and unlatched the iron bar. "And you let me lay about for so long? Where's the king?"

Aethra, followed by a gaggle of giggling young women, tumbled through the opening. "We were instructed by the king to let you sleep." Her maids quickly went about pulling gowns from cupboards, jewels from boxes, and ribbons from baskets. "It would be rude to keep the Prince of Troy waiting much longer."

"You speak as if the king were absent from the palace. Where's my husband?"

"The king has gone, my lady."

Helen dropped the golden circlet from her hands onto the table where it clanged against the marble. "Gone? What do you mean gone?"

Aethra shook out a dark red gown. "He's sailed for Crete, my lady. As soon as the sun rose. The winds favored."

Helen took the scarlet gown from Aethra's hands. "Crete? For the love of Zeus why Crete? Why was I not informed?"

"I beg your pardon, my lady, but his wish was not to burden you."

"Speak plainly, Aethra. What are you talking about?"

The enslaved queen mother of Theseus took the dress back from the Helen's hands. "A ship arrived before the dawn carrying a messenger. Catreus is dead, my lady. Will you be wearing the red gown?"

"Yes. It's fine." The maids pulled the night shift over Helen's head. "His mother's father. He was long in years, but not ill."

"My lady, he was killed by his son's own hand. A tragedy really. Althaemenes ran him through with his own spear. Mistakenly, of course."

Helen gasped. "Why would Althaemenes kill his own father? Surely he knows the gods punish such heinous actions most severely. Mistakenly? What riddle are you telling?"

"When Catreus arrived in Rhodes, he was apparently not recognized by anyone. His face altered by his travels, or perhaps the gods. Who can say? And so, Althaemenes killed him before his identity was revealed. Red is a good choice for you, my lady."

The queen paused, looking at her captive maid. "How is it you know so much of the comings and goings of the palace?" Helen wondered if the old crone knew about her tryst with Paris in the stable last night.

Aethra smiled. "I'm a keen observer. It's my duty to keep my Queen informed, is it not?"

Helen grimaced. "Yes, the red will be fine for today. I best not keep our guest waiting any longer."

Not long after, the queen swept from the room, the long train of her silken gown trailing behind her in a crimson cloud.

———————

Paris paced the stone floor in the main hall. The memory of Helen's kisses haunted him. "What have I agreed to?"

"My Lord Paris."

The Trojan prince turned. "Helen. My Queen." His heart pounded.

"Apologies for keeping you waiting. It wasn't my intention to be inhospitable."

"Your hospitality …" Paris lost his thoughts under her intense gaze.

Helen extended her hand. "Come. I believe I have something to offer you."

Paris took her hand in his and she curled her fingers between his. "I—"

The young queen whisked him from the hall and from the eyes of servants into a darkened corridor. "Kiss me."

Paris obeyed despite the dishonor of the act. *"Take her, she is yours …"*

"Your husband, the king …"

"Has left for Crete. The gods open a way for us to be together."

Paris kissed her passionately, his blood pumping furiously through his veins. "Aphrodite makes the way for us." He plunged a hand between her breasts. "I want you more than I have ever wanted any woman."

Helen returned his lust with equal measure. She smashed her body against his. "I would have you now. Here."

"Someone may see us," Paris protested.

"And if they do? Who will stop us?"

"You take risks, my lady." His raging blood pushed his cock to standing.

Helen lifted her gown and wrapped a leg around him. "Now." They made love quickly, not as they had the night before.

The prince rested his forehead against hers. "How will I live without you? You're the very breath of me."

"We won't be parted, my love. I'll show you the way."

"It goes against the laws of men and gods for me to take you. Yet, a searing pain binds me when I think of leaving your side. Aphrodite is bewitching me with your love." *Helen doesn't understand.*

"Then she's doomed us both. Or blessed us. Come." Helen led them down a series of stone walled corridors. She stopped at a set of large double doors framed on either side by torches. "The guards will be away for some time. We must hurry."

"Where are you taking me?"

Helen laughed. "Into the treasury, of course." She pushed open the doors. Darkness filled the space before them. The queen pulled a torch from its sconce, holding it high into the void. Slowly the glitter of gold and jewels came into view. "The riches of Sparta," Helen said.

Paris stood speechless at the sight of such wealth. What he beheld could rival the vaults of Troy. "How has Menelaus—"

"My husband is well rewarded by his brother in Crete for his service. Crete, you know, is the wealthiest kingdom in the seas. That and my dowry."

"I'd heard rumor of Sparta's wealth. I've never believed it. Until now that is. Always considered the whispers to be based on legend or lies."

"It's as real as the air you're breathing."

Paris ran his hands through his hair. He shook his head as if to shake the reality of his sight. "It's real enough." He turned to Helen whose green eyes sparkled with mischief. "Helen, how does this bring you to Troy?"

"We'll take half of the treasury and offer it to your father. He'll take it as reparation for the capture of his sister ... that and my presence in Troy as your captive bride should satisfy."

Paris was astonished by her plan yet equally impressed with her scheme. "It may work. If Priam is agreeable."

"How could he not be? You'll have brought half the gold of Sparta and its queen and placed them at his feet. All without bloodshed."

The Trojan prince considered the plan from every possible angle. "I'll do as you've said. It's a daring move, especially if we can pull it off ... if I'm ever to be seen as worthy among my brothers in my father's eyes."

Helen reached for Paris' hand. She kissed each knuckle and wrapped his arm around her waist. "I would have no other man, save you."

A sharp thought pierced his mind's veil. "My wife—"

The queen placed a slender finger over his lips. "We needn't speak of her now. We belong to each other. That's all we must know. All we must cling to."

Paris stared into the enormous chamber. Gold coins filled clay jars to overflowing. Jewels spilled from boxes on to table tops and onto the ground. Discs of silver were stacked here and there.

"What if Priam refuses?"

"He won't refuse, Paris. He can't refuse such a gift. His honor will demand nothing less than full acceptance."

"How will we move such treasure?" Paris asked.

"Send as many of your men as you deem truly loyal to you. I will send my personal guards as well. They will move the dowry portion of this as it belongs to me, and a bit more. Wherever I go, my gold goes. And I choose to go with you."

Paris nodded agreement.

"There's no time to waste. We must leave before Menelaus returns or gets word of what we've done. We must make it safely back to Troy, before he has a chance to catch us."

Helen held her daughter in her arms, stroking her soft cheek as she slept. All of her life she'd never dreamt the dreams of young girls, dreams of marriage and bearing children. She'd yearned for freedom and, in honest quiet moments with herself, she dreamed of love. She'd always been under guard or the watchful eyes of her brothers and father. Then, she was given to Menelaus, an older, ruddy-faced man with a barrel chest and legs like oak trees. Many of her household maids flitted around her husband. She knew they found him handsome and desirable. But she felt nothing. All of the women spoke of how the act of lovemaking with a husband, if done with proper enthusiasm, was enough to bring even the wildest dog to heel, and if done particularly well was a pleasure rivaling a hot bath. Bedding with Menelaus gave no such pleasure, no matter how rigorous. He always smelled of leather and wine, and moved awkwardly when he heaved his body on hers and he sweat too much. The act with him only disgusted her. But, her contrived willingness to accommodate her husband's voracious appetite for her gave him enough cause to grant her more freedom. He'd gradually relaxed his guard for her and she'd found other men to share her body with, bringing momentary pleasure, yet the desire to run free remained. She'd thought motherhood would perhaps fill the void growing within her, but that had been wrong as well.

Motherhood surprised her. She loved Hermione in her way. Now, on the precipice of leaving the babe behind, her heart softened for the girl. Helen loved her mother, although Leda was always a distant and cold figure more concerned with propriety and duty than in joyful expressions of love. And that had become the dream she chased more than anything else. The freedom to be and to love and have that love returned in equal passionate measure. As she peered down into her daughter's tiny face, she thought that perhaps, one day, this child could hold such affection for her. But her emptiness cried out now. It would not wait to be satisfied. What if Menelaus dictated horrors for Hermione that would steal the love she waited for the child to return? The way her father had stolen Clytemnestra's joy, distancing mother from daughter. She would be old and disappointed. And lonely.

Guilt pricked her heart, because she knew it was wrong forsaking her husband and abandoning her child for Paris like this. How could she ever explain that the promise of love Paris offered her cried louder against the present remorse? How would she explain that the Spartan crown had made her lonelier, or that marriage to Menelaus slowly suffocated her? There was not a single person in her world that could understand the turmoil she lived with on a daily basis. Women were not supposed to want anything that their husbands didn't already want for them. Life was supposed to be complete.

"I'm sorry, little one, that I could not be the mother you'll need me to be," Helen spoke softly. "I'll always be longing for something more than what I can possess if I remain in Sparta." The child kicked her feet at the blanket. "You're a princess of Sparta, little Hermione. I can leave you that at least." The queen kissed her daughter for the final time and laid her down in her cradle. She glanced one last time at Hermione as she passed through the door, heart torn, but determined, as she left to meet Paris for an uncertain future.

FIFTY EIGHT

lost at sea

EGYPT—1251 BCE

Helen vomited a mouthful of foamy bile into a bowl beside her bed. Winds howled. The ship pitched violently. Paris entered the small aft-chamber soaking wet, catching Helen heaving her empty stomach contents again into the bedside bowl.

"We're being carried off course by the winds of Aeolus," Paris announced.

Helen wiped her mouth with the edge of her gown. Her throat ached. "Will we make land before I die?"

"Where's Aethra? Why isn't she here to help you?"

"I sent her away. I don't want her to see me laid so low. I believe she delights in these small inconveniences I have to bear."

"Someone must empty your chamber pot."

Helen heaved once again. "The entire world is spinning." She laid her head down on the damp pillow. "I wish I would die."

"I'm afraid, my love, that you won't die." Paris sat next to her. "In time, you'll be up and no longer sickened by the rolling sea."

Helen groaned. "How does one ever get accustomed to the constant motion? Impossible."

Paris brushed a golden strand of her hair from her pale face. "The storm makes it worse. If the gods allow, we'll either make land or be on our way across the Aegean for Troy."

"The gods will allow nothing for us. We've taken our fates into our own hands and they will punish us for that."

"Aphrodite deemed it so. We can't be reproved for obeying her."

"The other gods must not agree with her. Look at us. Not even Aeolus will help us."

"Land!" a voice rang out above them. "Land!"

The prince kissed Helen on the forehead. "Answered prayer. I'll send someone to empty this bowl." Paris left the cramped quarters and the queen to her unfortunate misery.

Paris surveyed the horizon. "Where are we?" he asked the master helmsman.

"The gods help us, but we've landed at the Salt-Pans of Egypt."

Paris' lips tightened to a thin line. "Egypt." He'd dealt with Egyptian traders before. They were a difficult lot. Rigid. Trading relations were steady and stable, but there was certainly no great affection between Trojans and Egyptians.

"A hard people, these Egyptians," said the helmsman.

"Aye." Paris gripped the rail of the ship and studied the sky. "Dark clouds. The wind's steady at our side. The storm's not over, yet."

"Aye, my lord. On that we agree."

"Keep the men aboard. With any fortune, we'll be able to set sail before contact is made. Send someone to see to my Lady Helen. Her chamber bowl needs emptying."

"Aye, my lord. I'll see it done."

Under the gray light of the moon, a small band of sailors, having swum the cold distance between the Trojan ship and the Nile Delta's shore, followed the faint glowing light in the distance.

Polon—the short, fat one—spoke, "Do you think they'll spare us?"

"Shut your fucking trap, Polon. Anything's better than serving that conniving bastard, Paris. Prince or no," Linos said.

They trudged across wet sand, their feet sinking with each step. Their progress sounded like a giant beast slurping its way along the shore. As they grew closer to the light, the structure rose clearly into view. The towering columns and palisade marked it as a temple to a powerful god. An enormous hammered bronze bowl held a perpetual fire in homage to the divine, lighting what appeared to be a hundred steps to the entrance.

"Do you think it's a temple to Apollo? Or Zeus?" Phokas—the tall, lanky slave—blurted out, as they stood dumbfounded by the scale of the building.

Linos shook his head. "We're in Egypt, you dumb fucks. They've their own gods to contend with."

Phokas sneered at Linos. "What kind of high born are you

pretending to be? You're as low as the rest of us."

Linos rubbed the back of his head and spat back, "I may be low born by my mother, but my father was lord of the house. He made certain I was taught to read and that's more than you can say, Phokas. You scrawny bastard. More than the lot of you can claim."

Phokas answered the taunt by slinging an insult. "You're still a bastard slave like the rest of us. Deciphering scratch makes you no expert in a foreign land. You've no more idea what this place is than we do."

"Why have you come along? Linos already told you to shut that gaping hole in your face," Straton said.

Polon hooked his fingers into his belt hidden partially by his rounded belly. "The only way to know anything at all is to climb the steps and see for ourselves."

The men all nodded agreement and ascended the massive incline to the top.

As they crossed the threshold of the temple, a tall, dark man greeted them in Egyptian. His robes were colorful and swept the floor as he walked. His face and head were shorn of hair and his eyes thickly lined with kohl. He paused in their path, waiting for a response.

Straton spoke, "We're from Troy."

The priest nodded. "Your disheveled appearance obscures your place of origin."

Straton was taken aback by the priest's ability to slip so easily into their native tongue. "You know our language?"

"I'm gifted with the knowledge of many tongues of many people. We're Egyptians. We're the center of the world. Not barbarians, like some."

Phokas asked the obvious question, "Which god lives in this

temple? Will we be granted sanctuary if we ask?"

The priest nodded his head slowly, understanding dawning on him. "You're runaway slaves. Not shipwrecked sailors."

Straton narrowed his eyes at Phokas. "You idiot."

"Peace, captain of slaves. You've nothing to fear here in the temple of the great Osiris."

"Is there sanctuary then? For the likes of us?" Phokas asked.

"If your reasoning is sound, Osiris may grant you safety from your master." The tall priest gestured with a long arm and a tapering finger for the retched group to enter. One by one they eyed each other, silently agreeing to take their chances with the foreign god.

Once inside, the Trojan slaves walked in awe behind the priest, deeper into the forest of golden columns.

Polon spoke, "I swear by all of the gods I know, I've not seen anything like this in my entire life."

"The pillars touch the sky," Linos said.

"Aye. We've nothing to compare in Troy."

Over his shoulder the priest replied, "Many traders from your realm believe only the gods themselves could construct such a magnificent structure." He stopped before a door so large they couldn't see the top of the lintel. "Wait in this ante-chamber. You'll be heard."

The slaves entered as the door pulled open from the inside. Having nowhere to sit, they remained standing.

"Are you sure we've done the right thing?" Linos asked.

"We'll soon find out," Straton said, as a different priest entered the chamber.

"Greetings, I am Thonis, Warden of the Delta. I'll hear the transgressions of your master. If your protest is just, your wish to remain with us will be granted. Your safety guaranteed."

Straton spoke first. "We're from the kingdom of Troy, in the service of Prince Paris."

"Go on," Thonis instructed.

"What he's done will surely bring the wrath of the gods on us."

Phokas threw his hands up. "Look at what they've done so far! We've been blown off course, before the fool can even make it back to Troy! The gods will see us all dead for our part in this."

Thonis nodded. "What crime has your master committed that you fear for your own life?"

"He's kidnapped the Queen of Sparta."

The Egyptian raised his eyebrows. "Helen of Sparta?"

Straton scratched his head. "You've heard of her?"

"Her beauty is known throughout the world. How did your master come to possess her?"

"He was a guest of King Menelaus. When the king was summoned to a funeral, he left his wife and child behind. In keeping with hospitality laws. Our master raped her and bound her and brought her aboard our ship."

Thonis clasped his hands behind his back. "Heavy, grievous accusations."

Straton added, "He took half of the king's treasury as well."

"Grievous, indeed," Thonis sighed. "Proteus, the god, must be consulted. Your Poseidon favors him and he shall determine the consequence."

"What of us? What will become of us? If Paris discovers our mutiny, he'll surely kill us!" Polon shouted. "I've no wish to die."

Thonis answered, "You'll not die today. At first light, we will make for Memphis. Proteus resides there. He'll want to hear your accusations straight from your slave captain's lips."

The slaves of Paris stood in awed silence before the god. They'd not have believed Proteus existed had they not been presented to him. Even seated, he towered over them by half a body's length. His skin shimmered with the pale silver-green scales of a fish. His hair, as black as a winter's night, swam about his shoulders. His eyes—two sparkling, black orbs—pierced the veil of mortal men's lies.

Thonis asked, "What shall we do with Paris? Seize him or release him?"

Proteus, in a voice as deep as thunder, his words cracking the air, stated, "There is mostly truth in their words. The winds favor the Trojan Prince. Bring him and the Spartan queen and the gold to me, before he slips away on the open sea. Egypt has peace with the Hittites and we've no desire for a vicious raiding triad of Argives, Danaans, and Achaeans uniting against us. The king of Sparta may come and claim what is his by right, the woman and the gold. Paris, disgraced as he is, can't be harmed by my own word. I've spoken that none who land in Egypt by sheer accident may be put to death. The winds carried him here. Let the winds carry him back to his people. They may do with his empty hands what they will."

"It will be done, Proteus," Thonis promised.

The god added, "He has three days to depart from this land, or I will consider him an enemy of Egypt."

Thonis bowed low, his hand sweeping the floor. "Your command."

Paris and Helen lay in a tangled heap of naked legs and crumpled linen. A cool breeze passed over them, freeing their limbs from the coverings. Paris stirred. His eyes fluttered open. In the unfocused moment between sleep and full awareness, he saw her. *Aphrodite …*

"*Paris.*"

Have you changed your mind? Have you come to punish me?

"*No. I have come to save you from the wrath of Proteus and the Egyptians.*"

How?

"*Sleep, Paris. Sleep. For when you awake, the shores of Troy will be in your sights.*"

His eyelids grew heavy with unnatural sleep and Aphrodite went to work on the prince's behalf. She would maintain her bargain with this mortal. She would not tolerate accusations by Athena that she broke her oath with Paris, jeopardizing the judgment. When all aboard were safely slumbering under her spell, the goddess caused a great shroud of mist to fall around the ship, rendering it invisible to mortal eyes. She drew a deep breath and blew a fast wind to speed the Trojans home.

FIFTY NINE
the return of Paris

TROY—1251 BCE

Paris woke with a headache, rubbing the slumber from his eyes. His limbs were heavy with over-long sleep. He groaned, bending his legs over the bedside. *Have I become an old man so quickly?* He glanced over his arm at Helen. She slept soundly, pale against the linen and peaceful like death. Paris cocked his ear toward the upper deck, listening for the sailors. *Odd, all I can hear are the waves sloshing against the hull.* He gently shook Helen's shoulder. "Helen … Helen, wake up." She turned on her side with a moan. "Helen," he said, a bit more sternly. "You must wake up."

Helen's eyes fluttered open. "Good morning, my love." She propped herself up in the bed. "I'm so tired. I feel as if I've been asleep—"

"For days?" Paris asked.

Helen smiled. "Yes, how'd you know?"

Paris ran his hands through his black, curly hair. "I woke with the same feeling. Do you recall a face or voice before you slept?"

Helen shrugged her shoulder slightly. "A silver light. I saw a silver light, but I've no memory after …" She sat all the way up now. "I'm no longer ill."

"That's good news indeed. I need to see to the crew. It's much too quiet up there. Something isn't right. I believe we've been helped by Aphrodite. If I am correct, we will be home soon."

Helen got up out of bed and stretched her arms over her head. "The goddess? Why would she wish to help us? Why would any of the gods wish to help us?" She rubbed her stomach. "I'm famished. What a strange feeling to be so hungry after food sounding like poison for so long."

"It's a long tale, one that stretches back before you were born."

"I should like to hear this story, I think."

"I'll tell it to you one day, but for now, I must see to the crew." Paris kissed her dry, cracked lips. "I'll send some food for you."

As he left the sleeping chamber for the deck, he wondered if he should ever tell Helen the story entirely. He wasn't sure how much of her desire for him was due to Aphrodite's magic, or her real desire for him as a man. Paris didn't want to know if she only wanted him out of magic. All men lusted after Helen, but it certainly didn't work in the reverse.

Oenone couldn't believe her eyes. The sails of her husband's ship had pierced the horizon's line as soon as the sun rose. Each day since his departure, she'd come to the rocky shore, waiting for a sign of his return. She'd watched what felt like a thousand sunrises with no sign of Paris. Now, he was here. He'd returned for her. The nymph climbed down the rocks to reach the water's edge. She intended to swim out to his ship and greet him, ending the constant ache in her chest since his departure.

The ship drew closer, making for the narrow passage leading to the bustling royal port. As her foot touched the water, she saw Paris on deck, his hand gripping the rigging, his eyes focused on the path before the prow. She waved her arms in greeting, trying desperately to catch his attention. *Why is he wearing the royal purple? He abhors it.* He'd sworn to her that as long as he was an outsider, he'd never don the color of Trojan princes.

Oenone waded in up to her waist, readying to dive beneath the choppy cold green, when she saw the woman. Gold hair flying in the wind. Oenone's breath caught in her throat, and her heart pounded painfully against her ribs, as the woman wrapped her arm around Paris' waist and he wrapped his arm around her shoulders, pulling her close. In horror, she watched Paris kiss the top of the woman's head. She recognized that dance of his ... his love dance. The protective posture and gesture of love, and he was giving it to another. She froze when the ship passed by her, Paris blind to her.

As she walked from the water, her husband's parting words came to her ... *'You've no wish to live in Troy?'* She'd reminded him her home was in the wood. He'd tried to say something ... *'I'm afraid ...'* Did he know about this woman before he left? Had he planned this all along? Her anguish rose in her throat like a wind howling on a winter night. Her love for Paris ripped itself from her heart and she grasped at its departure. Oenone tore at her garments as she made her way back to her forest and her meadow, knowing now that Paris wouldn't be returning for her or their son. Not this day, and perhaps not ever. The hollow ache of betrayal laid her heart bare. She didn't know how she'd survive, when every breath stung, every tear burned, and every step took her farther from the only man she'd ever loved. Her premonition had unfolded into reality, despite Paris' repeated denials that he could never love another.

"Who is that wretched woman with my love? Who could take my love from my arms? Take my son's father?" She screamed at the sky, "What have I done to deserve this punishment?" Grief blurred her vision and she stumbled, falling hard on her knees. She was numb to the rocks digging into her skin. Oenone buried her face in her hands and wept until her eyes could shed not a single tear more and her hands were filled with crystals. "I'm alone again. Why do I desire his arms around me still? What curse is this that the one who has broken me is the only one I need to comfort me?" She tossed the crystals to the ground.

Slowly, the nymph rose and walked solemnly to the nearest river bank. "Father, are you there?"

"Yes, my daughter. Why do you weep so?"

"My husband has found another. Father, why didn't you tell me the pain of love is as deeply rooted as the joy?"

"My child," the River God's words bubbled across the water's surface. "There's always a darkness that follows the light. It's the way of the world. If the light never dimmed, how would you know it existed at all?"

"Love is a curse," Oenone said, misery hanging on each word.

"Love is a poison," her father responded. "One you grow accustomed to, but does not kill you."

Oenone knelt on the silky grass. "How long will my heart grieve and ache?"

"Given time, my gentle daughter, it will subside."

"I curse that woman that one day she'll know the pain of losing the one she loves."

"Beware of raising curses to life. The gods have ways of turning them against you."

Hecuba sat silently next to Priam as Paris recounted the tale of sacking Sparta's treasury and taking Helen. *It was a brave, if not foolish thing to do*, she quietly thought. The queen kept Priam's face in her peripheral view. She watched for any telltale signs of his displeasure—the clenching of his jaw, the slight frown at the corner of his mouth—she worried her husband might deem Paris' actions too reckless. Worse than that, however, would be if the king judged Paris' failure to retrieve Hesione as a weakness of character and prowess. Hecuba was well aware of the delicate balance required to maintain steady trade throughout the Troad and beyond, and Paris tipping that balance against Troy could be seen as a traitorous act. More than the strange Greeks from far off islands, she worried how Priam would react regarding the Hittites. They were friendly enough, but they were also allies to Egypt. If Paris' sudden departure against the wishes of their oracle-god and their pharaoh was interpreted as an insult or a threat, then the Hittites might direct their outrage at Troy.

Paris had stopped talking. Priam was nodding, his hands clasped behind his back as he paced the polished marble floor. "I'll send envoys to the Hittite kings, ascertaining and securing our mutual friendship. We've no desire to stir up rivalry and competition with people near our lands." He stopped pacing and gave a critical eye in Helen's direction. "You, young Queen of Sparta, have presented me with a conundrum. I'm caught between my own guilt and the pride of Troy. I could easily send you back, treasure and all." He sat heavily on his throne. "It's doubtful your Menelaus will take you back without severely punishing you, perhaps putting you to death for your betrayal." Helen opened her mouth to speak, but the king silenced her with his hand. "Make no mistake, young queen, that what you have done is a betrayal not only to your king, but to your father, Tyndareus, and his legacy. Do you think the red king will keep your infant daughter as your heir? Do you think he will not obliterate your name and remarry, remaking Sparta as his alone? He is king."

"But my brothers—" Helen protested.

"How long have you reigned as queen? Have you experience enough in this world of men and crowns to question me, King of Troy?"

Helen shook her head. "I have not."

"Menelaus has no kingdom of his own. That's why he agreed to marry you," Priam said.

Hecuba watched as the truth of Priam's words struck the young beauty. The queen asked, "How old are you, girl?"

Helen visibly bristled. "I've seen nineteen summers."

Hecuba raised an eyebrow. "Nineteen?" She looked to Paris, who refused to meet her gaze. "Paris, you've allowed a mere slip of a woman to rule you. No matter her beauty, she's but a spoiled dog masquerading as a queen. No true queen would abandon her husband and her people for another land entire." Hecuba's disappointment was clearly evident with every word she spoke to her beloved son.

"I've made my decision, Paris," Priam announced. Helen nervously wrung her hands in her lap. "I sent you on a mission to redeem the honor of Troy. To redeem my honor for having lost a Trojan princess to the Greeks. You've accomplished neither task." Paris hung his head, shamed by his father's words. "But only the gods could have aided you in this … this abduction of Sparta's queen. Under that fat, red-beard's nose, impressive. I've no desire to stand against the will of the gods. If Troy can't have Hesione returned, then Troy will keep its prize in Helen and her gold."

Paris took a step back. "Thank you, Father."

Priam embraced his son. "I welcome your return."

Hecuba was relieved by Priam's declaration and embraced her son, as well. "And I also welcome your return to Troy." Pulling her son aside, she asked gently, "What of the nymph and your son? Have you given thought to them, now that you bring a second to your bed?" She couldn't help but think that Hektor would never put Andromache aside, and neither had Priam cast her aside once their mutual passions cooled.

Paris met his mother's eyes. "I haven't seen her or my son. She doesn't know I've returned."

"She will soon enough. Be kind. Be truthful. Anything less will tarnish what you have with her."

"I will," Paris said hesitantly.

Hecuba's tone carried a warning tone. "It's cruel, my son, not to honor her as your first wife."

"There's only one wife to each husband in Sparta," Paris said.

The queen shook her head slowly. "You're saying that you will give up the nymph and your son for this Spartan girl?"

"The choice wasn't mine. Oenone has made it clear the woods and foothills are her home. I don't wish to live forever in a cave among the trees and meadows. I belong here in Troy. I belong with my family, among my brothers and my sisters."

"Very well, then," Hecuba said. "Very—" A vision of black smoke and falling ash pierced the veil of her waking mind. Then, she saw, once again, the burning log between her thighs.

Paris caught her as she fell to the ground. "Mother!"

SPARTA

Menelaus strode through the halls, his weighty footsteps ringing against the stone, as servants scurried away from him. The palace was conspicuously void of its usual market place sounds. He thought it odd that Helen hadn't greeted him in the hall, as he'd sent a messenger ahead with word of his return. Menelaus took the corridor leading to the queen's chambers. As he reached her door, opened it, a tingle of fear wormed its way into his gut. It hadn't occurred to him until this moment that there could be something within he'd no wish to discover. His eyes found Helen's bed, and he let out a sigh of relief as he'd half expected to see a man bedding his wife. He looked around the chamber.

It was then that he realized it was cold, signally no fire had been lit to warm it, meaning Helen hadn't been in this chamber at all last night. The thin thread of fear grew. He thought of their daughter, Hermione—perhaps she'd taken ill and the queen had spent the night in vigil over the girl. The king made his way to the nursemaid's chamber. A single torch lit the doorway. He entered to find the nursemaid rocking the child at her breast. He scanned the room. The queen wasn't there either. His eyes found the woman's stunned face. The fear now gripped his bowels, twisting painfully.

"Where's Helen?" Menelaus asked, his voice low and angry.

The nursemaid stumbled over words, clinging tightly to the baby.

Menelaus tensed his jaw, barely keeping his rising anger at bay. "I asked, *where is my wife?*"

The nursemaid's voice squeaked out, "Gone."

"*Gone?*" Menelaus roared incredulously.

The baby startled and began crying. The nursemaid frantically bounced and rocked the child to comfort it. "She's gone, my lord. Gone with that prince."

His eyes narrowed. Anger flushed his already ruddy complexion to bright red. "That fucking Trojan. I'll kill him!" He stormed from the room, his death threats booming before and behind him.

The nursemaid heard the king calling out for his ship to be readied for Crete. "At least he'll be gone and you'll be safe." She gently brushed a golden wisp of hair on Hermione's head as she settled the baby at the other breast. "You'll be safe for now."

Word of Helen's departure had reached Agamemnon before his brother arrived. He wasn't certain what his brother wanted from him. Clytemnestra had already begged him to be merciful if Helen were found, reminding him that she'd been made queen when she was barely a woman.

When Menelaus entered the hall, Agamemnon could see the

anger and confusion on his younger brother's face. "Travel has brought no clarity for you."

Menelaus shook his head. "I want her back."

Agamemnon scoffed. "Why would you wish her returned? She's a traitorous bitch. She left your heir behind, did she not?"

"How did you know?"

"I've ears and eyes in many places."

Menelaus tugged angrily on his red beard. "She's humiliated me, brother."

Agamemnon placed a firm hand on his brother's arm. "But she has left you the kingdom."

"How long before Tyndareus rescinds his abdication as a result, naming one of his own sons as king to replace me?"

"He won't … not as long as he desires peace with Mycenae."

"You'll help me, then, brother?"

"I will. But not for Helen's sake. Once a dog has run away, the only way to keep it is to leash it. The bitch, if returned, will bring you nothing but agony."

"I don't care. I won't be humiliated in my own house. I'll invoke the oath."

Agamemnon nodded his head. "Yes, the oath. Clever. Almost as if Tyndareus knew this would eventually happen."

Menelaus bent his head to his brother in deference. "You have my gratitude."

"Brother. My love for you is true. But, have no doubt I *will* take the lion's portion we reap along the shores of Asia. If I travel at your side, I go for plunder not Helen. Besides, the coastal cities hang like ripe figs ready to be plucked of their sweetness. And Troy …"

Menelaus laughed heartily. "The fattest fig of all!"

SIXTY
Ithaka's oracle speaks
ITHAKA—1251 BCE

Odysseus stood with his dog before the entrance of the cave to Ithaka's oracle. Ground water seeped along the walls in soft cascading sheets, forming shallow puddles along the pathway, eventually disappearing into the crevices of the stony floor. The wetness glittered in the flickering torch light, like the noon sun flashing off the tumultuous sea far below. From here, he could still smell the salty air. Tired and hot from the long morning hike through brush on the dusty path, Odysseus reached down to scratch Argo behind the ears. "Wait here. I won't be long."

A young woman wearing a thinly spun sun-bleached chiton approached. A crimson stripe of dye bled unevenly into the whiteness of her dress. The hem at her feet was damp and ragged from dragging along the ground. She stood as pale as a nymph might be. Her eyes focused on the earth beneath her bare feet. Her long, dark hair hung undone around her shoulders.

"Remove your sandals and lay down your sword. You don't need it here."

Odysseus reluctantly obeyed because in this cave he was not the young king of Ithaka, but simply a man who'd been summoned by the gods. He knelt to undo his leather lacings and held his sandals out to the waiting attendant.

"Your sword. I will keep it until you return."

Odysseus complied, unwilling to offend the oracle. He undid the clasp securing his short sword to the leather belt and handed that to her as well.

"She'll see you now." The young lady bowed her head deeply and stepped to the side.

The coldness of the rock path chilled his feet and numbed his toes. He nervously glanced around, expecting something to happen. Bird song and the ocean crashing far below sounded faintly in his ears. Odysseus glanced back at Argo patiently waiting. The dog raised his head a little higher and wagged his tail. He turned back to the woman. "Where's the oracle?"

"Follow the torches. She's waiting … down there."

Never once catching the attendant's face, nor the color of her eyes, Odysseus obeyed her outstretched hand. Walking through the shadowy cave, careful not to lose his footing on the slippery path, he wondered where the water came from. There was no natural water source above. He detected the distinct tang of fresh earth and rust … and something else, something bitter at the back of his throat. He coughed. Torch flames flickered as he walked by, sending dancing shadows all around him.

The path widened, eventually opening into a large antechamber. The light dimmed to near blackness and a loud buzzing filled his head. It was the sound of a thousand voices all at once, chanting his name. The sound dizzied him, and a great wave of sleepiness washed over him. As quickly as it had begun, the noise subsided, leaving his body feeling heavier than before. A light grew and pierced the veil of his eyelids.

When he dared open his eyes, he realized he was on his knees and he struggled to stand. He stood in a circular room surrounded on all sides by smooth rock. A single boulder, chiseled from the rock served as a natural altar. The oracle sat on the altar, her legs and bare feet dangling over the edge. Her head was bowed and her long, red hair completely obscured her face. Each palm rested flatly against the altar's surface. She wore nothing but the shadows.

Odysseus looked anxiously at the ground. *I'm the king, damn it, speak!* "Why have you called me here?"

The oracle's voice was a raspy whisper. "It's not your place to question why you're called by the gods, Odysseus. It will be your downfall."

"I assure you, I can endure whatever the gods lay at my feet."

The oracle looked up, just then, meeting his gaze with eyes as black as onyx. Her thin lips spread in an uneasy smile. "Such arrogance, Odysseus. It will bring you to your knees soon enough."

"I'm a king. I've been blessed with a strong son. A faithful wife. Athena herself keeps watch over me, guides me. What do I have to fear?"

The oracle slid form the altar, her tangled hair covering her sacred nakedness. In the flickering light, Odysseus could see that she was once beautiful before the gods invaded her. "For how long, Odysseus? You should practice humility and reverence for the winged world above your head."

"What do you mean by that? How long what? The hour grows long, the message?"

The oracle lifted a slender, golden arm, pointing directly at his chest. "Here it is, as plainly as it can be spoken." Closing the small gap between them, she rested her fingertip on his chest. Odysseus stumbled backward. "You'll travel far for the sake of a king much greater than yourself ... soon, you'll go to war."

"I've gone to battle many times. I've no fear of fighting. My sword and spear are able enough. My shield hangs upon my hearth."

She dropped her arm, stepping close enough the sweet smell of the wine and honey on her breath filled Odysseus' nose. Her eyes glittered with knowing things beyond this world, things of ether and dreams and fears. He looked away. "This war will launch a thousand Greek ships across the Aegean. Fair winds will carry you and your men to Troy, but they won't favor your return."

"Troy? Ithaka has no complaints against the Trojans. What could the Trojans possess that all of the Greeks should go to war?"

"The most beautiful woman in the world."

"The most beautiful?" *Who is she speaking of?*

"You know of whom I speak."

The King of Ithaka raised his eyebrows in disbelief. "Helen, Menelaus' wife? Impossible."

The oracle's laughter echoed eerily around the stone chamber. Narrowing her eyes, she said, "Yes, Helen."

Odysseus recalled the oath he'd spoken, half-forgotten since he'd returned from Sparta with a wife of his own. "You have my ear."

"You'll be called upon this very day to fulfill what you have sworn."

"Who's taken Helen ... this time?" Odysseus asked.

"Paris, son of Priam. Mycenaean and Spartan ships are already anchoring in the bay. You're being summoned even as I speak."

"Can I avoid this war? Give me some trick or magic to release me."

"There's no magic for honor, as you know, only a shield, your spear, and … your word."

Odysseus spat out his anger. "Menelaus should've kept a tighter leash on his wife! That unfaithful bitch will undo us all. He should've kept her out of sight."

"Perhaps, men should be less influenced by their cocks? Regardless, there's more, King of Ithaka."

Odysseus clenched his jaw, bracing for the next revelation. "Speak."

"You'll not return for twenty years, once you step foot off this island."

"By the balls of Zeus! What punishment is this? What of Penelope and my newborn son? I can't leave them now. I'll miss my son's entire life!"

"You made a promise. You gave your word."

"I won't go."

"You'd risk war with Sparta by breaking your word? Where would your honor be then? Or your family? Are you certain Athena would protect an *oath-breaker?*"

"I won't be gone for twenty fucking years. Athena will not allow it!"

"We'll see, King of Ithaka, who is right and who is wrong. Learn to respect the will of the gods. They control your fate. Athena alone can't save you. Heed my warning: remember your place in our universe. Mortal." The oracle backed into the shadows and disappeared.

With her words ringing in his ears, '*mortal, mortal, mortal,*' he turned on unsteady legs and ran. He slid up to the motionless attendant who was still holding his sandals and sword. Grabbing them roughly from her hands, he clasped his sword in place and then his sandals. *This can't be happening to me! A plan! I need a plan. Why do the gods fuck me with curses and threats?* It would take him nearly three hours to get back down the hill and to his palace. It was just enough time to hatch a scheme. *Think, man. Think!*

Passing Argo, he said, "Come, boy." The king and his faithful hound bounded down the hill, a trail of dust behind them.

SIXTY ONE

a feigning madness

ITHAKA—1251 BCE

Odysseus passed the outlying edges of his land. In the northern orchards, red pomegranates and apples fruited with small red and green orbs. In the western orchards, sweet purple figs and silver tipped olive trees thrived in the rich soil. On the eastern rockiest side of the royal lands, terraced grape vines stretched as far as the eye could see. Fields of barley and wheat covered the low lying southern lands. His father, Laertes, was right about planting the land in this strange way. Something was always ready for harvest, as the next crop was beginning to push into bloom or fruit. The aging king had abdicated his throne to his son to pursue his love of agriculture. He'd told Odysseus he liked the smell of the damp earth on his hands, the feel of sweat on his brow, and took pride in drinking wine or eating fruits that he himself had nurtured from stem to harvest. Laertes said he'd tired of the smell of blood and men. Anticlea, his wife and Odysseus' mother, chose to remain in the palace, helping the young queen, Penelope.

As Odysseus passed the last row of olive trees with their roots like arthritic fingers gripping the dry earth, he stopped at a lookout point above the bay. Mycenaean and Spartan ships sailed into his harbor, the white water breaking against each hull. The bright sails and insignias of the royal brothers were unmistakable even at this distance. Agamemnon's All-Seeing-Eye blinked as the main canvas sail billowed in the breeze. The sail of Menelaus the Red King shone bright red trimmed with black against the surrounding blue. These brother kings had no shame displaying their wealth over the other tribes. The wedding of Helen to the younger had solidified their position and rank among the mainland and the islands. Together they commanded the most powerful kingdoms in all of Greece.

As Odysseus approached the outer wall of the farthest courtyard, his caution heightened. He didn't want anyone to discover him, forcing his hand before he was ready. Ithaka was no match for a united Mycenae and Sparta. The oracle had been right. *Years before I return? Can she be right about that, too?* No doubt a messenger was already seeking audience with him at this very moment.

The young king went straight to the barn, keeping close to the wall. Argo at his heel. It was quiet and he was thankful Eumaeus wasn't around. That old man would've questioned him to death. The shepherd had likely taken the sheep out to clean the recently harvested barley fields. Odysseus robbed his own storage hut of a bag of sea salt and picked up a seeding bag, slinging it familiarly over his left shoulder. In the barn, he pulled the oxen yoke down from the wooden posts where it had hung since spring time planting was completed. He hefted it onto his other shoulder and carried it to the oxen pen.

The huge beasts were grazing contentedly on remains of the barley brought in by donkeys and stored just for them. They were stronger than horses for plowing the rockier ground and were treated as well as any fine horse. The oxen were reluctant to leave their comfort, but followed Odysseus' lead with Argo nipping at their tails. He hooked them with deft hands into the yoke, before picking up a plough. He stepped to the edge of the stable making certain he remained undetected. *It's too quiet.* Then, it occurred to him that Agamemnon or Menelaus might both be within the palace not out on their ships. He needed at least one of them to see him put his plan in motion or it wouldn't work. *Why have you allowed this to happen to me, Athena? Why?*

With his seed bag full of salt crystals and a planting team hooked up in front of him, he set the plough to the ground and commanded the oxen to move. The well-trod pathway was hardened by years of foot and animal traffic. The plough scored a shallow groove in the earth all the way down to the beach head.

"Stay," Odysseus commanded his faithful hound. The dog sat, cocking an eye at his master. "What?" Argo tilted his head. "Pray this works, old friend."

Once on the sandy shore, he set about planting his field of salt. The oxen pulled row after row along the entire length of the shoreline, while be sowed the salt. Apollo's light burned the skin on his neck a deeper shade of bronze. Sweat spiraled down his black ringlets, stinging his eyes as it dripped down his face. He kept on plowing and planting.

SIXTY TWO

sacrifice of madness

ITHAKA—1251 BCE

Penelope walked to her window overlooking the bay and watched as the uninvited ships anchored. *What do they want? What could Sparta want with Ithaka?* Penelope looked around her room, silently grateful her husband had taken such pains to make sure she'd always feel safe here. In the darkest corner of their room, she'd erected an altar for Athena with Odysseus' help. It was smaller than the household shrine in the center of the main courtyard. This one was for their private thoughts and thanks. Odysseus believed that Athena would always protect them and it had sometimes, she noted privately, made him brash and overly daring. In public, she would never shed a tear. But in this sanctuary, in front of their Athena, she felt free to shed as many as she needed for comfort. She knelt before Athena now. A rapid pounding on the heavy oak doors drew her away from the shrine.

"Open up, my lady. It's me."

Penelope quickly unbolted each iron slide and Eurycleia rushed in followed by two strange guards with swords drawn. "I'm sorry, my lady, but there's no other way." The old woman walked to the cradle and picked up the newborn prince, swaddling cloth and all. Without a word of explanation, she hurried out shouting over her shoulder, "Lock the door!"

The queen reached for her maid, but the guards roughly blocked her way. "Wait! Eurycleia! Where are you taking Telemachus?" she screamed, as the guards pulled the heavy doors shut. Penelope slid the iron latches back into place, leaning against the door. Confusion and fear overwhelmed her and she sank to the floor in tears. She recognized the Spartan armor and red capes of Menelaus. *Why has Helen's husband come here? What's happening?* Odysseus had been urgently summoned to the oracle. Foreign ships anchored in the harbor, and if she wasn't mistaken, the distinctive sail of the great king Agamemnon accompanied his brother. *What does all of this have to do with my son?*

Penelope sat on the edge of her bed waiting for someone to return her son and explain what was happening. *Athena, help me.* Her stomach grumbled. She'd missed the midday meal. Her usually bustling household now hushed to mere whispers.

"*Sleep, Penelope, sleep.*"

"Athena?" Penelope whispered, as she lay on her bed with its secret post.

"*It is me, daughter. Sleep until Odysseus returns.*"

Penelope's eyes closed and slumber took her from her worry.

From the bow of his anchored ship, Menelaus watched the King of Ithaka. He hit the elbow of Thalpius, as he pointed to the shore. "What's he doing? Look. There. Isn't that Odysseus?"

Thalpius, mouth agape, asked, "Is he plowing the beach?"

Menelaus shook his head. "What an idiot."

"The gods must have stirred his mind to madness," Thalpius concurred. A small group of curious rowers crowded around Menelaus to watch the lunacy on the beach.

Menelaus grabbed Thalpius by the forearm. "Look! Palamedes is coming. What's that in his arms?"

"It looks like a bundle of cloth."

The Spartan king leaned over the rail, squinting his eyes against the sun. "He's laying it on the ground in front of Odysseus' plough. What in Hades is he up to?" All of the spectators were riveted to the scene, watching intently as Palamedes walked clear of Odysseus' next pass with the plough.

"Whatever it is, Odysseus is going to turn it under the sand with his next row," Thalpius said.

Menelaus held his breath. "He stopped! By the balls of Zeus! He's stopped the oxen!"

"Why's he just standing there?" Thalpius asked, confusion wrinkling his brow. The onlookers murmured amongst themselves.

"Gods! I wish I could hear what they're saying!" Menelaus said.

Odysseus hadn't anticipated this maneuver. He'd heard the thin cries of a newborn baby coming from the gift Palamedes ceremoniously placed in front of him. He'd recognized the purple trim on the weaving and knew instantly it was his son, Telemachus. So, Agamemnon was putting him through a test of his own. The choices were plain enough to Odysseus. He could kill his son and remain with Penelope, losing everything he held most dear forever, or he could reveal his sanity, save his son, and save his family only to lose them for twenty years.

He pulled the seed bag off his shoulder, letting it sag to the ground, spilling the precious salt. He dropped the oxen's reins, their hooves sinking into the soft sand. The heavy beasts snorted and their nostrils flared, sniffing the tangy sea air. Slowly, Odysseus approached the swaddled bundle, gently scooping it up in his arms. With a hand calloused by war and fighting, he gently lifted a corner of the blanket. His tiny son's face squinted in the bright light, before wailing loudly. Odysseus left the salt bag, the oxen, the plough, and his hopes of avoiding war on the shore behind him.

As the young king walked up the beach, cradling the baby with one strong arm, he locked eyes with Palamedes, who stood with arms crossed over his chest in smug satisfaction. When Odysseus was shoulder to shoulder with him, he stopped and faced him. "You've cost me my wife and my son. Watch yourself, my friend. I might be gone for years, but you'll never see home again. By Athena, I'll make sure of that."

Palamedes' eyes rounded, but he said nothing.

Penelope awakened to familiar footsteps in the hall. She hurried to unbolt the door. There stood Odysseus with Telemachus cradled securely in the crook of his arm, sleeping peacefully with his little fingers in his mouth. Nothing could've pleased her more. She stood on tiptoes to kiss his sweating temple and gently took the child from his arms, placing him in his proper bed.

"Penelope, come sit by me."

"What's happening? How did you get Telemachus? Eurycleia took him and told me to lock the doors. I feared you'd been given some direction from the oracle to … to kill our son."

Odysseus took her hand. "Even if Zeus himself had given me such an order, I would not obey."

"Why was I locked in our room with only Athena's company?"

Odysseus sighed deeply. "Penelope … I'm leaving for Troy."

"Troy? Why are you going to Troy? We've no business there, do we?"

"No … and *yes*. I've business there."

"Is this why Spartan ships gather in our harbor?"

"Yes. I'll be joining the fleet with my own men. We sail to Aulis, then for Troy," Odysseus confirmed.

"Aulis? What will you do in Aulis? Odysseus, it sounds more like a gathering of warriors than a trading expedition …" Her voice trailed off, as the truth dawned on her. "You haven't mentioned a word of trading."

"We're going to war with Troy."

"Troy? Why? The Trojan walls have never been breached. By any enemy."

"True. That's the account given by Trojans."

Telemachus woke with a gentle whimper that quickly turned to a hungry wail. Odysseus stood to pick up his distraught son and laid him in his mother's arms. "That's a familiar cry. You'd better feed him before he runs out of breath."

Penelope opened her chiton, and her son's hungry mouth turned toward her soft flesh and latched onto her nipple.

Odysseus brushed his hand gently along his son's face. *I'll miss his journey to manhood.* It wasn't long before little Telemachus was again asleep with milky droplets spilling at the corners of his round mouth. Penelope wiped them away with the corner of her gown.

"Why do you have to go, Odysseus?"

"Helen has slipped away with a Trojan prince. Some younger brother of the Prince Hektor. I haven't heard of him. Paris, I think. And I took the oath before Tyndareus, promising to protect Helen. Now, I must honor it."

Penelope's eyes watered. "I thought you wished for me as your bride? I didn't know you took the suitors' oath. Was I simply your second choice?"

"I didn't take the oath for Helen's sake. I took it for you." He tilted her chin to face him. "Did you think your father would hand you over to me so easily? Tyndareus aided me, for aiding him." Odysseus pulled his wife into his arms, smashing the baby between them. "Put him down for a while …"

"Why did Helen go to Troy?"

"That question is without clear answer. Menelaus claims she was kidnapped. There's rumor he won her by his charm and she left willingly. I was told that Helen also took half of his treasury."

"Menelaus doesn't need all of the best captains of Greece."

Odysseus kissed her forehead. "Beloved, I've already tried to secure release from this commitment and failed. Only by killing our son could I prevent my departure. You must promise me something."

"I can deny you nothing."

"It will be difficult to hear," he cautioned.

"Ominous words, my husband. You frighten me."

"I don't mean to, my love." He stroked the back of his hand against her cheek. "If I should not return before—"

"Stop. I won't hear it."

He placed his fingertips lightly on her trembling lips. "If I don't return by the time Telemachus has grown the beard of a man, you must remarry and let our son claim his rightful place as king."

"Athena wouldn't keep you away so long."

"I'd hoped she'd never allow me to be sent away. But, you must promise this."

Penelope nodded. "When will you leave?"

"At dawn. First light."

"Then, let's not waste time, my lord husband. Come to bed. I want to make certain you remember me." Penelope lay back against the pillows and soft linens. Odysseus needed no more invitation than that.

In the morning, Odysseus didn't wake his wife or his son as he readied for departure to Troy. He wanted to remember her sighs, the way her hair tangled in his hands, the soft slope of her hip, as she lay on her side cradling their son. He hadn't been able to tell her it might be an entire lifetime, before he saw them again. He hoped the oracle was wrong on that account, or that he'd find favor with the gods to steer the direction of his own course. The king took his shield off the wall and his spear from the corner.

Odysseus stepped quietly over Argo sleeping at the door, but the hound's ears perked and he raised his shaggy head. Reaching down, the king scratched the dog behind the ears. "Take care of them while I'm gone," he whispered. "I'll be back soon. I promise." Murmuring a silent prayer to Athena, he turned, taking one last look at his family. *I promise.*

Then, he was gone.

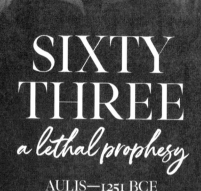

SIXTY THREE

a lethal prophesy

AULIS—1251 BCE

Agamemnon scowled as Kalchas spoke, his thick fingers laced tightly behind his back. He wanted to stuff his fist into the prophet's flapping lips speaking words he'd rather not hear.

"The signs are clear, my lord. You'll gain much from this raid against Troy, yet whether the Spartan queen returns can't be seen."

The Great King cleared his throat. "She'll return dead or alive to Sparta."

Kalchas grimaced. "There's more. You must take Achilles, if you intend to sack Troy and return."

"Return? What do you mean? Without Achilles we'll not take Troy or return?"

Kalchas' dark grey eyes found Agamemnon's hardened face.

"Without Achilles, no king who now sits upon a throne will return to claim it. No prince will live to succeed his father. And you will never sack Troy."

Agamemnon's fist slammed the table. Bowls and platters clanged against the wood. "Such words, Kalchas! I believed the gods favored us, now I see they only wish to fuck us." Agamemnon stood quickly, sending his chair flying behind him where it broke into pieces against the heavy tent wall. "You couldn't have delivered this prophecy before we left Mycenae? You had to wait until this very fucking moment? When we're far from home, between Charybdis and Scylla?"

Kalchas bristled at the insult to the gods. "It's the gods who speak when and where they will."

The Great King was pacing now. "Yes, the fucking gods. Spreading our ass cheeks and fucking us."

Kalchas grew nervous because the final portion of the vision revealed an even more heinous act that must be performed. *How can I tell him? Should I tell him? What if he turns back … the gods will surely punish us all.*

"Do you trust Kalchas that much?" Menelaus asked. "Are you sure the prophecy is about Achilles?"

"We can't win this war if Achilles and his Myrmidons aren't with us," Agamemnon said flatly. All of the captains, fulfilling their oaths, stood silently regretting they'd ever considered Helen as a bride in the first place, forcing the oath that bound them to this expedition of war. They all feared the final outcome if Agamemnon's words proved true. And if that were the case, they were all dead men and they knew it. It wasn't a secret that the ancient city of Troy was nearly impossible to overrun. Hektor, guardian of the great walled fortress, had a reputation as a fierce combatant, a warrior whose only rival was Achilles himself. How were they to defeat a city protected by a man who rivaled the gods? Rumors of Hektor's stealth and skill with a blade created doubt in the assembled captains' minds.

Ajax shoved a stick into the dying flames of the fire, shifting the sputtering driftwood to smoky curls. "How can we get Achilles to fight for us, when we don't even know where his nymph mother has hidden him? He's all but fallen off the edge of Gaia."

They all stared into the burning wood, as the flames reignited and shot into the night. Red hot cinders floated up into the black night like fiery moths, ending their lives as black specks dotting the sand.

Odysseus knew that Achilles was not only the key for their victory, but also his best hope of returning home before his family could forget him. As he stared into the fire, Odysseus heard a distant humming in his ears. He glanced around the camp circle. No one else seemed aware of the droning growing louder by the moment. He opened his mouth to speak but no words came out. The hum pulsed through him like the heat of too much red wine. He was aware of the heaviness of his limbs. He tried to raise his arm, but it wouldn't obey his command. He remembered a similar sensation in the presence of the oracle. He thought it strange to sense the oracle so far from Ithaka.

"It is not the oracle, my loyal Odysseus."

Then who are you?

"Do you not recognize me?"

A sparkling light filled Odysseus' waking eyes and he caught a glimpse of a helmet crested with shimmering golden horse hair. He closed his eyes against the burning image.

Athena.

"Go to Skyros."

Why, my goddess?

"Always questioning. Trust me."

What will I find at Skyros?

"Your golden warrior, of course, hiding among the women."

"Odysseus, are you well?" Diomedes asked. "Look at him!" All of the captains turned to watch Odysseus. "As still as a corpse he is. Look! His eyes look like two sparks of coal."

The King of Ithaka shook his head. "At first light, I leave for Skyros."

"Have you forgotten you're not the commander of this army?" Menelaus sneered.

Agamemnon purposely avoided looking in Odysseus' direction. "What duty draws you to Skyros? Your own interests or mine?"

Odysseus stood and walked into the night, leaving the Greek captains and the brother kings in stunned silence. "I go so that I may fulfill my oath."

"He must have a plan," Ajax offered.

"I hope so," Agamemnon warned. "Palamedes …"

"Yes, my lord?" The king's servant stepped forward with his head forever bowed.

"In the morning, go with Odysseus. Make sure it's the shores of Skyros he sails for."

Palamedes nodded. "I'll do as you command, my lord."

SKYROS

Nothing was as blue as the wide open Aegean Sea, reflecting the depth and mystical powers of Poseidon. When the god was angry the sea churned and thrashed, swallowing ships whole, burping up splintered twisted timbers and burying the dead and their belongings in the ancient muddy basin. Sometimes, the Sea God sent the sirens out to sing unsuspecting sailors to their doom. Their sensual supplications drove men mad enough to race on speedy winds to save them. Instead of becoming saviors, their ships and dreams were dashed on rocky reefs never realizing until the very end that they'd been enraptured and sung to their deaths.

Dozens of islands dotted this region of the Aegean like the very knuckles of Poseidon's own hands. In the midst of a string of Sporades rocks, the island of Skyros rose like a citadel, punching its presence from the undulating azure like a hand reaching for the empty sky. Mount Olympus stretched high into the living clouds in the north with lush forests disappearing into its thunderous heights, while Mount Kochila, barren and rocky, scratched its loftiness from hard volcanic earth in the south. The two-day trip from Aulis to Skyros passed uneventfully with fair winds to fill the sails. Odysseus prayed a silent thanks to Athena.

Many years had passed since he'd laid eyes on the boy, Achilles. He hoped he'd recognize him now. Even as a youth, Achilles was clearly blessed with the golden beauty of the gods themselves, something he'd inherited from his mother, Thetis. From his father he'd inherited strength, broad shoulders, and his noble bearing. Achilles, even in his youth, was what every man feared and loved all at once. Rumors abounded of the young man's speed and agility. Even as a child, under Chiron's tutelage, he'd fought without fear. Loved women as fiercely as he fought. Moved as the wind. In hand-to-hand contest, while still a youth at his father's court, he remained undefeated until his disappearance. One day he'd become a king of Phthia, if he ever returned to Peleus' court.

Odysseus and his crew anchored the sailing vessel behind the breaking waves and rowed the small boat along the northern shore and pulled its hull deep into the sand of the shallow bay. They'd have to return before the tide swelled, loosening their ship back to sea without them.

"Where will you start, Odysseus?" Palamedes questioned.

Odysseus' jaw ticked at the very sound of Palamedes' voice grating in his ears like a screeching hag. "If Thetis has taken her son up the sacred mountain, we're doomed. The hospitality of King Lycomedes and his court is logical." Odysseus hefted the water bladder over his shoulder and set off in the general direction of where he thought the palace might be. There was no trailhead from their landing site, but he was certain any palace built on this side of Skyros would have a clear view of this minor inlet. Odysseus reasoned that if he were king of this place, he'd build his house where he could see every entry point from the sea. So, they traveled straight up the hill.

Achilles pulled Deidamia into his arms and kissed her hard. When his mother had brought him here, he was a beardless boy. The princess was the first to befriend him, and became his first conquest on the island right beneath her father's nose. Achilles' reputation for combat rivaled his growing appetite for sex. He craved lovemaking and fucking almost as much as he craved battle. Blood sport would always be held in higher regard for there glory was won. Achilles desired that more than anything else. He was born to fight. As he kissed the soft body beneath him, he pushed the thoughts of war aside to concentrate on pleasing the woman.

"Do you remember the first time you kissed me, Achilles?"

He smiled into the face of the dark-haired woman in his arms. The deep color of her skin intoxicated him. Her almond-shaped eyes sparkled like polished obsidian, the pupil barely distinguishable from the iris. Her enticing glances rendered him *almost* helpless. "Yes."

"Well?" Deidamia asked.

"Well, what?" Achilles teased. He reached his hand through an opening in her chiton, cupping her full breasts in his hand, then rolling the nipples between his fingers, and pinching them until she squealed.

She slapped him. "Did you love me then?"

Achilles thought for a moment. *Love. What is there to know about love?* He'd learned enough about women to know avoiding this question served his needs better, so he held her tighter in response. *Deidamia does keep me from being too lonely. But love? Why do women always want to know about love?* "I married you, did I not? Isn't that enough?" *If I love anything, it's the open sea and war, not domestic life and its comforts.*

Deidamia grew unsettled by his silence and avoidance of the question. "Will you ever return to Phthia?

Achilles brushed her chin with his hand. "Soon, I think."

A commotion in the courtyard caught their attention. The clattering of wheels over stone was unmistakable. Achilles' smile disappeared as he moved quickly to the window. He watched a man, shoulders stooped with old age, wearing a frayed and thin robe with its hem trailing behind him, guiding a rickety wooden cart brimming with brightly colored textiles and shiny baubles swinging from various pegs.

"What is it, Achilles?" Deidamia asked.

"Just some poor peddler selling cloth and trinkets," Achilles answered, turning in time to see his wife running out the door. He watched as Deidamia entered the courtyard below, squealing with delight along with her sisters and cousins. They pulled at colorful lengths of cloth, holding them up to themselves and each other, admiring this one then that. One of them picked up what looked to be a sword hilt and tossed it back into the pile of unbound cloth. He heard it clatter against the wood. "I think I'll examine this cart more closely."

When the Achilles entered the courtyard dressed in a woman's robe and veil, the old man looked up, motioning him to examine the contents of his wares. Achilles fingered an edge of purple cloth. Its softness and quality were meant for royalty. *Odd that a beggar has such cloth. Cloth fit for a king.* He let his hand slip deeper into the pile of fabric and the point of a blade pricked his fingertip. His hand slid carefully along its edge, until it curled around the hilt. Like a bolt of lightning, Achilles pulled the sword free, slashing the blade and checking the balance of the weapon.

The old man watched. His eyes narrowed with knowing. "Achilles," the old man finally spoke, his voice deeper than the young prince expected.

Achilles watched the old man's guise magically fall away and in the peddler's place stood an imposing figure of a warrior. Achilles leveled the sword directly at the intruder. "Who are you to dare entry into this court?"

"I am Odysseus, King of Ithaka." He reached into the cart, pulling the purple trimmed himation from the pile, draping it across his shoulders.

Achilles lowered his sword. "I've a cloudy memory of you from my father's court years ago. What business brings you to Skyros, my lord?"

"You do."

The Golden Warrior laughed, pulling the veil from his face. He tugged at the woman's chiton with his free hand, ripping it from his body, never once letting his guard or the shining blade in his hand down. "You're far from your home, Odysseus. What business do you have with me? Has my father sent you?"

Odysseus flashed Achilles an engaging smile. "No, your father hasn't sent me. It's King Agamemnon who summons you." Odysseus eyed the young woman hiding behind Achilles, taking the warrior's hand familiarly in her own. She may have kept her eyes diverted toward the ground, but her regal presence wasn't lost on the beggar-king. "Perhaps, we should talk privately."

Achilles whispered something to the woman who then walked away, giving one backwards glance at Odysseus. The other women silently followed suit, leaving the two men alone.

Odysseus leaned casually against the cart, gesturing at the discarded robe on the dirt. "It seems that you've been living quite comfortably among the woman."

Achilles flashed a brilliant smile and shrugged his shoulders, divulging nothing, denying nothing. "How'd you find me?"

Odysseus shrugged. "I have my ways."

Achilles put the sword back in the cart. "What's the King of Ithaka doing so far from his kingdom? And why are you in the company of Agamemnon?"

"What's the future King of Phthia and Commander of the Myrmidons doing living here dressed as a woman?"

Kicking at a pebble, Achilles said, "Surely, you haven't traveled hundreds of miles to spar words. What do you want with me?"

"That you accompany me to Aulis," Odysseus answered.

"What does Aulis have to do with Agamemnon or you?"

"All of the captains are gathered there."

The soft hairs on Achilles' neck stood on end. "Speak plainly, Odysseus. No more banter."

Odysseus nodded. "Do you remember Helen, wife of Menelaus?"

"I've heard the rumors of her bewitching beauty. Of the oath her suitors took."

"She's been kidnapped, once again, and we go to free her."

"Who took her?"

"Paris, son of King Priam. We sail for Troy."

There it was, the city of his glory and his doom, beckoning him with an imposing finger. *This is the moment my mother tried to keep from me. My glory. The immortality of my name …*

Achilles stood still for a moment. For the first time, the weight of his decision tugged at him. He looked at the stone path beneath his feet. *Here is safety. I could just stay with Deidamia. Be a father, farm, live a long life.* "Troy," Achilles said, meeting Odysseus' gaze, his eyes sparkling with battle lust. "When do we leave?" *Glory. I.Choose.Glory.*

"Before the sun sets. My ship's a short hike from here." Odysseus shoved the linens strewn across the ground back into the cart. "She'll wait for you, Achilles. It's what women do." He clapped the young warrior on the shoulder.

"She's my wife."

Odysseus' pearly grin shone brighter against his grimy face. "I see. All the more difficult to leave then."

"Don't judge me harshly, but I long to go. Confinement here has taken all but my life."

Odysseus nodded understanding. "Home and hearth is not for all men. Some long for it and marry young. Some only imagine they want it, putting it off until their fathers force them to choose a wife. Some men want only to sail the open seas and fight."

"Which are you?"

The King of Ithaka clasped his purple himation securely with a golden pin fashioned into an olive tree. "I'm the man who wants it all."

Achilles embraced the messenger. "I must take my leave of King Lycomedes. Then make my way to Phthia and my father. If we're to win this war, I'll need the Myrmidons behind me. Their allegiance is only secured by my father's word. By my honor, I'll follow you to Aulis. My fate is tied to Troy."

"Then go quickly. Agamemnon isn't a patient man. But I'll follow you to Phthia, and then we'll make for Aulis."

AULIS

Menelaus stood at the cliff's edge, his eyes squinting out across the horizon. He could see nothing but the blinding sun bouncing back at him. Three days had passed since Odysseus' messenger had returned promising that Achilles would soon follow. The messenger reported that Achilles intended to return to his father's land to request the admiralty of the Myrmidons and would meet with the assembled army waiting at Aulis to head for Troy and war. The bright sky gave

Menelaus a throbbing ache behind his brow.

Standing next to his king, Thalpius asked, "How long will we wait, sire?"

"As long as it takes. We can't win without Achilles. If I have to retrieve him myself I will. By the balls of Zeus, I'll bring him back in chains …" Menelaus' voice trailed off. Until he'd uttered it aloud, he hadn't feared facing Achilles. But now, the lack of wind, the suffocating heat, and the lapse of days made him uneasy. *What if I have to force Achilles here? Could I do it?*

Thalpius scratched at the sweat dripping down the back of his neck. "What if the wind doesn't pick up? Isn't that a bad sign? Perhaps, the gods inform us of something … something we're doing wrong."

Menelaus gripped the pommel of his short sword. "He'll come. The winds will come. I *will* have my wife back." Menelaus' confidence slipped a bit. "Keep your lookout."

SIXTY FOUR

the long farewell

PHTHIA—1251 BCE

Years had flown by since Peleus had laid eyes on his son. Achilles had been on the verge of manhood, when Thetis whisked him off to seclusion at Skyros. Gone, now, was the lanky golden boy with a wide smile. He'd been replaced by a god among men. Standing taller than almost any man present, his azure eyes blazed fire beneath a handsome brow. His hair, catching the light, shimmered with gold and tumbled about his wide shoulders in long, twisted locks and tight braids. His stride was long, his gait easy and confident.

"Surely, the gods have had a hand on you since the womb," the King Peleus said, as he greeted his son.

Achilles grasped the king's hands. "Father."

Peleus pulled him into a warm embrace. "You've become a man, while you've been away."

Achilles released his father, turning his gaze to his beloved mother. A knowing look passed between them.

Thetis reached for her son. As he leaned to kiss her cheek, she whispered, "I hear the whisper of the sea behind you." She smiled up at Achilles, although joy failed to reach her eyes.

"Mother." His eyes spoke the words: *You know why I've come.*

"Forgive me, I must ask—"

"No." It was a simple answer. No hesitation. No fear. No way of asking more. "It's no small matter the course I've chosen. Don't be saddened by it."

The king interrupted the tender moment, declaring, "I've waited far too many years for this day. Tonight, we feast and drink to the Prince of Phthia's return!"

"We accept your invitation." Achilles' grin stretched wide across his face, a secret glinting in the corner of his eye.

The king asked, "We?"

"My wife and I," Achilles said.

Peleus looked to Thetis, but could see by her surprised expression that she knew nothing of the marriage either. "Wife? You've married Iphigenia? I wasn't informed you traveled to Mycenae to claim her."

Achilles' laughter roared across the marble hall. "Not Iphigenia, Father. Deidamia of Skyros."

Thetis gripped the arm rest of Peleus' throne, as her legs gave way beneath her.

"Mother!" Achilles flew to her side, catching her before she tumbled down the steps of the dais.

Thetis pushed her son's hands from her. "Truly, I'm fine. You've given us a shock, nothing more." She smoothed her gown. "Why keep such news from us? I don't understand."

"It's a long story. We're happy. That's all you need to know." Achilles' face revealed nothing to his parents of the scandal Deidamia's father had quieted. It served no purpose now, revealing his recklessness and breach of hospitality.

Peleus blustered. "But ... but what of Iphigenia? I swore an oath years ago with Agamemnon—"

"It wasn't meant to be. Agamemnon will no doubt find a more suitable prospect for his daughter." Achilles glanced at the over-sized cedar doors. "Escort my wife into the hall."

Deidamia entered, her purple silk gown flowing like a soft cloud behind her, as she took her place beside her husband.

"You can see, Father, I'm quite pleased." Deidamia slipped her delicate hand into Achilles'. "Mother, Father ... I present to you Princess Deidamia of Skyros, daughter of King Lycomedes."

Thetis stepped forward first, greeting the young woman who bowed her head with gentle ease. "And now, Princess of Phthia. Come here, child, let me look at you." Achilles' mother took in the visage of her new daughter—the olive skin a stark contrast to Achilles' golden hues, her hair black as still water, and eyes the deepest black framed by exquisitely long dark lashes. Thetis took her son's young wife's hands firmly in her own. "There's no need to stand on ceremony with me. I'm grateful you've brought happiness to my son while he was ... away."

Deidamia bowed her head. "Thank you, my lady."

"Call me as Achilles does. I've gained a daughter."

The young princess nodded. "Yes, Mother." Deidamia bowed her head to her father-in-law. "My lord."

Peleus embraced his daughter-in-law. "My dear, you've brought much joy to my heart … even if it forces a renegotiation with Agamemnon. I don't look forward to that, but I do welcome you."

"Thank you, my lord."

Achilles took his mother's hands in his own. "One gift yet remains."

"What, more wives?" Peleus laughed.

"My son," Achilles said.

The king's mouth hung open. "There's a child? A prince?"

Thetis beamed, her eyes glittered with tears. "A grandson."

Peleus echoed her joy. "A grandson, indeed, you present the kingdom with a legacy."

"We call him Neoptolemus. He's all of two summers." Achilles turned to the guards once again. "Bring my son."

A young nursemaid entered, holding a small, golden-haired boy in her arms. She put him down and he ran with an off-balanced gait to his father, who scooped him up with a flourish. "There's two people you should know, Neo." He took the boy to his father. "Little Neo, this is your grandfather, King Peleus of Phthia."

The boy held out his hand to the king. "Pappoús."

Peleus choked back tears, taking Neo's hand, and then lifting him from his son's arms. "Yes, Pappoús."

Achilles, pleased with the greeting, swept Deidamia into his arms. She squealed in surprised delight. "We're off to our chambers, Father! Perhaps, we'll extend your legacy once more! We leave Neo and his nurse with you for the afternoon." Achilles winked and flashed a roguish grin at his parents. The ever-present slaves pushed opened the great hall doors before Achilles could command it, leaving Peleus and Thetis staring after him with their grandson between them.

Peleus took Thetis' hand in his spare one. "Many years have passed since Achilles was born … it seems a lifetime ago. Now, he stands before us a grown man with a child of his own."

Thetis pulled the child to her arms, kissing his chubby fingers. "It has been a lifetime and far too long since these halls have echoed with a child's laughter."

The king reached for Thetis' arm, regret filling him. "The burning … I feared for our son's safety. I was angry, when I sent you away."

"And after?" Thetis asked.

"After … my anger subsided, I realized you'd never harm our son." His eyes burdened with melancholy, met hers. "But my pride was too great to say so."

"And now?" Thetis asked, as she kissed her grandson's soft cheek.

"Is there a chance you might forgive an old fool? Would you be willing to take your place, once again, by my side … as my queen?"

"Perhaps, there's a way, Peleus. The distance between who we were and where we are is no small space. For now, we've a feast to prepare and a brand new person to get to know. Shall I command the kitchens, then? Boar or lamb?"

"Both. We're celebrating our son's return home, a wedding … and an heir for Phthia." The king kissed Thetis lightly on the cheek. "Do as you wish." With rough fingers, he swept a stray tendril of hair from her forehead.

"What is it, Peleus? There's something more you wish to say?"

"Nothing. Nothing, but this." Peleus took her free hand into his own, brushing her fingertips with his lips. "Let's take the boy to the gardens."

The palace hall shimmered with laurel and olive garlands entwined with strands of sea pearls. Delicate alabaster lamps hung from the ceiling, lighting every corner of the hall where the shields of Peleus' forefathers hung with pride and honor. The hammered bronze shone as brilliantly as if each shield had been newly forged for the celebration. Amphorae of sweet pomegranate wine and spiced honey wine flowed freely into every guests' cup. The tables overflowed with wooden and silver trays stacked high with sticky dates, apples, honey glazed figs, oranges, olives cured with garlic and rosemary, and flat breads, bowls of olive oil steeped with wild sage, and fresh goat cheese by the slab. Lamb and roasted boar on spits sizzled and sputtered over the fire, the scent filling the air and making mouths water in anticipation of the main course.

At the high table, the king and queen sat overlooking their company. Achilles and Deidamia sat to the right of them in a place of honor with little Neoptolemus cradled safely in his mother's arms.

"You've out done yourself, my lady," Peleus whispered in Thetis' ear, teasing her as he used to do.

She squeezed his hand beneath the table and smiled. How could she tell him that this feast was not only welcome for their son, but also a farewell? Once away to Troy, their beloved son, the Golden Warrior of Phthia, would never return to the land of his birth. Thetis knew Achilles came home not only to introduce his family to the court, but to leave them under Phthia's protection.

Busy slaves served the roasted meat by the platters. Hungry hands dug into the greasy meal. In the house of Peleus, guests were accorded the first portion with the king and his family serving themselves last. Hospitality was only satisfied with full bellies. Late into the night, the stars spiked high against the mysterious dark. Many guests slumbered where they'd fallen or laid their heads down, sleepy with drink and food. Only the most distinguished guests were afforded private chambers. A balding singer plucked tiredly on a lyre, reciting ballads of Titans and heroes long since dead.

At long last, Achilles pulled Peleus away from the few remaining guests. "Father, there's more you should know of my return."

Peleus sat back, satisfied with the headiness of his wine and too much food. "More?"

"You've heard of the fleet gathering at Aulis, haven't you?"

"Yes, but what's that to me? I made no dim-witted oath for Helen's hand." He poured himself more wine, offering some to Achilles, who refused. "One wife at a time, I say. It's more than enough for most men."

Achilles leaned an elbow on the table, and rubbed at his chin. "Agamemnon has summoned me to join his army."

"Of course he did. Why, he never—" Peleus choked on his wine, remembering the words Thetis revealed years ago about Achilles' fate, and the reason he'd sent away. "What did you answer?"

"That I'd fight in his army, of course. And bring the Myrmidons with me," Achilles said.

"Bad news follows good. You've returned. You're married. Have a son. Now, you say you're off to war."

Achilles clasped his hands beneath his chin. "I wish to take the Myrmidons, if you'll allow it."

"Years ago, I went to war, among other things, with heroes come and gone. I'd always hoped you'd return from Skyros and take your rightful place as Prince of Phthia. But I see that must wait. The

Myrmidons are yours. I have only one request."

"What's that, Father?"

"Take Phoenix with you. And my man, Patrokles."

Achilles drained his cup of wine. "The man who lost his eyes for whoring and got a kingdom from you? Surely Phoenix would rather any other detail than this. And that's two requests."

"So it is. Phoenix will go. He owes me much."

Achilles arched an eyebrow. "He owes everything to Chiron." He grabbed a half-filled amphora and drank directly from the vessel. "Who's this Patrokles?"

Peleus pushed his diadem from his head. "He's a noble man. A few years older than you. He's loyal. Reads people better than most. He's skilled somewhat in the healing arts, as well. He will be a good companion for you. All captains need their second."

"I'll see it done," Achilles said.

Peleus stood. "It seems age calls the night short."

"It's almost morning, Father."

A thin beam of golden light filtered through the eastern windows.

"So it is." Peleus stood with a groan. "So it is."

Achilles stared after his father. They'd spent years apart, yet he loved him. He realized in that moment how hard it would be to say farewell to those he would leave behind forever ... *Deidamia, Neo*. It was a small mercy that he chose to keep his destiny between himself and his mother. *The stars may yet change; uncross their course, if Zeus commands it.* False hope, he deemed, was better than having none at all.

He walked the long, quiet hall to his chamber where he found Deidamia sleeping soundly with Neo cradled safe in her arms. He stood silently watching them. His heart filled his chest with binding affection. *I hope they'll remember me.* Achilles extinguished the flame of the oil lamp burning at the bedside table and climbed into bed beside them. He wrapped his long arm around them both, pulling them close. In her sleep, Deidamia nuzzled into his shoulder. Achilles kissed the top of her head and closed his eyes. A tear slid down his cheek. *Farewell, my wife. Farewell, my son.*

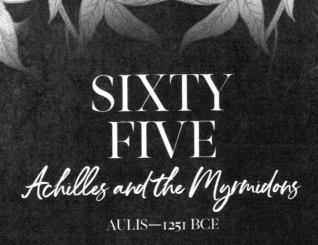

SIXTY FIVE

Achilles and the Myrmidons

AULIS—1251 BCE

The black hulls of the Myrmidons appeared silhouetted against the faint pink light of dawn. Palamedes rubbed his eyes; he couldn't believe he was actually seeing Achilles' fleet. So many days had passed that he'd begun to wonder, privately of course, if the Golden Warrior would come at all. He'd been commanded to watch the horizon and send word to Agamemnon directly at any sign of Achilles. Palamedes sent the boy, Nax, straightaway to the Great King's tent.

Nothing stirred in the camp. Nax heard snoring and occasional coughs, as he ran passed several unattended campfires smoldering to their last embers. He ran the entire way to Agamemnon's tent, his lungs burning and his breath short when he was stopped by the two guards posted at the entrance.

"What do you want?" grumbled one of the guards. "It's fucking early to be waking the king, don't you think, Cletus?"

"Too fucking early to be bothering anyone. Go away. The king's not interested in boys. At least not ugly ones!" Cletus chuckled and poked the boy with the butt end of his spear. "Get out of here before—"

"Palamedes sent me," Nax said, unmoving.

Cletus straightened. "By the balls of Zeus, why didn't you say so in the first place?"

The boy stood silent.

"Well, speak up. What does Palamedes want?"

"I'm only to tell the king. No one else."

Cletus rolled his eyes at his comrade. "Do you believe this shit? Who does Palamedes think his is? Better than the rest of us?"

Nax crossed his arms. "If I don't see the king now, I'm sure he'll be happy to beat you later, when he discovers you two kept the news he's been waiting for from his ears."

Parting the tent flap, Cletus roughly shoved Nax into the darkness of the tent. "By all means, enter at your own risk, you little shit."

No lamps were lit. The air reeked of sour sweat, stale wine, vomit … and sex. He pinched his nose closed. Standing for a moment, he allowed his eyes to adjust to the dimness. He heard a groan on his left and figured that to be where Agamemnon was sleeping. He took tentative steps in that direction.

Out of the dark, the sharp point of a sword blade pricked his chest. "Who are you? And what are you doing wandering about in my tent?" The voice thick with wine and sleep fell heavy in the shadows.

"I'm Nax. Palamedes has sent me."

Agamemnon sat upright, rubbing the stupefied haze of night

from his eyes and pulled up a clay pot from under his pallet to piss away the previous night's wine.

"Is it Achilles? Has that son of a sea hag finally decided to grace us with his fucking presence?"

"Yes, my lord. Palamedes has seen the black sails on the water. Achilles is coming."

"Take this." Agamemnon shoved the stinking piss pot under Nax's nose. "Don't just stand there. Hurry up you little blood rag. Go!"

Nax gagged at the steam rising from the dark yellow contents and bolted out of the tent without looking back, cursing under his breath as the piss splashed over his hands. He could hear Agamemnon roaring orders behind him.

"Where in Hades is Kalchas? Bring him here!"

Achilles and the Myrmidons anchored at Aulis as the sun slipped past its zenith, beating heat into the sand and rocks until the ground blurred with mirages. The arriving fleet rowed ashore, sweating and exhausted and headed for the main encampment in want of food and strong drink with Achilles leading the way. Talk of Achilles had, until that very moment, been more myth than reality, and to see the Golden Warrior walk among them bolstered the Greeks' courage and commitment to the war. The Prince of Phthia, son of Peleus, carried himself like a god.

Patrokles elbowed his lord. "It seems you have admirers."

"I've asked for none," Achilles said flatly.

"Clearly, you left your mirth back at the ship."

Achilles frowned. "Indeed, I have."

"My lord, you'll survive Agamemnon."

"Of that, I have no doubt." Achilles didn't wait for the guards to announce his arrival at Agamemnon's tent, he simply walked passed them and entered.

The Great King turned, and seeing Achilles, fell to pleasantries. "Greetings, Achilles! At long last you've arrived."

Achilles took in the sumptuous surroundings of Agamemnon's tent. Silk panels divided the tent into large rooms set with lavishly decorated and inlaid furnishings. Achilles shook his head. He wasn't impressed by this show of wealth, disregarding the morale of the gathering armies. "Greetings, Agamemnon. I see you've brought your palace with you. I'm sorry I've only brought my shield and spear."

Ignoring the reproach, Agamemnon replied, "It pleases me that you've come to our aid."

Achilles approached the Great King. "It pleases you," he said flatly. Then, he pulled a chair from a nearby table and sat down. He motioned Patrokles to take the seat next to him. "Do you have wine? We've traveled far, rowing most of the sea beneath us without the wind. What curse have you brought upon yourself?"

Agamemnon took a seat opposite his guest, again ignoring Achilles' accusation. "Bring the good wine."

"My men are also tired. They require food and wine, as well."

"A good captain always looks after his men. Palamedes will see to your crew. How many are your numbers? Palamedes!"

The servant entered. "Yes, my lord?"

"See that all of Achilles' men have what food and drink they require."

"Yes, my lord." Palamedes disappeared as quickly as he'd arrived.

"I haven't come because you summoned me. I made no oath on

your brother's behalf. I owe you no allegiance or obeisance."

Agamemnon's jaw twitched. "Then, why have you come?"

"It's my destiny to fight at Troy. Your cuckold war suits my purpose."

The Great King drained his cup. "More wine." A boy filled his waiting bowl. "You mean to lead your Myrmidons as a separate contingent?"

"I do."

"That won't sit well with the other captains. They've relinquished their authority to me, as commander of this army. You'd set yourself above the rest?"

Achilles leaned across the table, looking the Great King in the eye. "I *am* above the rest, Agamemnon."

"You've too much pride. Too much gall for my taste."

Achilles pushed his chair back. "We can leave by first light, if that is your final word." Patrokles followed suit.

Agamemnon held up his hand. "Patience, Achilles. Sit."

"There's nothing further to discuss." Achilles signaled the boy for more drink. He took the amphora and drank straight from the jar. It cooled his rising anger and irritation with the fat king. Once drained of the scarlet nectar, he handed it back to the waiting youth. "What is your name, boy?"

"Nax. They call me Nax." The boy stood in awe, wide eyes staring and mouth agape at the legendary warrior who asked him personally for his name.

"Close your mouth, boy, flies will gather and put worms in your belly," Achilles teased. "I am but a man." He tussled the boy's already disheveled hair. Nax immediately closed his mouth. "We are with you, *if* I command my men. If you can't abide that, then you go to Troy without me. Remember, I wasn't fool enough to bow before

Tyndareus and promise my life for the chance to fuck a whore." Without formal dismissal, Achilles left the tent, Patrokles following close behind.

"The gods truly fuck me," Agamemnon said to himself. Nax poured more wine. "Get out!" Agamemnon bellowed. "Get out!"

For the second time that day, Nax ran as fast as his scrawny legs could carry him. He ran as far as he could get from Agamemnon's tent. He ran all of the way to the beached ships lined up in rows in the bay. Since Achilles' arrival, the gathering fleet looked like an island of floating wood. The blue-green sea peeked between the gaps of the rounded hulls held fast by the soft sand. Affixed over each skillfully crafted prow sat a carved fish or bird pointing the wind's direction. Wiping at the sweat dripping down the side of his face, Nax realized there was still no breeze to speak of. He guessed that was why the fleet was still here at Aulis.

None of the soldiers took notice of him. And he didn't care. They busied themselves with drinking and gambling, polishing their shields and greaves, while some simply lay napping, sprawled out on their himations, catching the thin shade cast by the hulking beached ships. Nax walked beyond the fleet of triremes, farther from the encampment than he'd ever been.

The bay of Aulis was protected by a half circle of rocks stretching out to sea on either side. Nax walked until he reached the farthest rock wall and climbed up it. The open ocean, flashing blue and green, beckoned him and he jumped down into the wet sand. He looked up the rocks, backed up several steps, trying to see if he could catch sight of the Greek ships. He couldn't see them, not even the tops of the masts. He turned his attention to the deserted beach ahead of him. The white sands called to him, and he took off running for joy, for freedom. He ran through a flock of sea birds sleeping in the sun. They flapped wildly around him; some took flight, some squawked and circled back to scold him. The boy picked up a small pebble and threw it at a bird, pegging it squarely on its back. It flapped its wings at the insulting blow. He picked up a larger rock. *Something that can't hurt me back.*

Just then, a female voice whispered in his ear, "That's not very nice, you know."

Nax turned his head and saw no one, except a very large white bird with a long, narrow beak. Shrugging, he resumed pestering the sea birds with pebbles.

"I told you that's not very polite." The silver voice was sterner this time.

When Nax glanced over his shoulder, he saw a beautiful woman sitting directly behind him where the bird had been. He dropped the stones from his hand. "I meant no harm. They're just birds."

"You're just a boy, but you don't see me hurling rocks at you. Intent matters very little, in the end. Whether mortals intend to offend the gods or not, doesn't excuse the offense." The woman stood with a gown shimmering blue and silver in Apollo's light. It cascaded as thin as a waterfall over her nude body. Seashells and pearls were braided through her black hair, and her eyes glistened as green as moss-covered rocks. Bangles of pearls hung from her earlobes and about her neck. She laughed at his wide brown eyes. "Fear me not, child. I am Thetis, mother of Achilles."

The boy's eyes grew even larger. "A goddess," he whispered.

The nymph smiled. "You'll catch flies or worse with your mouth open."

Remembering what Achilles said about the worms, Nax clamped his lips tightly together. He gagged on the idea. "I hate worms."

"I see Achilles has already spoken with you."

Nax threw himself on the sand before her. "Yes, my lady. Well, sort of ... I mean about the flies. I gave him wine in Agamemnon's tent. Are you immortal?"

Thetis bowed her head at him. "So many questions. Yes, I'm immortal. Stand. You've no need to bow to me."

"By the balls of Zeus!" Nax jumped up. "My first goddess! I never thought a goddess would show herself to me. I'm just a slave. I've never been to a temple. Never offered anything to the gods ... I don't even have anything of my own. I figured what would a god ever need with me?"

Thetis' laughter sounded like bells. "We don't always appear the way you expect."

Nax stood dumbly smiling at her. *Achilles' mother caught me throwing rocks at birds. If Agamemnon hadn't yelled at me ...*

"Will you help me, Knaxon?"

"How'd you know my real name?"

Thetis placed a cool arm around Nax's shoulder. "Will you help me guard my son?"

"Me? Guard Achilles?" The boy laughed so hard snot blew from his nose. Without thinking, he wiped the slime on the hem of his tunic. "How am I supposed to do that?"

"My son keeps very few friends, Knaxon. What's your age, do you know?

Nax stretched as tall as he could. "Fifteen winters."

"Good. My son will need an attendant smart enough to watch those who'd plot against him. Are you loyal, Knaxon?"

"I do as I'm told. Don't like getting beat."

"That's honest." Thetis nodded understanding. "Come here, Knaxon, I've something for you."

Nax stepped toward her. Instinctively, he held out his hand. The nymph touched his outstretched hand, leading him to the water's edge. The water washed over his feet. With fear and confusion in his eyes, his mind swam with incoherent thoughts. The water rushed up to his waist and then, without warning, the goddess pulled him under completely. He hadn't taken a breath, so he panicked and fought against her hold on his arm.

"Don't struggle, Knaxon."

His body obeyed the nymph without question. *But, I'm afraid.*

"Don't be. As long as you're connected to me, I protect you."

Nax squeezed his eyes tighter against his rising fear. *I don't believe you.*

"Open your eyes."

No.

"Knaxon, open your eyes."

No. It will burn.

"You're safe."

Slowly, the boy opened his eyes under the water. It didn't sting. *She's right.* A few blinks later and he could see clearly. Thetis was no longer a woman, but a fish-woman. Her hair swam around her face and shoulders. Instead of legs she had a silver tail. Her breasts were bare. He'd never seen a naked woman before.

"Now, you see me as I am. And I will see that you are blessed as well."

With that, Thetis pulled him up to the shore. Nax sputtered

and coughed as Thetis helped him stand. The fish woman was gone and the nymph with two legs had returned.

"Let's look at you." She turned him around in a circle like a prized jewel. "Your hair is clean. Your skin is gleaming. You're not so lean now. That's very pleasing. Let me see your teeth."

Nax grimaced as he curled his lips up so Thetis could inspect his mouth. She reached down into the sand and picked up a very large pearl. Gently, she rubbed it against his decayed and chipped teeth. "You're complete."

The boy touched the smoothness of her magic pearl on his mouth. "Why did you do that?"

"Consider it a gift, Knaxon. My son should have a shining attendant to match his own countenance." Pleased with her work, Thetis said, "Now, take this bag to Palamedes."

Nax narrowed his eyes. "Why?"

The nymph leaned close to his ear. "To purchase your freedom, of course. All men have a price," she whispered. Thetis placed her cool hands on the young man's shoulders and squeezed him firmly, but with gentleness. "Go to Achilles straight after. Tell him I've sent you as my eyes and ears."

Thetis handed him the small, leather pouch. It weighed heavy. He shook the purse; the contents rang dull and metallic. His fingers probed inside. He could feel the rounded gemstones and heavy coins. "I'm not worth as much as this." He handed the purse back to the nymph.

"It will appease your current master. Now, off with you." Thetis spun Knaxon on his heel and shoved him back in the direction of the camp. He turned around to thank her, but she'd already disappeared. Only the sea birds remained. He shrugged his shoulders and went to do exactly as commanded, having no desire to anger the beautiful nymph.

———

As the glory of the day faded and the stars blinked into existence one by one, Menelaus found it impossible to push away thoughts of Helen. His wife had always looked her most glorious in this golden light. *That bitch has cursed me with her beauty.* He slammed his fist against the map table, scattering random items. *I know the men mock me behind my back. They think me weak ... cunt ravished. Fuck them all. They'd be no different if they'd bedded her even once.*

The thought of her lying cold beneath him stirred his loins. Helen had never seemed to enjoy the games of love, but he spilled his seed into her as often as he could. Just the wisp of her gown against his hand or the smell of her fresh from the bath was enough to drive him mad with desire. He wanted to conquer her heart, but she was an unwilling partner in the art of love. Other women had eagerly wrapped their legs around him and begged for more or mercy. He had given all and none. With Achilles' arrival he took hope that the voyage to Troy would soon begin. *I'll bring my fucking wife back and make her mine again, even if I have to bruise her mind and body into submission.*

Palamedes interrupted his brooding. "Excuse me, my lord. But your brother wishes a word with you."

"Tell him I'm on my way," Menelaus replied.

"Yes, my lord." Palamedes bowed and disappeared so quickly, it seemed to Menelaus that he'd vanished into the deepening night air.

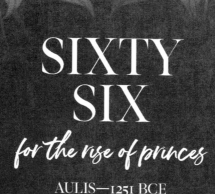

SIXTY SIX

for the rise of princes

AULIS—1251 BCE

All of the captains of war filled Agamemnon's tent. Kalchas, the seer who'd led them this far, stood with Agamemnon in a far corner engaged in heated back and forth whispers. The assembled captains grew anxious. Not one of them knew the reason the Great King had called them forth. Menelaus noted with disdain that Achilles was absent.

"The goddess demands it! You have no choice!" Kalchas shouted, his voice breaking the mounting tension among the men.

All eyes turned toward the seer who dared raise his voice to Agamemnon. Idle banter ceased. The warlords watched as Agamemnon's head sagged to his chest in resignation. His shoulders slumped with some burden or other. They waited.

"First, I'm forced to tolerate Achilles. Now, this? At every turn the gods fuck me. Every turn!" He paced. "I'm bound by my own oath to avenge my brother, my very blood! If I turn back now, I'm no better than that fucking Trojan traitor. I'll have gathered the western tribes at my feet for nothing. Wasted resources. No rewards to carry home. Who'd heed my call after that? No one I tell you, no one!" His sigh was grave. "You're certain, Kalchas? There's no other way?"

"None." Kalchas' voice resonated grimly.

Agamemnon turned to the expectant warlords. "Palamedes, fetch the wine." The hovering wraith of a servant had anticipated his master's request and was pouring bowls of wine before the words finished tumbling from Agamemnon's mouth. "Captains, it's well known that the winds haven't favored our departure. Indeed, there've been no winds at all," Agamemnon began with the obvious. There was a general round of agreement and the king continued, "But tomorrow that will change."

"How can you be certain?" Ajax asked. He was practical, not a great believer in the readings of bird signs or animal innards. And in particular, not an admirer of Kalchas. "The gods of wind do what they will, when they will. I think it a bad omen."

"It's not a bad omen, brother, but rather a warning," replied Agamemnon.

"What kind of warning?" Odysseus asked. "Perhaps we should all return home. Let Menelaus nurse his own pride. A wife who abandons her husband makes him not only a cuckold, but a fool for wishing her return."

Agamemnon coughed. "Yes, we all know how you preferred to stay in Ithaka." A round of laughter went about the gathering. "But that was not the oath you took."

"Then, why no wind? Why are we still here if the cause is just?" Odysseus was exasperated.

"Kalchas has informed me that it's the goddess Artemis who is angered and has stopped the winds as punishment."

Odysseus set his wine down. "Punishment? For what wrong doing? Who does the goddess fault?

"Brothers, it falls on my shoulders to right the situation. Kalchas has told me how her favor can be regained. I'll do as commanded and the winds will follow and we will leave for Troy."

"I will need more explanation than that, Agamemnon. Kalchas says many things. How do you know he is right? I swear, if the winds do not gather in our favor, I will row my warships all the way back home," Ajax thundered.

"Patience, Ajax. His readings are truth," the Great King reassured the towering warrior.

Odysseus placed his hands on the table, leaning in toward Agamemnon. "You have yet to tell us what the goddess demands."

Agamemnon's eyes shifted to the ground. He couldn't quite meet the gaze of his captains. "I must marry off my daughter. A great sacrifice."

Odysseus glanced around the tent at the finest men from across all of the western city-states. "Who is she to marry? Wasn't she betrothed to Achilles?"

"At break of day, five dawns from now, the demands of the goddess will be revealed," Agamemnon said. "No more questions."

With that, the drinking continued along with talk of the coming war and the prizes waiting to be claimed. Night approached with thousands of flickering stars. One by one, the generals of war retreated to their separate quarters to sleep off the heady effects of the wine, until only the royal brothers remained.

They sat in cushioned chairs, the silence between them tense. Menelaus suspected that his brother needed to speak of something. He was too cautious to raise the subject first. Only Agamemnon seemed to understand his predicament, that Helen had slashed his pride to the core. She'd left Hermione behind. Knowing that Paris ignited the fire between Helen's thighs, where he could not, damaged his manhood more so than being thought of as a cuckold. Helen placated him, that he'd always known, but he'd convinced himself that her light affection was genuine. Now, it was plain to the world that she loved him not at all. *What mother leaves behind her only child by a man she loves? She's put my claim to Sparta at risk by her recklessness.* He tugged nervously at his red-gold beard.

Agamemnon slammed his golden kylix on the table. "Stop fretting, brother. It annoys."

Menelaus sat up straighter. "It's difficult *not* to think of what that Trojan is doing to my wife *against* her will."

"Against her will? You cling to that notion? That your whore wife was kidnapped by the handsome prince and is now being ravished rather than wrapping her legs around his fucking thighs?"

Menelaus' mouth hung open at the stinging insult. "I ... she ... when—"

"Whether or not Helen is fucking that Trojan is the least of my concerns. I've graver issues to deal with now."

"Now? What do you mean?"

"The sacrifice," Agamemnon said quietly, almost too quietly. "It's a price I'm not convinced I should pay."

Menelaus blustered, "B-But ... certainly we've come too far to turn back, because you're unwilling to give up your daughter in marriage. All women must marry. You knew that—"

"I have only one eldest fucking daughter, Menelaus. One!" Agamemnon rose from his seat, his face shaking with fear and anger. "One! And is your whore of a wife worth Iphigenia's life? Tell me, you cunt ravished blood rag!" Agamemnon's spittle flew across the space between them as he bellowed, "Tell me!"

Menelaus sat in stunned silence.

Agamemnon sank back into his chair, his wits wracked with indecision, his hands gripping the arm rests until his knuckles whitened. Finally, he met his brother's stare. "It's my fault. This sacrificial horseshit. I killed a stag … a stag! I boasted, in jest mind you, that I was a better shot than Artemis." He shook his head in disbelief. "The gods truly enjoy bending me over a table and fucking me."

"It can't be as bad as that. Is the match for Iphigenia so undesirable?"

"It was a *sacred* stag." The Great King wiped an angry tear from his eye. "The marriage is a ruse."

Intrigued, Menelaus sat up. "A ruse? For what?"

"I must sacrifice Iphigenia to the goddess. Or we're lost."

Menelaus sat back, disbelieving. "That can't be so. Kalchus is wrong."

"It's the truth."

Menelaus reached for his brother's arm across the table. "You cannot do this, brother. I will not allow it. No one will forgive me or you."

"You won't allow it. You? Menelaus? You won't allow *this*," Agamemnon mocked. "You're no god to defy the command. The gods test us … torment us. If I refuse Artemis, do you think she'll stop tormenting me? No goddess will be satisfied until her request is fulfilled."

"Forgive me, brother. I meant no offense. Perhaps, well, as I said, Kalchas is wrong?"

"He's never wrong. Leave me. Get out of my sight. I must think."

Menelaus stood and left without finishing his wine. He thought nothing could be worse than his public humiliation, but now, he knew he was wrong. He'd be blamed. Hated. Despised. Menelaus rounded a dark tent and clutched his gut, before vomiting the wine he'd drank. *Poor Iphigenia. I'm so sorry, child*. He knew, even as he prayed, it'd make little difference. Agamemnon was right. The gods delighted in tormenting their prey.

The appointed morning burst with brilliant light. Iphigenia had hardly slept at all. Three days ago, one of her father's ships had arrived late in the evening bearing the good news. Artemis demanded the seal of her marriage to Achilles before the blessing of fair winds to Troy would be granted. Since the arrangement had been made years before, her father had given his immediate consent and blessing. And she was to make haste for Aulis. The fleet would make way as soon as she and Achilles consummated their marriage.

The very thought of Achilles bedding her made her blush. She'd never felt a man's touch before. And it was well-known among all women that Achilles walked as a god among men. Humor abounded regarding his prowess. Women jested that merely being in his presence caused the womb to flutter with life. Indeed, there were dozens of women around the Aegean claiming to have borne his children. In the weaving room, the women talked of sweet, lingering kisses, lips drenched in honeyed wine. And much to her curiosity and embarrassment, they spoke of the glorious taste of a man's seed, and learning to crave the tang of its saltiness that lingered on the tongue. The women teased one another about that delicacy being an essence requiring time to truly appreciate. They also spoke of the act as a necessity to keep one from having too many babies. They joked how Trojan men must not enjoy their cocks being sucked, or maybe they enjoyed other men more. Talk of this nature usually ended in rounds of laughter and sly smiles.

It was strange, Iphigenia noted, that when weaving in a gaggle, women tended to speak openly of their personal lives. It was while carding wool or spinning threads that she had learned of the delights between a man and woman during lovemaking. Only a man planting his seed deep inside of a woman could cause her legs to shake and her belly to quiver, if she was a fortunate bride. One woman, who'd been newly married, had said her husband could bring her to such ecstasy over and over in a single night, so much so that walking the next day was nearly impossible. The women teased her hobbling gait from time to time since she'd been married. Sometimes, when Iphigenia awoke at night, she'd reach her hand to her sacred cross and finger the soft folds. But, she dared not share how she'd rubbed herself many times until it tingled and pulsed with wetness. She hoped Achilles would satisfy the desire she'd felt at those quiet times for something deeper inside her.

A gentle knock sounded at her door. "Iphigenia?"

"Enter, Mother." Iphigenia turned to greet Clytemnestra. Iphigenia had always thought her mother the most beautiful, rivaling even her younger sister, Helen. Where her aunt was golden splendor, her mother was darkly exotic. It was like comparing the sun to the moon and stars.

Clytemnestra carried a gown wrapped in bleached linen draped over her arms. "Here, my darling, I set the women to work as soon as word came that you were to be wed." She held out the gift. "Take it, my sweet girl. I'd hoped for more time to plan, that this day would follow tradition. That you'd have seen more than fifteen springs. I didn't see it coming in such a rushed manner. But, war changes everything."

Iphigenia laid the gift on her bed and slowly unfolded the covering. She held the gown up against her body. "Do you like it, Mother? Is it what you imagined?" Each saffron layer was so finely spun it was practically transparent. A magnificent golden broach, encrusted with blue and green gems, pinned the shoulder on one side; the other exposed a bare shoulder. A golden belt would gather the sheer layers into concealing folds leaving her nude outline a mystery for her husband alone to discover.

"It only pales in comparison to you, my sweet girl," the queen said, wiping a tear from her eye. "I still can't believe I'm to lose you." In that moment, she recalled the words the goddess spoke on the day of Iphigenia's birth … '*She is yours … for a time. Treasure your days with her …*' A chill shivered through Clytemnestra.

"It's only in marriage. My husband will be gone to war, as will Father. I'll stay with you until he returns. Nothing will change. At least not now." Iphigenia smoothed the gown with her hands. "It's truly lovely, Mother. Gratitude. I hope Achilles will be pleased."

"How could he not be?" Clytemnestra fussed at the gown's folds. "If the goddess favors, perhaps we shall have your son to help us pass the days, until the men return."

Iphigenia blushed at her mother's implication. "Such talk."

"My darling girl, you'll be the envy of every woman. If Achilles is as skilled as his reputation, he might give you twins."

"Mother," Iphigenia giggled.

"I'll have the maids stow this carefully for our journey. In two days time, you'll be a married woman and I'll have gained a son." Clytemnestra kissed her beloved daughter good night and swept from the room, as if her feet never touched the stone floor.

Iphigenia embraced her father warmly, as she stepped from the boat to the soft sand of the Aulisian shore. Her arms encircled Agamemnon's neck with great affection. "Father! I've missed you so much. It's so good to see you again."

Agamemnon's arms wrapped around her tightly. "And I, you, my sweetest daughter."

Iphigenia held him at arm's length. "Are you sad to lose me, Father? That I'll soon be a woman?"

The king's heart sank. His eyes welled with unshed tears and his head pounded. "More than you'll ever know."

"Father! No tears! Here's Mother to cheer you."

Clytemnestra leaned to kiss her husband on the cheek. "You've gone more gray since I last laid eyes on you. It hasn't been that long, husband. Has it? And why the grief? You bargained this arrangement years ago. You're reacting as if it is only now news to you."

Agamemnon brushed his wife's admonishment aside. "How was your journey? Are you tired? Hungry?"

Clytemnestra patted Iphigenia's arm protectively. "Uneventful. Where's our tent? There's much planning to do and not much time."

"You go on, Mother. I'll catch up. I promise."

"As you wish, my darling girl."

As the queen followed a pair of soldiers with her retinue of attendants, Iphigenia turned her full attention on her father. "Tell me about Achilles. Why did you choose him for me?"

Agamemnon smiled sadly. "He's a proper prince. Worthy of our household. Worthy of you."

Iphigenia giggled. "But is he as handsome as they say? Is he kind?"

The thought of what he must do made it easy to tell the small truths. "He is handsome, as men go. Kind to those he loves, I suppose."

"Will you be happy to have him as a son?"

The king clicked his jaw, holding back the curses he wished to hurl at the sky. "Yes, what king wouldn't be?" He took her hand as they walked. "Do you remember when we'd walk the country paths of Mycenae?"

"Yes, and you'd let me make you crowns of flowers."

"That's our secret. No warrior could take me serious if he knew I wore flowers on my head." He brought their entwined hands to his lips. "You know I've loved you since you were born. Even when they told me you were a girl, I loved you."

"Of course. Why?"

"After you're … married, remember that I've always loved you."

Iphigenia's brows knit in concern. "Why would I forget that? Achilles isn't so great that he could make me forget my own loving father."

Agamemnon shook his head. "No man will ever love you more than I do."

"Father, you're frightening me. It's only a wedding."

"Promise me, you won't forget my love for you."

Iphigenia smiled warmly up at her father. "If it will make you happy, I promise. Now, show me where I'm to wed." She scanned the beach stacked with rows of ships. "I certainly never thought I'd marry in the midst of a war camp."

The king kissed her forehead. "I'll build you a beautiful altar. One worthy of a princess."

Hugging Agamemnon tightly, she said, "Thank you, Father."

"Now, go and find your mother. I'm sure she has a thousand tasks to complete."

As Iphigenia ran off to plan her wedding, Agamemnon's heart shattered. There was no turning back. He would do what must be done.

Agamemnon summoned all of the captains to a giant pavilion erected just outside of the main encampment. The Great King and Clytemnestra stood near a hastily erected altar adorned with garlands of field flowers and boughs of slender olive branches. Menelaus stood nearby as did Palamedes. The captains, except for Achilles, stood in ranked order, opposite the royal family members of Mycenae and Sparta. The gathering crowd of soldiers speculated among themselves about what Agamemnon's purpose could be. When Iphigenia appeared, veiled and glowing in a golden gown, it became clear Agamemnon intended to marry his eldest daughter to someone. The soldiers looked to each other, wondering who'd been chosen as groom; since it was well known in camp that Achilles had taken a bride in Skyros, breaking his betrothal oath to Agamemnon's daughter.

Iphigenia, crowned in yellow soldier's flowers, walked the short distance toward her father. The golden threads of her veil shimmered in the sun. Her saffron gown fluttered softly as she walked the short distance to the marital altar. Iphigenia dared a quick glance at the men nearby; none bore the appearance of Achilles. As the she approached the sacred alter, Palamedes gripped Clytemnestra's arm with the speed of a snake stunning its helpless prey, and two soldiers stepped forward, grabbing Iphigenia roughly by each arm. The princess looked to her father, confused. He made no move to help her.

"What are you doing?" Clytemnestra shouted.

Iphigenia sank to her knees in fright. "Father? Father! What's happening?" The men dragged her screaming across the hard sand and rocks to the altar.

The crowd shouted its confusion and concern. Agamemnon ignored them all.

The queen's shriek cut through the air, raising the hairs on men's arms. "My lord? I beg you! Stop what you're doing!" Agamemnon flashed an angry glare, chilling her blood. His face was all fire and stone. She knew that look—years ago on Mycenae. Her child … her husband. "Why? Why?" she screamed, struggling frantically against Palamedes' iron hold of her. "No! No! No! Iphigenia! Run my girl!" Clytemnestra slumped helplessly against her captor. "Run. No … no … no."

Agamemnon pulled a gleaming silver dagger from his belt, holding it aloft. "*Artemis!*"

Clytemnestra twisted again in desperation against Palamedes. "Please, my lord, not again! Don't take her from me! She's *our* daughter, Agamemnon … ours. Please, take me instead."

"Artemis has spoken!" he shouted so all could hear. "She has spoken and must be obeyed," he said, softer than before, the burden of the act weighing on him now.

The assembly stood in shock at the drama playing out in front of them. They openly questioned Agamemnon who answered them, "Artemis demands the sacrifice of my daughter to raise the winds for Troy."

Clytemnestra howled in desperation. She freed one arm and managed to scratch Palamedes across the face, before he could subdue her in his grasp again. "Husband, my lord! I beg you!"

Only now could Iphigenia see that her father's eyes were swollen and rimmed blood red. His smile faded to a thin line of determination. Searching his face for any sign of the love he'd born her, she found only a gray coldness. Iphigenia's heart pounded. "Where is Achilles?" Her voice cracked with fear. Agamemnon refused to meet her eyes. "Please, Father! What have I done to offend you?" She struggled vainly against the hard arms holding her captive.

Clytemnestra screamed, "You take our daughter's life to retrieve that whore, Helen?"

Odysseus sprang forward, reaching for the silver blade in Agamemnon's hand. "You can't do this!"

Agamemnon punched Odysseus with all his weight behind him—his heavy fist sent the young king sprawling back into the sand. "It's not for you to say!" He turned to the throng of horrified men. "Do you, any of you, dare oppose the will of Artemis? You would spare one life to sacrifice thousands? Artemis has spoken through Kalchas and I will obey, even if it tears my heart in two. I'm no match for the goddess. Let any man, I dare you! Let any man step forward and save my dear, sweet daughter from the wrath of the goddess." Purple veins pulsed on his forehead; his face blotched with fear and determination. He held the slicing blade aloft. "Save us all! Confront the goddess!"

The dissention in the crowd hushed to a great silence. A lone voiced cried out, "Is it true, Kalchas?"

The seer, who'd been standing by in abject silence, stepped forward, holding his hands out in peace to the men. "Artemis withholds the winds to carry us to Troy …" He hesitated, before laying the final stone in their path. "And denies all princes and kings safe passage home if this sacrifice is not made."

There it was, the awful truth revealed, forcing each man to assess his own life before that of a single girl. The stillness of the assembly spoke volumes to the queen. No one would step forward and save her daughter now. No one would dare challenge Artemis for any reason.

"Hold her down," Agamemnon commanded coldly. The guards obeyed. Agamemnon arched the dagger in the air, intending to drive it deep into Iphigenia's chest, when on the downward stroke the blade flew from his hand with a metallic ping. A second arrow passed his head, piercing one of the guards through the eye. The guard screamed as he went down in a lifeless heap of bone and blood. Agamemnon whirled in time to see Achilles launching himself over the line of captains, coming straight for him. Achilles took Agamemnon to the hard ground with a heavy thud, as he cracked the king's face with his iron fist, sending a shower of blood from the king's nose. He pummeled the Great King again and again until there was no more fight between them.

Covered in blood, Achilles turned to free Iphigenia … and caught Palamedes pulling his own blade across Iphigenia's throat. The thin red line turned to a gaping wound as her blood poured out, staining the front of her golden gown crimson. Her eyes wide with shock glazed over and her body fell slack in the slave's arms, before he let her slip to the ground. Her crown of yellow flowers fell from her head, as the sand drank her blood like a thirsty desert.

An eerie silence fell across the assembly. No one moved. Mouths hung agape. Apollo's light warmed the air.

And then it happened. A gentle breeze from across the sea reached the shore.

Achilles spat on Agamemnon lying unconscious on the ground. "There, you have your wind. You have your war. But you'll never have my allegiance. Or my respect." He stormed from the gathering, as all eyes rested on the horror before them. Clytemnestra's agonized wailing filled the air, drowning out even the roar of the sea. Slowly, one by one, the warriors left for their ships.

With Iphigenia's blood freshly spilt, the assembled Greeks readied the rigging of their galleys and checked their sails. Men mumbled that the bloody sacrifice had given them the promised winds, despite the awfulness of it. It confirmed in their minds that it wasn't their place to question the gods. And after such an iron display of determination bordering on madness by Agamemnon, not a single man, king, or prince wanted to stand against him save one. Achilles.

With tender care, Clytemnestra wrapped Iphigenia in a dark shroud and sailed for home. As the ship sped through gentle waves, her heart filled with renewed hate. Her arms ached with the weight of Iphigenia's lifeless body. The long buried grief for Tantalus and their son crashed with this new agony, sweeping over her like a wild fire. Everything she'd worked to build, her entire existence, lay in ashes all around her. Hugging her daughter's body to her chest, she wept knowing what she must do, what she should have done long ago. *I will be their vengeance. I will wield the blade that takes Agamemnon's life myself, if he ever dares set foot in Mycenae again ...*

KEEP READING FOR A SNEAK PEAK:

RISE
OF
PRINCES

CAST OF CHARACTERS

THE GREEKS

Achilles: Phthia, son of Thetis and Peleus, Captain and Commander of the Myrmidons

Aegisthus: Sparta, half-brother to Agamemnon and Menelaus

Aethra: Aethra, mother of King Theseus, forced to serve Helen

Agamemnon: Mycenae, King of Mycenae, husband to Clytemnestra

Ajax the Great: Salamis, also known as Telemonian Ajax, he is son of king Telemon and the Prince of Salamis, cousin to Achilles

Anticlea: Ithaka, mother of Odysseus, wife of Laertes

Antilochus: Pylos, son of Nestor

Chiron: Mt. Pelion, centaur, half-brother to Zeus, mentor to generations of warrior-kings

Clytemnestra: Sparta, Mycenae, daughter of Tyndareus, widow of Tantalus, wife of Agamemnon and mother of Iphigenia

Deidamia: Skyros, princess of Skyros, daughter of King Lycomedes, wife of Achilles, mother of Neoptolemus

Demius: Gythium, friend of Patrokles, helped Patrokles escape Gythium murder

Diomedes: Argos, king of Argos, immortal weapons granted by Athena

Elektra: Mycenae, daughter of Clytemnestra and Agamemnon

Helen: Sparta, daughter of Tyndareus and Leda, Queen of Sparta, wife of Menelaus and Paris

Hermione: Sparta, daughter of Menelaus and Helen

Hesione: Troy and Salamis, sister to Priam, taken captive by Herakles and given to Telemon of Salamis. Her sons fought against Troy.

Iphigenia: Mycenae, daughter of King Agamemnon and Queen Clytemnestra

Kalchas: Mycenae, seer for Agamemnon and the Greeks

*Knaxon: Aulis, Achilles' servant and mentored by Thetis

Laertes: Ithaka, retired king of Ithaka, father of Odysseus, husband of Anticlea

Leda: Sparta, Queen of Sparta, mother of Clytemnestra, Pollux, Castor, and Helen

Lycomedes: Skyros, king of Skyros, father to Deidamia, grandfather to Neoptolemus

Menelaus: Sparta, brother to Agamemnon, husband of Helen

Nauplius: Euboea, father of Palamedes

*Neola: Mycenae, trusted servant of Clytemnestra

Neoptolemus: Skyros and Phthia, son of Achilles Nestor, Pylos, old king of Pylos, in Messenia, wise council warrior

Odysseus: Ithaka, King of Ithaka, husband to Penelope, father to Telemachus

Orestes: Mycenae, son of Agamemnon and Clytemnestra

Palamedes: Mycenae, personal servant to Agamemnon

Patrokles: Phthia, guardian and elder cousin of Achilles

Peleus: Phthia, King of Phthia, father of Achilles

Penelope: Sparta and Ithaka, cousin to Helen and wife of Odysseus

Phoenix: Phthia, friend to Peleus, guardian of Achilles

Pirithous: Athens, helped Theseus kidnap Helen, he wanted Persephone as a wife

Tantalus: Mycenae, Prince of Mycenae, murdered by Agamemnon and first husband of Clytemnestra

Telemachus: Ithaka, son of Odysseus

Telemon: Salamis, traveled with Herakles, father of Ajax, took Hesione as concubine

Theseus: Athens, King of Athens, kidnapped Helen

Thrasymedes: Pylos, son of Nestor

Thyestes: Mycenae, King of Mycenae defeated by Agamemnon

Tyndareus: Sparta, King of Sparta, father of Clytemnestra, Pollux, Castor, and Helen

THE TRO ANS & THEIR ALLIES

Aeneas: Troy, Trojan warrior, nephew of King Priam, and founder of Italy Agelaus, Troy, royal bull herder and breeder, foster father of Paris

Andromache: Hypoplakia Thebe and Troy, daughter of Eetion and Mira, wife of Hektor

Astynome: Chryse, daughter of Chryses, prize concubine of Agamemnon

Briseis: Pedasus and Lyrnessus, daughter of Briseus and Shavash, widow of prince Mynes, concubine and wife of Achilles

Briseus: Pedasus, father of Briseis, King of Pedasus

Cassandra: Troy, daughter of Priam and Hecuba, cursed priestess of Apollo

Chryses: Chryse, priest of Apollo, father of Astynome

Corythus: Troy, son of Prince Paris and Oenone

Eetion: Hypoplakia Thebe, King of Hypoplakia Thebe, father of Andromache Euneus, Lemnos, King of Lemnos and infamous wine trader, son of Jason and Queen Hypsipyle

Eurypylus: Tenedos, Son of King Telephus and a physician

Evenus: Lyrnessus, king of Lyrnessus

*Hapeshet: Methymna, Seer and wise man to King Mikares

Hecamede: Tenedos, war prize gifted to Nestor

Hektor: Troy, eldest son of Priam and Hecuba, the Golden Prince of Troy and Commander of the Trojan army

Helenus: Troy, son of Priam and Hecuba, twin brother of Cassandra

Hypsipylos: Methymna, commander of King Mikares army, betrothed to the Princess Peisidike

*Kebriones: Troy, bastard son of Priam by Melita

*Korei: Tenedos, distinguished warrior in King Telephus' army, father of Valparun

*Lateke: Methymna, hand maiden to Princess Peisidike

*Lexias: Troy, wife to Agelaus, foster mother of Paris

Lykaon: Troy, half-brother to Hektor and Paris

Megapenthes: Troy, bastard son of Menelaus by Teridae

*Melita: Troy, concubine to King Priam

Mikares: Methymna, King of Methymna, a kingdom on Lesbos

Mira: Hypoplakia Thebe, Queen of Hypoplakia Thebe, mother of Andromache

Mynes: Lyrnessus, prince of Lyrnessus, first husband of Briseis

Oenone: wood nymph married to Paris, mother of Corythus

Paris: Troy, second son of Priam and Hecuba, the Forgotten Prince of Troy

Peisidike: Methymna, princess and daughter of King Mikares

Polyxena: Troy, youngest daughter of Priam and Hecuba

*Shavash: Pedasus, mother of Briseis

*Sidika: Lyrnessus, Queen of Lyrnessus

Telephus: Tenedos, King of Tenedos, a province in Mysia

Teridae: Troy, concubine of King Menelaus, mother of Megapenthes

Troilus: Troy, youngest son of Priam and Hecuba

*Valparun: Tenedos, son of Korei

*denotes characters I have imagined where the myths have left a void

THE GODS

Aphrodite: Goddess of Love and Beauty

Apollo: God of the Sun and Healing

Ares: God of War

Athena: Goddess of War and Wisdom

Artemis: Goddess of Hunting and Chasteness

Cebron: River god, father of Oenone

Eleithyia: Goddess of Childbirth

Eris: Goddess of Strife

Hera: wife of Zeus

Hermes: Messenger of Zeus

Poseidon: God of the Seas

Thetis: sea nymph, Goddess of Water; also, wife of Peleus, beloved of Zeus, and Achilles' mother

Zeus: father of the Olympians, true father of Pollux and Helen

TIMELINE FOR
HOMERIC CHRONICLES

1295 BCE   Hektor is born in Troy

Agamemnon is born in Mycenae

1290 BCE   Paris is born in Troy

1288 BCE   Clytemnestra born in Sparta

1285 BCE   Andromache born

1282 BCE   Briseis is born in Pedasus

Menelaus is born in Mycenae

1279 BCE   Odysseus is born in Ithaka

1272 BCE   Wedding of Thetis and Peleus

Paris fights Ares' Bull

The Judgment of Paris (15 years old)

1271 BCE   Achilles born to Thetis and Peleus

1270 BCE   Penelope born

Cassandra's Curse

Leda raped by Zeus

Clytemnestra (18) marries Agamemnon (25)

Helen born

1269 BCE   Briseis (13) meets Hektor (26)

1268 BCE   Hektor (24) meets Andromache (18)

1267 BCE   Briseis (15) meets Mynes (25)

1266 BCE   Iphigenia born to Clytemnestra & Agamemnon

Achilles (5) with Chiron the Centaur

Hektor (29) meets Andromache (19)

1265 BCE   Hektor (30) marries Andromache (20)
            Briseis (17) marries Prince Mynes (27)

1263 BCE   Orestes born to Clytemnestra & Agamemnon

1262 BCE   Phila born, daughter of Briseis (20) and Mynes

1260 BCE   Elektra born to Clytemnestra & Agamemnon

1259 BCE   Phila dies of illness

1257 BCE   Achilles (14 yrs) returns to Peleus

Studies under Phoenix

Corythus born, son of Oenone and Paris

Achilles (14) sent to Skyros by Thetis

1254 BCE   Achilles (17) marries pregnant Deidamia (16)

Helen kidnapped by Theseus and Pirithous

1253 BCE   Neoptolemus (Achilles' son) born

1252 BCE   Helen (18) marries Menelaus (30)

Odysseus (27) marries Penelope (18)

1251 BCE   Hermione born to Helen and Menelaus

Paris quests to rescue Hesione

Menelaus attends funeral of Catreus of Crete

Paris (39) takes Helen (19)

Telemachus born to Odysseus and Penelope

Gathering at Aulis for Troy

Odysseus retrieves Achilles (20) at Skyros

Iphigenia (15) at Aulis

** A note about the timeline. I have tried to the best of my ability to incorporate as many myths as necessary into this series. The process has uncovered several surprises for me, first as an historian, and secondly as a writer. Sometimes these two halves of me clashed in the process. I have tweaked a few dates so the stories make the most chronological sense. If you want a detailed discussion of how I arrived at the timeline, listen to my "Greek Mythology Retold" podcast, episodes 1-3.

MY MYRMIDONS

So many people helped me in so many ways, big and small, to complete this book and stay focused. I call them "My Myrmidons" after the warriors who loyally served in Achilles' army. I want to give a huge thank you to my beta readers: Veronica G., Jennifer M., Kristine R.H., Linisha T., Nicole T., Tricia R., Isabel N., and Chris D. They re-read *Song of Princes*, provided critical feedback, and helped me make the final decision to re-title this book: *Song of Sacrifice*. I wouldn't have had the courage to make this change without them.

As an indie writer, I rely on social media a lot. Maybe, too much. Thank you, Lina, for helping me figure out what I was supposed to be doing with Instagram, and then steering me in a more focused direction. (If you've liked my posts over there recently, it's because of her). I'd also like to thank Charles, who edits the *Greek Mythology Retold* podcast, which is instrumental in helping me define and develop my characters. It certainly takes a village. Thank the gods I have one.

I've never met Ryan Stitt @greekhistorypod, but I'd know his voice in a crowd. Thanks for your encouragement with my podcast and all the helpful episodes you have available on Ancient Greek history and culture. You're my listening reference library.

Getting the eBook and paperback put together requires a team of specialists. I'm fortunate to be able to work with some very talented women. Regina designed the most beautiful cover. And I'm excited about her plans for the rest of the series. Nadège designed the equally impressive interior pages. (She also has a YA Sci-Fi-Fantasy series called the *Bionics Saga* you might like to check out.) I'm very grateful to both of them for their thoughtfulness in creating the new imagery for the *Homeric Chronicles*.

My editor, Melissa of There For You Editing polished the manuscript and any remaining errors are completely my fault.

I'd like to thank *you* for reading my work. Hopefully, you enjoyed *Song of Sacrifice* and want to read the next one, *Rise of Princes*. Let's stay in touch on my social media accounts. I'm there probably more than I should be, but hey … what's a writer to do? I invite you to join the Myrmidon Crew Letter on my webpage and/or leave a review at your favorite book seller.

Much Gratitude,
Janell Rhiannon

TURN THE PAGE FOR A SNEAK PEAK:

RISE
OF
PRINCES

ONE

promises

MYCENAE—1251 BCE

"I promise." Clytemnestra stared with unseeing eyes at the lifeless form of Iphigenia. The blood had long been washed from her daughter's body, yet the queen could only see red. Red was the color of her hate. Red was the color of her revenge. Black was the color of her heart. This new grief ripped open the old wound. She remembered with tender pains the son Agamemnon had cruelly taken from her, whose death had been only slightly softened by Iphigenia's birth. Now, both children were gone, and their precious lives taken by her husband's hand. She reached pale, trembling fingers out to touch the gold coins on her daughter's eyes.

"Promise what, Mother?"

The queen dropped her hand and turned around, her black gown gathering around her feet like a dark pool of water. "Elektra. I thought I was alone." The flickering light of twin oil lamps couldn't lift the descending darkness of the mourning hall.

The princess shifted her weight to one side, waiting. But Clytemnestra remained as still as if carved from stone. "May … I enter?"

Clytemnestra turned back to face her dead child. "It's a grim business. Mourning your sister."

Elektra approached softly, practically tip-toeing, until she was just a step behind her mother. "Since you've returned, I've hardly seen you, except in here." She scratched at her nose. "I heard someone talking about the ghost queen -"

"I've also heard that. Pay it no mind."

"Her gown is beautiful, Mother."

"It is."

Elektra tugged at a fold of her chiton. "Mother, is it true? About Father, I mean? What they say …"

Clytemnestra sighed under the heaviness of her grief. "All of it, dear child."

"But, why would he do something so —"

"Because, he's a murderer."

An icy cold finger slid up Elektra's neck. "What were you promising to Iphigenia?"

"Revenge."

Elektra's voice cracked. "Against my father? It's not fair!"

Clytemnestra whirled around and her hand shot out like a viper, grabbing her second daughter's chin. She lifted her Elektra's face to hers. "It's not for you to worry about."

Elektra's mouth quivered awkwardly in her mother's grip, as fresh tears sprang to her eyes. But her mother's hand remained unyielding.

"She was my blood. Do you understand that? My. Blood. She was taken from me in the cruelest way." Clytemnestra dropped her hand, rubbing a thumb into her palm. "It will not go unpunished."

"Please, Mother—"

The queen's icy voice cracked with restrained rage. "He is a *murderer*. I'll hear no more from you."

Elektra sprinted from the room, tripping on the hem of her chiton. The woman who'd returned from Aulis wasn't her mother. Tears blurred her vision as she ran to the kitchen. *Neola will stop her*. When she reached the lower steps leading into the cookery, she saw Neola pulling hot rounds of bread from an open oven.

The nurse maid wiped sweat from her brow. "What now, child? Why are you crying?"

Elektra bounded down the short flight of stairs and leapt into the old woman's arms. "She's going to hurt my father."

"What? What are you talking about?"

"She told me. Just now. In the mourning hall. She said she would make revenge for Iphigenia." Elektra buried her face in Neola's neck, her slender shoulders shaking.

"Shah, child. Shaaaah. It's only a mother's grief to speak this way."

"She told me it was true. What he did was true. How could he do it? How could my father kill Iphigenia?"

Stroking the girl's hair, Neola pressed her wrinkled cheek to the princess' head. "I don't know why the gods punish us with such tasks."

"The gods are evil, then, to ask my father to do that."

Neola looked Elektra in the face. "It's best you never utter such things aloud for the gods to hear. Do you understand?" She leaned closer to her ward, her lips brushing against the young girl's ear. "They are hard. Cruel. And will punish you for loyalty, as well as betrayal. Keep your thoughts of them to yourself. Go unnoticed by them. Life is easier, when they don't see you."

Elektra dried her nose on Neola's tunic. "I loved my sister."

"I know you did, little one. I know."

"Father loved us, didn't he?"

"Yes, if a man as hard as King Agamemnon was capable of love … yes, he loved you all. No doubt."

"What could make him do it?"

"It's war, Elektra. War has a way of changing everything."

Clytemnestra stood before Athena's statue in the temple, her face heavily veiled from the world. Her children, heirs to Agamemnon's throne, stood with her. The priest mumbled through the appropriate words and the funeral procession began. Attendants carried Iphigenia's body on a gold filigree pallet, her blue gown fluttering in the breeze. Clytemnestra walked with her head held high, her children trailing her like cygnets gliding after their mother swan. Behind the royal mask, each step broke her heart over and over again.

How will I breathe freely again? Death pressed his cold lips to her cheek. *I'm broken into a thousand pieces. Why have the gods cursed me? I want to die.* The procession halted at the pyre where her precious daughter's ashes would kiss the sky. Blinking, Clytemnestra focused on the world through the black gauze of her veil.

The tallest of the king's guards stepped forward and spoke, his words burning through the fog of Clytemnestra's grief. "My queen, when you are ready. Give the word and it will be done."

"I will never be ready," she whispered, her voice sounding weak in her own ears. A small hand reached for hers, and her fingers curled around it without thinking. Clytemnestra glanced down to see Elektra's sad eyes gazing up at her. *They are his eyes.* After giving the little hand a squeeze, she found the guard's face and nodded.

As they laid her beloved daughter's body on the pinnacle of the fire bed, her heart pressed painfully against her chest. The torch was set to the wood and sections of the bed smoked. Smoke turned to flame. *My beautiful girl.* Fire licked the edges of Iphigenia's gown. Clytemnestra panicked. She knew Iphigenia was dead, but watching the fire devour her body grieved her all over again. *She is dead. She can feel nothing.* A breeze whirled around the pyre, encouraging the flames to rise higher. In dazed horror, Clytemnestra stared into the dancing orange and red blaze as the visage of her daughter disappeared. *Iphigenia.* Her knees buckled beneath her and she crumpled to the ground.

The king's guards rushed to Clytemnestra's side, as she released an agonized wail. The funeral assembly stared at their queen, on her knees, weeping and howling. The rumors whispered on the wind about King Agamemnon sacrificing the Princess Iphigenia had been too awful to believe, but upon the queen's return from Aulis, all speculation had been proven *fact.* The people wondered about the fate of the royal family. Would the queen lead them? Would she abandon them for her home in Sparta? They'd grown to love her over the years. Her kindness was known throughout the city. Her pity of the poor had gained Mycenae's heart. She was beloved by all.

―――――

Neola offered Clytemnestra a cup of watered wine. "Drink, my lady. You must take some nourishment."

Clytemnestra pushed the wine away. "I want nothing."

Neola set the cup on a nearby table. "Perhaps, later."

"Do you recall the day Iphigenia was born?"

"How can I forget?"

"The goddess warned me … warned me of this day. She said Iphigenia would be mine for a time. I should have *seen* this coming. I should have *known*, he'd do something."

"There's no way you could've known, my lady. You shouldn't torture yourself with such talk."

Clytemnestra sighed heavily, slumping back against her chair. "I rarely thought of my old life. Before Agamemnon. I buried that pain long ago. But now … now it has returned. It mingles with this new horror that my life has become."

"You still have Orestes and Elektra."

"Should that lessen the pain I feel?"

Neola shrugged. "I only meant —"

Clytemnestra stood. "I know what you meant. I can hardly think of them." She walked to the table and picked up the wine. "I know what I must do. I'm just uncertain how it can be done."

"What must you do?"

"What I should have done years ago."

Neola shivered at the ice in Clytemnestra's voice. "Should I send for your mother?"

Clytemnestra scoffed. "For what purpose?"

"Perhaps, she can help you?"

"No one can help me, now."

REFERENCES & INSPIRATIONS

Aeschylus, *Agamemnon*.

Alexander, Caroline. *Iliad*, translation. HarperCollins Publishers. Reprint edition (November 24, 2015)

Arnson Svarlien, Diane; Scodel, Ruth, translator. *Euripides: Andromache, Hecuba, Trojan Women* (Hackett Classics) (March 15, 2012).

Cassandra. Retrieved from https://www.greekmyths-greekmythology.com/the-myth-of-cassandra/

Claybourne, Anna. "Achilles." *Gods, Goddesses, and Mythology*. Tarrytown, NY: Marshall Cavendish Reference. Retrieved from https://search.credoreference.com/content/entry/mcgods/achilles/0

Cuypers, Martine, *Ptoliporthos Akhilleus: the sack of Methymna in the Lesbou Ktisis, Hermathena*, v.173-174, 2005, pp. 117-135.

Hanson, Victor Davis, *On Barry Strauss's The Trojan War: A New History*. Retrieved from www.newcriterion.com.

Hauser, Emily. 'There is another story': writing after the *Odyssey* in Margaret Atwood's *The Penelopiad Classical Receptions Journal*, Volume 10, Issue 2, 1 April 2018, Pages 109–126.

Hesiod, *The Homeric Hymns and Homerica*, H.G. translated by Evelyn-White

Higgins, Charlotte, The Iliad and what it can still tell us about war. Retrieved from www.theguardian.com.

Homer, *Iliad*.

Homer, *Odyssey*.

Hyginus, *Fabulae, Cassandra* 65. Retrieved from http://www.theoi.com/Text/HyginusFabulae3.html#65.

Hyginus, *Fabulae, Palamedes*105. Retrieved from http://www.theoi.com/Text/HyginusFabulae3.html#105.

Mark, Joshua J., *Oenone*, Ancient History Encyclopedia, 2009.

Mason, Wyatt. https://www.nytimes.com/2017/11/02/magazine/the-first-woman-to-translate-the-odyssey-into-english.html (On Emily Wilson's *Odyssey* translation)

Mendelsohn, Daniel, Battle Lines: A Slimmer, faster Iliad. Retrieved from www.NewYorker.com.

Muich, Rebecca M. *Pouring out tears: Andromache in Homer and Euripides* https://www.ideals.illinois.edu/handle/2142/16755

Ovid, *Ars Amatoria*.

Ovid, *Herois 5*, translated by R. Scott Smith.

Parada, Carlos, *Peleus*, Greek Mythology Link. Retrieved from http://www.maicar.com/GML/Peleus.html

Parada, Carlos, *Agamemnon*, Greek Mythology Link. Retrieved from http://www.maicar.com/GML/Agamemnon.html

Parada, Carlos, *Paris*, Greek Mythology Link. Retrieved from http://www.maicar.com/GML/Paris.html

Polyxena: *Encyclopedia Mythica* from Encyclopedia Mythica Online. Retrieved from http://www.pantheon.org/articles/p/polyxena.html. Accessed March 03, 2017.

Reardon, Tyler (Dramaturge) https://pacifictheatrearts.wordpress.com/ancient-burial-customs/

Seneca, *Thyestes*.

Stewart, M.W. *Achilles*. Retrieved from https://mythagora.

com/bios/achilles.html (now available in Kindle format)

Stitt, Ryan. The History of Ancient Greek Podcast. http://www.thehistoryofancientgreece.com/2016/04/hello-im-ryan-stitt-and-welcome-to.html

Strauss, Barry, *The Trojan War*.

Thyestes and Atreus. Retrieved from http://www.classics.upenn.edu/myth/php/tragedy/

Wilson, Emily. *Odyssey*, translation. W. W. Norton & Company; 1 edition (November 7, 2017).

Printed in Great Britain
by Amazon